THREE WEEKS TO WED

Worthington's heat, his scent, seemed to drift across the desk to her. Reminding her of how good it felt to be in his arms. God help her, all she wanted was for him to touch her.

The next thing she knew his strong arms lifted her from the chair and drew her close to him.

"Grace, I know you don't think I still want to marry you, but I do." His lips brushed her forehead. "I can't live without you. I like all of your brothers and sisters. I want to take care of all of you. Please let me."

"You don't"—her blood roared in her ears—"you cannot know what you're saying. I have seven, *seven* brothers and sisters. The youngest is only five."

He grinned as his lips made their way to her jaw. "She'll be six in summer."

Grace wanted to sink into him, have him sink into her. She fought the urge to cant her neck, giving him easier access.

This would not do!

Rubbing her temples, she gazed into his mesmerizing lapis eyes. "I don't understand you at all. Why do you want to take us on?"

"To make you happy. To make us a family."

He reached out and curled one of her locks around his finger. She stared into his eyes. The blue depths combined humor and hope. He made her want to hope. Although he didn't touch her, she was drawn toward him.

He bent his head. "Let me love you."

Grace was in his embrace again and somehow her arms were around his neck.

Their lips met in a kis

D0963809

Books by Ella Quinn

The Marriage Game

THE SEDUCTION OF LADY PHOEBE

THE SECRET LIFE OF MISS ANNA MARSH

THE TEMPTATION OF LADY SERENA

DESIRING LADY CARO

ENTICING MISS EUGENIE VILLARET

A KISS FOR LADY MARY

LADY BERESFORD'S LOVER

MISS FEATHERTON'S CHRISTMAS PRINCE

The Worthingtons

THREE WEEKS TO WED

Novellas

MADELEINE'S CHRISTMAS WISH

Published by Kensington Publishing Corporation

EEKS
to WED

ELLA QUINN

ZEBRA BOOKS
KENSINGTON PUBLISHING CORP.
http://www.kensingtonbooks.com

ZEBRA BOOKS are published by

Kensington Publishing Corp.
119 West 40th Street
New York, NY 10018

All Kensington titles, imprints and distributed lines are available at special quantity discounts for bulk purchases for sales promotion, premiums, fund-raising, educational or institutional use.

Special book excerpts or customized printings can also be created to fit specific needs. For details, write or phone the office of the Kensington Sales Manager. Attn.: Sales Department. Kensington Publishing Corp., 119 West 40th Street, New York, NY 10018. Phone: 1-800-221-2647.

Zebra and the Z logo Reg. U.S. Pat. & TM Off.

First Printing: April 2016
ISBN-13: 978-1-4201-3955-6
ISBN-10: 1-4201-3955-X

eISBN-13: 978-1-4201-3956-3
eISBN-10: 1-4201-3956-8

10 9 8 7 6 5 4 3 2

Printed in the United States of America

To my husband,
my hero of over thirty years,
who sits on the helm
while I write.

Acknowledgments

Every book takes a journey from the author's first words to publication. I have a lot of people to thank. To my beta readers, Doreen, Margaret, and Jenna. You ladies always give me such fantastic advice and guidance. To my lovely agent, Elizabeth Pomada, and my wonderful editor, John Scognamiglio. To the Kensington publicity team, Jane, Alex, Vida, and Lauren, for all their hard work promoting my books. To the fabulous authors in The Beau Monde for answering my questions quickly and accurately. And last, but not least, to my fantastic readers. I have no words to express how much your support means to me.

Chapter One

End of February 1815. Leicestershire, England.

The sky had darkened and wind rocked the carriage, causing at least one wheel to leave the road. Hail mixed with freezing rain battered the windows. Lady Grace Carpenter pounded on the roof of her coach, trying to make herself heard over the storm. "How close are we to the Crow and Hound?"

"Not far, my lady," her coachman bellowed over the wind. "I'm think'n' we should stop."

"Yes, indeed. Make it so." She huddled deeper into her warm sable cloak. When they'd started out this morning, the weather had been dry and sunny, giving no indication a storm of this magnitude would come on.

She was only an hour or so from her home, Stanwood Hall, but they wouldn't make it. It was better to trust in the Crow and Hound's innkeeper's discretion than risk her servants and cattle to this weather.

A few minutes later, they turned off the road, and her coachman bellowed for an ostler. Moments later, her coach's door was quickly opened and the steps let down. Her groom,

Neep, hustled her from the carriage to the open entrance of the inn.

The innkeeper, Mr. Brown, was there to greet her. Saxon blond, with blue eyes and of middling height and age, he shut the heavy wooden door against the weather. "My lady," he said in a surprised tone, "we didn't expect to see you this evenin'."

"For good reason." Grace whipped off her damp cloak and shook it. "I didn't expect to be here. I was visiting an elderly cousin, and the storm blew up on our way back."

"It's as they say, my lady," he said, nodding, "no good deed goes unpunished."

"Well," she blew out an exasperated huff, "it certainly seems like that at times. Thank God, we were close to you. I have my coachman, groom, and two outriders"—Grace grimaced—"but not my maid." She prayed no one would discover she was there without her lady's maid, Bolton, who was sure to give Grace her *I told you so* look when she finally made it home. "I shall require the use of one of your girls. It should go without saying you have not seen me here."

"Yes, my lady." He nodded, tapping the side of his nose. "You were never here. Don't expect to see anyone else in this weather. You and your servants will sleep warm and dry tonight." He pointed to the door next to the stairs and within easy reach of the common room. "I'll put you in this parlor for dinner."

She gave him a grateful smile. "Thank you. That will be perfect."

Susan, one of Brown's daughters, showed Grace to the large chamber at the back of the inn on the first floor. She handed the girl her cloak to dry, then shook out her skirts. "I'll call for you when I am ready to retire."

"Yes, my lady. Anything you need, just pull the bell." Susan bobbed a curtsey and left.

Grace glanced around. Although she had stopped here any number of times on family outings, she'd never spent the night. The inn had been in the Brown family for several generations. The building was old, but it was clean and well maintained.

She took a book and Norwich shawl from her large muff before descending the stairs to the parlor. Although it was early, not much past two o'clock, Mr. Brown had closed the shutters, and a fire was lit, as well as sufficient candles to brighten the room.

An hour later, warm and dry, she was engrossed in *Madelina,* the latest romance from the Minerva Press. Over the storm, sounds of another carriage arriving could be heard. Grace lowered the book, wondering who the newcomer could be.

The inn door slammed opened. Moments later, Mr. Brown's agitated tone and that of another man, a gentleman by his speech, reached her.

Her heart skipped a beat. Worthington? Could it really be him? She hadn't heard his voice for four years, but she'd never forget it.

Opening the door slightly, she peeked out. It was him. The man she'd wanted to marry her whole first Season and had never seen again. His dark brown, almost black, hair was wet at the ends where his tall beaver hat had failed to keep it dry. If he turned, she knew she would see his startling lapis eyes and long lashes.

"Could you not just ask the traveler in the parlor if I might share it with him?" Worthington asked the landlord, his tone strained, but still polite. He was probably already cold and wet, and the common room would be chilly at best.

The kernel of an idea began to form. Swallowing her trepidation, Grace stepped boldly into the hall. "Mr. Brown, his lordship is welcome to dine with me."

"If you're sure, my . . ."

She flashed him a quelling glance. If he said "my lady," there'd be too many questions from Worthington. Whatever happened, he could not know her identity.

"Ma'am."

She tried not to show her relief. "Yes. You may serve us after his lordship has had time to change." Grace dipped a slight curtsey to Worthington and returned to the parlor.

Closing the door, she leaned back against it. This was her opportunity, maybe her only one, and she was going to take it.

"What are you doing, my girl? Are you out of your mind?" her conscience berated her.

No one will know. Brown will deny I was here.

"How do you expect to preach propriety to the children when you are—"

"Oh, do be quiet," Grace muttered. "When will I have another chance? Answer me that. All I want is to spend some time with him. What is the harm in that?"

Water dripped off the greatcoat of Mattheus, Earl of Worthington, as it had dripped off his hat earlier. A puddle had to be forming at his feet. He was not particularly impressed with the small inn. Although he'd passed it every time he made the trip to Town, he'd never stopped here before. If it weren't for the weather, he wouldn't have done so now.

"I can add more wood to the fire in the common room, my lord," the landlord said. "But me parlor's already got a guest."

He glanced over at the fairly large space. Even with the shutters closed, the windows rattled. Cold and drafty. "Would you please ask your guest if he will share the parlor for a short time?"

"Couldn't do that, my lord." The older man shook his head. "I could send the meal to your room, but I ain't got an extra table. Once it warms up, you'll be right comfortable in the common room."

He sincerely doubted that would be the case.

"Mr. Brown . . ."

Matt turned at the sound of the low, well-bred, no-nonsense female voice. He suspected it would belong to an older lady, perhaps a governess, most definitely not the vision of loveliness standing before him. Before he could even thank her, she gave a curt nod and closed the door.

"I'll show ye to yer room, my lord." The landlord grumbled as he picked up Matt's bag.

"Thank you. It will be nice to be dry again." Halfway up the stairs, he stopped as a memory played hide-and-seek with him. He knew her, but from where? London. During the Season. He shook his head trying to knock the memory loose, but nothing more came to him.

"This way, my lord."

"Coming." It was her hair that stuck in his mind. It shone like a new guinea coin.

The landlord held a door at the end of the corridor open. "Thank you."

"I'll send one of my boys up with warm water."

"I would appreciate that."

Brown set about lighting the fire.

Matt didn't know many ladies who would offer to share their parlor with a complete stranger. The feeling that they had met before grew stronger. Who the hell was she?

"There ye be, my lord."

Once the door closed behind the landlord, Matt began shedding his damp clothing. The sooner he got back downstairs, the sooner he'd know who his mystery woman was.

Less than a half hour later, Matt made his way downstairs and knocked on the parlor door before entering. He bowed. "Thank you for agreeing to share your parlor and your meal. Permit me to introduce myself. Worthington, at your service."

Nothing like sounding pompous.

He was almost surprised when she smiled and rose instead of turning her pretty nose up at him. "How could I refuse to assist a fellow traveler and in such dreadful weather as we are having?"

Graceful.

That was the first word that sprang to mind as Matt watched her glide to the bell-pull. When he had entered the parlor, the table had already been set up for tea. She took a seat, motioning him to the chair opposite her. "Please. There is no need to stand on formality."

She handed him a plate, and in a few moments a young girl brought in a pot covered in a brightly colored cloth, set it down, then left.

"Do you take sugar?" the lady asked, glancing from beneath her long gold-tipped lashes.

It was clear the lady, for she was certainly gently bred, had no intention of telling Matt her name. "I do, Miss—"

"Milk or cream?" she responded hastily.

"Two lumps of sugar and a splash of milk if you would." The corners of her lush lips tilted up slightly.

He made a point of looking around the room as if searching for something. "Are you traveling alone?"

A deep rose crept up into her face. Though, under the circumstances, that wasn't surprising.

"Sometimes one cannot order the weather to suit one's convenience." Her voice was tight as if she did not approve of either his question or the weather.

Her long, slender fingers showed no indication of a wedding ring. A fleeting memory of seeing her before niggled at him once more. How could any red-blooded man forget that glorious hair, gold glinting with burnished copper in the candlelight? On the other hand, the hair he remembered. It was her name he'd forgot. Her brows, a little darker than her golden curls, arched perfectly over eyes that tilted slightly upward at the corners. He'd never seen a more beautiful woman.

He wished he could make out the exact color of her expressive eyes, but the light was too dim.

Blue. That was encouraging. Now if he could only remember the rest. Damn the devil. He had seen her before, but where and when, and why couldn't he remember? His gaze was drawn to her mouth, deep rose and a little wider than what was considered fashionable. What would it be like to taste her, to feel her soft lips on his and where had that desire sprung from?

Grace's heart was in her throat by the time Worthington joined her. In the short time he had been gone she'd changed her mind a dozen times at least about inviting him to join her.

Mattheus, Earl of Worthington.

Grace allowed her eyes to trail over his perfect form, adding to her still-clear memories of him. He was tall and broad-shouldered, his jacket was cut to perfection. His cravat perfectly tied. He had always been so well dressed. She never thought she'd see him again, or if she did, he probably would be married with several children. Come to think of it, even though he wasn't wearing a ring, he could still be married . . . Oh, he was speaking.

"Miss . . . ?"

When she did not give him her name, he looked at her curiously. Grace walked over to the bell-pull, giving a sigh of relief when a few moments later Mr. Brown's daughter entered the room.

She'd have to do better than that if she wanted him to . . . well . . . She fought the blush rising in her cheeks. "Please take a seat. I shall enjoy the company."

There, that was much better. Remember you are five and twenty, not eighteen.

This was not going to be as easy as Grace had thought it would be.

Worthington took a sip and his almost-black brows drew together. "This is extraordinarily good tea for an inn."

"It is my blend. I travel with it." She only had it this time as a treat for her elderly cousin who professed to love Grace's tea, but would never allow her to leave the canister.

Now what was she to say? With the exception of her vicar, it had been so long since she had spoken with any non-family-member male and those had not been pleasant discussions. "Have you family that will worry about you?"

"Only my sisters and stepmother and they do not know when I plan to return home." He took another sip of tea. "I imagine your family will be anxious."

They would be frightened to death. She should have been home long before now, but her cousin was lonely and had needed the company. "A bit."

"Do you have far to travel?"

Grace studied him over the rim of her cup. She had thought there'd been a spark of recognition in his eyes, but it was clear he did not remember her. That was not surprising. It had been several years since they had seen each other. He had probably danced with thousands of ladies since her one dance with him. In any event, she did not want him to know who she was. It would only complicate her already overly complicated life.

"Within a day," she finally answered. True, but misleading. She had to turn the course of this conversation to a safer subject. "What do you think about the progress of the peace treaty?"

A small smile formed on his well-molded lips. "That the process has gone on far too long and that the new French government is not as strong as it needs to be."

Mr. Brown tapped on the door, then entered with another

of his many daughters. "Come to clear the tea away, if you're ready."

Grace tore her gaze from Worthington's mouth. Oh, my. If she'd thought he was mesmerizing before, it was nothing to what he was doing to her insides now. She had to pull herself together. "Yes, please. We shall dine at six."

Mr. Brown bowed. "That's perfect, my—"

She gave the man a sharp look.

"Ma'am."

Enough was enough. Just being around Worthington was turning her mind into a bowl of jelly. The landlord and his daughter left, leaving the door slightly open. She met Worthington's steady gaze. She would probably never see him again and might as well talk about what she wanted to. "I do not mind discussing politics, though you should know that I'm a Whig."

Chapter Two

That was certainly throwing down the gauntlet. Matt had a feeling this was going to become an interesting conversation. If only he could either remember or discover who she was. It would be even better. "My party as well. On the left side."

The lady's eyes sparkled with pleasure. "Then we should have much to discuss . . ."

During the meal and afterward, their conversation ranged over politics, philosophy, and estate management. In fact, any topic that came into their heads, except the weather. Hours later they had not even had to search for subject matter to discuss. He had not had such an interesting conversation in months, maybe years, and never with a woman. She was as well or better informed than any man he had ever met. He'd never been so taken by a lady. Suddenly Matt wanted to know everything about her.

"Are you an adherent of Wollstonecraft?" she asked.

He leaned forward, placing his elbows on the table. "Completely. I find her views on the rights of women interesting in the extreme, and I am pleased to see that the numbers of Wollstonecraft and Bentham followers have grown in political circles."

A far-off expression crossed the lady's face. "I've not been in London much of late, though I do keep up a lively correspondence with my friends."

Perhaps this was his opportunity. "Do your friends hold the same ideas as you do?"

"Most of them." A note of caution entered her tone.

"We might know some of the same people."

"Have you joined the group attempting to help the war veterans?"

Drat it all. That hadn't worked. "I have."

They discussed some of the proposals being batted around. She was certainly knowledgeable. He peered at the large armchair near the fireplace. A book with a marbled cloth cover lay on the seat. "Is that one of the Minerva romances you have there?"

"Yes, it is." She lifted her chin a little. "I find them excessively diverting."

Based on their conversation, no one could accuse her of muddling her mind with romances. She was as well informed as any bluestocking, but she didn't have the acerbic tone of one. "My stepmother reads them. Although, she tries to hide them from my sisters." Matt grinned. "I'm not sure she always succeeds."

A smile played around her lips, and she tilted her head a little to the side. Much like an inquisitive bird. "And you, my lord?"

He wondered, not for the first time this evening, what it would be like to kiss those lips. To tug lightly with his teeth on her full lower lip. She was beautiful, intelligent, and he had to answer her question. Damn, now he wished he had read the books. "Not yet."

"You might enjoy them, some gentlemen do."

"On your recommendation, I shall most definitely read at least one."

She colored prettily, as if pleased that she had made a potential convert.

Before he knew it, the clock struck half-six.

He came to his feet as she rose. "I must tidy up for dinner."

"Of course. I'll meet you here shortly."

She left the room, and he poured a brandy from the decanter on the sideboard. Never in all his years had he been as drawn to a woman like he was to his mystery lady. They agreed on almost everything, and when they disagreed, she stated her opinions clearly and intelligently.

Yet, how the devil was he to discover her name and direction? The only idea he could come up with was to offer to escort her to her home to-morrow, provided the weather cleared. But what if she refused? He could follow her. He tossed off the brandy. Somehow, some way, Matt was determined to court her.

Grace shut the door of her chamber behind her and leaned against it. For years Matt Worthington had been nothing more than an infatuation, but now, he was rapidly becoming so much more. It had been years since she had allowed herself to feel angry at the hand fate had dealt her. Yet, now, now she could do something just for herself. She would not leave here, leave him without knowing what it would be like to know joy with a man.

"What if someone finds out? Everything you've worked for will be for naught?" Her conscience popped up, just when Grace had thought it had given up.

Even with her family around, there were still times when she was so lonely she thought she'd die of it. Not being able to marry was the one thing she had never got over. "Am I to have no joy of my own? I just want one night. One night to last me the rest of my life, that's all I'm asking."

"Wanton!"

"So be it." Her hands trembled and her stomach lurched. If only she wasn't so ignorant.

"So much for your grand plans," her conscience sneered. *"You don't have any idea how to go about this."*

"I am sure he'll help. How hard can it be, after all?"

"He'll recognize you. Then where will you be?"

"He won't. Other than that one dance, when Lady Bellamny made him ask me, I am sure he never took a second look at me. I was just one of many girls who came out that year." He certainly did not remember her now.

"So you say. What if you get with child?"

"Would you cease! It must be fate. After all, what were the odds that we would both be here at the very same time with no one else in the inn?"

Wishing she had something nicer to wear, Grace gave up arguing with herself and washed her hands. When she had returned to the parlor, she called for wine. By the time Worthington arrived, she'd calmed her jangled nerves, and her conscience had decided to leave her to go to perdition in her own way.

He had changed his linen, but not his suit. "I apologize for dining in boots."

"I do not mind at all." She handed him a glass of claret. "As you see, I have no other clothes with me. This was only supposed to be a day trip."

"I expected to be home as well and sent my valet ahead with the rest of my kit." He gave a rueful grin. "A lesson to me to keep a bag with me." He took a sip. "This claret is excellent."

"Yes, Mr. Brown keeps a well-stocked cellar."

She had wanted to confide in Worthington. Tell him that her father used to bring them all here because of the quality of the wine. Confide the difficulties she was experiencing now. Fortunately, before she revealed too much, the door opened and Mr. Brown entered followed by one of his sons, both carrying covered trays.

The savory aroma made Matt's stomach rumble.

"My misses thought you might like a nice cream of mushroom soup to begin. Then we have a haunch of venison, with Frenched beans . . ." By the time the man finished the dishes covered the table and sideboard. "And here is a trifle for desert."

Matt offered the lady selections from the offerings before filling his plate. They were silent for a few minutes as they ate. He, because he was ravenous. She simply appeared a bit shy. That was no wonder. She most likely never dined alone with a man before.

"I must tell you that at first I was not impressed by this inn, but the food and wine make up for it being a bit shabby."

"I have always found the place to be cozy."

He gazed at her, mesmerized by the dainty way she licked the cream from the trifle from her spoon. "I think I agree."

He asked her what she thought of the experimental farm in Norfolk and was surprised to find she knew as much as he did. The hours flew by as they had earlier. Soon the clock chimed ten, and she rose.

Matt stood as well, expecting her to make a hasty retreat. Yet rather than curtseying and heading for the door, she stood before him searching his face, waiting. That was all the invitation he needed.

Tentatively, he reached out and with the back of his hand slowly caressed her cheek. He had never wanted a lady as much as he did her. *What would she do if he kissed her?* Suddenly, where she was from or who she was didn't matter any longer. She was his. He knew it in his bones. Fate had created a storm and placed her here for him to find and claim.

She took a small step toward him as with one finger he traced her jaw. She closed the distance between them again.

This is like tickling a trout, but with a much greater reward.

Worthington had proven to be everything Grace thought he would be, and now . . . now even if she wished to resist him, she could not. She shoved down her rising anxiety. Her plan was coming to fruition, and now was not the time to be frightened. After all, what good would her virginity do her in her spinsterhood?

His eyes mesmerized her, and she wanted him. To feel his mouth on hers, his arms around her. How much else there was, she wasn't sure, but she wanted him to show her. Then he wrapped one arm around her waist, drawing her the few inches to him. He placed his hand on her cheek and brushed his slightly callused thumb over her lips. This was going just as she'd wanted it to. It would be the most perfect night of her life.

"You are exquisite." His voice was low and sultry.

A pleasurable shiver ran down her spine. She'd never thought to hear a man say that to her. She or fate had chosen well.

He bent his head and moved his lips softly against hers.

She rested one hand lightly on his shoulders. He took the other, encouraging her to wrap her arms around his neck. When he trailed his tongue over the seam of her mouth, she did not know what to do so she puckered them a little. He smiled against her lips. Had she done something wrong? She could not allow him to stop.

As bold as the lady had been when she had invited Matt to join her in the parlor and in their conversation, he had expected her to be experienced. She was not, and, for no reason he could understand, he wanted to crow. It was as if she had been waiting just for him.

Matt lifted his head and gazed down at her. "You've never been kissed before?"

A blush infused her cheeks. "Is it—is it that obvious?"

"No." Yes, but he wouldn't tell her that.

She lowered her long, thick lashes, and her unexpected shyness captivated him. "You are perfect."

Once again she raised her face to him. He leaned forward, breathing in her light, spicy scent. So different from the flowery perfumes other women used. Cupping both her cheeks with his hands, he kissed her again, nibbling her lush bottom lip, teaching her, urging her to open her mouth to him.

Her tentativeness gave way, and she held on to him tightly, returning his kisses with more vigor. As he stroked her back, he itched to untie the laces his fingers traveled over, and he paused for a moment. Too much too soon. This lady was the most remarkable woman he had ever known, and he needed to ensure he did not scare her away.

She sighed, sinking boneless against him.

Two of his good friends had recently married, and it was time he did so as well. He hadn't believed his friend Marcus all those years ago when he'd claimed to have fallen in love with Phoebe at first sight. Matt did now.

He had no brothers, and it was past time he wed. The idea to look seriously for a wife had been pestering him more and more over the past few months. Matt wanted to laugh. It never occurred to him that he would meet his future wife when they were stranded together in a small inn. He held her closer. Whoever she was, she was his. If only she would tell him her name. He considered ignoring all the manners he had learned and asking her for it. But he was afraid she'd flee. What did it matter, though, when he would spend the rest of his life getting to know her.

He supposed he'd have to wait until to-morrow to propose or to ask whom he should go to for permission to address her. Yet her countenance, conversation, and the mature curves of her body told him she was not a young lady. So much the better if she could answer for herself.

A knock sounded on the door. He broke the kiss and set her away from him. "Yes?"

Brown opened the door and poked his head in. "My lord, my—um, I mean ma'am. Your chambers are ready. I had one of my girls run a heating pan between the sheets and put hot bricks in them."

When Matt had released her, his lady had turned from the door to face the fireplace, leaving him to deal with the innkeeper. "Thank you, Brown."

"Ring if you need anything, and someone will answer straightaway."

"Thank you, again." Matt closed the door.

In two steps he was with her again. He placed a finger under her chin, tilting her head up. "I'll escort you to your room."

She nodded. Even in the candlelight, he could see the desire lurking in her eyes. He wished he could take her to his chamber, but there was time enough for that after they were betrothed.

Leaving her at her bedroom door, he went to the chamber he'd been given at the opposite end of the hall.

Matt was pleased to find a decanter of brandy on the bedside table. He stripped off his clothes and donned a serviceable dark green wool dressing gown the landlord had left for him. He stood staring into the fire, twirling the glass and trying to decide what he would say when he proposed. Finding out her name might be a good idea as well.

Grace could not believe he had kissed her like that and then left her at her chamber door. Good Lord, she had practically thrown herself at him.

"You see, he didn't want you," her conscience mocked.

"He did, I—I could tell by his—by his kiss."

Why did Worthington have to be such a *gentleman?* It was not the most helpful thing he could have done at the moment. He could have made it easier for her. After what he had said and the way he had kissed her, how could he have just left her here? Obviously if she was going to have her night, she would have to do something. There was nothing for it. She would have to go to him.

She called the maid and undressed. It had taken another glass of wine and several minutes to gather her courage. Then she threw the blanket around her shoulders and stepped out into the corridor to find him.

Fortunately, a light shone under the door at the other end of the corridor. It must be him. Except for her servants, sleeping on the floor above and in the stable, she and Worthington were the only two guests in the inn.

The old, worn floorboards were cold under her feet as she walked the short distance to his chamber. Taking a breath, Grace fought down the fear threatening to overtake her. Surely he would not turn her away. She knocked on the door and entered.

The pleased expression on his face told her she had not been mistaken. He did want her. Every bit as much as she had prayed he would.

Chapter Three

A cold draft heralded Matt's door opening. He turned and his heart swelled with joy, as he gave thanks to the deity.

The pristine white of his lady's chemise peeked out from beneath the wool blanket she had wrapped around her body. Her long hair hung loose, curling over her shoulders to her waist. There was a small, timorous smile on her lips. Even though she was clearly nervous, she had come to him.

He thought briefly about what his friends had gone through to wed and smiled. This had to be the easiest courtship in history. All he'd had to do was take refuge from a storm.

She blushed. "May I—may I come in?"

Three long steps brought him to her. "Yes." *Into my life, my home, my heart.* Part of him couldn't believe she was actually here. "Yes, you may come in."

As he picked her up, the blanket fell to the floor. Matt kissed her and stared into her eyes before he walked to the large bed and gently lowered her feet to the floor. His fingers hovered over the ribbons of her chemise, tingling in anticipation. "May I?"

His lady glanced up at him. "Yes."

He pulled the bows free, and the finely woven muslin fell

to her hips. Matt lost his breath. Her hair screened all but the light pink tips of her generous ivory breasts. They called to him, begging to be tasted and worshipped. Was there ever a more perfect woman? He captured her lips with his, as he pushed the garment down to her waist. He stepped back, her hips swelled gently out and a triangle of gold covered her mons.

Mine, tonight and forever.

Drawing the sheets aside, he lifted her, placing her in the middle of the bed. He removed his dressing gown and crawled in next to her. He'd make this night, her first time making love with him, perfect for his lady.

Matt hesitated. Perhaps he should propose now before they made love. No, best to do it right to-morrow. She must know what he intended, otherwise she would never have come to him.

His lady lay still watching him, her eyes wide and dark as he traced her body with his palms. He had to touch all of her, to make sure she was truly there. *With my body I thee worship.*

"You are the most beautiful woman I've ever seen."

She smiled a little and trembled.

"Don't be afraid. I'll be gentle." He stretched out next to her, encouraging her to touch him as well before pressing soft kisses on her neck down to the perfect mounds of her breasts. Touching her nipples as they furled into tight buds for him, Matt took one into his mouth, teasing it with his tongue and sucking. She quivered and pressed into him. Sighing as he kissed his way down to the light curls between her legs. Triumphant, he found her already hot and wet for him.

A quiet moan escaped her lips, but she didn't tense.

When his tongue made a long, slow stroke across her center she cried out and arched off the bed. His body shook with desire as he drank in her delicate flavor. He'd never received so much satisfaction in pleasuring a woman. Perhaps it was because this one would be the only lady he'd pleasure for the rest of his life.

Grace took in his muscular chest with its dusting of hair. It was even more impressive without clothes. She fought her embarrassment when he removed her chemise, but there was no room for maidenly modesty. If she were to have only one night of passion she wanted it all, even if she didn't know what that entailed.

Grace would have to trust him to lead her.

Then he called her exquisite, and her heart melted.

He chuckled and stared down at her. "Touch me if you wish."

She reached out, laying her hand on his chest, then couldn't resist playing with the curling, dark hair covering it. And though the hair was soft, his chest was hard, much harder than hers. She'd occasionally seen men in the fields without shirts, but none of them looked like Worthington.

He kissed her tenderly as he stroked her, everywhere. His hands, not soft like hers, but rougher, caused her skin to warm to his caresses. She didn't know how good another person's touch could be. A man's touch. Her breathing hitched as Worthington placed soft kisses where his hands had been.

"My lady," he whispered. "My love."

My love? Tears tried to fill her eyes, but she blinked them back, refusing to allow them. If only that was true, but even if she were to entertain the notion of staying with him, he would not want to take on her responsibilities. She wouldn't think about that tonight. It was probably just something men said when they were with a woman. And what did it matter, this was what she wanted.

Allowing him to retake her senses, Grace moaned as tension ebbed and flowed and he laid claim to her. Need flowered deep inside. Desire flooded her, overwhelming her senses.

Her breasts were heavy, and her nipples were so hard they ached. Worthington touched them, circling lightly with his thumbs. When he lifted his head, Grace tried to stop him from breaking their kiss. Then he took one nipple in his mouth and sucked. The sensation was like nothing she'd experienced before. She'd gone to heaven. He ministered to the other breast then placed featherlight kisses down her body to the sensitive spot between her legs. When he licked her lightly, she cried out, begging for more.

Worthington held her in place when her hips thrust up against him. Her body seemed to have more of an idea what to do than she did.

"Not yet, my sweet. You'll have your chance." His voice was deep, intoxicating.

Grace thrashed her head. Her body tightened with tension until she thought she couldn't stand it anymore then suddenly, wave upon wave of delight flooded her. Her heart pounded so hard she could hear it.

He made a groaning sound and, with fluid grace, stretched out beside her again, claiming her lips. He tasted different this time. There was an added layer of musk to his arousing tang.

Worthington reached for a glass and took a sip, and offered it to her. "It's brandy."

"Thank you."

He raised her in his arms, and she took a sip, it burned. *Fool's courage.*

Worthington gazed down at her. The place between her legs throbbed. "Are you sure you want to go further, my love?"

How could she not? Some part of her was still empty, and she only had tonight to last for the rest of her life. "Yes, I am positive."

His deep voice caressed her. "Tell me if you want me to stop."

Stop? *Never.* Not now that she'd gone so far. She nodded. "I will."

Hard lips teased hers and his tongue grazed her teeth. Moaning, she met his caresses with her own. His hand stroked the apex of her thighs, placing one finger inside her. The fire burned deep in her core and he held her to the kiss as she cried out. Nothing had ever felt so good or so right.

Worthington chuckled lightly, as if he was enjoying this as much as she. Grace was wet where he touched her and wondered why. He shifted his body over hers, slowly entering, filling her. Then he thrust, and a sharp pain spiked through her, and he stopped. Worthington's lips moved on hers and ravished her mouth, sending her into a whirling inferno that ripped away her wits.

The heat was so great Grace could only try to respond to him, to appease Worthington's need as well as her own. He kneaded her breasts, and she cried out through the kiss, wanting more.

When his lips left hers, he was fully inside her and gently thrusting.

"How do you feel, are you all right?" he murmured.

"Yes, I feel . . ." Grace couldn't find the words. The pain had receded and he, his body possessed her fully and she'd never known such joy.

"Well loved, I hope. You'll feel even more so. I promise. Wrap your legs around me."

She did as he asked, and he took her even more fully. Flames danced and she sizzled. Grace was in the storm raging outside, but somehow hot, waiting for an explosion. Suddenly sparks shot through her.

I'll pleasure you for the rest of your life, she thought she'd heard him say.

Matt swallowed her scream with a kiss. Her legs squeezed him like a vice, and her sheath tightened around him as he held on, with no hope of withdrawing. Thrusting deeper still, he spilled his seed. His lady had clung to him and was now slowly relaxing. He pressed soft kisses in her hair. This wonderful woman was his.

Before they'd climbed the stairs he'd decided to marry her because he needed a wife and she was everything he'd been looking for. Now he knew she was necessary to his future well-being. He needed to be with her for the rest of his life. They'd wed as soon as he could arrange it and nothing would separate them.

Matt arranged her next to him in the place that would be hers for the rest of their lives "Sleep, my love."

Tears choked her. Grace wanted to say something to Worthington and couldn't. He'd done everything perfectly. Better than she could have ever imagined. She was such a fool to have thought she could give herself to him with no consequences. Still, she didn't know she'd fall in love. What was worse, he called her his love as if he meant it. The pain in her chest grew as her heart ripped in pieces. Even if he did love her, nothing could come of it; she'd given her oath and could not marry.

Hours later, a beam of white light streamed through the window waking Grace. The air was still. Bright stars twinkled in the antelucan sky. The storm had passed, and she was tucked into Worthington's side, warm and protected. She wanted to stay here for the rest of her life. Yet, she had to leave. Slipping out of the bed was harder than she'd thought it would be. He was so much larger than she, and she had to climb up out of the mattress's indentation. When he reached for her, she thought he'd woken. Stilling, she waited until he snored softly again.

Quickly donning her chemise, she grabbed the blanket, wrapping it around her. She glanced at the bed, memorizing Worthington's strong features, wishing she could risk kissing or touching him one last time.

Grace moved as silently as she could back to her room.

She judged the time to be about four in the morning. Washing, she dressed as best as she could before ringing for the maid.

A soft knock fell on the door and Susan entered, rubbing the sleep out of her eyes. "Yes, my lady."

Grace cast the girl an apologetic look and wished she had worn a gown with buttons in the front. "Please just tie my laces, and you may go back to your bed. I am sorry to disturb you so early, but I must be on my way. Please tell your father we'll be leaving."

A few minutes later, Grace reached the ground floor. Mr. Brown handed her a cup of tea. "My lady, we'd be happy if you'd break your fast with us."

Grace took the cup and smiled, but shook her head. "Thank you, but I must go home. My family will be worried."

"Wait a bit, and I'll get you some bread and cheese. You can eat it on the way."

Considering the amount of food she'd consumed at dinner, she was amazingly hungry. "Thank you."

Shortly thereafter, Grace walked through the door and out into the frozen landscape to her coach. Heavy frost covered the ground and snow decorated the inn's windowsills. Thankfully, the moon was bright enough to guide them.

Her groom helped her into her carriage and a few moments later they were on their way. "We'll be at the Hall well before daylight, my lady."

Pulling her cloak around her, Grace turned to Neep. "Thank you. Did any of you eat?"

"Some bread and ham. Good enough 'til we get back."

Grace nodded and snuggled back against the soft, but cold, squabs, grateful for her cloak and the warm bricks under her feet.

As the coach lurched forward, she gazed out to the window of the inn's first-floor bedchamber where Worthington slept. The only man she'd ever wanted to love her did, and it was too late. Wishing he still held her in his strong arms, she tried to hold back her tears, yet they slid silently down her cheeks as she cried for what might have been and for what could never be.

A little more than an hour later, they turned into the drive of Stanwood Hall. She wiped away all traces of her sorrow and assumed a bright smile that would hide her misery.

Entering the large, airy Georgian hall, Grace was greeted by her concerned butler, Royston, who took her cloak. A moment later, an explosion of noise as six children, ranging in age from eighteen to five, ran to her. Pandemonium reigned as they poured their concern and fear into her ears.

She should have known they'd panic when she was de-layed. "What are you all doing up so early? Here, I haven't had my breakfast yet. Let me eat and, if you will all quiet down, I can tell you what occurred to delay me."

They escorted her to the breakfast room.

Eighteen-year-old Charlotte handed her a cup of tea while Walter, age fourteen, piled food on a plate and brought it to her. Alice and Eleanor, twins, age twelve, and Philip, eight, sat around the table staring at her, waiting. Mary, the youngest at five years of age, climbed into Grace's lap. The only one missing was Charlie, now the Earl of Stanwood, who was at Eton.

"I thought you had gone away like Mama did," Mary said, her bottom lip trembling.

Grace hugged her sister tightly. "There is nothing to be afraid of. I'm here now."

After taking a bite of toast and a sip of tea, Grace steeled herself to remain calm as she answered their questions. No one could know anything about Worthington or suspect there was anything wrong. "I was on my way home from Cousin Anne's when a storm hit. Fortunately, I was close to an inn and able to take refuge. Nothing more exciting than that occurred. Quite a dull trip all in all." Nothing at all except meeting Worthington and spending the most wonderful night of her life in his arms. "Now, we have three weeks before we leave for London. I expect all of you to behave so that we may get off in good time. Royston"—she turned to her butler—"do I have anything in the post?"

"Yes, my lady. I put it in the study."

Grace glanced around the table. "Charlotte, I shall meet you there in an hour. If you've finished eating, please practice either your singing or the piano until I send for you. The rest of you have lessons."

They left the table as one and the room became suddenly quiet. Only her cousin Jane, who'd acted as Grace's companion for the last four years, remained.

Jane gave Grace a concerned frown. "Grace, you look tired. Didn't you sleep well?"

"Well enough, considering the storm. I suspect when I've bathed and re-dressed I'll look more the thing."

Her cousin smiled softly. "Of course. That must be it. Have you given any consideration to reentering society yourself? It would be a shame for you to miss all the fun."

Grace pressed her lips together. She'd not been in London for the Season since her mother died in childbirth along with the baby. "What would be the point? I am not free to marry until Charlie is one and twenty and able to take over the guardianship of the children. That is still five years away. Even then, he will require me to raise them." She shook her head. "When Mary is ready to come out, if some gentleman is looking for an ape-leader then, I'll consider it. Until that time, I shall go to teas and entertainments of that sort, but not to balls. You and Aunt Herndon can be gadabouts. She is sponsoring Charlotte and must attend in any event."

Jane scoffed. "Surely, you will go to Lady Thornhill's drawing rooms."

Lady Thornhill had the most interesting gatherings in the

ton, drawing from artists, writers, and philosophers for her guests. Grace picked up the pot and poured more tea. "Yes, I may do that and perhaps some of the political parties."

Her cousin rose. "I shall leave you now. I know you have much to do."

Jane was as kind as she was undemanding. In her late thirties, her blond hair was beginning to show some silver. She'd lost her love at sea and had never been tempted to marry another. Perhaps she would find someone this Season, though that would leave Grace seeking another companion.

A deep bark came from the hall, and a one-year-old Great Dane, towing a footman, bounded into the breakfast room. Finding her mistress, the dog went to Grace and placed its huge head on her arm.

"Good morning, Daisy, did you miss me?" She glanced up at the footman. "Do I want to know how walking lessons are going?"

He grimaced. "We was doing better, my lady, until she heard you."

Grace patted the dog, stroking her soft ears. "You'll have to be left behind if you cannot learn to walk on a lead."

Daisy gave her a sidelong glance and directed her attention to the beef on Grace's plate.

Grace grinned. She was probably too lenient with the dog. "No. I will not have you eating from the table."

Daisy looked back up at her with large, hopeful eyes.

"You are incorrigible." Grace ate the last of her egg then gave Daisy the small piece of meat. "Go find something to do that won't get you into trouble. I must change."

Wagging her tail, Daisy followed her mistress to her room, dragging the footman with her. Grace sighed in resignation. "George, you may leave her with me for a while."

He bowed. "Thank you, my lady. We'll try the walking again later."

She stared down at Daisy and wrinkled her brow. "Very well, you may come with me, but you must behave."

By the time she'd repeated the story of her absence to her maid, Bolton, the tub was ready.

Sinking into the warm water, Grace found twinges in muscles she didn't know she'd had until making love with Worthington. Her throat tightened, but she stopped herself from weeping again. She'd gotten what she wanted and more, much more than she expected. She would just have to remember him with happiness and affection. That is the only way she could think of him now.

Worthington was perfect in every way. If she could marry, he would be the one. But if she wed, she would lose the guardianship of the children she'd fought so hard for and they'd be separated from one another. She clinched her teeth remembering her aunts' and uncles' scorn in thinking she could raise the children. The court battles that had cost so much in money and emotional pain. Yet, she had made a promise to her mother that she would keep the children together. Even if she had not, she would have fought to keep her family whole. They had already lost so much. They would not have survived being separated from one another. What joy could she have found if she'd left them? Thank God her grandfather had finally taken her side and ended the contretemps in her favor.

By the time Grace entered her study, Daisy was lounging in front of the fire, and Charlotte sat at the other end of the partner's desk working on accounts. "I thought you were to practice your music?"

Charlotte pressed her lips together. "I wanted to see how much I could get done without your help. After all, once I marry, I'll have to do it on my own."

"Humph. Well I suppose you have a point. Do you have selections ready that you can play and sing without your music?"

She started to roll her eyes. Grace glared and Charlotte stopped. "Sorry. Yes, I have a few ready, and Dotty and I have been working on a duet we can play together."

Grace took her seat and opened the letter on top. For several minutes the only sound was the scratches of Charlotte's pen. Once Grace had gotten through all the business correspondence, she started on her personal letters. "Charlotte, listen to this. My friend Phoebe, Lady Evesham, is increasing. She'll be in Town but not going about much. She has given us a letter of introduction to Madame Lisette, whom, I will have you know, is the most exclusive modiste in Town. If we arrive a couple of weeks before the Season, Phoebe has arranged for Madame to design all your gowns." Grace put down the letter and glanced at her sister. "Isn't that good news?"

Charlotte's face was wreathed in smiles. "Yes, indeed. Dotty told me Miss Smithton wanted to go to her last year and could not get in."

Grace resisted a grin. Dotty, Charlotte's best friend, was coming out this Season as well. Miss Smithton, a year older than Charlotte and Dotty, had considered herself the reigning neighborhood beauty until Charlotte and Dotty began going to the local assemblies and some private parties. Miss Smithton was indeed beautiful and knew it, which put off many of the young men. Charlotte's fair hair contrasting with Dotty's black tresses made a stunning pair, which caused many young men to gather around them. Grace was glad they would come out together.

Her sister picked up a heavy glass paperweight, lifting it up and down for a few moments. "Grace, do you think Dotty may come with us to Madame Lisette's?"

"My dear, I am sure Lady Sterne will have sorted Dotty's wardrobe." She saw no reason to remind Charlotte that the Sternes were not quite so plump in the pocket as the Carpenters. "You may go shopping with her at Pantheon's Bazaar." Grace took out her calendar. "We must bring our trip forward by a week."

Charlotte glanced at her pensively. "Grace, wouldn't it be nice if you and I left early, and the children could come as planned?"

Sitting back, Grace toyed with the feather end of the quill, passing it over her cheek and lips until it reminded her of Worthington's kisses. She put it down. "I'd love to be able to give you that treat. Let me talk to Jane and the others. If they think they can handle the rest of the children without me, we'll do it."

Jumping up in a very unladylike fashion, Charlotte rushed to Grace, hugging and kissing her. "Oh, thank you, thank you, thank you! I love them all, but sometimes . . ."

Grace returned her sister's embrace, pushing a stray curl behind Charlotte's ear. "I understand, my dear. No one could think badly of you for wanting some time without all of them hanging on one and listening at the doors."

Charlotte stepped back and frowned slightly. "Do you ever wish it?"

Smiling, Grace took her hand. "Of course I do. But I wouldn't give any of you up. Not for anything." *Not even for Lord Worthington*. "And we are very fortunate. Unlike many, we have the funds to order life as we will. All of you girls have good dowries, and the boys have easy competences. Indeed, I could not wish for more."

"We're lucky we have you." Charlotte grinned and squeezed Grace's hand. "I've finished the accounts and they all balance. May I ride to Dotty's house?"

There'd be no gallops for her sister in London. Grace

glanced at her and nodded. "Yes, as long as you dress warmly and take your groom."

Charlotte kissed Grace again and skipped, before remembering to walk out of the room at a sedate pace.

She put her head in her hands, which was how Jane found her. "Grace, my dear, *are* you going to tell me what is bothering you? You've been in a brown study all day."

She glanced up. "It is nothing, really. There's just so much to do, and now I must take Charlotte to London a week early for her wardrobe. Do you think, between you, Nurse, Miss Tallerton, and Mr. Winters, you could manage the rest of the children yourselves for that week?"

"I do not see why we cannot." Jane's brow wrinkled. "The boys mind Mr. Winters well and the girls love Miss Tallerton. Where will you stay? You'll not want to be alone at Stanwood House with Charlotte."

Grace shook her head. "No, that would not be at all proper. I shall write Aunt Herndon and ask if we may visit with her for the week. It will be a good way for Charlotte and her to get to know each other better. My sister is a good girl, though one could hardly call her biddable."

Jane eyes sparkled with laughter. "None of the girls could be called biddable, my dear, including you."

"No, I think it's in the blood." Grace grinned and picked up another letter. "Oh look, it's from Charlie." She read his hastily scratched missive. "He's doing well and thinks I shall be happy with his marks this term. He asks if he may come to London during the holiday. Well of all the chuckleheads. Where else should he go?"

Her cousin gave a laugh, shook her head, then left Grace alone with her correspondence. Yet other than reading a few letters from friends with whom she maintained a large correspondence, she accomplished nothing else. She turned in her chair and gazed out of the window at the rosebushes.

Many of them were still covered in frost and sparkled under the midday sun.

She shouldn't have done it. She'd thought if only she could experience it once, she'd be satisfied to live out her life as a spinster. Now she was anything but content. Every time she thought of him, her body tingled and she imagined his hands stroking and teasing her. And it was not only the lovemaking. And it wasn't simply the way he made her body feel, she'd so enjoyed talking with him throughout the day and evening. They agreed on almost everything. When they had differed, he'd listened to her point of view respectfully and even agreed she had good reason to think as she did. She would miss that more than his touch.

She had to stop thinking about him. Going to Town early would be a good change. She could settle Charlotte's wardrobe and forget Worthington.

Grace reached out for a piece of elegant pressed paper and dipped her pen in the standish.

> *My Dearest Aunt Almeria,*
>
> *Charlotte and I are so looking forward to our visit with you. An opportunity to have Charlotte's entire wardrobe for the Season made by Madame Lisette has arisen. Therefore I do most earnestly hope you will not mind if we come a bit earlier . . .*

Yet even as she wrote her aunt with plans for their visit, the emptiness inside her wouldn't leave.

Chapter Four

Dawn had still not broken when Matt awoke. He grinned to himself. Soon he would be an engaged man. Finally, he understood the looks of love and possession he'd seen in his friends' faces when they glanced at their wives. That was exactly what he wanted with his lady. Later, after the sun had made an appearance, he'd discover her name and how soon they could wed. Reaching for her, his hand found nothing but a cold, empty sheet. He listened for any sign of her in the chamber, but there was nothing. Hmm, she must have gone to her room, but why? There was no one in the inn but them. Perhaps she was concerned about servants. Although none of them seemed to appear until called.

Rising, he donned his dressing gown, walked down the corridor, then opened the door to her chamber. Empty. Nothing to even indicate she'd been there.

The clock on the mantel showed five o'clock. He went back to his room and tugged the bell-pull. In a few minutes, the boots brought hot water for him to shave.

Matt waited until the water was poured into the basin. "The lady who was here last evening, is she downstairs?"

"I dunno, my lord. Ain't seen no lady," the lad mumbled, and left.

Matt finished dressing and descended the stairs. His groom, Mac, was in the common room eating. "Where are the others?"

Mac finished chewing and swallowed. "Gone, my lord. Their coach ain't in the yard."

Something wasn't right. Why would she have left and not told him? "Be ready to leave in half an hour."

He looked around for the landlord and, not finding him, entered the parlor. Covered dishes set on the table, with one place setting. He wished he was sharing the meal with her and conversing as they had the night before. *Hell*. He wanted to be in a warm bed with her next to him.

Mr. Brown knocked on the door before entering. "My lord, you was wishful of seeing me?"

Now Matt would get some answers. "Yes, I want to know the lady's name."

The innkeeper opened his eyes wide. "What lady, my lord?"

Matt bit the inside of his lip and tried to keep from losing his temper. "The lady who was here last night. The one I shared dinner with."

The landlord started backing out of the parlor, shaking his head. "Weren't no lady here, my lord."

Matt choked back an angry response. Losing his temper would do him no good. He must attempt to reason with the innkeeper. "I can understand she would not want it known she was here alone and without her maid. But you may tell me who she is. I plan to marry her, and I need to know her direction."

"I'd like to help you, my lord, but I can't." The man closed the door.

Matt stood so quickly his chair crashed to the floor, but by the time he got to the hall, the innkeeper had prudently taken himself off.

"You there."

The young woman glanced at Matt wide-eyed. "Yes, sir?"

"Where is Brown?"

"Me da had to go to the farm."

"When will he return?"

She furrowed her brow. "No tell'n how long he'll take."

"Do you know the lady who was here?"

"I just got here meself. I only work during the day and weren't here at all yesterday."

Matt stalked off. "Damn the man."

He strode outside to find his curricle ready and Mac standing next to it. "Did any of the lady's servants mention where they live?"

"No, my lord. One of the younger men said something about a hall, but the others shut him up right quick."

Matt clenched his fists. "*Hall!* Hall does me no good at all. Half the bloody houses in England are called the Hall. How the devil am I to find her?"

Mac closed one eye and stared at Matt. "You sure she weren't married?"

He glared at his groom. "Yes, quite sure."

"Jus asking." Mac shrugged. "Suppose we could stop along the way and ask."

Matt rubbed his cheek. Why hadn't he thought of it? "Good idea, Mac, we'll try finding her that way."

For the next few hours, they asked at every inn and coaching house along the road home. But by the time they stopped for luncheon, Matt knew no more than he had that morning. No one remembered seeing a coach carrying a golden-haired lady.

Where had she gone, and why did she leave him? The idea that he could just forget her was immediately shrugged off. No, he was the first man to have touched her, and she was his. What if she was with child? *His child.*

He ground his teeth. By God, somehow he'd find her.

By the middle of the afternoon, he'd driven up to the

front door of his home, and was in as foul mood as he'd ever been in. Matt jumped down from the curricle.

"Why do you look so milligrubbed?"

He narrowed his eyes at Theodora, his eight-year-old sister. "What did I tell you about talking cant? If you cannot stop repeating everything the grooms say, I shall have to discover who's teaching it to you and dismiss him."

Blue eyes the same color as his widened. "You wouldn't make Curry leave?"

He stared down at his youngest sister. *Probably not.* "I will and you shall have it on your conscience. Is that what you want?"

Theodora's long, dark brown braid flipped around as she shook her head. "No."

Curry was her personal groom and Theo was very fond of him. "Then see you mind your tongue."

She nodded her head emphatically. "Yes, Matt. But you haven't answered my question."

He picked her up. "And I don't intend to. Where's your mother?"

Theo screwed up her face in thought. "She was in the morning room the last time I saw her, but that was a long time ago."

He stopped and frowned. "Don't you have lessons?"

She gazed up at the sky and kept her mouth firmly shut.

"I thought so."

Swinging her up onto his shoulders, he carried her into the house, setting her on the stairs. "Go, now."

"Thorton," he said, addressing his butler. "Where is her ladyship?"

His butler bowed. "We are very happy to see you home, my lord. Her ladyship is in her parlor."

"Thank you." Taking the steps two at a time, he quickly caught up with Theodora's much slower progress. Matt flung her over his shoulder and finished climbing with her giggling in his ear. He set her down on the stairs to the school-room. "There you go, little one, up to the school-room with you."

He stood watching her until she was at the top and then turned toward his stepmother's apartments. After knocking on her door, he entered.

His father had married Patience barely a year after his mother had died in childbirth. Matt had learned of the marriage from one of his schoolmates. At first he was inclined to be resentful, but when he went home for the long summer holiday, he found his father's new bride was a shy, scared seventeen-year-old. A mere five years older than he and she already breeding.

His father had stayed around long enough to introduce them and left for Bath, where he spent the remainder of the summer before decamping to Town for the Little Season. The new Lady Worthington didn't see London again until one year after her husband had died.

Although he had encouraged her to re-marry, she would not. Patience truly loved her daughters and, as Matt was his sisters' sole guardian, re-marriage would mean leaving them at Worthington Hall.

She glanced up, set aside her embroidery, and smiled. "Worthington, I'm so glad you're home. The girls have missed you horribly."

He gave her a peck on the cheek. "How have you been?"

"I'm well. We are all excited about Louisa's come out. Do you need anything?"

He'd known she would ask. "Yes, I've fallen in love. The only problem is I can't find her."

Patience went off into a peal of light laughter. "Mattheus Worthington, what will you say next? Isn't this rather sudden? Did you meet her in Town?"

"It may be, but it's true, and I wouldn't be the first man to fall in love at first sight. I met her at an inn during a storm. She left before I could discover her name. I need your help finding her." He described in careful detail his love's most important features.

She pressed her lips together as if she would argue, then her countenance softened and she nodded. "Very well, but my dear, why do you not draw her for me?"

"That's a good idea." Why hadn't he thought of it? Ever since he'd discovered she had left him, his brain had stopped working. Matt took her leave going immediately to his studio.

Using a pencil, he sketched his lady's face and hair, careful to use the style she had when it was up, and colored it in. Once he was satisfied, he took it to Patience. "What do you think? Do you recognize her?"

Patience squinted over the drawing and tapped her cheek. "I have seen her. I just don't know when. It must have been a few years ago, because her cheeks were rounder. Like that of a younger lady, still"—she held the paper up to the light—"I am sure it's her."

He was so close. He tried not to dance a jig. His breath caught. "Who? Who is she?"

Her brows drew together. "That's the problem, I don't remember her name. May I keep this? When we get to Town, I'll ask a few discreet friends."

"Yes, of course. Though I don't want her name bandied around."

Her eyes twinkled in amusement. "I shall be very careful. I am leaving for London with the girls in two weeks to purchase Louisa's clothing. When will you join us?"

"I'm off to Leicestershire hunting, but I should arrive in Town around the same time you do." He paused for a moment. "If you need to hire an additional maid to keep Theodora under control, you have my permission."

Patience pulled a face. "Cant again?"

"Yes." He frowned. "I hope I have impressed upon her

that if she cannot control her tongue, I'll have to dismiss her groom. I'll have Mac speak to the lad as well. I've no objection to her learning the words. But she doesn't have the discretion not to spout them out at the wrong times."

"How extremely large-minded of you," Patience replied sarcastically. "You may not care that she learns such vulgar language, but I certainly do. What do you think will happen when she comes out, pray?"

His mouth twisted into a grimace. "Let's get through the other three before we worry about Theo. I'll see you at dinner."

Matt went back to his studio and sat at his drawing table. Again putting pencil to paper, he drew his love's perfect oval face and long, curling hair, her slim, elegant neck and slightly sloping shoulders. Once he allowed his memory to take him back to the feel of her full breasts, his pencil reverently made them appear. By the time he was done, carefully leaving her facial features blank, he'd drawn his lady naked, the way he remembered her as she waited to give herself to him. He would have liked to have drawn the passion in her beautiful blue eyes and the smile of delight on her lips when he kissed them. But if anyone found the picture it would ruin her, and she was his to protect.

Excitement over Louisa's come out turned dinner into a raucous affair causing him to threaten to leave the younger girls at home with an army of servants to watch over them. "I will not have my sisters acting like a bunch of sad romps. In two days, I shall depart to go hunting." He fixed the three younger girls with a firm look. "If your behavior has not improved by then, only Louisa will go to Town."

From the corner of his eye, he saw Patience's lips twitch and had to clamp his own tightly together. "Louisa, you may excuse yourself and take your sisters with you."

Louisa opened her mouth, shut it, and glanced at the other girls. "Come along. We can play jackstraws until it's time for bed."

Once they'd left, Matt glanced at Patience. "To whom are you going for Louisa's gowns?"

"Oh, I thought Miss Lilly."

"No, she's not fashionable enough. I'll write to a friend of mine and arrange an introduction to Madame Lisette."

Patience's jaw dropped. "Worthington, I—why did you never tell me you could—Madame Lisette. Hardly anyone can get in to see her. But could you manage it?" She eyed him closely. "Is your friend respectable?"

He sat up, affronted. "Of course she's respectable. It's Lady Rutherford. She buys all her gowns from Madame. Lady Evesham does as well."

"But they are two of the most—"

"Yes, fashionably dressed young matrons on the Town. I am not such a fribble as you think, ma'am."

"I never thought any such a thing." Patience lifted her chin. "I just didn't realize you were so interested in women's fashion."

Not understanding her, he drew his brows together. What man wouldn't be fascinated in the clothing that allows women to be so enticing? "Many men are. Why should I be any different?"

Patience shrugged. "I just never think of you being in the petticoat line, but thank you very much. Who wouldn't want her daughter dressed in the latest style?"

He grinned. "It is a matter of family pride. She is my sister after all." Matt broadened his smile. "Whoever she marries may not thank me though."

His stepmother's eyes twinkled. "Madame Lisette is very expensive. You're a good brother."

Matt signaled for the port to be set on the table. "Now that that's settled, you can help me find my bride."

He rose when Patience left, then sat back down and poured a glass of port. Who else could he ask who was discreet enough to help him find her? Anna would, although if his lady hadn't been to Town in a while, she might be too young to know her. Phoebe would probably have met his lady. He'd talk to her when he got to Town.

Matt twirled his glass. If he had to go out of London to find her, then he would need to ask some of his friends to keep watch on his sister, Louisa. Harry Marsh would be in Town for the legislative session, both he and Emma would help and Rutherford. It wouldn't do for any fortune hunters to think Matt didn't take his role as guardian seriously.

He turned his thoughts back to his lady and scowled. Whoever was protecting her wasn't doing a very good job at it. She wasn't married: She wore no ring on her left hand, nor was there any indication she'd ever had one. And, until she'd come to him, she was a virgin. What could make a gently bred lady go to a stranger? But he wasn't a stranger to her. She'd addressed him as my lord. Where did he know her from? Did she think he was the type of man who would take her innocence and leave her? This brought him back to the question of why she'd given herself to him at all. He threw his head back against the chair. Why the devil had she disappeared?

Damn it all. There were too many unknowns and not enough answers.

Chapter Five

Two weeks later, Grace hugged and kissed each of the younger children. "Behave, and I shall see you in a week. I had better not hear that you tried to run wild."

"Yes, Grace," they chorused angelically.

She gave them a stern look.

Already in the coach, Charlotte called out, "Come on, Grace. Let's go!"

"Yes, my dear." Jane hugged Grace. "We'll all be fine. Enjoy your shopping."

The children were herded back into the house. This was the first time she'd left for so long since before her mother had died. Well, no point second-guessing herself now. She put a foot on the carriage step, then glanced back. "Write to me."

Jane grinned. "Every day. Whether you want to hear about them or not."

"Thank you."

Before Grace changed her mind she took her seat and gave the order to go.

"Think of it, Grace." Charlotte practically bounced on the opposite seat. "A whole week to shop and be by ourselves."

Settling back against the plush velvet squabs, she removed a book from her reticule. Visions of sick children and broken bones flashed through her mind. "Yes, just think about it."

Rather than make a push to London in one day, Grace had decided to spend a night on the road. It would make for two days of leisurely travel rather than one hard day. She'd ordered a guidebook depicting all of the most interesting historical places along the route. Never before having been to a larger town than Bedford, Charlotte agreed to everything Grace suggested. They spent a pleasant day sightseeing and having luncheon at a very good tavern.

Several hours later, they pulled into the yard of the King's Head Inn, in Hunton Bridge. Her groom, Neep, handed her down first. She was shaking her skirts out when Charlotte came up beside her. "Grace, this is so exciting. A real inn."

Grace resisted the urge to tell her they couldn't very well stay at an imaginary inn. "Yes. I've been told the rooms are comfortable and they have a good cook."

"They must, look how lovely the building is."

She hid her smile. Wondering if she'd ever been so impressed by an inn. "Er, yes. Well then, shall we go in?"

The innkeeper came out to greet them. "My lady, your maids arrived some time ago. I'll have one of my daughters take you to your chambers."

She inclined her head. "Thank you for letting me know." When she reached the top of the staircase, she squeezed her sister's shoulder. "Charlotte, meet me in the parlor after you've changed."

The door to Charlotte's chamber opened, and her lady's maid, May, held it open. "Oh, Lady Charlotte, come see. It's ever so nice."

Charlotte turned to Grace and grinned. "I'll see you downstairs."

Across the corridor, Bolton, Grace's lady's maid, opened

the door for her and shook her head. "That May's got nothing but feathers for brains."

Grace laughed. "Yes, I understand. Well, neither of them have stayed in an inn before. They'll calm down in a few days."

Bolton pursed her lips. "I hope so, my lady, or she and I will have to have a talk. She can't be acting like a skitter-brain in London."

May would come out on the losing end of it, Grace had no doubt. "Come, I must wash and change."

"I'll go order your wash water."

Left alone in her chamber, Grace thought back to the last time she'd spent the night at an inn and glanced at the large four-post bed with longing. A too vivid picture of Worthing-ton lying next to her touching and kissing her raced through her mind. Her body responded to the memory, and an ache between her legs made her want him even more. If only he could hold her just once more. If she could watch him sleeping and not have to leave.

She sighed.

"If you want to lie down, I'll tell them to push dinner back."

Goodness, Grace hadn't even heard her maid return. She needed to stop all this mooning about. It would do her no good at all. "No, I'm just a little fatigued from the travel. Not being in a coach until to-morrow is what I need."

That and to stop thinking about Worthington.

"What the devil's wrong with you?"

Matt glanced to his side as he made his way to the stables. A large bay gelding pranced prettily next to him. Mounted on the horse was the Marquis of Kenilworth. "Good morning, Kenilworth."

"Aren't you going with the hunt to-day?"

For some reason, chasing after a small fox did not hold its usual interest. "No. As a matter of fact, I'm leaving for Town."

"Why the deuce would you want to do that?" The man glanced at the group starting to form around the Master of the Hunt. "Only thing there this time of year are mamas getting their girls ready for their come out. Better off staying here." Kenilworth raised a brow, and drawled, "Unless you're in the market, that is."

Mac was leading the curricle out of the coaching house, and Matt was in a hurry. It hadn't been until he'd arrived that he realized he was in completely male company. If his host's ladies were in London, so might his lady be. Though he'd be damned if he would let Kenilworth know anything about her. He gave the marquis a chagrined look. "My sister's coming out."

"I don't envy you that." Kenilworth gave a shudder. "Remember hearing what my mother had to go through with my sisters. Never been so glad to be the youngest. I made sure I wasn't sent down from Oxford the whole of their Seasons."

Matt grinned. "I look forward to seeing you in a few weeks."

"Oh no, you won't." Kenilworth looked at Matt as if he'd lost his mind. "I'm there for parliament and other entertainments. You're not going to catch me around the types of parties you'll be attending." The other man tipped his hat as he rode away. "Might see you at Brooks though."

Matt climbed into his carriage, saluting the hunters as he drove toward the main road. He had no idea if his lady would attend the Season or not, but someone there must know who she was. As soon as he made sure his sisters were settled, he'd visit Marcus and Phoebe.

* * *

Charlotte and Grace had finally reached Mayfair. She rapped on the roof of the carriage. "Take us by Stanwood House if you please."

"Are we go'n in, my lady?"

"No, I merely wish to show Lady Charlotte where it is."

Ever since they'd reached London's outskirts, Charlotte had been excitedly pointing out all the people, conveyances, and buildings.

"This is really much different than some of the areas we went through."

"It is," Grace agreed, wishing there was some way she could help those less fortunate. "Anyone who has pretensions of being in Polite Society lives in Mayfair. Here we come into Berkeley Square. Our house is the fourth one in from the end."

Charlotte clapped her hands delightedly. "I can't wait to live here. That one floor looks to be all windows. Is that the school-room?"

"It is." Grace craned her neck to be able to see it. "I'm exceedingly proud of how it turned out."

A few minutes later, they arrived at Herndon House in Grosvenor Square.

As the coach rolled to a stop, her uncle's butler opened the door, and soon they were being led down a long corridor to the back of the house and announced.

"My dears." Aunt Herndon rose from her desk and bustled toward them, a harried expression on her face. "I wasn't expecting you until closer to dinner. Not that it matters, my housekeeper has had your rooms ready for days." She hugged Grace then said, "Dear Charlotte, how you've grown. Let me look at you." She held Charlotte's chin with two fingers, turning her face one way then the other. "Perfect." Aunt Herndon dropped her hand and smiled at Grace. "I could not have asked for better."

Charlotte's chin firmed and Grace smothered a sigh.

This was not the time for her sister to become miffed. It was very fortunate they were only spending one week at their aunt's house. "Charlotte?"

Charlotte curtseyed gracefully. "How pleased I am to meet you again, Aunt Herndon."

Their aunt smiled again, glancing at Grace. "Despite what everyone said would be a bad result. You've done a wonderful job, my dear. You should be proud."

Grace's throat tightened. "Thank you for that and all your support."

Until her aunt had given her approval, she hadn't realized how concerned she'd been about Charlotte's come out. Other than her maternal grandfather, Lord Timothy, none of her relatives thought she was capable of raising her brothers and sisters. Her heart contracted at the memory of panic and nightmares her younger brothers and sisters had when, for a short time, it appeared they would be parceled off in ones and twos to family members. If it hadn't been for his and then Uncle Herndon's support, she would not have been awarded guardianship.

Aunt Herndon turned back to Charlotte. "Call me Aunt Almeria, my child. I predict you'll have a wonderful Season with many offers."

A few moments later, Charlotte and Grace were shown to their chambers, urged to rest, and informed that tea would be served at four o'clock in the back parlor. Grace removed her hat and gloves, handing them to Bolton. She'd not been able to cast off the lowness of spirit that had affected her since her rendezvous with Worthington, but her aunt's words strengthened her resolve. There was more to her life than lying contented and loved in his arms. As hard as it was, her main focus must be on Charlotte and the rest of the children. Not Worthington and the way he made her laugh or agreed with her about political issues close to her heart. And

God help her, not the way he held and kissed her and called her his love.

Yet whenever she thought of him her body burned with remembered pleasure. That could not happen any longer. This whole matter had become much more complicated than she'd expected. Drat the man. Why couldn't he leave her alone?

Bolton helped her change moments before Charlotte fairly flounced into Grace's chamber. "I cannot believe she did that." Charlotte seethed with indignation. "As if I was some sort of prized horse. I should have shown her my teeth."

Grace passed a hand over her brow, then fixed her sister with a look. "You may as well calm down now. It will not be the last time something of the sort occurs."

Charlotte frowned and her lower lip thrust out. "Did you have to go through it?"

Drawing Charlotte to the small sofa set before the marble fireplace, Grace placed her arm around her sister as she thought back to her first Season. "Yes, of course. It won't last long and fighting it will only make you appear churlish. It is for this exact reason we practice our manners. So that no matter the provocation, one is able to respond with proper restraint."

She might have been better off recalling that at the inn with Worthington.

Charlotte took Grace's hand and rubbed it against her cheek. "Oh, Grace, I'm so sorry. You must think me the most spoiled creature in nature. I didn't mean to upset you. I'll do everything you taught me, I promise."

She gave her sister a hug. "Thank you. Just remember, it won't last long." She tried to smile. "I'm sending a note round to Lady Evesham. If she is receiving, we shall visit her."

Charlotte glowed. "I would love to go and thank her for recommending us to Madame Lisette."

"Well then, return to your chambers and dress for tea."

Charlotte gave her a hug and a kiss then rushed out of the room. It was hard to imagine now that Grace had ever been that carefree. Tilting her head from one side to the other, Grace tried to loosen the kinks in her neck.

Bolton rubbed her shoulders, digging her fingers expertly into the knots in Grace's shoulders "By the looks of it, my lady, you're going to have your hands full with Lady Charlotte."

Grace closed her eyes briefly. "I forbid you to even think such horrible thoughts." She grinned wearily. "I must have a word with my aunt. If she was expecting a shy, missish young lady, she'll be dreadfully disappointed."

She began to rise, but Bolton made Grace sit while she worked on her shoulders. "What you need to do, my lady, is come out of the mopes. You've been walking around blue-deviled for weeks now. While you're getting Lady Charlotte's gowns, you should buy some for yourself. There's nothing like a new gown and a pretty bonnet to perk you right up."

Some of Grace's tension eased under Bolton's hands. "Yes, you have a good point. I shall speak to Madame Lisette."

After a few more minutes, Bolton went into the dressing room.

Grace moved to the pretty burl-inlaid desk and searched for paper, a pen, ink, and wax. Once she'd gathered them together, she wrote Phoebe a note. She sealed it, then rang for a footman. "Please take this round to Dunwood House and wait for an answer."

"Yes, my lady."

He returned about twenty minutes later. "My lady, Lady

Evesham would be honored to receive you after tea, or to have you join her for tea. Whichever it is you desire."

"Please tell her as we have arrived just to-day, I must take tea with my aunt, but I shall do myself the honor of waiting on her immediately afterward."

"Yes, my lady."

Grace grabbed her cloak, descended the stairs, and slipped out of one of the French windows to take a turn in the garden at the back of the town house. A flagstone path meandered around the fountain, a much smaller version of one at Versailles, strolling over to the roses on the other side of the fountain. The garden was surrounded on three sides by a tall stone wall. Rose canes scrambled up trellises and the two arbors with seats nestled in them. Grace peered closely at the bits of green springing forth from the brownish-gray stalks. How lovely this would all be come late spring. Perhaps she should plant more roses at Stanwood House. She looked at the watch pinned to her gown. It was almost four o'clock. Retracing her path, Grace arrived as tea was being brought in.

By the end of tea, caught between her aunt's oppressive solicitude for her situation and her sister's spirited defense, Grace had the beginnings of a headache and wanted nothing more than to be alone.

"Grace, my dear child, I'm very proud of you. But no one, I'm sure, would blame you if you sent the older children off to school. Many parents do, you know. Then you would only have the youngest, what is her name? Oh, it doesn't matter . . ."

"Her name is Mary," Charlotte said with aching sweetness.

Their aunt blinked. "Yes, my dear, I am sure it is. As I was saying, if you would send them off and allow your steward to handle the estate . . ."

"But Aunt Almeria"—Charlotte intervened once more—

"you must know that our papa always said one must care for one's own land. It wouldn't be right of Grace to ignore his advice."

"My dear Charlotte." Her aunt blinked several times. "How you do take one up. I was merely suggesting that if Grace rid herself of so many burdens, she might have time to find a husband."

This time when Charlotte opened her mouth to respond, Grace quelled her with a stern glance and turned to her aunt with a smile. "You mistake the matter. I am not at all burdened. After fighting for so long to gain guardianship, I cannot imagine you think I would give it up. I would no sooner send my brothers and sisters to boarding schools than I would have to various family members. Until such a time each one is ready to leave the nest, we shall all remain together." Grace went to her aunt and hugged her, softening her tone. "Please understand, that is really all I desire. Now if you'll excuse us, Lady Evesham would like me to bring Charlotte round to meet her."

Lady Herndon returned her embrace. "Yes, of course. Very good of her to offer to take you to Madame Lisette."

Grace bussed her aunt's cheek and signaled to Charlotte to do the same. "We shall see you before dinner."

When they reached the door to Grace's chambers, she whisked her sister inside and passed a hand over her eyes. "Charlotte, my love, I appreciate you trying to defend me. Still please, for the sake of my nerves, do not. If I have to go through that again, I shall have strong hysterics."

"But you don't have hysterics," Charlotte pointed out.

"Charlotte," Grace said warningly.

Her sister hung her head. "Yes, Grace. I won't do it again. It's just that . . ."

"Thank you. I am perfectly capable of defending myself. Now change into a walking gown and pelisse and meet me back here. I'm almost afraid to step outside. I have the greatest fear we'll both look like country dowdies."

Not more than a quarter of an hour later, Grace and Charlotte were shown into a room with a view of the gardens in the back of the Dunwood House. Phoebe, Countess of Evesham, rose to greet them. "Grace, how glad I am to see you again. It has been an age." Phoebe clasped Grace closely and kissed her before greeting her sister. "This must be Charlotte. How beautiful you are. You look very like your sister did when she made her come out. Come and sit, then you may tell me how you've been."

Grace studied her friend for a moment. Phoebe had changed little over the years. She was still a small lady with bright red-gold hair and sky-blue eyes. "Phoebe, you look wonderful. I see married life suits you."

Phoebe grinned. "Thank you, I am very happy."

"The baby is due in the summer?"

Her friend touched her stomach. "Yes, in July. We'll not entertain in a grand way this Season, and I've promised Marcus to restrict my gadding about. But we will still attend the political parties, and I shall hold a few drawing rooms. You, though, will be extremely busy."

Busy didn't begin to describe it. With the children and Charlotte's activities, it wouldn't be a surprise if Grace collapsed at the end of the Season. "Yes, my brothers and sisters, except Charlie, who is at school, will be here. My aunt Herndon is sponsoring Charlotte. I want to thank you for arranging the introduction to Madame Lisette. We have an appointment to-morrow morning."

A servant silently entered and Phoebe motioned for the tea to be set before her. "Wonderful. All the ladies in my family give her their custom. I know your mother admired Madame Fanchette."

"Yes, though she retired last year. Nevertheless, I'm

happy to make the change. You and your sisters are always so well dressed."

Phoebe pointed to the teapot and Grace nodded. "Allow yourselves to be guided by Madame, and I promise you'll be delighted with the results. Shall you set up your stable?"

Charlotte's eyes lit up. "Yes. My favorite hack is being brought down, and Grace taught me to drive." She clasped her hands together. "I am to have my own phaeton and pair."

Phoebe handed Grace a cup. "Famous. Who will help you buy the horses?"

Grace drew her brows together slightly. "I think my uncle Herndon might help, although, I have not had an opportunity to ask him."

"If you will trust me, I can take care of it for you." Phoebe glanced at Charlotte, including her in the conversation. "I happen to know of a well-matched pair of grays that are going up for sale. Marcus and I shall escort you to the carriage maker."

The pressure on Grace's shoulders and the ache in her head eased. "Yes, thank you. That will suit us perfectly. Do you not agree, Charlotte?"

"Yes. I'd love to have a pair of matched horses, and grays are so elegant."

Phoebe narrowed her eyes a little then said to Charlotte, "Would you like to look at the latest *La Belle Assemblée*? It is in the parlor next to this one down the corridor."

Charlotte cast a sidelong look at Grace.

"Yes, my dear. Go if you'd like."

"Well, if you wouldn't mind," her sister said shyly. "I would like to see it. Ours is a few months old."

Phoebe pointed to the corner. "Tug on the bell-pull and the footman will show you to the room."

Once Charlotte was gone, Phoebe turned to Grace, concern lurking in her eyes and took her hand. "Now, tell me what is wrong."

Chapter Six

Tears started in Grace's eyes, and her voice trembled. "I am not sure I should tell anyone. I—I don't know what you will think of me. In fact, I wouldn't blame you if you cut my acquaintance. Oh, Phoebe, I've done something so stupid and incredibly wrongheaded."

Phoebe tightened her grip on Grace's hands, holding them firmly. "My dear, dear friend, we've known each other since we were children. Even if it turns out that I do not agree with what you've done, I'd not turn from you."

Grace regarded her friend. The burden of her secret was weighing on her much more than she ever thought it would, and she really didn't have anyone else she would even consider telling. "I am in love."

Phoebe's laugh was a musical tinkle. "Grace, falling in love isn't the end of the world. It complicates things for you, to be sure. Yet there must be something that could be worked out."

Removing her hands from Phoebe's, Grace hid her face in them for a moment, before finally meeting Phoebe's steady gaze. "You don't understand. He doesn't know who I am."

Phoebe tilted her head, puzzled. "I think you'd best start at the beginning."

Grace nodded. If nothing else, maybe she would feel better if she could talk about it. She told her friend about the night at the inn, and when she burst into tears, Phoebe held Grace until she was calm enough to continue. "I thought, if I could have just the one night, I'd know what it was all about, and never being able to marry wouldn't bother me so much."

"Grace, are you—?"

That was the only blessing. She wasn't breeding. "No."

Phoebe let out a sigh of relief. "Well that is something at least." She rubbed her forehead. "All of this makes much more sense now. My dear, there is no easy way to tell you what I'm about to say . . . Worthington is searching for you."

Grace sat up with a start. Why would he do that and what if it got out? "*Oh no*. He can't be. This is terrible. Phoebe, how do you know?"

She handed Grace another cup of tea. "He came to see Marcus when I was on morning visits and described you. Marcus, of course, has never seen you, so he was unable to help him. Later he gave me Worthington's description. I knew who it was immediately. Worthington is a very good artist and has an eye for detail. I just couldn't, for the life of me, figure out why he wanted to find you."

Grace's chest tightened, and she had trouble breathing. The thought that he wanted her as his mistress was too horrible to consider. "Why—why is he searching for me?"

Phoebe raised her brows sympathetically. "He wants to marry you."

All the breath in Grace's body left in one fell swoop. *Marry me*? Oh no. This couldn't be happening. "I—I shall have to find a way to avoid meeting him." Rubbing her temples, she tried to think. Unfortunately her brain seemed unwilling to cooperate. "I don't plan to go about much. At least not to entertainments where gentlemen are likely to be."

Phoebe regarded her dubiously.

Grace really was going to have strong hysterics. "What?"

Phoebe took Grace's hands again. "It's been my experience that gentlemen in love turn up just where one does not expect them to be."

She was right, of course. Men were so unpredictable. They never behaved the way one wished. Why couldn't he have just forgotten about her? "Phoebe, this is horrible. What shall I do?"

Despite her large middle, Phoebe rose gracefully and seemed to float over to a small side table with a decanter and glasses. She poured two and handed one to Grace. "Sherry, not as strong as brandy, but effective nonetheless." Phoebe sank back down next to Grace. "You had better be prepared to explain to him that you do not intend to give up guardianship of the children. The law is very unfair to women in many respects and this is probably the worst example." Phoebe's brows drew together in thought. "I don't suppose you might consider that, as your husband, Worthington could be their guardian?"

Grace drank half the glass in one swallow. It didn't help. "I cannot conceive of any man willingly taking on seven children." She took a small sip. "Even if he thought he wanted to, what if something happened to change his mind? I would be helpless to do anything about it. If he were to send the boys off to school before they are ready or send the girls to school at all. I have no great opinion of girls' schools and want them to remain at home." Grace stopped, her voice suspended by tears. She put the glass on a side table and dropped her head in her hands.

Phoebe rose, refreshed Grace's glass, then handed it to her. "I understand. In your position, I'd likely feel the same."

Grace sipped her sherry. "Thank you."

"For what?" Phoebe's lips curved up. "Being your friend? Let me remind you, my friend, you stood by me when I refused to marry."

Yet that wasn't nearly as bad as what Grace had done. "No, for not thinking me an abandoned woman."

"Nonsense." Phoebe gave Grace a rueful look. "You've been half in love with Worthington for years. I remember the offers you turned down hoping he'd ask."

She sighed miserably. "He never even noticed me."

"No, probably not. Young men are like that. But, my dear, how on earth did you think you could make love with him and not fall in love?"

Well, that was a reasonable question. Still, she'd only seen him that one Season. Grace dabbed her eyes. "I might not have done it, if he hadn't been so wonderful."

Phoebe grinned. "Apparently he was quite taken with you as well."

Grace took a large sip of sherry. It really was very good, and she was feeling a bit better. Why had she been so stupid? She sat up straighter. "That, unfortunately, doesn't do either of us any good at all. I cannot marry. Not him, nor anyone else."

"It's a shame he didn't figure out he was in love with you before your parents died. Though really, men can be such big noddies."

She finished the glass, stood, and started to pace. "I must avoid him. There is absolutely no conceivable way I could ever tell him I only wanted one night."

"No, I can't see him taking that well at all." Phoebe shoved a small cushion behind her back. "Though Grace, I shall own myself surprised if you *can* avoid meeting him. You'd be better occupied deciding what you will say when you do see him."

Grace had reached the end of the room and turned. He'd

never understand. Men could do what she'd done, but ladies, at least unmarried ladies, could not. "Yes, you're right, of course."

Charlotte knocked on the door and came in carrying a largish magazine.

Grace quickly brought herself under control and smiled. "Well, my love, did you find anything?"

"I found several wonderful gowns," her sister said, with a sly grin. "If only you will allow me to have diamonds sewn onto the bodices and wear silk."

Grace held out her hand for *La Belle Assemblée* to look at the pictures Charlotte was mooning over. The ball gown depicted was in a pale lavender with a darker color under-skirt. The narrative recommended small diamonds or some other gemstone. Grace assumed a prim expression. "If you wish to dress in diamonds, you will have to set your cap at a very wealthy gentleman who will agree to give you a large allowance."

"Oh pooh. I don't care that"—Charlotte snapped her fingers—"for such fripperies. Although I did think it was extremely droll."

Grace laughed. No, she'd never give up her brothers and sisters. "Well, we had better be on our way. Aunt Almeria plans to serve an early dinner until we get used to Town hours." She held out her hands to Phoebe. "Thank you for our conversation. Will you join us to-morrow?"

Phoebe grinned and glanced down at her stomach. "Yes, I think I shall. I'll very soon need new gowns, again."

As Grace and her sister strolled arm-in-arm across the square to their aunt's house, she thought of and dismissed ways to tell Worthington she could not wed. Somehow she'd find a means to convince him, if she couldn't avoid him altogether, that was. Which was a much better plan.

* * *

Matt sat in the large leather chair behind his desk in his study, staring out the window overlooking the still-empty garden. In another month it would be green again, and his sisters would be out there playing rather than running up and down the corridor over his head. He was glad there were only four of them. He hoped his lady liked children.

A light knock sounded on the door. It opened to reveal Patience carrying a small basket. "What is that?"

She set it on his desk. "Invitations. All the ones you told me to accept for you. Really, Worthington, it is time for you to hire a secretary."

He'd asked her to accept any invitation at which she thought his lady would appear. Swallowing, he asked, "How many?"

She huffed in frustration. "If you attend four events an evening, every evening except Sunday, you will not have met all your obligations."

He glanced at her expectantly. "I don't suppose you would be willing to . . . ?"

"No." Her lips firmed and her chin jutted out a bit. "*I* am not looking to be carried off to Bedlam. Louisa and I will attend only the entertainments most suited to finding her a husband."

Diverted, Matt frowned. That was not what he and Patience had discussed. Louisa was to be given time to mature before she wed. "Patience, do you really want her to marry this year?"

She sat on the chair in front of his desk and sighed. "If she finds someone she loves and who returns her love, then I shall not have any objections. Of course, I would like her to wait another year or so, but, unlike me at her age, she has her own opinions." Patience's eyes sparkled softly. "I know you won't make her wed."

He shook his head, remembering all too well the story

she had told him about being pushed into marriage before she was truly ready. "No. I shall not."

The running and thumping sounded again. "I do wish they would not choose the corridor over my head to play."

She glanced up at the ceiling. "Oh, dear. They are not directly over your head, but in the school-room."

Two floors up? Matt scrubbed his face with his hand. How did they manage to make so much noise from that distance? "Tell them to get their pelisses, hats, and gloves. I'll take them to the park. I want two foot . . . no make that three footmen, and Duke may come as well."

The massive light brown lump that had been sleeping on the rug in front of the fireplace raised his head.

Matt grinned. "Would you like that, boy?"

The Great Dane's tail thumped lazily on the floor.

"I shall tell them." Patience rose. "Will you take the town coach?"

God forbid. "No, they'll walk. I want them tired out by the time we return."

Her eyes lit in amusement. "Indeed."

Once she'd gone, Matt turned to regard his garden again before ringing for his coat, hat, gloves, and Duke's lead.

By the time he arrived in the hall his sisters were waiting impatiently for him. He fixed them with a gimlet eye. "On our way to the Park, you will each remain next to a footman. Louisa, you shall walk next to me."

Smiling, they all nodded. Deceptive little things, his sisters. They'd be trying to break free after a block. But he was ready for them.

Shortly after they left Berkeley Square, Theodora and Madeline decided to have a race. Matt congratulated himself on his forethought. The two footmen assigned to the girls glanced at him for direction. "Stop them. I do not intend to allow my sisters to be the talk of London. They may run when they reach the play area and not before."

By the time he and Louisa caught up to the miscreants, their hands were held firmly by the footmen. When they arrived at the edge of the Park, Matt nodded. "Let them go and stay with them."

The girls went running off, laughing. "Don't tell me it was just the two of them making such a racket?"

Augusta blushed. "No, I was running with them."

"You may do so now as well. Much better to run here than *over my head*."

"Oh Matt." Her face scrunched up in distress. "I'm sorry. Did we disturb you very much?"

"No, not very much." He smiled at her and chucked her chin. *Only enough that I needed to bring you here.* "Go play."

Augusta grinned. "May Duke come with me?"

Matt released the Great Dane. "If he'll go."

"Come, Duke, come." Augusta clapped her hands and took off running with Duke loping after her.

Louisa squeezed his arm. "This was a very good idea, Matt."

He glanced down at his sister. She was a beautiful girl. This Season was going to be hell. He finally understood what his friend Harry Marsh went through when Anna came out. "Why thank you. I do have them at times."

She smiled up at him, clearly delighted. "Will we see you more now that we are all in Town?"

He started them ambling toward the other girls. "Yes, I shall be living at Worthington House this Season, and I'll attend many of the same entertainments as you." He tapped her nose as he'd done since she was a baby. "If for no other reason than to keep all the gentlemen in line."

Louisa took a breath, and she suddenly looked very young. "Do you think I shall be a success?"

Matt took out his quizzing glass and pretended to study her. She was taller than average with sable-brown curls and blue eyes. Her nose was straight and her complexion clear. Her generous mouth curved up excitedly. "I predict you will be a Diamond of the First Water."

She smiled ecstatically. "Truly?"

"Without a doubt." His grin faded. "Louisa, you must promise to tell me if any man makes advances toward you, or makes you feel uncomfortable. If any of them wish to address you, they must speak with me first."

She nodded. "Yes, Matt, I promise."

He would introduce her to Phoebe and Anna. Both ladies waited until they'd found the right gentlemen to wed. "And don't worry about marrying this Season unless you meet someone you love deeply and he loves you."

Louise tucked her arm in his. "I shall do everything you tell me to do."

He didn't believe that for a moment. Not that she'd purposely do something he didn't like, just that some gentleman might overcome her good sense, and she had a tendency to want her own way. He patted her hand. "Good girl. Then we shall come off without a hitch."

He fervently prayed he would find his lady quickly so he could watch over his sister and keep her away from the rakes, rogues, and fortune hunters lurking around innocent young ladies, hoping to take advantage.

Matt arrived home to find a note from Anna asking if his stepmother and sister would like to accompany her to Madame Lisette's on the morrow. He glanced at his butler, Thorton. "Please ask Lady Worthington to attend me in my study."

"Yes, my lord."

A few minutes later, Patience knocked. "What is it? Not the children, I hope."

Matt grinned and handed her the note. "Only one of them. Anna Rutherford would like to know if you and Louisa are able to go to Madame Lisette's in the morning."

Chapter Seven

The following morning, the bell on the door of Madame Lisette's shop tinkled as Grace, Phoebe, and Charlotte walked in.

"*Ah, bonjour, miladies.* Lady Eves . . . ah, bah, *excusez-moi.*"

Phoebe's eyes sparkled with humor. "Madame, you may still call me Lady Phoebe."

"*Non, non,* it is not proper. I shall practice." She turned to Grace and Charlotte. "These are the ladies about which you wrote me?"

"Yes, Madame. Lady Grace Carpenter, Lady Charlotte, allow me to introduce you to Madame Lisette. Madame, Lady Grace Carpenter and her sister, Lady Charlotte."

Madame curtseyed gracefully. She was a small, energetic lady. Her dark hair laced lightly with silver.

Madame studied them with an experienced eye. "You will both need everything, *non?*"

"I will not be attending many balls," Grace responded. Particularly if Worthington was searching for her. That meeting, if it ever occurred, would be on her terms. "My aunt is sponsoring my sister for her come out. Please concentrate on her first."

"*Ah oui?*" Madame said. "Well then, Lady Charlotte, come with me."

Charlotte glanced quickly at Grace, who shooed her after Madame. "Go on, my dear. I'll wait for you here."

"Come let us sit." Phoebe took a place on a plush velvet sofa.

A servant appeared offering cups of coffee. Phoebe accepted one as she asked Grace, "Tell me, which of the entertainments do you plan to attend?"

Grace took a sip. The coffee was quite good. "I would dearly love to go to at least one of Lady Thornhill's drawing rooms, and I'd like to pick up some old threads with friends I haven't seen lately. Probably most of the teas, maybe an afternoon rout party."

Shifting on the sofa, Phoebe frowned. "I hope you plan to come to the small parties I shall hold."

Though it was a risk, Grace couldn't refuse her friend. "Yes, I wouldn't miss them." She gazed out the window. Carriages, footmen, vendors, ladies, and other women filled the street. She'd forgotten how exciting London could be. No matter what occurred, Grace vowed she'd have fun this Season. "Phoebe, I so enjoy being back in Town."

"I find it pleasant for a few months." She rubbed the small of her back. "After that, I'm happy to be back in the country."

Taking another sip, Grace wondered where Madame found her coffee. "Do you never go to Brighton?"

"No." Phoebe's eyes narrowed slightly. "I find very little to admire there since certain parties decided to switch parties."

Ah yes, Prinny switching sides had been a blow. "That was disappointing." Grace took another sip of coffee resolving to discover where Madame bought it. "I had hoped our next sovereign would be more progressive."

"My dear, have you decided what you'll do when you see *him* again?"

Hide. Grace shook her head. "I think I've been praying it won't happen. I—I just don't know what I *could* say." She sighed again. It seemed that was all she did these days. "Maybe I should take the other children home and leave Charlotte with my aunt."

"Of course," Phoebe responded in a dry tone. "Then you could wear a path from Bedfordshire to London checking on Charlotte or worry yourself to death."

Grace rubbed her brow. "You are right. It wouldn't do. How could I have been so stupid?"

Phoebe patted Grace's knee. "None of us are particularly bright when it comes to love. It is a form of insanity."

"But you were. I can tell that your husband loves you very much."

Smiling mistily, Phoebe said, "Yes, though we had our problems as well." She glanced at Grace ruefully. "And I have to say, once one has experienced the physical side of love, it's very hard to resist it."

No matter how hard Grace tried not to think about it, somehow the feel of his hand on her slipped through, and she had to resist moaning. Yet that memory had to be enough. She could never do it again. "Very true." She must change this conversation. "Phoebe, I've never known you to drink coffee."

"I acquired the habit on my honeymoon in Paris. Outside of France, Madame Lisette's is the only one I like."

In a little while, Charlotte joined them, her face wreathed in smiles. "Grace, she said she has some gowns already made up. How can that be?"

"I sent your measurements to her."

"Of course. I didn't think of that."

One of the bright spots of Grace's life now was seeing

Charlotte's joy at being in London and preparing for the Season. "You goose. Did you think it was magic?"

Charlotte blushed. "It was silly, I guess."

Madame joined them with a tablet of drawings. "Milady Grace, I think these gowns *comme il faut pour la jeune fille.*"

Grace flipped through the pages. Each gown was perfect for Charlotte. "I agree. These are excellent, and you have some garments already completed?"

Madame's lips formed a moue. "A few minor alterations. I shall send them round this afternoon, unless you need something sooner?"

Grace couldn't remember her aunt mentioning any plans. "No, this afternoon is fine. If you could give me fabric samples and recommendations for hats and alike, we may start on the other things she'll need."

Madame inclined her head. "But *naturellement,* milady. But, now it is your turn."

Phoebe nudged Grace. "No time like the present, as they say."

She rose and followed Madame behind the black curtain where she was made to stand on a raised platform to have her measurements taken. Then, based on the ones she'd sent earlier, Madame brought out several gowns, spencers, and pelisses for her to look over. They were lovely. Grace hadn't had such beautiful gowns since she'd last been in London. After all, there was no reason she should not dress fashionably. Even bluestockings, such as Lady Thornhill and the Misses Berry, dressed well. Bolton was right. A new gown was just the thing to make one feel better. "I shall take them all, including the ones in your drawings."

After Madame showed Phoebe some designs and re-measured her, they were ready to leave. Grace put on her hat, being careful to tuck her hair up. It had always been her most recognizable feature. They left armed with samples and descriptions.

When they reached the pavement, Phoebe was hailed by a very pretty matron with chestnut curls. Accompanying her were two other ladies, one older with blond hair and a young lady with striking, sable-brown hair, who for some reason reminded her very much of Worthington. "Phoebe, we will meet you at the milliner's down the street." Grace grabbed Charlotte's arm and whisked her away before the others reached them.

Phoebe nodded in acknowledgment. "I shan't be long." She turned to the ladies walking toward them. "Anna, my dear . . ."

Charlotte, despite casting Grace a confused look, had not demurred. Grace's bosom heaved with relief. If she was a gambling woman, she wouldn't have wagered a groat against the chance that the younger woman was Worthington's sister. Her heart pounded. She finally managed a shaky breath. "Do you have the samples?"

Charlotte narrowed her eyes. "Yes. Grace, what was that all about?"

"What about? Why nothing. We mustn't let the day catch up with us. We're expected back in Grosvenor Square for luncheon."

"Aunt Almeria said we'd be alone for luncheon."

"Did she? I daresay I've forgotten." Grace cast desperately around for another topic of conversation. "Here is the clerk wishing to help us."

She gave Charlotte a small push. "We will need bonnets for the Season."

Phoebe entered a few minutes later while Charlotte was with the clerk. "That was a good escape you made."

Glancing out the window, Grace pressed her lips together. "I knew it. Worthington's sister. She is so much like him."

"She is indeed."

Charlotte turned to her. "Grace, what do you think about this one?"

It was a satin straw bonnet decorated with ribbons and artificial flowers. The hat would be perfect with some of her walking gowns. "Excellent, my love." Grace glanced at Phoebe. "You know so much more of what is in fashion. Will you help her?"

Phoebe grinned. "Of course, but Madame has had a partnership of sorts with this shop, and trusts them to enhance her fashions." She leaned closer. "Calm yourself. The others will be at Madame's for a while yet."

Grace bit her lip and tried to focus on the bonnets. "How wonderful that she can offer such a convenience to her customers."

Phoebe nodded. "I quite agree. It saves a great deal of time."

The rest of the day was spent in buying the other articles of clothing and accessories that a lady of fashion needed. They had luncheon with Phoebe before sallying out again that afternoon.

Concerned about Phoebe's condition and the pace she was keeping taking them around, Grace insisted her friend rest. "My dear, you'll soon be knocked up."

Phoebe just chuckled lightly. "I have a great deal of energy. Though I am told my last three months will be a little dreary and I shall tire more easily."

"I suppose you know best. You won't overdo it, will you?" Grace drew her brows together before she knew what she was doing. Good Lord, she was getting as bad as the older ladies, mothering other people.

Phoebe grinned. "You have become quite the mother hen."

Grace smiled wryly. "I was just thinking the same thing. I suppose it comes with the territory."

Once back at Herndon House she took the one package she'd decided to keep with her to her chamber. Opening the box, she drew out a straw bonnet with a high crown, which made her look taller, and a brim trimmed in gathered straw silk that hid her face from a side view.

Grace donned it and studied her reflection in the mirror. Unless one came upon her from the front, they would not be able to recognize her. The only problem was that she could only see what was directly in front of her.

It would have to do. At least now, she could shop without fear of being taken unawares.

Bolton came out of the dressing room and stopped. "I take it that's the newest style?"

Grace met her dresser's gaze in the mirror and lied. "Yes, do you like it? I think it very fashionable."

"If you don't want to see what's around you." Bolton shook her head. "Several of your gowns have arrived. Now those I like. As I've said anytime during the past four years, there is no reason you can't dress like a fashionable lady even if you are in the country."

It was true, there were some things Grace need not deny herself. After all, no one was going to take the children away because she dressed well. "Yes, I believe you're right. Just because I'm not spending time in Town doesn't mean I need to look like a provincial."

Bolton put away the garments. "You still need to buy stockings, material for chemises, and more gloves."

"I'll attend to it to-morrow. Get a list from May for Charlotte." Grace removed the bonnet, handing it carefully to her maid. Until she could come up with something better, that hat was her only form of disguise.

The week passed quickly. She bought a phaeton for Charlotte and a curricle for herself, as well as one large town coach and a smaller one. She also gave in to her temptation for a landau. Even if *some people* thought it was an old woman's carriage. "Truly, Phoebe, it will be so practical with all the children."

Phoebe's eyes danced. "If you say so."

Grace snoodled around the pale yellow conveyance. "It is, and it seats six, maybe even seven. The top goes up and down, so it may be used no matter the weather. I assure you, it's just what I need, and I'll require more horses as well."

"You're in luck, my uncle Henry is in Town, and he has a very good eye. Make a list of what you want, and I shall ask him to procure them for you."

"Thank you. I don't know what I would have done without your help."

Her friend laughed. "No, no, it's my pleasure, and I have had a lot of fun."

Grace leaned back against the landau. "I shall also need more grooms."

"Sam, my groom, shall help you. I'll send him round to Herndon House."

One day when Charlotte and Aunt Almeria were on morning visits, Grace visited Stanwood House to reacquaint herself with the London housekeeper, Mrs. Penny, an old retainer Grace could not bear to let go. After all, she would rather have the house occupied when the family was not in residence.

Other than coming to London to inspect the renovations last autumn, Grace had not been in Stanwood House since before her mother died. Mrs. Penny had done the best she could with only a skeleton staff. Though they'd need at least a dozen or so more servants for the Season, Grace had agreed to hire the contingent of maids Penny needed to reopen the large town house a few months earlier.

Two days before her brothers and sisters were due to arrive, Grace inspected the house and was pleased to see Royston in residence.

Mrs. Penny curtseyed. "It is all as it should be now, my

lady. I've already had the house cleaned and aired. I hope the maids I've hired meet with your approval."

"Thank you, Penny. I was in a worry we wouldn't have it all done before the children got here. Lord knows we can't do it afterward." Grace turned to her butler. "Please hire more footmen if you find a need. Neep has taken the new grooms and stable boys in hand. With Cook remaining at Stanwood Hall, I've hired a French chef for the Season. He'll come this afternoon. Ask him to have the menus ready for my approval to-morrow."

Penny glowered. "If you're sure, my lady."

Grace raised a brow. Penny, for good reason considering one of her nephews died in the war, may not like the French, but insolence was one thing Grace would not tolerate. "Yes, quite sure. He is the relative of Lady Evesham's chef and known for his steady temperament. I'll go back to Grosvenor Square and have our trunks sent over."

After taking a quick tour of the house, Grace set off on foot, followed by her footman, Harold. Resisting the temptation to amble along the tree-lined path through the square, which was lovely, but would take her longer, she dutifully turned left toward Davies Street. She was only two houses down the street when a gentleman, several girls, and a large Great Dane exited one of the houses on the opposite side of the square from Stanwood House.

Oh, no. It took her only the matter of a second to recognize the man.

Worthington.

He and his sister were striding in the same direction Grace was. Her heart raced and she averted her face. Grateful for her bonnet, she picked up her pace, hoping to pass out of the square and toward Mount Street before Worthington reached the corner.

But then the brim of her hat hid them. Her footman was too far behind her to ask where they were, and what could she say in any event? *How far away from the other group am I? I'm running away from the man who wants to marry me?*

Grace bit her lip. If she dashed down the alley behind the houses Worthington would see her. Her mouth dried, and she couldn't swallow. Fervently praying she'd reach the corner of Davies and Mount Streets before they did, she clasped her reticule more tightly and sidled toward the inside of the pavement.

It was then that everything went horribly wrong.

As she tripped over a massive paw and started to fall, a strong hand caught her arm. Heat seemed to radiate from him, drawing her to him.

"Duke, stand. I'm terribly sorry, ma'am, he wasn't paying attention to what was in front of him."

Worthington's deep voice caressed her. It was all Grace could do to keep from turning toward him. Her arm tingled from his touch, and the rest of her wanted to fall into his arms.

Then fear, her familiar companion of late, pushed aside her desire for him. She'd lose everything that was important. If she spoke, he'd recognize her voice. All Grace could do was nod and mumble, making sure to keep her hat-brim between them. She made a motion to wave them on.

Worthington hovered over her, concern coloring his voice. "Are you sure you don't need any help?"

Oh God, why didn't he leave? Her heart raced and she was sure she'd faint. Taking large breaths of air, Grace shook her head and tried to pull her arm away.

"I shall help her ladyship," her footman, Harold, said.

"Very well. I wish you a good day." Worthington, sounding confused, released her and turned toward the Park.

"My lady, are you all right?" Harold asked.

Holding a hand to her chest, Grace nodded. "I'm fine. Let's go, shall we?"

Walking straight ahead, she crossed Mount Street and didn't stop until she reached Herndon House. Her hands shook as she tried to untie the bow to her hat. Finally the ribbons came undone. Tearing the hat off, she tossed it on her dressing table and fell across the bed before she collapsed. Too late did she remember he lived on Berkeley Square.

Matt and his sisters were halfway down Mount Street heading toward the Park, and he was still trying to understand what was so unusual about that lady.

Louisa frowned. "That was very odd. She wouldn't even look at us or talk to us."

"Maybe she was horribly disfigured and is afraid to let any see her face," Madeline piped up.

"Don't be ridiculous," Augusta, in her know-it-all-voice, said. "If she'd been disfigured, she'd have worn a veil."

"Well, no matter the reason." Louisa gave her younger sisters a superior look. "I still think it's strange."

Matt lowered his brows. "Very strange, indeed."

And very familiar. Glancing down at the hand that had touched her, he realized his fingers were still warm. Then it hit him as if he'd been punched. *She is my love.* She had to be. He'd never had that sort of reaction to another woman. Turning quickly back, he searched the street, but she was nowhere in sight. Then he started to walk toward Berkeley Square.

"Matt, what are you doing?" Louisa tugged at his arm. "If you want to go back, we must also."

Damn. His sister was right. He couldn't leave them, especially Louisa. And Matt wasn't going to take them on a chase through Mayfair to find his love. Still, she'd been in Berkeley Square. Who lived in there? Had he ever known? Matt had rented his own rooms for so long he had little idea who his neighbors were. Patience would know. If not, he'd knock on every single door if he had to. "Where is your mother?"

Louisa shrugged. "I believe she is attending a tea or visiting a friend." She gazed up, her eyes shining. "Matt, we are going to a soirée at Lady Bellamny's house to-morrow evening. It will be my first London party."

He summoned a smile. "I know you'll have fun."

"Will you be there?"

"I doubt it. I'm dining with friends at my club." He'd speak with his stepmother this evening.

He was so close to finding her, and, when he did, he'd discover why she ran away from him.

Grace's heart had finally stopped thudding so hard she was sure it would fly out of her breast, when Aunt Almeria knocked on her bedchamber door. "My dear, would you like to attend Lady Featherton's at home with Charlotte and me?"

Grace rose. "I am sorry, but I cannot. The children are arriving to-morrow. I must attend to some additional details at Stanwood House. This evening, Charlotte and I will dress there and come round to fetch you for dinner." She glanced at her watch. "If I have time, I must go to Bond Street to exchange some ribbon that is not quite right."

"If you are sure, my dear."

"Quite sure." Grace bussed her aunt's cheek. "You and Charlotte have a good time."

Aunt Almeria's eyes grew misty. "I'm certain we shall. Oh Grace, she is so beautiful. Just what your mother looked like at that age."

Suddenly, Grace's throat hurt. A portrait of her mother, not much older than Charlotte was now, hung in the Hall's gallery. "Yes, I know."

Charlotte came into the room. "Aunt Almeria, are you ready to go?"

She blinked a few times. "Yes, my love. Grace, I'll see you this evening."

There was much too much to accomplish before dinner for Grace to allow Worthington to disturb her so greatly. She gave herself a shake. Surely their meeting earlier was an aberration.

A half an hour later, she, Bolton, and May took the town coach to Stanwood House. Once they were settled and she had met with the chef, Grace sallied out to Bond Street followed by Harold to exchange the ribbon. She stepped out of the haberdasher's, then stopped. Worthington was across the street engaged in conversation with another gentleman. For a moment, she stood, frozen to the pavement.

He stopped speaking, and as if he could sense her presence, turned. The next thing she knew he had stepped purposefully into the busy street. A coach driver shouted, bringing his vehicle to a halt, and blocked her view of him.

This could not be happening. She was not prepared to speak to him. Not yet. Possibly not ever. "Harold, oh my, look at the time, we must return home immediately."

She hurriedly turned down a little-used alley leading to Bruton Street.

The footman trotted to catch up to her. "My lady, why are we going this way?"

Grace faced straight ahead. "This was the shortcut, was it not? Ah, see, here is Bruton Street now, so much quicker than the other way."

She stared straight ahead, not slowing to see if Worthington was following.

After striding swiftly down the pavement, passing a group of ladies, she slowed her pace and continued on calmly down the street until they came to the crossroad leading back to Berkeley Square.

As soon as she attained her room, Grace took off her hat and fell into a chair. Her heart was pounding, again. She was going to have apoplexy at this rate. How the deuce was she to avoid him for the rest of the Season?

* * *

Matt and his friend Rutherford had emerged from Jackson's Boxing Salon and stood on Bond Street talking when his neck began to tingle. He turned and saw a lady with a poke bonnet and blue ribbons. The same color ribbon as her eyes, how did he know that? It was also the same blue as the trim on the bonnet he'd seen earlier. He'd wished he'd seen his lady in the daylight. Still the female's height appeared right. She wouldn't get away from him this time. "Rutherford, I must go. I'll see you this evening."

Rutherford raised his brows. "Yes, of course, see you then."

Dodging carriages and carts, Matt strode rapidly across the street, but when he'd reached the other side, she was gone.

Where the devil did she go? It was like trying to find a phantom.

Chapter Eight

Grace smiled with pride as Charlotte pirouetted for her sister. "Very pretty indeed."

Charlotte beamed. "I'm so glad we went to Madame's. This gown and all the others are so lovely. You look beautiful."

"This is your evening, my dear. I am merely a chaperone."

"But . . ."

"No, no." Grace shook her head. "No arguing."

This evening was Lady Bellamny's soirée for the young ladies making their come outs. Charlotte would be one of the most beautiful young ladies of the Season. Her pale yellow muslin evening gown, embroidered with small butterflies in green, blue, and gold, was perfect.

Grace clasped a single strand of matched pearls around her sister's neck and handed Charlotte a pair of small pearl earrings suspended on gold wire. It was hard to believe she was already making her come out.

If only Mama and Papa were here to see it. They would have been so proud of Charlotte. Tears pricked Grace's eyes. *Silly goose.* She was not going to cry.

A spangled shawl, delicate brisé fan, and a reticule completed her sister's ensemble. "Come, we do not want to be late. We must fetch our aunt before dinner with Lady Evesham."

A short carriage ride later brought them to Herndon House where they joined Aunt Almeria in the drawing room.

She studied Charlotte, then nodded approvingly. "Well, you two will certainly do me credit."

Charlotte would. Grace wished her aunt would give up including her in the husband hunt. "Thank you, Aunt. Shall we walk or take my town coach?"

Aunt Almeria's brows drew together in thought. "It's always tempting to stroll. Dunwood House is not so very far, but one would not want to walk across the square in evening slippers. They become ruined so easily." She paused for a moment. "I'm sorry, my dear, but I have decided not to attend with you."

Grace frowned. This was a surprise. "Is anything wrong?"

Aunt Almeria smiled gently. "No, no. Not wrong. It is just that your uncle is arriving home this evening, and I am always here to greet him when he returns. You have it well under control, and Lady Evesham will be with you. It is not necessary that I attend. I've already sent a note to Lady Bellamny. Do not fear. Once the Season is under way, I will help you decide which entertainments would be best to attend, and accompany Charlotte to all of them."

How very sweet of Aunt Almeria to want to be home for her husband. At least this evening, there would be no chance of Worthington attending. It was ladies only. "I shall hold you to that. Come, Charlotte, we shall be off."

"I'd like to walk. May I?" Charlotte asked.

"No, my dear, when I made the suggestion, I hadn't considered. Aunt Almeria is right, if your slippers got wet, they'd be ruined. We shall take the coach."

"Yes, of course." Charlotte straightened her shoulders, looking every inch a young lady. "How silly of me. Will there be dancing at the soirée?"

"Not at a soirée," Aunt Almeria said. "That is a party for mingling."

Grace kissed her aunt and took Charlotte's arm as they walked to the front door. "Besides which, dancing is not the purpose. It is for you girls just out to meet each other. That way when the balls begin after Easter, you will have friends." And so the mamas can look over the competition, though her sister did not need to know that. "You must be on your best behavior. The patronesses of Almack's will be there as well."

Charlotte's countenance became serious. "This is no longer practicing. It really is important."

"Yes, it is." Grace squeezed her sister's fingers. "But do not allow it to worry you. You'll be fine."

Once at Dunwood House, she and Phoebe decided to take two carriages. One would return to Grosvenor Square and the other to Berkeley Square. When she and Charlotte were announced, Grace was surprised to see only Phoebe in the drawing room before dinner.

Phoebe came forward to greet them. "Since gentlemen are not expected at Lady Bellamny's, I sent Marcus to dine with his friends. Sherry?"

"For me, please," Grace responded. "Charlotte will have lemonade."

Once they had their glasses, Phoebe led them to a seating area in front of the fireplace. "A toast then to Charlotte's come out."

After taking a sip of lemonade, Charlotte turned to Phoebe. "Why will there be no gentlemen?"

"There may be a few." Phoebe grinned. "Yet not until later in the evening and only to escort the ladies home. Once the Season begins, you'll meet gentlemen aplenty. At present, you are better served by meeting other ladies your age and a few that have already had a Season or two."

Charlotte tilted her head to one side, considering. "Yes, I suppose you are right. There is so much to learn."

Grace suddenly wished she could be with her sister at all

her events. Perhaps Worthington would give up attempting to find her, and she could be.

Matt had been unable to speak with his stepmother the previous evening. He'd left a note to be given to her when she arrived home, desiring a meeting as soon as it was convenient. The following afternoon, she sent a message asking Matt to meet her in the drawing room before dinner.

When he stalked into the room she placed her glass on the small side table next to her. "What has got you in such a taking?"

Matt paced the room. "I saw her again to-day, and she hid from me."

Patience frowned. "What did she do?"

He stopped and scowled. "She wore a deuced—a—one of those large hats that hides a lady's face."

"Well, Matt," Patience laughed lightly, "they are fashionable."

Rubbing a hand over his face, he tried to keep his frustration under control. It would do him no good to take it out on his stepmother. "She knew it was me and didn't acknowledge me."

"It seems to me you are taking a lot for granted." Patience seemed to study him for a moment. "How, pray, do you know that she is avoiding you?"

When he opened his mouth to speak, she stopped him. "No, no, start at the beginning."

Matt told her how the lady tripped over Duke's feet when she'd tried to move closer to a house wall.

"Really, Worthington." Patience cast an exasperated glance at the ceiling. "What lady wouldn't have wanted to hide herself after that embarrassing incident? I think you may find it is not at all what it seems."

He frowned. "She was also on Bond Street earlier."

Patience widened her eyes. "Did you see her face?"

"No, I saw her hat." He began pacing again. "It had the same blue ribbons on it."

"Blue is one of the more popular colors this Season. It could have been anyone. Aside from that, you told me she had not been to Town in a while. Why are you so sure she is here now?"

He opened his mouth and closed it again. There was no point in arguing what he only felt. Patience might not believe him, but he knew his lady was here.

"What are you doing this evening?"

"I'm dining with Evesham and Rutherford." He stopped and glanced at her. "I'll meet you at the soirée later to escort you home."

"Mind, do not come before supper." Patience's lips tilted up. "You know Lady Bellamny's rule, no gentlemen until then."

"I won't." He grinned and gave her a brotherly peck on her cheek. "Evesham and Rutherford are probably under orders as well."

"You have fun at your club. Louisa and I are dining with Lady Rutherford."

The door opened and Louisa stepped into the room. "Mama? Matt?"

Matt glanced at his little sister. The pale blue muslin gown embroidered in silver and dark blue was perfect. And it didn't make her appear too grown up. He'd have to keep a very close watch over her this Season. He took her hand and kissed it. "Louisa, you are beautiful. I'll have to hire more footmen. Large ones to protect you. Have a good time this evening."

"I shall." She smiled brilliantly. "Thank you for everything."

He left the drawing room, and after donning his hat and gloves, strolled to Brooks. Matt had not had a chance to ask

Rutherford about his mystery lady. Perhaps he might know who she was.

Grace and Charlotte made their slow way through the receiving line behind Phoebe.

The formidable Lady Bellamny was even larger than she'd been before. She now had three chins instead of two. Her eyes lit up when she held her hand out to Grace. "Lady Grace, I haven't seen you in a dog's age. How are you, my dear?"

Grace curtseyed. "Very well, my lady. May I present you to my sister Lady Charlotte?"

Charlotte curtseyed.

Lady Bellamny inclined her head. "Very pretty. Very pretty indeed. The gentlemen will have a hard time resisting you." She turned to Grace. "What's her portion?"

Grace allowed a slight smile to play on her lips. "Thirty thousand."

Lady Bellamny nodded sagely and glanced at Charlotte. "Stay away from the fortune hunters and rakes."

Charlotte smiled politely. "I will, my lady."

"Pretty manners." Lady Bellamny turned to Grace. "You've done a good job. She didn't even blink an eye."

Charlotte refrained from grinning, but her lips twitched.

Nodding, Lady Bellamny patted Charlotte's shoulder. "You'll do, my dear. Follow your sister's lead."

"Yes, my lady." Charlotte's lips deepened into a grin.

Grace took her arm as they joined Phoebe.

"Grace?" Charlotte whispered.

"Not now." Grace smiled politely and nodded to acquaintances. "We will discuss everything when we are back home."

It was just like Lady Bellamny to test the young ladies as they walked in the door. By the end of the evening, she'd have every girl's measure.

Grace and Charlotte were announced and descended into the already crowded ballroom where Phoebe awaited them with a look of enquiry on her face.

Proud of her sister, Grace grinned. Even though Charlotte had been skittish at first, Grace had known her sister was ready for her come out. "She did well."

Phoebe smiled warmly at Charlotte. "Excellent."

"Thank you."

They accompanied Phoebe to meet new ladies and renew old acquaintances, including Phoebe's mother-in-law, Lady Dunwood, and her aunt, Lady St. Eth.

The dark-haired young matron Grace had seen outside of Madame's shop glided toward them.

Phoebe took Grace's hand and turned to the lady. "Anna, come meet my friend, Lady Grace Carpenter, and her sister, Lady Charlotte. Ladies, this, my good friend, Lady Rutherford."

Anna lightly bussed Phoebe's cheek and extended her hand to Grace. "My pleasure. May I present Lady Louisa Vivers? She is also making her come out."

Worthington's sister? Oh my. Did that mean Worthington would be here later? Grace kept her countenance calm as Lady Louisa curtseyed to her. "A pleasure to meet you."

"And you." Turning to Charlotte, Grace said, "You girls may take yourselves off to meet more of the young ladies coming out this Season."

Phoebe nodded. "Yes, do."

"Look for us later," Anna added, then turned to Grace and Phoebe. "She and her mother dined with me this evening, but a message was brought round that one of Lady Worthington's other daughters was complaining of an upset stomach. As a result I volunteered to escort her."

Grace let go of the breath she'd held. Thank the Lord she'd have more time to decide what to do about Worthington.

During her musings, she remembered that she had met

the second Lady Worthington during her first Season. Although Grace didn't expect the lady to remember her, she did not want to take the chance and was glad the lady wasn't here. They arrived at a small sofa with two comfortable chairs flanking it. She encouraged Phoebe and Anna, who was also increasing, to sit. "There seems to be a remarkable number of good-looking girls."

Phoebe settled back against the cushions. "Yes, but I've seen none more beautiful than the two we just had with us. Not only their faces, but their manners as well."

Grace blushed. "I'm so pleased you think so."

Soon the ladies settled into a comfortable coze. Old friends and some she'd kept up a correspondence with stopped by and visited. She'd forgotten how isolated she had been at Stanwood Hall, and wished she would be able to attend more of the parties this Season. Yet with Worthington searching for her, it was simply too dangerous. How incredibly reckless she'd been with him. Although she couldn't bring herself to regret the night, only the consequences.

Before Grace knew it, it was time for supper. Glancing around, she saw Charlotte and Lady Louisa with a group of other girls.

"Shall we go down to the supper room?" Phoebe asked.

"Yes, let's." Anna rose from the chair. "I am famished. It's amazing how my appetite has grown along with my waist."

Several moments later, Grace was enjoying a lobster patty and taking a sip of champagne when Phoebe exclaimed, "Oh, here is Marcus, and Rutherford."

Yet when Grace looked up, Lord Worthington was staring down at her. Her hand trembled so much, her champagne sloshed in the glass. He plucked it from her numb fingers and set it on the table. Concern shadowed his eyes.

He bowed. "My lady. I can't tell you how happy I am to see you again."

The room spun. This was too soon. Much too soon. Suddenly she couldn't breathe. "I—I think I need some air."

Grace rose and quickly strode toward the terrace doors.

Phoebe started to rise. "Grace, shall I . . ."

Worthington stopped Phoebe by putting his hand on her shoulder. "I'll go with Lady Grace."

Oh, no. He can't follow me. She pushed open the door and darted down the terrace searching for a way back into the house and the front door. She had to escape. Her mind whirled, while her body tightened and tingled.

Traitorous senses. This was not the time. A low light flickered through a French door. Now if only she could make it before he found her.

A strong arm caught her around her waist and pulled her gently against a hard male body. Her heart beat so fast she thought she'd swoon. She couldn't move. A frisson of desire started in her back and spread throughout her body.

"Lady Grace." Worthington's deep voice caressed her.

She gasped for breath as she leaned back against his firm chest. Sheer longing and desire speared her. Her breasts tingled in anticipation and the place between her legs grew hot and moist with need. His warmth radiated through her. Tears slid down her cheeks, and she nodded. How mortifying to be found out. To have her weakness exposed.

His voice was gentle but stern. "We have some things we need to discuss. Such as the reason you left so early that morning." He paused. "Will you look at me?"

Unable to put together a coherent answer or even move, Grace closed her eyes.

Worthington bent over her. His lips near her ear. She shivered and shook her head.

His thumb caressed her cheek, and stopped. Concern infused his voice. "Why are you crying?"

She couldn't answer him. What would she say? That she'd been so horribly wanton, making love with him when she knew she couldn't wed? That she loved him and couldn't marry him? That she so desperately needed to feel him inside her, but the obligation to the children took precedence over him? Nothing she did or said would make what she had to do any more palatable. He'd be so angry. What man wouldn't be?

"Come with me." Not waiting for an answer, he swept her up into his arms and carried her to the empty parlor through which she'd hoped to escape. Worthington set her back on her feet, locked the door, and closed the curtains.

Grace stared down at her shaking hands. All she could see of him was his evening pumps. Drawing her into his arms, he tilted her head and kissed her.

Fire roiled through her as she clung to him, desperately returning his kisses. The last one, she vowed. When he deepened the kiss and his tongue played with hers, Grace wrapped her arms around him, pressing full length against his muscular body.

Trading breaths with him, she pressed closer. A shuddering sigh escaped her. Oh, how she wanted this. To be in his arms, to let him possess her, to possess him.

Just one once more. Just this, a kiss, no more.

She needed him in the same way she needed to breathe. Her breasts, her nipples hardened and ached. He groaned. His palms moved down her back, then over her breasts, caressing them. Grace pressed against him.

Well, maybe a little more than a kiss.

Her hands moved greedily over his strong back and the ache between her legs intensified. Her dreams and remembrances were nothing compared to being here with him. She pressed her hips into Worthington's body and moved one hand over his hard buttock bringing him closer. Grace tried to focus on the kiss, frantically caressing his tongue with hers, trying to ignore the memory of his hard shaft inside her.

Maybe just once more.

Then she'd explain.

Chapter Nine

Grace. Her name fitted her. Matt reveled in their kiss. The feel of her soft body in his arms drove him mad with desire. This lady, Grace, his love, was the only woman he'd ever need, ever want. Why she ran from him or cried and refused to speak to him, he didn't understand. But this need they each had for the other, he did. Since their meeting at the inn, he'd played their lovemaking over and over in his mind. He hadn't even thought of another woman since. He wanted no one but her, and he had to have her. This time, he'd make sure Grace knew she was his. This time, he wouldn't let her go.

When her hand reached his throbbing shaft, he backed her to the chaise next to the fireplace and tenderly laid her down. Without breaking the kiss, he raised her skirts, trying not to crush the silk, and unbuttoned his breeches. Grace's legs parted as he covered her, and she wrapped them around his waist.

Thank God she wanted this as much as he did.

Special license. To-morrow.

He plunged into her wet heat. Silk, that's what it was like, the softest silk.

Growling with intense possession, he felt like a medieval

knight claiming his prize. Pressed against him, she moaned and sighed softly, a symphony to spur him on. Using long, slow strokes to increase her pleasure, he reveled in her frenzied panting and her hands holding him tighter as her sheath convulsed around him, bringing him with her.

Matt pressed soft kisses to her neck, yet Grace was quiet, too quiet. Perhaps they should not have made love here, but she'd seemed to want him as much as he needed her. Rising, he tucked his shirt back in and rebuttoned his fall. He helped Grace to her feet and smoothed her skirts, straightening her bodice. All the while she said nothing. Finally he sat and placed her on his lap. Holding her, he rained soft kisses on her cheeks and lips, and nuzzled her hair, breathing in her scent.

Never, never again would he let her go. "I'll purchase the license to-morrow. We can be married as soon as you like."

"I cannot." Grace sobbed and burst into tears.

That wasn't the response he'd expected. Matt stroked her back. What did she have against a special license? Perhaps she wanted a large wedding. "Then we'll have the banns read. As long as we marry, it matters not to me."

He kissed her tears and pulled out his handkerchief to dry her cheeks. "I'll call on you in the morning and do this properly. I love you and want to marry you. But right now, you should go home. Is your carriage here?"

Still unable to speak, Grace nodded. How had she done this? Again? It was only supposed to be a kiss, and she'd let him take her. No, that wasn't fair, she encouraged him and desired him every bit as much as he seemed to desire her. But now everything was so much worse. And he thought it was just a matter of how a wedding was to take place. She'd have to explain it to him to-morrow, when she could think rationally. Grace let him smooth her skirts once more and guide her into the hall.

His arm was around her, as if she was ill. Leaning down,

he touched her ear with his lips. "I'll tell the others you're not well and have gone home. Better yet, I'll send for Phoebe."

By the time her carriage and Phoebe arrived, Grace had herself at least a little bit under control. Well, that might be overstating the case; at least she wasn't weeping any longer.

Phoebe took her arm. "I'll take her home. Worthington, go back and ask Anna to watch Lady Charlotte and bring her home."

"I'll help you into the coach first. She's very pale." He started to pick Grace up.

"Worthington, stop," Phoebe hissed in a harsh whisper. "You cannot simply carry her. It is bad enough that people will have seen you rush out after her." She walked Grace toward the door and huffed. "She will be fine."

Apparently, he was not convinced. He remained with them, accompanying them to the carriage and helping her and then Phoebe into the coach before closing the door.

The coach gave a small lurch as it rolled away. Phoebe chaffed Grace's hands as she attempted to understand what came over her this evening. How was she going to explain herself, and what if she got pregnant? Right now she couldn't even remember when she'd last had her courses.

Soon they were at Stanwood House.

Royston opened the door and bowed. "Are you all right, my lady?"

Grace repressed a hysterical giggle, and lied, "Just a little faint. I'll be fine."

Phoebe stayed with her as she mounted the stairs, then entered her parlor.

Oh God. Phoebe was going to think Grace had lost her mind, and she'd be right.

"Sherry or hot milk?" Her friend tugged the bell-pull.

Grace sighed. "Sherry. It is on the sideboard. This has gone beyond hot milk."

Handing her a glass, Phoebe sat down next to her. "Now,

what happened? He seemed more concerned than angry. Did you tell him you cannot marry?"

Grace shook her head. Her heart was breaking all over again. "I—I didn't get a chance. We . . . and then I—I tried. But he said he'd get a special license, and I told him I couldn't, but he thought I wanted the banns read . . ."

Phoebe put her arm around Grace's shoulders. "Grace, did it happen again?"

Tears rolled down her cheeks. "Yes, and he's coming in the morning to propose properly."

Her friend sighed. "And you still plan to tell him you cannot marry him?"

Sobbing again, Grace nodded. "I must. I do not have any other choice."

A knock sounded on the door. She really couldn't face anyone else now. "Come."

Royston cracked the door open. "My lady. The Earl of Evesham is waiting for Lady Evesham. He said not to rush."

Grace sat up and took her friend's hand. Enough was enough. She had to pull herself together. The children would be here to-morrow, and they'd sense something was wrong if she didn't. "I'll be fine. A good night's sleep should do me."

Drawing her brows together, Phoebe looked at Grace dubiously. "If you are sure?"

She tried to smile, but didn't quite manage it. "Go to your husband. At least one of us can have one."

She broke down into tears again.

"I'll stay a while longer. Marcus won't mind at all." Phoebe turned to the door. "We shall need a mug of hot milk with honey and her ladyship's maid. Please tell Lord Evesham I'll be some few minutes yet."

"Yes, my lady. There is also a Lord Worthington asking after her ladyship."

Grace gulped air and tried to breathe normally. *Not tonight. I cannot see him now.*

Shaking her head, Phoebe glanced at Grace. "Tell him to go home."

Royston bowed and left only to return a few minutes later. "Lord Worthington says he'll do himself the honor of calling on her ladyship in the morning."

At least Grace wouldn't have to deal with him tonight. To-morrow, she would tell him.

Phoebe stayed until Grace finished her milk and tucked her into bed. "Phoebe, thank you."

"You'll feel more the thing in the morning." Her friend kissed Grace's forehead, then left the room.

Grace slept fitfully between bouts of tears. She'd never thought of herself as a watering pot, but she was doing a fine job of acting like one. She tried and failed to find the words she must say to Worthington.

When she woke, the sun streamed through her windows. What time was it? She never slept much past dawn. That was the reason she had her curtains left open. She rose onto her elbows, then flopped back. *Worthington*. Merely thinking about him made her body hum. What was she going to say to him?

Hushed voices crept past her bedchamber. *The children are here?* She could not have slept through the day. Grace reached over and tugged the bell-pull.

The next moment, Mary opened the door. "Are you all right? Bolton said we must be quiet, a'cause you weren't feeling well."

Grace held out her arm and Mary crawled in bed. One of the seven reasons Grace could not wed. Her sister hugged her and gave her a wet kiss. Worthington would just have to understand. Mary nestled next to Grace. She stroked her sister's hair, allowing the homely motion to soothe her. "When did you arrive?"

"Last night. We stopped for dinner, and Mr. Winters said

he'd be blessed if he'd keep the whole pack of us in an inn overnight."

Repressing a chuckle, her lips tilted up. "Oh dear. Who was involved?"

"Alice, Eleanor, and Walter. They just wanted to take Daisy for a walk. Then there was a cat that Daisy wanted to see, and some horses attached to a carriage."

Grace struggled not to laugh. The dog could never understand why cats didn't immediately like her. "I understand. Was there much damage?"

"I don't know. There was a lot of shouting." Mary concentrated on retying a bow that had come loose on her gown. "I couldn't see very much. Mr. Winters and Miss Tallerton made us get back into the coaches right away, and we left. I didn't even have time to finish my milk."

"I see. I shall have to commend them for their quick thinking." Grace sat up. "Time for you to leave. I must wash and break my fast."

Mary scrambled off the bed as Bolton came in the room. The maid waited until the door shut and grinned. "I ought not to laugh, but such a story Mr. Winters and Miss Tallerton had to tell last night. Luckily, the horses had been changed and were ready to go when Miss Tallerton gave the order. No real damage. Just an angry young man who took off running after them. John Coachman said the man's horses were scared but not hurt."

"Well, that's a relief. I would not care to shirk my duties if his horses had been injured."

"No, my lady. They arrived here not long after you'd gone to bed. I didn't want to wake you."

Smiling, Grace rose from the bed. "I'm happy they are here. It is one less thing to worry about."

Jane poked her head in the room. "How are you feeling this morning? I heard you were taken ill?"

"Not ill, precisely." Grace donned her robe, then padded

over to the wash-basin. "I'm looking forward to hearing about what happened last night from an adult perspective."

A broad smile appeared on Jane's face. "It was quite an interesting story."

Due to the children having broken their fast earlier, Grace took breakfast in her study. There, at least, she could stay busy and try not to think about Worthington. She nibbled her toast and sipped tea while she reviewed the household accounts that had been brought on the baggage coach last night.

An hour later, Grace sat back in her chair and sighed. This wasn't working. She couldn't concentrate on anything. He was going to come here to-day. She briefly considered denying herself, but he deserved to know the truth. Promising herself that she'd remain calm, she glanced back down at the column of figures and resisted the growing urge to throw something.

For the thousandth time, she wished her parents hadn't died. Though this time it was for a completely selfish reason. She wanted to marry Worthington, and she could not.

Royston knocked on the door and poked his head in.

"Yes, Royston, what is it?"

"My lady, Lord Worthington presents his compliments and asks that you speak with him in private."

There's no avoiding it. Grace bit her lip. Maybe it wouldn't be as bad as she thought. After she'd told him about her responsibilities, he would be happy she must refuse him. "Very well, I shall be right there."

Matt had presented himself at Stanwood House late the following morning and handed his card to the butler. He couldn't believe that this whole time she'd been right across the square from him. "Is her ladyship feeling better?"

The man bowed in that stately way butlers had. "To the best of my knowledge, my lord."

God knows Matt had never been able to trick his butler into descending to the level of a mere mortal.

"I would like a private interview with her."

"If you will follow me, my lord." The butler bowed again and led Matt to a parlor overlooking the street. "I shall inform her ladyship you are waiting."

He clasped his hands behind his back, stood staring out the window. Sounds reminding him forcibly of a herd of elephants, or more accurately his sisters, came from the corridor. Then he heard an older, sharper voice, and the herd moved in mass up the stairs. He turned as the door opened.

Lady Grace entered, closed the door behind her, and curtseyed. "My lord, how may I help you?"

She was still a little pale, but as beautiful as ever. Grace clasped her hands in front of her. Bowing, he smiled as he approached her. "You can help me by darn well marrying me. I meant to ask you that first morning, but you forgot to tell me you'd planned to leave so early."

A light blush crept from her slim throat into her cheeks. She refused to meet his gaze. "There is no need for a proposal. It was merely a pleasant rendezvous, my lord. Nothing more."

He unclenched his jaw and found himself clenching his fist instead. After last night, that was *not* the answer he was expecting. What was going on here? No woman of her obvious quality, not to mention only recently former virginity, would make love with a man and try to pass it off as nothing.

Matt tried to relax his churning stomach and maintain an unruffled countenance. He kept his slow pace and now stood only a few inches from her. "For you, *perhaps*, but not for me." He raised a brow. "Even if I thought you were telling the truth about the first time, last night was not nothing."

The blush deepened and Grace's gaze flew to his face. "I—I do not understand."

Pleased to have caught her off guard, he noted her quickened breathing and the confusion in her lovely deep blue eyes. Taking her in his arms, he kissed her. Her lips opened to him as he—*he* had taught her. No other man would ever touch her. Lady Grace Carpenter was his. Matt lifted his head. "Not nothing. No mere rendezvous. I think it is time you tell me what you're playing at, my lady."

Grace couldn't believe Worthington was in her parlor kissing her. What was infinitely worse, she was kissing him as well. What kind of power did he have over her? It was as if she had no control, her arms reached over his shoulders and her hands clutched the back of his neck as if she were clinging to him for life, again. The door opened and feet shuffled in. *He,* not she, broke their kiss. Why did she have no resolve when it came to him?

"Why are you kissing Grace, sir?" Mary asked.

"That is an answer I would like to have as well," Walter added.

Worthington held her so close the rumble of his deep chuckle vibrated through her.

"I'm trying to convince Grace to marry me."

She shook her head trying to clear it.

Philip frowned. "Well, if one has to kiss a lady in order to marry her, I don't think I shall."

The last thing she needed was to have her overly curious brothers and sisters involved in this. "All of you, leave now, and do not open this door again unless you've been given permission to enter."

They backed up out of the room. Alice and Eleanor pulling Mary with them. The door closed.

Grace swallowed. Maybe now he'd understand. "My

lord . . ." His mouth captured hers again. Her tongue tangled with his, savoring his taste and the soft caresses. Once again his wicked hands lit fires under her skin.

He lifted his head and her lips followed. "Will you do me the honor of being my wife?"

Grace fought herself to let go of him and back up, yet he refused to release her hands. "My lord, thank you for your very kind offer, but I find I cannot accept."

His expression rapidly changed from humorous to confused and then severe. "Why?"

She closed her eyes and fought to steady her voice. "All those children, they are my brothers and sisters."

Frowning, he shook his head as if trying to make sense of what she'd said. "Very well. Many families have a number of children. What does that have to do with anything? I have sisters myself. I've been hoping you liked children."

Tears stung her eyes as Grace bit her lip. This was the hardest thing she'd ever had to do, but do it she must. Her throat tightened, threatening to choke her. "I am—I am their guardian. I will never give up that position."

Wrenching her hands from his, she fled the room, closing the door with a *snap* behind her.

Matt stared down at his empty hands and then at the closed door. He found a chair and sat. Numbness washed over him. *How* many children were there? He should have counted, but it never occurred to him that she . . . He put his elbows on his knees and dropped his head into his hands.

Guardian? She's their guardian? How can that be?

He'd lost track of how long he sat there trying to think when the door opened.

The youngest girl walked in, a mulish cast was about her mouth, and her determined chin trembled a bit. "You made Grace cry."

That was fair. He felt like crying as well. "I didn't mean to. I meant to make her happy."

The child creased her brow and nodded wisely. "Made a mull of it, did you?"

Despite himself and Grace, and this damnable problem, Matt found his lips twitching. "Yes, I suppose you could say that. What is your name?"

Eyeing him, she moved closer. "Mary. What's yours?"

"Worthington, but I would consider it an honor if you would call me Matt."

She sidled next to him. Her blond hair was in two braids, some of it escaping their confinement and curling around her face and neck. Her deep blue eyes, just like her sister's, stared up at him. "Now what're you going to do? Grace told our cousin Jane that she can't marry anyone. Not until Charlie is older."

Trying not to frown, Matt rubbed his chin. "Charlie, I take it, is your eldest brother?"

Mary nodded emphatically, causing her braids to bounce.

Matt held out his hand. Mary took it and climbed into his lap. "How old are you?"

"I'm five." She smiled, showing a missing tooth. "But I'll be six this summer."

"Five is a good age." He needed to know, so he may as well ask now. "How many of you are there?"

Counting on her fingers, she said, "All of us are seven. Charlotte is eighteen. She is the reason we are in London. Charlie is sixteen, he's at Eton; Walter is fourteen; Alice and Eleanor are twelve, they're twins; and Philip is eight."

Matt felt a little light-headed. "Other than Grace, who cares for you?"

"Nurse, Mrs. Tallerton, Mr. Winters, and Cousin Jane, but we have to listen to Mrs. Penny and Royston and anyone else Grace tells us to mind."

Something wasn't right. "Do you not have an uncle that is also responsible?"

Mary shook her head. "No, I heard my aunt say once it is a very good thing her brother, that's our uncle, is not here because he's a ne'er-do-well and a bounder."

Matt laughed. "In that case, I agree with her, but I'll bet my boots you're not to be repeating what she said."

Mary looked up at him with eyes that reminded him of a puppy's, albeit blue, not brown. "Are you going to tell on me?"

Matt gave her his most serious look. "No, never. I am true blue and will never stain."

He was rewarded by a trusting smile. "I like you."

"I like you, too."

The door opened and a pair of twins with the same gold hair and blue eyes entered.

"Alice in yellow and Eleanor in green," Mary whispered. "Thank you."

Identical looks of disapproval turned on Mary. "There you are. You know you are not to be in here." Alice held out her hand. "Come along."

Mary shifted closer to him. "But he's my friend."

Eleanor heaved a dramatic sigh, and Alice gave her a look of long suffering.

"Matt wants to marry Grace." The mulish chin made another appearance.

Alice rolled her eyes. "And she refused."

"How do you know?" Mary's eyes grew wide. "Oooh, you were listening at the door."

Tapping her foot, Eleanor pressed her lips together. "Yes, now come with us."

Fascinated, Matt asked, "Do you all eavesdrop?"

Alice turned to him. "Well, how else are we to know what is going on? No one tells us children *anything.* Mary, come *now.*"

Before Mary could obey, the door opened once more to admit, he counted them, three more, including the eldest girl—Ah yes, there was the eldest boy at school.

"What are you still doing here, sir?" a boy asked. Matt placed him as Walter. "I thought my sister turned you down. Though I don't know why she did when she's made herself deuced unhappy."

The only pair of eyes not staring at him was Mary's. Interesting. This is what it's like to be a circus freak. He wondered how it would be to live with such an embarrassing and outspoken group of children. He had not a doubt that if he married their sister, that would be his lot.

"If you ask me, I think Grace does want to marry him." That was Philip. "Except we're rather a lot to swallow."

This was Matt's cue. He could either leave now and lose her forever, or attempt to enlist Grace's brothers and sisters to aid him in securing her hand.

Walter's brows furrowed. "If you'll take my advice, sir, you'll think on it. You can send us word if you still want to marry Grace."

"And how, pray, is he to do that?" Lady Charlotte gave her brother an exasperated glance. "Grace would find out the instant a note came. No, we shall have to be cleverer than that." She pressed her lips together in thought.

It occurred to Matt that they all shared not only their distinctive hair color and eyes, but determined chins as well.

Charlotte glanced at him. "Is one of your sisters out this year?"

"Yes. Lady Louisa Vivers." What had that to do with anything?

She smiled, pleased with herself. "I thought so. There is a resemblance. I met her last evening. You may send a message through her." Charlotte glanced out the door. "Now you must go before someone finds us all in here with you and tells Grace."

"Is she a hard task mistress?"

Shooing the younger children out, Charlotte turned back to him. "She is the best of sisters. If it was not for her, we'd not be together."

Maybe now he'd discover what's going on. "Why is that?"

Charlotte stared at him for a few moments. "When Mama died, none of our relations would take all of us. We were to be piecemealed out. Grace promised Mama that wouldn't happen, and she fought to keep us together." She glanced out the door again. "Now you really must go."

Matt stood. "I'll send word."

A sad smile appeared on her lips. "We don't really expect you to and won't hold it against you. Grace said no man would want to be saddled with seven children, and she wouldn't trust it anyway." Charlotte bit her lip. "I think it is very sad, because she's given up everything for us."

Putting her hand over her mouth, Charlotte turned and walked quickly away.

He couldn't imagine life without Grace. Still, he would be responsible for eleven children including his four sisters. It was not a decision to make lightly, though it was one he would have to make soon.

Chapter Ten

Grace ran into her room and threw herself upon her bed. At least it was out. Now Worthington knew why she couldn't marry him. And he'd seen the children. He'd let her go easily enough after she'd told him she was their guardian, which proved he didn't truly want her. Or at least not with her brothers and sisters.

He was probably relieved that she had refused him. Now she could go back to the way she'd been before they'd made love. Touching her lips, still swollen from his kisses, tears coursed down her cheeks. Something shriveled up inside her as she realized Worthington would never hold her or kiss her again. She dried her eyes and rolled over, staring at the bed canopy.

The only time she'd been more miserable was when her parents had died. She shuddered to think what her mama or papa would have said about her behavior with Worthington. Then again, under the circumstances they might have understood, at least a little. They loved each other so very much, and loved her and the other children. She had been able to talk to Mama and Papa about anything. They would have been able to advise her. Then again, if they had not died, she would not be in such a muddle.

One lone tear escaped from the corner of her eye. In its own way, what she was going through with Worthington was worse. Far worse. For she would meet him everywhere and never have him in her life.

Matt made his way across Berkeley Square, trying to grapple with the idea of having eleven children. He wasn't at all sure he wanted his sisters involved and was a little insulted that Charlotte and Walter had dismissed him as a potential husband for Grace. After all, how did they know what he could and couldn't accept?

Aside from that, Matt had taken her innocence. If he'd been enough of a gentleman to refuse, she'd still be a virgin. He rubbed a hand over his face as he entered the square and glanced back over his shoulder.

Gazing back at him was Mary's face squished against the glass of a first-floor window watching him. Next to her was Philip. The older children stood with solemn faces staring at him as he walked through the park. When he reached the other side of Berkeley Square, he waved away the footman and let himself into his house.

Once he reached his study, he poured a large brandy and took a swallow. He relished the familiar burn as it cleared his head. Seven and four, eleven children. No matter how many times he'd add the numbers, they would be the same. If he could persuade her to marry him, they'd start out with eleven children between them. If she was as fertile as her mother . . . the only decision would be the date of the wedding.

He could understand why she'd be leery about trusting anyone with her brothers and sisters. Could she learn to trust him with the children? Could he live without her? Bloody, bloody, hell. He hurled the glass at the fireplace.

Crystal shattered and the flame flared as the wine hit. It didn't feel as good as it should have.

It was midnight before Matt sought his bed, and still he couldn't sleep. Every time he closed his eyes, visions of Grace as he made love to her were replaced by hundreds of children. Giving up on slumber, he dressed and went back to his study.

Sometime later, Thorton brought breakfast. The rare roast beef turned to ashes in Matt's mouth and he had it taken away. Dropping his head to his hands, he groaned. Why couldn't he think? He rose and poured a glass of brandy.

For a reason he couldn't understand, whenever his mind reached the idea of not sharing his life with Grace, it stopped and refused to go any further. Living without her was not an option. She would have to learn to trust him with the children. But how was he to convince her?

A knock sounded on the door, and Patience entered. She regarded him for several moments before raising her brows. "Is it not a little early for that?"

He lifted his glass. "Under the circumstances, no."

"Matt, I've never known you to drink so early in the day. Do you want to tell me what is bothering you?"

He considered briefly telling her to go away, but there was no denying he needed help, and she was a mother. He turned his chair to face her. "Yes. Please, have a seat."

Taking the chair in front of his desk, Patience gazed at him expectantly. When he didn't say anything, she asked, "Does it have anything to do with your lady?"

He really had no idea exactly how perceptive Patience was. Matt couldn't help heaving a sigh. "It does. Her name is Lady Grace Carpenter."

"Ah." She nodded sagely. "I see."

It was good that at least one of them did. "You do? How?"

"I would have thought that was obvious. It is no great

secret that she won a hard-fought battle for guardianship of her brothers and sisters. It took her over a year to do it. Her maternal grandfather finally tipped it in her favor. He agreed to share guardianship with her, though he made it clear, the children would live with Lady Grace. He died several months ago. I don't know how or if that will affect the matter."

For one thing, it would cause Grace to think she could not wed. If Lord Timothy were still alive, she wouldn't have to give up control of the children. Matt rubbed his forehead. "I don't understand why no one helped her."

"Her aunts and uncles on the Carpenter side were more than willing to take a child or two . . ." He grimaced. Charlotte had told him the same thing. Patience continued, "She's been in fact, if not in law, their sole guardian for probably three years now."

That long. With no one other than servants and teachers to help her? He drew his brows together. "How old is her brother Stanwood?"

Shrugging her shoulders, Patience glanced around. "Where is your *Debrett's*?"

Matt went over to the bookshelf and pulled it out. After a few minutes, he glanced up. "Sixteen. Five years before he can act as guardian."

"He would still be too young to raise his brothers and sisters." Patience shook her head. "And you will never wrest the other children from her."

He replaced the book back on the shelf, returning to his seat. What he was about to say would affect his stepmother as well. "I have no desire to take her brothers and sisters from her. I am well aware I must be ready to take on her whole brood. They know it as well."

Patience's lips tightened. "In addition to the one you already have."

He knew this would come up sooner or later. It was best

to put her at ease now. "Did you think I've not considered that? None of us could live in a house with eleven children at each other's throats."

"Of course not." The lines around her lips eased. "Yet even *if* she loves you and *all* the children get along, you must still convince her you are worthy to be the children's guardian. That is where your challenge lies."

He scrubbed his face with his hands. "One of the many. I imagine she is not very trusting when it comes to her brothers and sisters."

"She has no reason to be. She fought her paternal uncles for guardianship. None of them believed she could raise them and, of course, they all thought she should do what a well-bred lady normally does and marry. It was the fact they wanted to divide the children among them that Lady Grace refused to accept. At least one point is on your side. You know the court prefers a maternal uncle to have guardianship. Fortunately her mother's only remaining brother is still overseas and cannot cause you any trouble."

Matt narrowed his eyes. "What do you know of him?"

"A ne'er-do-well. He can be very charming until he's crossed. Someone I believe you'd call an ugly customer. If he thought it would in some way benefit him, he would try for guardianship."

"Cant, Mama?" he teased. "I'll go bail you got that from Theodora. I'll have to have a word with her about corrupting her innocent mother."

Patience chuckled, then rose and shook out her skirts. "I shall leave you with your thoughts. Worthington, you will need to know what you are doing."

"I know. That's what makes it so deuced difficult. I'd marry her to-morrow, if she'd take me." He went back to his garden view as his stepmother closed the door.

Luncheon arrived, and he ate not paying attention to the food. His heart broke, buoyed, and sank again. He began to wish his heart had broken for good, like his friend Robert Beaumont's. But Matt wasn't so lucky as to want to eschew love and marriage. He'd never been in love before. Though that wasn't the problem. He knew she loved him, and he damn well loved her. It was the other things that came with it. Precisely seven of them, or rather Grace's fear for them.

A soft whine drew his attention away from the window. He glanced over to see his Great Dane focused on a bit of leftover beef. Reaching out, he plucked up the meat and gave it to Duke. "Well, boy, what do you think? Shall we add another seven children to our household?"

Duke thumped his tail.

"Yes, of course you'd think it a great deal of fun. More people to pet you. I don't suppose you've considered what would occur if they happened not to like you. Or were afraid of you?" The dog looked up with a furrowed brow. "No, I didn't think you had."

The pounding of running overhead disturbed Matt's thoughts. "I think it is time for our walk."

The door burst open, and Theo stood looking expectantly at him. "Matt, are you ready?"

She was the joy of his life. All the others had passed the age of childlike innocence. "Yes, tug the bell-pull." His thoughts turned to Mary, and the way she had so trustingly climbed into his lap. Did she even remember her father? At least Theo had him.

They were half-way to the Park when a loose Great Dane puppy, all legs and lead trailing behind her, ran past them followed shortly thereafter by a footman. High-pitched shouts followed the escapee. He glanced down at Duke, alert for the first time in ages. "Duke, fetch." Matt let loose the lead and called to one of his footmen, "One of you, give me your girl and follow him."

Madeline took his hand. Her cheeks flushed, she had a wide smile on her face. "What's going on?"

"Runaway dog."

"He's really pretty."

Matt grinned. "Well, my dear, I think you have the adjective correct, but not the gender. That's a female."

"Really?" she breathed.

"Really."

A block from the Park, they caught up with the miscreant.

"We've got her under control, my lord. She got away from this poor fellow here." The footman he'd sent pointed to a footman who was bent over, trying to catch his breath. "But Duke brought her to."

Matt regarded Duke, who was clearly in the process of either falling in love or flirting heavily. "Duke, here."

Duke glanced at his lady friend and ambled over to Matt. She followed. "At least one of us is lucky in love."

"Daisy, Daisy, you bad dog." Lady Charlotte came hurrying up. "How could you go off like that?"

Alice wagged her finger. "You know Grace will be angry."

Offering his hand, Walter bowed. "Thank you, sir, for catching her."

Turning, her eyes widening, Lady Charlotte seemed to finally notice him. "Lord Worthington."

Louisa peeked out from his other side. "Charlotte, is that your dog?"

Just stopping herself from rolling her eyes, she glanced at Daisy. "Yes, and unfortunately she is not nearly as well behaved as yours."

"Well, Matt—I'm sorry—Lady Charlotte, my brother, Lord Worthington, but I'm sure it's all right if you call him Matt. He trained Duke. Matt can do anything."

Charlotte looked impressed. "Can he indeed? Well, I wish he'd train Daisy. You wouldn't believe the trouble she caused when the children were on their way to Town. Here the rest of them come now."

Before Matt could glance around, he was surrounded by a sea of children.

"Matt?"

He looked down to see Mary. "A pleasure to see you again."

She tucked a confiding hand in his.

Theodora looked daggers at Mary. "Who's she?"

Worthington tried not to groan. "Theodora, this is Mary. Here, take my other hand. It's just as good. Maybe even better."

Mary moved closer to him. If Patience was correct about the length of time Grace had had guardianship, Mary probably didn't remember her father. At least his sisters had him as a father figure.

"Who is she and how do you know her?" Theo demanded.

Louisa scowled. "For goodness' sake, Theodora. Do stop. She is a friend's sister and if you don't behave, I'll tell Mama."

Theodora grumbled.

"Oh, do you have a mama?" Mary asked as if it was a novel idea.

Theo frowned. "Everyone has a mama."

Shaking her head, Mary stared at Theo. "I don't. I used to have one, but she died. I don't remember her because I was too little."

Theodora stopped walking. "Who takes care of you?"

"My sister and Nurse and Miss Tallerton."

Glancing at Louisa, Theo drew her brows together. "I don't think I'd like to have my sister take care of me."

Mary nodded her head. "Well, if it was Charlotte, I'd agree, but it's Grace."

Matt, tired of tripping over them as they leaned forward to talk, said, "Tell you what. You can both be on one side of me as long as you hold hands."

They looked at him with identical frowns. "No."

Thankfully, they'd reached the Park. "There you go. Off with you."

The girls darted away, and Matt stretched his fingers. For little girls, they had strong grips. "Why did I have to fall in love with the only single woman in England who had charge of her seven brothers and sisters?"

He followed them at a leisurely pace. The dogs were playing together and some of the children as well. The two eldest sat together on a bench, heads together talking. It could be worse. And then came the sound of unhappy shouting. The older boy—what's his name? Matt's gaze followed the contretemps. Walter, that's it—was fighting with another lad.

Good bottom, glaringly abroad.

Walter needed to keep his arms in closer to his body. At least that was something Matt could remedy. Smiling, he took off toward the fight. This was the answer to his problems. He'd show Grace how much she needed his help with the children.

Grace had been in her office since she had finished breakfast. Shortly before noon, she heard a commotion coming from the front of the house.

"Daisy! Duke, heel," a strong male voice commanded.

"I'd pay good money to see that." Grace rose and hurried to the entrance hall. Both dogs stood by Worthington's side and hundreds of children milled about. *Chaos*. She covered her eyes, looked again, and counted. Ten children? Two Great Danes? And Worthington. What was he doing here? "I don't understand."

His eyes smiled, and her heart tried to melt.

"Philip, Theodora, Mary, and you"—he pointed to a footman—"what's your name?"

"Hal, my lord."

"Yes, Hal. Take the dogs into the back garden. Walter, come with me."

Walter detached himself from the crowd, glanced up at Grace, and hung his head. One eye was turning an interesting shade of purple, his shirt was torn, his hair was messy, and he appeared as if he'd been rolling around in the dirt.

Grace sighed. "Walter, what have you been doing?"

Worthington put his hand on Walter's shoulder. "Nothing but a bit of cross and jostle work. If we can be private, Walter will explain."

"Of course. My study." Grace led them down the corridor. Once in her office, she offered Worthington a chair and sat behind her desk. Walter stood in front of the desk facing her.

He glanced at Worthington, who nodded.

Her brother swallowed and nodded back. "You see, it was like this. There was some other boy, and he was teasing Philip, then the other boy took Philip's ball. And I decided to get it back, and he swung at me, so I swung back and the next thing I knew, we were fighting. I'm sorry my shirt got ripped."

As hard as Walter was trying, he couldn't keep his eyes from shining. *Boys, all of them.* She glanced at Worthington and raised her brows. "And how did you become involved?"

"I—um—I helped them get Daisy back."

Oh, no. Grace widened her eyes. "What did she do?"

Walter grinned. "She got away from Hal and took off down the street. We gave chase, but then Matt told Duke to fetch her. Well, Duke didn't exactly bring her back, but he did stop her."

Pinching the bridge of her nose, she said, "Indeed, my lord, it seems I have you to thank for rescuing both my dog and my brother."

"That's not fair, Grace. I was doing fine. Just glaringly abroad."

Worthington frowned. "What did I tell you about repeating that to your sisters?"

"But this is Grace," Walter protested.

She gave a short laugh. "Walter, go get cleaned up. You didn't start the fight, so I shan't blame you."

Grace shook her head as her brother left the room then turned her attention to Worthington. "Now, will you please tell me what actually happened? And what, pray, does 'glaringly abroad' mean?"

Chapter Eleven

Worthington grinned boyishly at Grace. "The term means that his arms were too wide. As for the rest of the fight"—he shrugged—"it was very much as your brother said. When I saw the clash, I broke it up, then sent a message that if Mr. Babcock, the other boy's father, wished a precise accounting he could contact me. I gave my card to the lad's nursemaid."

She opened her mouth and closed it again. Ending the contretemps was helpful, but Worthington should not have sent his card. It indicated that he might have a right to—to. Grace couldn't think about that now.

In her most repressive tone, she replied, "I thank you, but Walter is my responsibility."

"After that I taught Walter some boxing moves."

She struggled to keep her jaw from dropping. The dratted man acted as if she hadn't said a word. What did he think he was doing? Gazing up at the ceiling for a moment, she blew out a puff of air. He should not involve himself with the children. It wouldn't do for them to become attached to him. Nothing could come of it. Not for them and, most certainly, not for her.

Worthington's heat, his scent, seemed to drift across the

desk to her. Reminding her of how good it felt to be in his arms. God help her, all she wanted was for him to touch her. She would order him out of the house. Not seeing him was the only way she could retain her sanity.

The next thing she knew his strong arms lifted her from the chair and drew her close to him.

"Grace, I know you don't think I still want to marry you, but I do." His lips brushed her forehead. "I can't live without you. I like all of your brothers and sisters. I want to take care of all of you. Please let me."

"You don't"—her blood roared in her ears making it hard to think—"you cannot know what you're saying. I have seven, *seven* brothers and sisters. The youngest is only five."

He grinned as his lips made their way to her jaw. "She'll be six in summer."

Grace wanted to sink into him, have him sink into her. She fought the urge to cant her neck, giving him easier access.

This would not do!

Somehow she found the strength to take one step back, out of his arms. "Yes, and she has another twelve years before I'll present her." Grace covered her brow with a hand. Her temples began to throb. "Do you have any idea how much attention they need?"

"I got a taste of it to-day," he murmured against her lips, "and it didn't bother me at all. In fact, I quite enjoyed it."

She closed her eyes in frustration. Why was he being so—so stubborn? "You have spent what? One day with them? Not even that, one trip to the Park, and what if we have children? I'd be taken up with a baby, and the others would have to rely on you." She closed her eyes at the memory of suddenly becoming mother and father to her brothers and sisters. "I know what that's like. Mary was barely in leading strings when my mother died." Glancing at him, she shook her head. "You cannot want that kind of responsibility."

"I don't want you to die, if that's what you mean, but I'm perfectly ready to take on your brothers and sisters, as well as our children."

Grace had to have more distance from him. She retreated to the other side of the room. What he said didn't make sense. Why would he want to have the responsibility for her family? What sane man would?

Worthington began slowly closing the distance between them, his tone soft and compelling. "Grace, I'd be an excellent guardian. I won't promise you that I'll suborn all my decisions to you. I wouldn't do that with our children. Still, I will treat them as if they are ours. No differently from the children we'll have or my sisters."

Rubbing her temples, she gazed into his mesmerizing lapis eyes. "I don't understand you at all. Why do you want to take us on?"

"To make you happy. To make us a family."

Standing only inches in front of her, he reached out and curled one of her locks around his finger. She stared into his eyes. The blue depths combined humor and hope. He made her want to hope. Although he didn't touch her, she was drawn toward him.

He bent his head. "Let me love you."

Grace was in his embrace again and somehow her arms were around his neck. Their lips met in a kiss. "I shouldn't do this."

"Do what, my love?"

"Any of this. I meant to speak with you rationally."

"You are speaking rationally. You just haven't come to the realization that I've made my decision." He dragged her closer and plundered her mouth. "I think I forgot to tell you I love you."

This felt too good to be right. "That is not enough, my lord."

"Matt." He nibbled her ear. "I want to hear you say my name."

Why wasn't he listening to her? He couldn't want all of them. He must be mad, or he simply did not have a good understanding of what was involved. "Matt, it's not enough."

"Grace, we'll make it enough." He kissed her deeply, laying siege to her senses.

Matt couldn't be in Grace's presence without wanting her. Wanting to possess her, help carry her burdens or anything else she required of him. He would find a way to change her mind.

She responded to him, yielding so that no space remained between them. He feathered his thumbs over her nipples. She shivered and caught her breath.

"We should cease this," she said, yet that wasn't what was in her eyes or in the huskiness of her voice.

"Tell me you don't want me, and I'll stop." He gently rubbed the undersides of her breasts as she moaned.

He loved touching her and her responses to him. When he covered a breast with one hand, she pressed it into his palm. He swooped and captured her soft lips again. Lifting her to the desk, he sat her on it. Grace's legs parted as she tried to press closer to him. He slowly, lovingly caressed her tongue with his, and she clung to him.

Grace's fingers tightened on the back of his head. Her mouth demanding everything he could give her. She shivered, and a deep primitive part of him rejoiced.

Matt eased back and whispered, "Tell me you want me to stop, and I will."

Grace panted. "I—I don't know."

She was so beautiful and appeared vulnerable. Yet, against all odds, she'd been strong enough to keep the children together. He needed her, to make her his, and, even if she didn't know it, she needed him in return.

"Grace, let me in. Let me into your life." Stroking her

back, he pressed kisses from the tender part under her ear, down her throat and back to her lips. Her skin was warm, and her small breathy sounds of desire urged him on. Her tongue stroked his frantically, and he moved his hand down her legs, kneading and caressing her. "Grace, my only love, I need you."

She trailed her palms from his back down over his buttocks. Matt slowly lifted the edge of her skirts, the fine muslin rising as his fingers made a slow path up her inner thighs. She moaned and tilted her hips even closer to him.

If nothing else, he'd pleasure her. But when he reached her curls, she unbuttoned his pantaloons and released his erection.

Thank God for managing women.

He slid Grace back a little more on her desk and slowly sank into her. She was hot, wet, and ready for him. Her legs wrapped around him, and her whole body trembled.

He withdrew, then thrust inside her again. It was as if they were made for each other, and no one else.

Grace tightened around him. Matt smothered her low keening cry with his mouth. She was on fire, and her climax spun out like fine crystal until she shattered, carrying him with her.

Afterward he held her, kissing her hair and temple gently, tenderly, before carrying her to the large leather sofa placed in front of the fireplace. He sat, shifting her to his lap.

Mine.

Even if Grace couldn't quite bring herself to accept the fact at the moment. If need be, he'd worm his way into her life until she could no longer deny she was his.

Matt didn't know how long she sat cuddled on his lap, her head against his shoulder, pretending to sleep.

Innumerable minutes passed before she opened her eyes. "I have failed."

Surely she could not have thought of another reason to keep them apart. "What do you mean?"

Her worried countenance was only inches from his face. "I had every intention of telling you we could not go on. That our loving each other wasn't enough, you would never be able to cope with the children. As it is, I am still not sure this is a good idea."

Finally. He resisted the urge to smile. He'd made some progress. "I'm not going to lie to you. I thought about it all of yesterday, last night and to-day. Grace, I just couldn't see past having a future that didn't include you." He lightly kissed her hair. "It was serendipity that my sisters and I and your brothers and sisters were all going to the Park at the same time, not to mention Daisy getting loose."

Grace shuddered. "As much as I love that dog, I could happily throttle her at times."

Matt chuckled. "They are all like that when they're young." He placed his palm on her cheek, she nuzzled into it. "I've never had brothers. I rather enjoyed it."

"What about the girls? How many sisters do you have?"

"Four. Louisa is the same age as Charlotte, Augusta is fifteen, Madeline, twelve, and Theodora, eight." He barked a laugh. "It was touch and go with Theodora and Mary, but they worked it out rather quickly. Charlotte and Louisa already act like they are the best of friends. There will no doubt be squabbles, but nothing we can't manage."

Grace raised wide, horrified eyes to his. "*Eleven children.*"

He smiled and kissed her again. "In addition to whatever we will have."

How could he remain so calm? She got up and stood before him, fists on her hips. "How do you propose are we going to manage eleven children?"

"If we want to be together, we will find a way." Matt reached out, wanting her soft warmth on his lap again. "We shall also have my stepmother's help."

Grace shook off his fingers and began pacing the room muttering to herself, then stopped in front of the window, her back to him. "I don't know. How do I know you won't tire of my brothers and sisters and send them off to school?"

Wiping a hand over his face, Matt studied her. She was right to be concerned. Although they had the deepest physical attraction he'd ever experienced with a woman, and they appeared to agree on most issues, she didn't yet know him well enough to completely trust him. "I would want to send the boys to school. I think it's a good experience for them."

She whirled around and glared. "Not when they are so young. I've heard stories about even the best boarding schools. They need to be old enough to know how to deal with the problems."

When Matt reached for her hands again, she whipped them behind her.

He stifled a groan. This was not what he wanted to be doing with Grace, but they may as well have the conversation now. "Walter is not that young. He should already be in school. I agree with you about Philip, he is not yet ready."

Raising her chin, Grace stared at Matt defiantly, as if she was looking for a fight. "And the girls?"

She would soon discover he was not easily provoked. "No, I'm not in favor of girls' schools. After hearing about flirtations with dancing masters and liaisons with gardeners' boys, they do much better at home with a governess."

Her mien as well as her tone softened. "Matt, do you truly wish to apply for guardianship?"

"Yes." Lord, how he wanted to hold her, comfort her, yet if he did, the issues would still hang between them. "I could never—would never ask you to give your brothers and sisters up. You are doing a wonderful job with them, still it occurred to me at the Park that I have knowledge to offer the children that you cannot, a different point of view, the experiences a man has."

She glanced up and though her face was still strained, a spark of humor lit her beautiful eyes. "Such as teaching them to box?"

"Among other things." He stood. "We will discover how to go about changing the guardianship." He closed the distance between them, placing his hands on her waist. "Please be my wife."

"I want to. I do. I—I just don't know. I cannot think how we are going to manage it all. There are so many problems to solve." She threw up her hands in defeat. He caught them.

"We will make it work." Perhaps if he continued to repeat that, she'd finally agree with him.

The sound of shuffling feet in the corridor intruded.

Matt grinned. "Someone's been keeping them out." He touched his forehead to hers. "It won't last much longer. Do we tell them?"

"Tell them what?" She tried to pull back. When he held her in place, she heaved a sigh. "I cannot make a decision until we have worked out all the details."

And to think Matt had once thought his would be the easiest courtship ever. Still, he wasn't giving up. "Tell them we're thinking about it. We must, Grace. We can swear them to secrecy until we are sure."

Her brows drew together, and he wanted to smooth the wrinkle it caused. Maybe it was wrong of him, but he knew once they mentioned it to the children, the decision would no longer be hers.

Closing her eyes, she gave a slight nod. "Well, I suppose we should get their opinions. After all, any decision we make affects them as well."

If it wasn't for their lovemaking, Grace thought she might have been able to resist him. At least that's what she told herself. She had made a strategic error when she'd chosen Matt, believing once would be enough. A lifetime wouldn't be sufficient. Yet she could never have given herself to another man. He seemed so confident everything would work. If only she could be as sure.

Grace sank onto the sofa while Matt opened the door. Ten curious faces stared up at him. He inclined his head. "Please, come in."

They piled into the room. Mary came immediately to Grace, crawling onto her lap. The youngest Vivers girl, Theodora, sat next to Grace. It appeared Theodora and Mary had already formed a friendship, just as Matt had said. Charlotte and Louisa took the two chairs across from the sofa, while the others formed a semicircle between the chairs and the sofa, and waited. Grace had rarely seen her brothers and sisters so solemn.

Matt took the seat on the other side of Grace. A smile tugged at his lips. "May we help you?"

"Well." Walter cleared his throat, glanced at the other children, and fell silent.

Grace hoped nothing serious had happened. She hadn't heard any loud horrifying noises. Then again, she'd been rather occupied. How long had they been in the corridor?

After a few moments, Mary tugged on Matt's coat. "We want to know if you and Grace are going to be married."

"Yes," Theodora agreed. "We want to know."

Grace glanced at Matt, then surveyed the children. "What would you like?"

Alice opened her mouth and closed it when Walter narrowed his eyes at her. He looked at Matt then Grace. "I, for one, would like it if you married." He flushed. "You'd be happier, Grace."

Augusta, Eleanor, Madeline, Alice, and Philip nodded.

The two eldest glanced at each other and Louisa said, "Yes, all of us would like it."

"Theodora?" Worthington asked.

"Me too." She nodded, smiling. "I won't be the youngest anymore, and I'll have more older brothers."

Grace nudged Mary. "What about you, sweetheart?"

"I like being the youngest, and I like Matt." She gazed up at Grace. "Are you going to get married?"

Grace sighed. "I don't know. We would like to, but there are so many problems."

A cacophony of voices broke the relative quiet.

"Silence," Worthington barked. "Listen to Grace."

The children stopped speaking so quickly, she could swear she'd heard teeth clicking together. "Our main concern is the guardianship." She addressed her brothers and sisters. "Matt will have to apply to be your guardian." Grace tried to steady her voice. "Once I marry, I am no longer allowed to . . ."

He placed his hand on her shoulder. "Once we wed, the law will no longer allow Grace to be your guardian. Therefore, you must decide if you want me to take her place, as it were. Children aged fourteen and above may make their own decision."

A slight line formed between Charlotte's brows for a moment. "I have no objection."

Walter nodded. "I have no objection. It's not as if you won't still be here, Grace."

Charlotte glanced at Grace. "Will you write to Charlie?"

Leaning down, Matt's lips brushed Grace's ear, causing her to repress a sigh. "If you'd like, my love, I can fetch him. Eton is not far."

Her head was in a whirl. This was all going too fast. She had not yet agreed to marry Matt. "We are getting ahead of ourselves," she replied tartly. "The guardianship is only one issue. We do not know where we will live or any number of other things. You children have only just met. How do you know you'll get along? And there is Lady Worthington to consider." She rubbed a hand over her forehead. "This is an extremely important decision. It will irrevocably change our lives. We should not rush into it. Once done, it cannot then be undone. Let us all consider the ramifications carefully. One more thing, until a final decision is made, I do not want a word said outside of our families."

Matt looked at each one of them. "Do you understand what Grace just said?" They all nodded. "Not a word to anyone."

Fortunately, the children were new to Town, otherwise she would have no hope at all of keeping it secret.

Chapter Twelve

"Louisa." Charlotte stood shaking out her skirts. "Let's take the children and give Matt and Grace some time to discuss this further."

The two girls shooed their brothers and sisters out of the room.

Once the door closed behind them, Matt turned to Grace. "My love, in fairness, you must still think of your other brother."

"I don't like taking him out of school, but yes, you're right. For this he must come home."

A knock sounded on the door and Jane entered. "Am I to wish you happy?"

"I wish I knew." Grace covered her face with her hands. This is what came of being selfish and wanting things she should not have.

Matt squeezed her shoulder. "There are a few details that must be put to bed first, but I believe we're making progress."

"Jane," Grace said, "let me introduce Lord Worthington. My lord, my cousin, Miss Carpenter."

She dipped a curtsey, and Matt bowed.

"I've met your sisters already, my lord. If you are to be part of the family, you may as well call me Jane."

"Thank you. For the same reasons, please call me Matt."

Jane focused on Grace. "My dear, I realize you and his lordship have not known each other long, and I am quite sure I do not wish to know how this came about." Jane's lips tilted up. "But if you want my advice, you will take this chance at happiness. His lordship has a reputation as a steady and capable man, a good brother, stepson, and the children like him already. It's as if the stars have lined up in the proper order for you." A sad smile lurked in Jane's eyes. "Love doesn't come along often. When it does, grab it and hold on. You might never have another chance." She bussed Grace's cheek. "Now, I shall leave the two of you to work it out and see what the children are up to."

Jane left, closing the door behind her. Not for the first time did Grace wonder what exactly had happened to the man Jane had loved.

"I think your cousin gives excellent advice."

Grace glanced up at Matt and was tempted to roll her eyes. He had the largest smile she'd ever seen on his face. "You would."

His countenance immediately sobered. "You can trust me. With your heart and your brothers and sisters."

Her paternal uncles' words sounded in her ears. *"No gentleman of substance will ever want you with all those children, Grace."*

Had she truly found the one gentleman who would?

"Charlotte," Louisa asked, "where are we going?"

Charlotte lowered her voice. "To the school-room, where no one can hear us. Come along, everyone. We have some things to work out."

She led them up the stairs to the first floor then up the

next set to the second floor where the school-room and the younger children's bedchambers, as well as those of Mr. Winters and Miss Tallerton and the nursemaids, were located.

One the way, they ran into May, who had a bundle of whites in her arms.

"May, can you please have tea, lemonade, and food sent to the school-room?"

The maid's eyes grew wide as she glanced down the stairs. "For how many?"

"Ten." Earlier in the Park and returning home, Charlotte had noticed the way passersby had looked at all of them. Well, people would just have to get used to it. Matt was perfect for Grace, even if her sister didn't quite see it that way yet.

"Right away, my lady."

Once they were all in the large, airy classroom, Charlotte clapped her hands, the way Grace did when she wanted their attention. "Alice, Eleanor, and Walter, please show Augusta, Madeline, and Theo around the floor. I shall call you when tea has been brought."

Louisa glanced at Charlotte. "I take it we shall do the same at Worthington House?"

"I believe that would be best." Charlotte drew her brows together. "If we inspect both houses, we will be able to make a recommendation as to where we should all live." She linked her arm with Louisa's. "I have a plan, but I do want you to be an equal part of it. It seems to me that settling Grace and Matt quickly will allow us to focus on husbands of our own."

"What a splendid idea." Louise grinned. "You make a great deal of sense. It will be much easier for them to chaperone us if they are wed."

Less than a quarter hour later, they were all armed with lemonade and jam tarts, and sandwiches. Charlotte called the meeting to order. "Now . . ."

"Why are you in charge?" Augusta asked.

Louisa rolled her eyes. "Because it is her house. When we go to Worthington House, I shall be in charge." She frowned. "We'll have to rethink that arrangement when we're all living in one place. Are there any more questions before we begin?"

The rest of the children shook their heads.

"Well then," Charlotte said, "as I was about to say, it is clear our sister and brother are in love."

Madeline sighed happily, clasping her hands together. "They make such a lovely couple."

Walter's lips twitched, and Philip looked as if he had eaten something rotten.

"I think Alice, Madeline, and I should start planning the wedding," Eleanor suggested.

Alice and Madeline agreed and the girls immediately began discussing what they and everyone else should wear. Walter and Philip started talking in hushed whispers, probably about boxing or some other horrid thing.

Could no one remain focused on the current issue? Charlotte rapped a ruler on the table until she had everyone's attention once more. "First, we need to ensure they agree to marry. If we are to help them along, we will need to anticipate the problems and address them. Such as . . ."

She glanced at Louisa, who shook out her skirts and glanced at her sisters. "Yes, such as getting along. We are only four to their seven. We need to agree to come to *Parlé* in the event we do not agree."

"What is *Parlé*?" Philip asked.

"It's from pirates," Louisa replied. "That's what they do to negotiate."

"Yes, indeed. I read that novel as well." Charlotte was pleased she and Louisa had so much in common. "We must form our own set of rules to negotiate any difficulties that arise."

She glanced around, making sure all the brothers and sisters understood. Madeline's forehead puckered. "Do you have a question, Madeline?"

"Yes, what's the purpose of the negotiations? We always go to Mama if we cannot agree."

Louisa took over. "If the disagreement is among ourselves, then we may still go to Mama, but if the disagreement is between—our—our new brothers and sisters, we cannot go to Mama because Grace is like their mama."

Augusta frowned. "Does that mean we'll have two mamas?"

"No," Charlotte said. "Let me try to explain. If, for example, Louisa and I disagree, we cannot go to either Grace or your mother, as that might cause problems between them. We must come to a compromise between ourselves. Our rules will help us to work out our differences without being a bother to Grace and Matt."

"Exactly," Louisa agreed. "And that is just one of the issues we should discuss. You heard Grace. She will not marry Matt until they have resolved all the issues. If we want them to wed, we must assist."

Walter stared at Charlotte skeptically. "Do you think they need our help?"

"Of course they do." Louisa's eyes opened wide. "It's obvious they need our aid. Otherwise we would have a wedding date instead of a possible betrothal."

Matt watched his betrothed wear a path in her Turkish rug. She'd been at it since Jane had left over a half an hour ago. Something in addition to the general mess they were in was clearly bothering her. "Grace, my love, open your budget. I can't help you if I don't know what has you so upset."

"I dislike uncertainty immensely." She threw her hands up. "And at the moment, it is all I seem to have."

He couldn't disagree with her about that. The only thing that was making waiting to marry at all tolerable was being able to make love to her. He conjured a vision of her naked, her golden hair curling down over her fabulous breasts . . .

"Matt, are you listening to me?"

He jerked his attention back to her. "Yes, my love."

"I said that we must stop having these—these—oh, I don't know what to call them. We must wait until we are married to—to have relations again."

He was nearly diverted by her beautifully crimson cheeks. "*What?*"

Grace stood rubbing her brow. "You must know how improper it is for us to be—be doing that—with the children around. If even a hint of it got out, my reputation would be ruined and the children taken from me."

She was right, of course. Worthington rubbed a hand over his face. Damn. He should have thought of that. It was his job to protect her. The chancery court wouldn't allow a woman of questionable morals to keep the children. He stifled a groan and his vision of naked breasts faded away. "Yes, my love, I agree."

Her face was anything but happy. "What next shall we discuss?"

Our wedding date. He'd better keep that thought to himself. As up to snuff as he considered himself when it came to the foibles of the *ton,* he needed help. "We should speak with Patience. She always seems to know what's going on and what to do in any social situation."

Grace stopped pacing. "Very well. When would you like to talk with her?"

"Immediately." He glanced at the mantel clock. "I hope she's at home. May I have a sheet of paper, pen, and wax?"

Stepping to her desk, she took out the writing implements. "Here you are."

Matt wrote his note and sealed it with his ring stamped in the wax.

Grace tugged the bell-pull, and a few moments later her butler appeared.

She handed him the missive. "Royston, please have this taken to Lady Worthington."

Seeing the butler's confusion, Worthington said, "It is the house directly opposite the square."

"Yes, my lord."

"If she is there, please have the footman escort her here."

Royston bowed and left the room.

Grace pinched the bridge of her nose. "We shall need to see my uncle Herndon as well. He has always supported me."

"Is he the children's trustee?"

Worrying her bottom lip, she nodded. "Yes. He must be told what we want to do. He was very helpful when I was trying to have the guardianship established."

A knock came and Royston opened the door. "My lady, Lady Worthington has arrived."

Grace glanced over in surprise. "Well, that was fast. Royston, please show her to the morning room and have tea brought."

Leading the way to the other side of the house, Grace glanced up at Matt at the same time he looked down at her. Would she finally have what she wanted and be able to keep the children together? His eyes were warm and loving. He would try, but would it be enough? What if his stepmother objected to the marriage? No one could blame the lady for not wanting seven more children added to her household. Perhaps this wasn't a good idea after all.

When Grace entered the room, Lady Worthington smiled, then her eyes widened. "Worthington, I didn't expect to see you here."

"Aren't you here because of my note?"

"Not at all." She raised her brows. "I came because your sisters and Lady Grace's brothers and sisters are at Worthington House inspecting the school-room."

Laughter burbled up inside Grace and tipped over. "Of course they are. I have no doubt they intend to help us solve our problems."

Matt's brow lightened. "Yes, with Louisa in the lead."

Lady Worthington glanced from Grace to Matt. "I rather think the position is held jointly by Louisa and Charlotte. Their heads were together, in what I can only describe as a plotting position."

Grace thought about the girls for a few moments. "That makes sense. Yesterday evening, they hit it off immediately."

Grinning ruefully, Lady Worthington said, "I'm very happy they are getting along, but may I be made privy to what is going on?"

"I wonder what the devil the children are planning now," Matt murmured to Grace. "Patience, forgive me. Do you know Lady Grace?"

Patience held out her hand, smiling. "We met when you first came out. I knew your mother. She was extremely helpful and kind to me after I came out of mourning."

Grace shook Patience's hand. "Yes, I remember her mentioning you. My lady, please take a seat and be comfortable. Tea will arrive soon. Then we may discuss what we need to without interruption."

Lady Worthington gracefully disposed herself on a French-backed chair. "Please call me Patience, my dear."

"Thank you, Patience."

Grace sat on the small sofa facing Lady Worthington. Once they were seated, Matt joined Grace on the sofa. Tea arrived almost immediately. Grace dispensed the cups and Matt the plates.

"Well." He glanced at her. "Grace and I have decided to marry." Next to him, she tensed. He prayed she wouldn't refute his statement. After a moment, he continued. "Considering the guardianship and the other issues, we are in a bit of a quandary as to when we should hold the ceremony."

"Other issues such as combining both houses?" Patience asked dryly.

Next to him, Grace tensed, but her face was a mask. "That, of course, is one of the matters we must settle."

Was Patience upset that he hadn't discussed the marriage with her first? Nonsense, she knew he intended to wed Grace as soon as he found her. Matt rubbed his chin. "We must discuss aspects of the guardianship with Grace's uncle and consult our respective solicitors. I would like to marry this week."

Patience's brows shot up. "That is certain to cause a deal of talk."

The hell I will wait. He scowled. If he had his way, they'd wed to-morrow.

"You will need to court her for at least a few weeks." Patience straightened her shoulders. "Then we shall plan the wedding. St. George's, I think. We may have the ceremony in six weeks."

She had lost her mind if she thought he'd wait weeks to have Grace to himself. Particularly now that he'd agreed to not bed her. "No."

Grace had been nodding in agreement with everything his stepmother had said. Now she stared at him. "No?"

Patience's lips formed a thin line. "A scandal would affect your sisters, Grace, and Lady Charlotte."

Think quickly. An idea began to form. Matt sat back

against the thick, soft cushions. "I do not intend to cause a scandal." Allowing himself a smug smile, he said, "I shall tell everyone I've fallen madly in love, which happens to have the benefit of being the truth, and shall pursue her relentlessly, until she agrees to marry me." He glanced over at Grace. "You, my love, will be suitably modest before you give in to my love-crazed desires."

Grace, who'd been taking a sip of tea, made a choking sound, which she turned into a cough. She held her hand over her lips, pitching her voice so that only he could hear. "I've never been modest with you and you know it. If I had, we wouldn't be in this mess."

He slapped her back a few times. "I beg to differ. It is not a mess."

Patience's eyes narrowed. "I'm sorry. I was unable to hear either of you."

"Grace said the tea went down the wrong way. Isn't that right, love?"

"Yes, thank you for your help," she replied primly before turning to Patience. "I have at least one friend in Town who knows I had a tendre for Matt when I first came out." Grace gave him a sidelong glance. "I think, with the proper placement of that knowledge, Matt's plan might work."

That was news! Matt had trouble keeping his jaw from hanging open. "When was this, and why did I never know about it?"

"Six years ago. You even danced with me and were very charming."

Charming and not in the market for a wife. What a fool he'd been. He searched her face. "Tell me about it."

Grace's cheeks and neck turned a vibrant shade of deep rose. "Maybe later, but not now."

Taking her hands, he said, "I'll hold you to that."

She gazed into his eyes, and it was all he could do not to kiss her right there in front of Patience. "Two weeks."

His stepmother cleared her throat, and Grace jerked her eyes away from him.

"Three," Patience countered.

"Very well. Three, and not a day longer." Three very long weeks. "Grace, do you agree?"

She hesitated a moment before answering. "Yes."

He didn't trust that she wouldn't find some reason to put it off longer. There must be a way to wed her sooner.

"It might work," Patience said. "Particularly after you followed Grace out of the ballroom the other evening, and the way you look at her. I must say, calling Lady Evesham to attend to her was inspired." Patience took a sip of tea. "Grace, how do you intend to chaperone your sister while Matt is pursuing you?"

Grace picked up her cup. "My aunt Lady Herndon is sponsoring Charlotte. When we tell her, she will be more than happy to help. She's had a difficult time accepting my decision not to marry."

"Very well"—Patience smiled with relief—"we may bring this off after all."

Grace leaned forward a bit. "Would you like to dine with us this evening?"

"I would, my dear, but I think I shall use this evening to find out what the girls have been up to instead. Worthington, though, should dine with you."

High voices and stomping feet echoed through the house.

Patience rose. "I shall extract my four from the menagerie and take them home." She took Grace's hands. "I am very happy you will be joining our family. You do understand my concerns?"

Clearly relieved that the conversation had gone well, Grace smiled. "Indeed, I do. For I have the same ones. As you said, any scandal would affect Charlotte as well. Which I cannot allow."

"You have a lady that is your companion, I believe?"

"My cousin, Jane Carpenter."

"Good. If Worthington plans to haunt your house, which he should, we must ensure the gossips know you are not alone."

"I am aware of that."

The children entered the morning room in mass. Patience blinked as though stunned, then said, "Louisa, Augusta, Madeline, and Theodora, come with me."

"But Mama, we've decided to dine together," Louisa said.

Patience closed her eyes for a moment. "Not this evening. Come with me, if you please. You may meet again to-morrow."

"Yes, Mama," Louisa, Augusta, and Madeline said in unison.

Theodora's mouth had a familiar mulish cast. "Mama, I promised Mary I would stay."

Patience's lips formed a line. "Theodora . . ."

Matt glowered. "Theodora, mind your mother."

"Yes, Matt." His sister pouted, but turned to Mary. "I'm sorry."

Mary hugged Theo. "I understand. I'll see you in the morning."

"We can all go to the Park together again." She returned Mary's hug and followed her sisters out the door.

Patience glanced at Matt and Grace. "Since Theodora's been born, I've earned my name."

Grace's brothers and sisters followed Matt's sisters into the corridor. There was much hugging on the part of the girls. Matt hid his smile when the girls tried to embrace the boys who instead offered to shake hands.

Raising her brow, Patience asked, "How long do you think this comradeship will last?"

"I wish I knew. Hopefully for the duration." He kept his eyes on the children. "Try to find out what they've been up to. I'm sure whatever it is, is well intended, but we might need to nip a few plans in the bud."

"I shall most certainly need to discover their plans. I shudder at what they could come up with."

"I have to say, I agree." Grace grimaced. "They are all bright and imaginative."

"As you say," Patience watched the children for a moment. "Grace, please come to visit me to-morrow."

"Thank you. I shall."

The ladies bussed each other's cheeks.

Matt blew out a breath. So far, so good. He just hoped the rest of his plan to marry Grace quickly was as much of a success. He glanced around. Something was missing. *The dogs!* Where had they got to?

Chapter Thirteen

Once back at Worthington House, Patience took the girls to the children's parlor. "I take it you are pleased with the prospect that Matt and Grace will marry?"

"We have never been so delighted," Madeline said. "Mama, isn't it so romantic?"

Patience nodded, romantic indeed. Though she worried it was too soon for the couple to know their minds.

"I agree," Louisa said. "Grace had decided not to marry because of her brothers and sisters. I think it was a very good notion Matt had of falling in love with her, because he is just what the boys require."

"Yes," Augusta added. "You should have seen him break up the fight Walter was in to-day. Not that Walter started it. It was that other horrid boy."

Patience didn't have to ask Theodora. For years, her youngest daughter had wanted a younger sister. Patience studied them for a few moments. "You seem to have given this some thought."

"We did." Louisa smiled and glanced at her sisters. "We had a meeting with Charlotte and the others and decided how to resolve any disputes that may arise."

Here it was. Afraid her knees would give out with shock,

Patience sank into the old rocking chair and inquired in a tone fainter than she would have liked, "Did you indeed? How is that?"

"Well," Augusta replied, "we shall negotiate the disputes between the two families. Right now, Louisa and Charlotte are the oldest, so they shall help resolve any arguments. As the older ones leave, the next oldest of each family will step in."

"Yes," Madeline piped up. "That way, neither Grace nor Matt will have to be involved. They will just be responsible for their own family and you for us."

"I see." That wasn't as bad as Patience had thought. Although she wondered how long their good intentions would actually work, and what Matt and Grace would have to say about it. Obviously Charlotte and Louisa were destined to be political or diplomatic wives. "Is there anything else?"

Louisa nodded. "Next we must decide where we should live."

Patience could not keep her lips from twitching slightly. "I'm sure you will take everything into consideration."

"Thank you, Mama, we shall," Theodora said solemnly.

"Now then." She rose. "You should all go wash and dress for dinner."

Her daughters obediently left the room. Patience tugged the bell-pull and gave orders that the girls would eat up here, and she'd have a tray in her chambers. If the children planned to dine together, this might be the last quiet meal she would have for quite some time. What else would they decide to help with?

She went to her parlor and poured a glass of sherry. This marriage would change all their lives. Still, Worthington was bound to have married at some point, and she liked Grace. The woman was down to earth and knew how to take on responsibilities. Matt had never looked happier. Patience tried her hardest not to be envious of the feelings he had for

Grace. Not that she was jealous of Matt. He had always been like a brother to her. She only wished she could have experienced that type of love with a husband. Well, there was no use thinking about what would never happen. After all, she had her daughters.

Grace's brothers and sisters followed Worthington's sisters out of the morning room, where Grace and he remained. "Where are the Danes?"

Her eyes widened. "The last I knew, you'd told Hal to take them outside."

"I also told some of the children to go with them," he replied ruefully. "That clearly didn't last long."

She moved to the French windows overlooking the garden. "Look."

Matt joined her. Daisy and Duke were rolling around together, playing, while Hal looked on. "It appears everyone is getting along well."

"At least the dogs won't make plans." She smiled up at him. "I am afraid to ask what the children have been up to."

"Leave it to Patience. She'll get it out of my sisters." He took Grace's hands and proceeded to kiss each finger one by one. "You know, they only want to see you happy."

Tears pricked her eyes. "I do know."

"Grace." His strong arm pulled her to him. "I'll be a good guardian. We will raise them together."

Taking her chin between two fingers and tilting it up, he dabbed the corners of her eyes with his handkerchief. "Trust me, please. I would never do anything to hurt either you or the children."

How much she wanted to trust him. Grace did believe that he would never do anything to purposely hurt any of them. If he did, it was her fault. Due to her own behavior, she had no choice but to pray he would keep his word. "I'll try."

A knock came on the door, and Jane peeped in. "I shall go if I'm disturbing you."

Worthington kissed Grace's lips lightly and stood. "Not at all, I must leave to change for dinner."

Casting Grace a reassuring look, he left the room.

Jane's eyes sparkled in merriment. "Am I to understand that Lord Worthington refused to take no for an answer?"

Lowering her gaze, Grace swallowed. She hadn't *actually* said yes. Then again, they could not go on as they were. As soft as his last kiss had been, her lips still tingled. He made everything sound so easy. Yet, three weeks to the ceremony was not long at all.

Smiling for her cousin, she raised her head. "Just so. His fortunes changed to-day. Daisy got away from the footman, and he was able to save her. Then he stopped a mill Walter was involved in and brought all the children back here to plead his case. I also took your advice to heart."

Jane wrapped her arms around Grace. "My dear, I am extremely happy for you. I do think you're making the right decision, and I am sure your parents would have approved."

Everyone seemed to be happy for her. Maybe if she could be sure she could trust him, she'd be happy as well. "Thank you. I never thought I would find a man who was just as concerned about the children as I am."

As she said the words, she realized it was true. Perhaps her fears had no basis in reason.

Taking a seat on the chair, Jane asked, "When will you marry?"

Grace gave a short laugh. "To-morrow, if Worthington had his way. But Lady Worthington has talked him into waiting for three weeks."

"You must tell me when you wish me to leave."

Her eyes flew open. "Oh, no, Jane, why would you? Do you want to go?"

"No, but you will no longer need a companion." Jane smiled gently.

"Jane, you are so much more than that."

Jane patted her hands. "Don't worry, my dear. We can discuss it later, when you are closer to your wedding."

Grace nodded as her cousin left the room. She had never considered that Jane might leave her. Her cousin had been a stalwart supporter since her father had died after he'd been thrown by his horse, and her pregnant mother fell ill. Perhaps Grace shouldn't marry. It had all been so sudden. She'd not been able to give this marriage as much thought as she should have. How was this going to affect her staff, many of whom had been with the family for years, and Jane?

Several minutes later, she approached the grand staircase.

Royston bowed. "The senior staff would like to wish you happy, my lady."

Summoning a smile, she thanked him and proceeded to her chamber. Of course her senior staff would have figured it out before she'd told them. The younger members of the staff probably knew as well. It had most likely even made it out to the stables.

She tugged the bell-pull for her maid, but just as she brought the pull down, Bolton appeared carrying one of her new gowns. "I think this one for dinner tonight."

"Perfect." Grace washed with the warm water already in the basin. She wished she could be as excited as everyone else seemed to be. After all, for years she had wanted to marry Worthington. Bolton put the gown over her head and Grace stood as her maid adjusted it. But was it the right thing to do now? Passing a hand over her eyes, she berated herself for not only making love to him the first time, but not being able to control herself once his arms were around her. Still, she hadn't actually agreed to the marriage. She just hadn't said no the last time he asked or when he'd announced it.

"My lady, do stop fidgeting." Bolton tied the laces.

It had finally dawned on Grace that when she'd not protested, she had inadvertently agreed. "Do you think I've made a mistake agreeing to marry Lord Worthington?"

"No, my lady, I do not."

Grace turned around. "But Jane talked about leaving."

"You have to allow folks to make their own decisions. If there is a place in the household that makes her happy, she'll stay, if not, she'll go. You can discuss all that with his lordship."

She handed Grace a missive that arrived. Breaking it open, Grace read the lines. Phoebe and Marcus would join them for tea this evening. Perhaps Grace would consult her friend. Phoebe always gave good advice.

Standing, she gave herself one last look in the mirror before she went down to the drawing room. Her gown was one of the new ones. A salmon-colored tussore silk with a deep V neckline in front and back. A braided cord in deeper salmon and gold was fastened by a brooch under her breasts. The three-quarter-length sleeves were unadorned. Two flounces decorated the bottom of her skirt. Madame Lisette knew her work. Grace thought she looked very well indeed.

Matt was handing his hat to the butler when Grace descended the stairs. His heart stopped as he sucked in a breath. Every time he'd met her before, except at the inn, when she'd worn a well-made but out-of-date twill gown, he'd been so intent on speaking to her, or kissing her, he hadn't paid attention to her clothing. Now that he had her promise, he could take the time to appreciate her beauty. It took his breath away. Her hair glowed under the candles and her gown, a silk, moved with her, discreetly accentuating her figure as she gracefully descended toward him. His chest swelled knowing she was his. A few curls spilled over her shoulders from a knot high on the back of her head. Every part of his body tightened. Yet his love appeared distracted and unsure. He needed to take her into his arms and kiss all her doubts away.

Why the devil did I agree not to make love to her?

Then Charlotte, Walter, and the twins appeared on the stairs. He held out his hand to Grace. "Chaperones?"

She placed her fingers in his palm, but she was tense. "We usually all dine together."

Tucking her hand in his arm, he grinned. "I think that's a wonderful idea, much better than you dining alone." What would dinner with seven, no ten, children be like? "You'll have to show me where to go."

She led him to the drawing room, where he noticed Jane already in residence sitting in a chair near the fireplace, speaking with a man and woman, both in their midtwenties. Jane rose. "My lord, good evening."

He bowed, and not knowing who the couple was, replied formally as she had. "Good evening. Miss Carpenter."

Jane grinned. "I'm glad you are joining us."

"Worthington." Grace directed his attention to the two other people, who'd risen. "Miss Tallerton, I must introduce you to Lord Worthington. Worthington, Miss Tallerton is the children's governess, and this is their tutor, Mr. Winters."

Matt inclined his head as the governess curtseyed and Winters bowed. The governess lived up to her name; she was indeed a long meg, but handsome in a firm sort of way. Winters was only slightly taller than she and had a very pleasant countenance. "A pleasure to meet you."

"And you, my lord," Miss Tallerton said.

Matt shook Winters's hand.

The rest of the children arrived and were given glasses of lemonade, while he and Grace had wine. They were remarkably well behaved. More so than his younger sisters. Even little Mary seemed to know how to go on.

She came to sit next to him on the sofa Grace had led him to. "We're glad you're here."

His heart tugged, and he gently pulled one of her braids. "I'm glad to be here too."

Bringing a chair closer to the sofa, Walter sat. "Sir, will you teach me more about boxing?"

Matt glanced at Grace, who gave what appeared to be a resigned shrug. He might have to go a little slowly when it came to teaching the boys the masculine arts. "If Grace doesn't mind."

"I am sure she doesn't. Do you, Grace?"

She'd been taking a sip of wine and lowered her glass. "Not at all. I suppose if Papa would have lived, he would have instructed you as he did Charlie."

Walter went off to tell Philip, and Matt glanced at his love. "If you don't want me to . . ."

Shaking her head, Grace sighed. "No, you were right. They need a gentleman to teach them how to go on. Though I don't approve of fisticuffs, I do realize it is one of those sports which gentlemen enjoy."

"Thank you. I appreciate your faith in me."

She pulled her full bottom lip between her teeth. Ah, maybe not so much trust yet, and possibly a reluctance to give up full control of her brothers and sisters. After all, they had been her entire life for the last few years.

Royston announced dinner, and Matt escorted Grace to the dining room, taking his place on her left. As he finished each course, he couldn't remember when he'd had such a tasty meal. They dined on *soupe à l'oignon,* followed by poached salmon, lobster en croûte, and roasted guinea-fowl. He did justice to all the dishes. The removes included French beans and peas tossed with a butter-thyme sauce, escalloped carrots and leeks, and pureed potatoes. He wondered if his cook could do half as well and gave up the thought. Not that he'd ever faulted Patience for it, but she was not the housewife Grace was. Various creams, jam tarts, grapes, and cheeses made up the last course.

Matt leaned toward Grace. "The chef is staying with us."

Until then, Grace had been very quiet, responding only when addressed. Now she smiled. "Jacques is very good. He is a cousin of Phoebe's chef. Oh, I forgot to tell you, Phoebe and Marcus are joining us for tea."

"Excellent. We'll be able to tell them our plans." With any luck, Matt would be able to enlist their support for an earlier wedding.

Straight after dinner, other than Charlotte, the children were sent up to the nursery. Tallerton and Winters went with them. Worthington raised a brow to Grace.

"Charlotte is not a little girl anymore. She will be at all the entertainments and, if our story is to be believed, she'll need to know it and know how to respond to the questions she is sure to receive."

He groaned. "Louisa as well?"

"Yes, of course." Grace gave him a slightly exasperated look. "Your sister will be in the same position as mine. I do wish she was present as well. I'll ask Charlotte to tell her whatever plan we come up with."

Not wanting to drink port in solitary splendor, he accompanied the ladies into the drawing room. Jane and Charlotte took chairs next to the fireplace. Grace strolled over to the long French windows at the other end of the room.

He stood behind her. His body crackled in anticipation, and he wondered what would happen if he touched her. Lifting a hand, he twisted one of her curls around his finger. A quiver ran down her back. He whispered, "Grace?"

She leaned back a little and her chin rose, giving him a perfect view of her slender neck. He traced her jawline with the pad of his thumb. She swallowed and the pulse at the base of her neck jumped.

A brief glance over his shoulder assured him Jane and Charlotte were deep in discussion. He lightly drew his thumb down her neck over the gold chain she wore and caressed the creamy mounds of her breasts. Her nipples were already hard when he touched them.

Bending his head, Matt blew on her ear. "Grace?"

"Matt, you promised."

"I promised not to make love to you. I didn't promise not to try to encourage you to make love to me."

Grace turned suddenly, her breasts brushed his chest. When her eyes lifted to his, instead of glowing with the desire he expected to see, they pleaded with him.

"Please don't do this. You know I've agreed to marry you." Tears glistened in her eyes.

What a dolt he was. He'd wanted to ease her burdens, and, instead, he was adding to them. "I'm sorry. Forgive me, please?"

"This isn't easy for me either."

Her hands fluttered in his as he led her to a sofa and sat in the chair next to it. His voice was low. "I am sorry. I will try not to do it again, but I want you so desperately."

"And you don't think I want you just as much?" She searched his eyes. "I yearn for you."

"I know you do. I can tell by the way your breath quickens and your skin glows." Bringing her hands to his lips he kissed one then the other. "Can you forgive me?"

"Yes, yes, but may we talk about something else before we . . . ?"

What a fool he was to have distressed her. "Tell me about this tendre you had for me."

A deep blush rose from her chest to her cheeks, and her summer-blue eyes softened. "As you already know, I'd just come out. Although we danced, I don't think you really ever noticed me. No other gentleman made my heart race like you did." Grace glanced at him from beneath her lashes. "Because of that, I didn't give up hope. I turned down a few offers and decided to wait until autumn. Yet for some reason I can't remember, we didn't come for the Little Season. The next Season, I didn't see you at all. Of course the following autumn and spring, I was in mourning for both my parents."

That must have been the year he'd eschewed all entertainments that included marriageable young ladies. Finally remembering when he'd seen her, he took her hand and kissed it. "I did notice you. I was young and not ready to marry."

"That is what Phoebe said."

Matt scoffed. "I'd wager it is not all Phoebe said."

She glanced up shyly. "But you didn't recognize me when we . . ."

"It would be more accurate to say I couldn't place you. I knew I'd seen you somewhere."

Grace smiled, and his heart lightened.

"My lady, Lord and Lady Evesham have arrived." Her butler bowed.

Grace rose. "Please show them in, Royston, and asked that tea be brought."

She and Worthington went to greet them.

Phoebe entered the room, glanced at him, and went straight to Grace. "Am I to wish you happy?"

"Yes, but we—we—well, it is so sudden."

"I understand." Phoebe took a chair. "You need a plan."

"Exactly so." Grace's smile trembled on her lips. "You've met Charlotte. I'd like to introduce you to my cousin, Miss Carpenter."

"My lady." Jane curtseyed.

Phoebe greeted Jane, smiling.

After the rest of them disposed themselves on chairs and sofas, tea was brought in and Grace poured.

Phoebe took her cup. "Tell me, do you have any ideas yet?"

Grimacing, Matt said, "Of sorts. My stepmother is not happy about it though."

Raising her brows, Phoebe took a sip of tea. "Yes well, Lady Worthington is a very high-stickler, and she is bringing out a daughter. One cannot be too careful. Tell me your scheme, and I'll give you my honest opinion."

"I plan to put it about—that's where you come in, Marcus—that I fell instantly in love with Grace and intend to pursue her. Grace will resist for a while." He glanced at her and couldn't keep his voice from deepening. "A very short while and then agree to marry me."

Grace took one of the ginger biscuits. "Phoebe, you may let it be known that I harbored a tendre for Worthington years ago, but we didn't meet again after my first Season."

"Hmm, it may work." Phoebe took a small cake and bit into it. "I have only a few details to add. Worthington, you must have had an attraction to Grace but, in the way of all young men, thought you had time. Then successive tragedies struck her family, and you did not meet again until you saw her at Lady Bellamny's soirée."

Worthington nodded. "I have no objection to that. Marcus?"

"Far be it for me to hinder a man in this path toward marriage." He grinned. "I'll help in any way I can."

Putting down her cup, Phoebe glanced from Matt to Grace. "When would you like to marry?"

"My stepmother and I agreed three weeks." Matt couldn't keep from growling. "I'd like to marry in two, or sooner."

Phoebe shook her head, Marcus gave a shout of laughter, Charlotte giggled, and Jane grinned. His beloved put her head in her hands. "Fine, three weeks."

"Yes, I think that will work," Phoebe said.

"If he can mange it." Marcus's eyes danced with amusement. "Worthington, what do you plan to do when another gentleman asks Lady Grace to dance?"

Matt's jaw dropped. Grace dance with someone else? No. He closed his mouth and snarled.

"As I thought. My love, you must allow them to wed sooner."

Phoebe sighed. "If you intend to act like a dog with a bone, you shall provide the *ton* with a good deal of entertainment."

"If it gets me what I want, I don't care."

"Has it occurred to you, my lord"—Grace's lips barely moved when she spoke—"that I may not wish to be a source of amusement?"

Suddenly, Jane set her cup down. "That is it. Lord Worthington here acts the way he wishes, and Grace shall behave with dignity. Suitably modest but happy that, after all this time, he has finally come to claim her."

Charlotte clasped her hands together and sighed. "*That instant his heart at her shrine would lay down. Every passion it nursed, every bliss it adored.*"

They all stared at her.

Her eyes rounded in shock. "What? It's Thomas Moore. The context may not do, but the sentiment is correct."

Poetry. Matt groaned. This is what comes of involving young ladies.

Chapter Fourteen

"Very romantic." Grace said encouragingly.

"Exactly so." Phoebe nodded. "And your romance *must* be seen as passionate. The *ton* adores a love story as much as a scandal. Let us give them the romance without the other." She turned to Grace and Worthington. "You must be seen in public together as much as possible. I suggest you go to the service at St. George's to-morrow. Drive in the Park during the fashionable hour. Grace, you may use your landau. I shall make up a list of the best entertainments for you to attend." She took a sip of her tea and nibbled a biscuit. "Charlotte, if you and Miss Carpenter tell your friends that Worthington haunts Stanwood House, that will help."

Charlotte gave an excited nod. "I can also tell them he takes all the children to the Park."

Phoebe's eyes grew wide. "Does he do so?"

Looking slightly bashful, Charlotte blushed. "Well, he did to-day. Accidentally."

"How did that happen?"

"Daisy, our dog, got away, and Matt sent Duke, his dog, to . . ."

Going into whoops, Phoebe laughed until she wept.

"Worthington, you'll have to make a habit of taking the children around."

Grace drew her brows together. "If it is known you are already taking charge of the children. That might help with the guardianship."

Taking her hand again, Matt kissed it. "I agree."

When Phoebe tried to hide a yawn, Grace stood. "Phoebe, you should go home and rest."

"I think I shall. We have busy days ahead of us."

Marcus helped her rise, and Grace started to accompany them to the door.

"No, my dear," Phoebe said. "Charlotte and Miss Carpenter may show us out."

Grace hugged her friend. "Thank you."

"I am happy to help." Phoebe kissed Grace's cheek. "This Season will be more interesting for it."

Although Grace had wanted a chance to speak with Phoebe alone, it helped that she didn't find anything untoward about Grace and Matt marrying.

After the door closed, Matt took her in his arms. "I cannot believe all that has happened in the past few days."

"I know." Grace lifted her eyes to his lapis-colored ones. "To think it was just yesterday morning that I refused you."

"Kiss me, nothing more. I know kisses will have to satisfy me until we can wed."

She brought his head down and moved her lips tenderly against his. When she teased them with her tongue, he opened his mouth to her. Her breasts rubbed against this chest, and her nipples became hard buds. She tilted her head, deepening the kiss, the throbbing need raced down her body and pooled between her legs. She wanted him so badly that her need scared her. It was as if she'd been starved for years and wanted only to feast.

"Matt, my love, we have to stop."

He lifted his head reluctantly. "I'll see you in the morning."

Grace nodded and walked him to the door. This was going to be the longest three weeks of her life, with him so close and always willing to touch her. If she could only stop thinking about his body and how he made her feel, they might survive.

The following morning, Matt was admitted into Stanwood House and informed, unnecessarily, that the family was all together in the breakfast room. He could hear the din from the front door and followed it toward the back part of the house. Footmen were running back and forth carrying plates of toast, glasses of milk, and fresh pots of tea.

"Good morning." At first, he thought he was seeing things. He pressed his palms to his eyes but when he dropped his hand, his four sisters were still present.

The room briefly became silent then choruses of greetings were spoken or shouted out.

Presiding over the table, Grace laughed and shook her head. "Good morning."

God, it was good to see her happy. He strode to her and kissed her lightly on the lips.

"Oooh." Mary's eyes rounded.

Grinning, Matt tugged gently on one of her braids and settled in the chair a footman had placed between Grace and Mary. "Yes, oooh. Now finish your breakfast." He took out his quizzing glass and focused it on each one of his sisters. "Did you tell your mother you were breaking your fast here?"

Louisa raised her chin slightly. "Mama wasn't up. We told Nurse. She was to have told Mama. We've"—she glanced at the other children, who nodded—"decided that since we'll all be living together, we should get used to it."

"It makes perfect sense," Walter said, "if you think about it."

Waving a piece of toast, Augusta added, "This way it's easier for us to help."

Worthington blinked. He didn't dare close his eyes longer than that. Lord only knew what they'd come up with next. He glanced at Grace. "When do you wish to start out, and will you take your town coaches?"

Grace swallowed her tea. "We shall walk. I'll not subject the rest of the parishioners to this bunch as they are."

"I am marrying a woman of superior understanding. It would not do for them to act up in church our first time out." They were going to cause enough of a stir as it was. "We cannot be late either. When will you be ready to go?"

"In less than thirty minutes. They are all dressed under their smocks."

He glanced around the table and for the first time noticed they all wore what looked like artist's smocks. He'd never heard of anything like it. "What a good idea."

"Thank you." She grinned. "At least they will leave the breakfast table without stains on their clothing. I make no promises after luncheon or tea."

His lips twitched. "Due, I imagine, to the jam tarts."

"Precisely. It should take us about fifteen minutes to walk to Hanover Square. Does your stepmother join us?"

"Yes, Patience will take her town coach. I am here to determine the method of travel."

He lowered his voice. "They really are getting along well."

"Indeed, but I don't know how long it will last. Have you eaten?"

"No." He stepped to the sideboard, served himself, and then returned to the table. "Have you heard from your uncle yet?"

She took a bite of her eggs and swallowed. "No. We'll probably see them at church. I looked at the calendar and realized that next Sunday is Easter. Charlie will come home for the full-term holiday."

"If we have a week left in Lent, that means none of this week's entertainments will have dancing."

Grace giggled. "How fortunate for you, my lord."

"Yes, isn't it?" Matt grinned. They must at least be formally betrothed by the start of the Season. "By the time we have the first ball, I'll have made my intentions known to every gentleman in the *ton*."

Shaking her head, Grace munched on a piece of toast. "I don't understand why it's so important to you."

"I can't explain it. Some primitive urge, I suppose." He tried to pass it off lightly. Yet with each passing day, the warrior in him had become more protective of her, and, by extension, her brothers and sisters.

The children were just finishing when Lady Worthington was shown in and informed they were walking to St. George's.

Matt rose. "Patience, I didn't expect to see you here."

She smiled at Grace who offered her tea. "Most likely because I didn't expect to be here. My curiosity won out." Patience smiled more broadly. "When I awoke, I was greeted with the news that the girls had decided to breakfast here. I have never seen a table with so many children. I also decided it might present an off appearance if I did not arrive with you. It is a pleasant day, and I haven't had a good hike since we arrived in Town."

Grace clapped her hands together twice. "All of you up to brush your teeth and wash your hands."

The table emptied. Once the children had gone, the silence was deafening.

"How long do we have until they return?" Matt asked, finishing his tea.

"About fifteen minutes or less. They all have their own washbasins."

"You have organized them well," Patience said. "I wanted to tell you both at the same time what my girls told me last night. It seems they have decided to relieve you of some of your worries . . ."

When she finished, Grace chuckled. "I must say, I am happy they've settled on a way to try to work out their own problems. Though I do not think they should decide where we are going to live."

The children started coming down the stairs, and she rose. "I must fetch my bonnet and meet you in the hall."

"My love." Matt stood, placing his hands on her shoulders. Glancing up at him curiously, she asked, "Yes?"

"Can you wear a hat that enables me to see your face?"

Her eyes widened as a blush rose in her cheeks. "How did you know?"

He ran his thumb along her jaw. "It took me too long to realize it the first time. The second time you disappeared into thin air. Someday, you must tell me how you managed it."

Grace bit her lip. "Oh my, and you still wish to wed me?"

"More than anything."

Patience laughed lightly. "I predict you shall have an interesting married life."

Matt glanced at his stepmother. "I'm looking forward to it. I don't know how I was stupid enough not to marry her when she was eighteen."

His stepmother flicked her fingers dismissively. "You both would have been too young."

"Maybe you're right." He took Grace's arm and led her to the main staircase.

When Grace reached her room, a small chip hat with netting and a feather was on the dressing table. She placed it on her head and tied a jaunty bow under her ear. The children were all present when she reached the hall. "I want everyone lined up two by two. Hal and Will, follow at the end."

Worthington offered one arm to Grace and the other to Patience. They set out the door and down the street.

They were not more than a block from the church when Grace glanced around to find people staring. "Maybe this was not such a good idea. I didn't think we would draw so much attention."

"I wouldn't worry about it." He tightened his grip on her and drew her closer. "We were bound to draw notice."

She smiled gratefully. "I suppose you're right. I couldn't go the whole Season without taking them to church. We attend every Sunday at home."

"It's like anything else." Matt's lips quirked up. "The curious will be interested for a time or two then we'll be old news."

Leaning around Matt, Patience said, "He's right, my dear. Do not worry over this."

Grace's aunt and uncle descended from a town coach and turned, seemingly arrested by their procession.

Lady Herndon's smile grew larger the closer they came. "Grace, Lord Worthington, Lady Worthington. How good it is to see all of you and the children. For once it appears that the rumors were correct."

Grace's eyes widened and her face drained of color. "Rumors?"

Aunt Herndon's smile faded. "Why, yes, my dear. This is what they mean, isn't it?"

Stilling her shaking hands, Grace took a breath. "I—I don't know. I don't know what the rumors are."

With great presence of mind, which seemed to have deserted her, Matt responded, "Yes, Lady Herndon. The gossip is correct. I am doing my utmost to convince your niece to marry me."

"Well, for my money"—her uncle shook Matt's hand—"you're going about it the right way."

"*Uncle Bertrand!*" Why was it family members insisted on embarrassing one?

He ignored Grace's outburst. "Is this the reason you wish to speak with me?"

"Yes, Uncle."

"Good, good, come to Herndon House for tea this afternoon." He glanced behind her. "No need to bring the children."

"No, Uncle Bertrand." Grace's head was spinning. The ringing in her ears wouldn't stop. This was going much too fast, and not for the first time Grace wondered why she was the only one to think so.

Her uncle turned away. "Lord Worthington?"

"Yes, my lord."

"This is a great responsibility and not one entered into lightly."

"I understand that, my lord. If I did not think I could do justice by both Lady Grace and all the children, her brothers and sisters as well as mine, I would not undertake it."

Lord Herndon glanced at the growing number of people entering the church. "We shall speak further this afternoon."

"We must go in and get the children settled," Lady Worthington said. "My lord, my lady, would you like to join us?"

"Yes, we would love to." Aunt Almeria's eyes danced with joy.

"Grace, are you all right?" Matt whispered in her ear.

"I'll be fine." She should be ecstatic. Why wasn't she?

He led her in and made sure the children were settled. Grace kept her eyes downcast, not wanting to see the interested stare at them. Once the service began, a homely sense of belonging and the familiar form of service calmed her.

She had just been thrown off guard for a moment, that was all. Nothing was really wrong. Matt sat next to her, a strong, steady presence. Their brothers and sisters behaved. God must have had a hand in that.

Almost two hours later, they filed out of St. George's, greeted a few friends, bid adieu to her aunt and uncle, and went home the same way they'd come. Grace was once again her unshakable self.

After sending the children up to their floor, she, Matt, and Patience went to the morning room.

"That went much better than I'd dreamed it could," Patience exclaimed.

Worthington squeezed Grace's hand. "What did you think?"

"I was shocked at first. I've spent so much time being careful to not be the object of any gossip, that at first it didn't occur to me a rumor could be good." She shook her head. "I'm not making any sense, am I?"

He kissed her cheek. "In a roundabout way you are making perfect sense. After all, most gossip is not helpful, and you have had a great deal to worry over. We will bring this off, see if we don't."

Grace smiled and wished they could be alone together. "We shall, won't we?"

"Yes, my lady. I'm looking forward to speaking with your uncle."

"First things first." She turned to her future mother-in-law before they forgot she was in the room. "Patience, would you and the girls like to join us for dinner?"

Patience grinned. "I've been hoping you'd ask, although I gather the girls have already decided to take their meals here."

Not only would the children and Jane be present, but Mr. Winters and Miss Tallerton. Sixteen for dinner. Fortunately she had already informed her cook that the Vivers girls would now be eating with them. At this point, one more would hardly matter. She made a mental note to herself to remind Royston to add two more leaves to the table, and not to remove them, at least until after the marriage and maybe not even then. They still hadn't decided where they would live.

Chapter Fifteen

Early that afternoon, Grace was thrilled that the first major meal by her new cook was such a success. The roast of beef studded with garlic was done to perfection, as was the pudding. No English cook could have done better and many a great deal worse. It was accompanied by a clear soup, Brussels sprouts tossed with shallots, that even the younger children liked, French beans with shaved almonds, a salad of greens with vinaigrette, new potatoes, and asparagus from her succession houses. The last course included cheeses, fruit, jellies, small tarts, and sweetmeats.

Patience sat back in her chair. "Oh, my dear Grace, I do not know when I have eaten so well. I must compliment your chef."

"Thank you, he is a wonder. I shall pass on your praise."

Other than the *click* of tableware against china, the children had all been quiet and were now picking over the sweets. "Matt and I must visit Aunt and Uncle Herndon. What would you children like to do while we're gone?"

"If no one would mind, we could play outside," Alice said.

"You'll have to change."

"Yes, Grace, but what about the others?"

Grace glanced to Patience, who then said, "I must change

as well. I shall take my girls home and, if you don't mind, bring them back. I am happy to remain here while you visit Lord and Lady Herndon."

Grace was glad that Patience seemed to be feeling at home around them. "I don't mind at all. It's a perfect idea."

Patience stood and called her daughters to order. At the same time, Grace's brothers and sisters went to their rooms to change.

Matt drew her up. "Alone at last."

"Yes." She stepped closer to him.

His brows drew together. "Do you want to tell me what happened at St. George's? You seemed lost."

"I don't know if I can explain it." Grace frowned. "We had made a plan, and I saw it all unraveling."

"How so?"

"It started going too fast. I expected some resistance from my uncle, at the very least. Since my mother died, life has seemed so much harder. Now it seems too easy and that makes me fear that something will happen to keep us from marrying." She put her hand on his chest. The steady beat of his heart reassured her. "I know it sounds silly. I'm fine now."

"You're not being silly." He nuzzled her hair. "Nothing will stop me from marrying you. We may not have decided where we're living or how you're going to manage Stanwood from a distance, or any number of other issues, but my marrying you is a certainty."

Gazing up at him she was bereft of words. She had to trust him and what he said. If she didn't, she'd be lost.

He nodded as if he could hear her thoughts. "If we are able, do you wish to marry earlier?"

Perhaps that was the answer. "Yes, oh yes. I want all this uncertainty to be over."

"Grace, my love, when you came to me at the inn . . ."

"My lady, my lord, Lord and Lady Evesham would like to see you," Royston said.

"Please show them here and bring tea." She wondered what brought their friends without warning. Was it wrong of them to take all their brothers and sisters to church? No, it couldn't be that.

Her butler bowed. "Yes, my lady."

She took Matt's hand. "I wonder what this is about. Did you see them to-day?"

"I did." He stroked her back. "You had your head down."

Grace sighed. "I suppose I did."

They stood as Phoebe and Marcus were shown in.

Phoebe could barely contain herself. "Grace, everyone in Town must have been at St. George's this morning. You and Worthington are all anyone talked about."

The room whirled and grew dark.

"She's fainted," Phoebe said calmly. "Marcus, I have smelling salts in my reticule. Please give them to me."

Matt looked down at the limp form of his betrothed in his arms. Fortunately, he'd caught her as she fell.

"Worthington, take Grace to a parlor and lay her on a chaise."

He did as he was told. "I don't understand. What happened to her?"

"No, I daresay you don't," Phoebe said. "Let's get her settled, and I shall explain."

Carrying his love to the chaise, Matt tenderly laid her on it. Then sat next to her and chaffed her hands.

Phoebe came over. "Grace was always shy. It's easy for her to talk with one or two people, but she has a tendency to panic in larger crowds. Since she came out, she's always been concerned about gossip. But after her parents died and the battle for her brothers and sisters began, I could tell, through her letters, that it had become almost an obsession. She is afraid, no terrified, that someone will start a rumor, and the children will be taken away and parceled out to various family members. Which, of course, means she'll have failed in her oath to her mother and in her duty to the children. I shouldn't have said what I did without preparing her." Phoebe took the salts from Marcus and glanced up. "Worthington, tell me you understand."

"Yes, I think so. Come to think of it, when she noticed the attention we were receiving in church, she seemed to go somewhere else."

"That's not surprising. All she needs is support, and she'll be fine." Phoebe passed the salts under Grace's nose, and she came around.

"Grace, my love." He held her to him. He hadn't fully appreciated the extent of the burden she'd been carrying, but he should have. All the more reason to get leg-shackled as soon as possible.

"Did I faint?"

"Yes, it's no matter." Phoebe handed Grace a glass of water. "I knew better than to shock you. Come sit up. Worthington, help her. Grace, you'll be right as a trivet in no time."

He held her as Grace drank.

Putting the glass down, she said, "I'm fine. Now, tell me your news."

Phoebe sat down, her lips tilted. "Everyone is talking about how Worthington swept you off your feet and is acting just as he ought. Some of the talk originated from Lady Bellamny's party, but some if it has to do with Worthington taking care of the little contretemps your brother was involved in."

The tea Grace asked for was brought in. Phoebe served them before continuing her story. "Mrs. Babcock has told anyone who would listen Lord Worthington is fixing his attention on you. And your aunt Herndon is putting it around that Worthington is speaking with your uncle this afternoon."

Grace's startled eyes flew to Matt's. He hugged her to him. "It's all right."

"But we still have so much to decide."

"Yes, and we shall."

Patience was shown in and greeted. "I've spent the last half hour with Helena Featherton and Sally Huntingdon. You are the romance of the Season."

Matt glanced down to see Grace had once again fainted.

"Is it something I said?" Patience asked with concern.

Marcus handed him the vial of sal volatile, and he brought Grace around. Phoebe took his stepmother aside, speaking softly to her.

"Oh, no, and I am afraid I haven't been very helpful. I was so concerned about a scandal, I did not think about Grace." Patience glanced at her stepson. "Worthington, I am so sorry. Grace, my dear, I would not for the life of me have hurt you. I'm thrilled with how this is turning out. Lady Sefton congratulated me and promised vouchers for Almack's for both Louisa and Charlotte."

Worthington handed Grace her water followed by a sherry. "What can I do to convince you it will all be made right?"

Grace's voice shook. "I feel so stupid."

He sat her up and held her to him and vowed to himself nothing and no one would ever hurt her. "You are anything but stupid. It's just been a bit of a shock."

"What time is it?"

"You have time to rest for a while before we leave." He cuddled her closer.

Marcus helped Phoebe rise, and she said, "Yes, indeed. It will not do for you to show Lady Herndon your pale face. Come, and I shall help you to your chamber."

"Here, I'll carry you." Matt rose and bent to scoop her into his arms.

"No, no, really, you shouldn't carry me through the house."

Grace laughed weakly. "I'm perfectly capable of going to my room. All I need to do is splash my face with some cold water."

Once she and Phoebe left, he regarded his stepmother. "I'm buying the special license to-morrow. As soon as she agrees, we shall marry."

"As you will." Patience had the grace to blush. "I freely admit I was in the wrong in thinking you should wait several weeks."

"I don't blame you. We still have many problems to resolve. Yet I want her as my wife as soon as possible."

Patience furrowed her brow. "Just the family and some friends at the wedding?"

Nodding, Matt firmed his jaw. "Yes. I'll not put her through a large wedding. Not with the guardianship hanging over her."

"That"—Marcus saluted Matt with his cup of tea—"is a wise decision. Let us know and we'll stand as witnesses."

Matt wrung his friend's hand. "Thank you. I'm going to see about Grace."

Matt strode to the grand staircase, taking the stairs two at a time. At the top, he looked around, wondering where Grace's chambers were. Fortunately, she and Phoebe emerged from a corridor. Phoebe wiggled her fingers at him and left.

Trying to keep the worry from his voice, he glanced down at Grace. "Are you well?"

Grace smiled weakly. "Yes, of course, I really didn't need to rest."

"You're sure?" He dragged her into his arms. "We can't have you fainting at your aunt and uncle's house."

"I'm certain, though I may faint from lack of breath."

Loosening his grip, he lightly kissed her forehead. "I love you."

"I've felt the same about you since that night. That is

what frightens me." She closed her eyes and small lines appeared in her forehead. "I cannot shake the feeling that something bad is about to happen."

He held her closer and kissed her brow. Grace trembled in his arms. "I will not allow anything or anyone to take those children from you. I promise you that. I'm not leaving you."

"Your stepmother is so concerned."

"No, not any longer. She's admitted she was in the wrong."

"Did she? That is a relief." Grace gazed up at him. "Is there anything else I should know? More rumors?"

He laughed easily, happy to have good news for her. "No, my love. All the rumors and speculation are helping us."

"Then I suppose we should go."

Worthington kissed her lightly on her lips. "Shall we walk to Grosvenor Square? The air might do you good."

"Yes, I should like to." Grace took his arm. "It's such a pretty day, and, other than to church, I haven't been for a nice walk since I arrived in Town."

When I wasn't dodging you or your family, that is.

Worthington retrieved his hat and placed her hand on his arm. "Shall we go, my lady?"

She nodded. Being with him was right. So many times she'd ached with loneliness and struggled with thinking she couldn't marry. He loved her, and he wasn't taking the children lightly. He knew how much work it would be. Everything would be fine.

Several minutes later, Worthington knocked on the large, shiny, black door of Herndon House. Her uncle's elderly butler bowed and showed them into the drawing room where her aunt and uncle rose to greet them.

"Grace, Worthington." Aunt offered Grace her cheek and her hand to Worthington.

Uncle Bertrand smiled broadly. "Worthington, come and sit. We have a great deal to discuss."

Her aunt kept up a steady stream of small talk until tea was served. The topic turned to Grace, the children, and Worthington.

"I don't mean to mince words with you, my lord," Uncle Herndon said. "I'll be happy to see Grace married." He glanced at her. "Since her grandfather, Lord Timothy, died, talk has gotten back to me that some of her father's relatives think it improper for her to hold the guardianship alone."

Grace's heart lurched. Had she been having premonitions? Her mother had them at times.

Matt squeezed her hand. "Will our marriage settle the talk, do you think?"

Her uncle rubbed his nose. "You are a respected and wealthy peer. Everyone knows you would not take on the responsibility of the children unless you wanted to." He took a sip of tea. "Masterful stroke bringing your stepmother with you to church. Everyone knows her reputation. She wouldn't countenance the match unless she was convinced all was proper."

Grace kept her breathing calm. It was a good thing Patience didn't know about the inn, or the other. "No, she wouldn't."

Her aunt smiled. "Have you set the date, my dear?"

Grace glanced at Matt. "Not yet. We were concerned that there would be just the kind of talk we wish to avoid if we married too soon."

"Very prudent of you." Aunt Almeria reminded her of a bird looking expectantly for a piece of bread.

"We had originally agreed on three weeks." Grace took a breath, steeling herself for her aunt's reactions. "But now perhaps less."

Aunt Almeria smiled warmly.

"My lord?" Matt asked. "How soon may I apply for guardianship?"

"Not until you are married." Her uncle rubbed his chin.

"They might accept the application based on the betrothal, but no action could be taken before you're leg-shackled."

"That's not good at all." She wanted the guardianship completed as soon as possible.

"Grace?" Small lines bracketed Matt's mouth.

She met his gaze. "If that's the case, we must marry as soon as possible. One week from Tuesday." She turned anxiously to her aunt. "If you do not think it too premature, Aunt Almeria?"

"You just want a small wedding, dear?"

Grace nodded. "Yes, family and close friends. That is all I want. Worthington?"

"I as well."

"Under the circumstances"—Aunt Almeria said briskly—"with the guardianship and two young ladies to bring out, I think what little talk the marriage might cause will die down quickly. It is not, after all, as if you are a young lady just out. I know the rector at St. George's quite well. If you'd like, I shall make the arrangements." She twisted the fringe of her shawl. "I shall leave you with the wedding breakfast to plan. As much as I hold all the dear children in affection . . ."

Grace laughed at the thought of eleven children trooping through Herndon House. "No, I'll be happy to arrange it."

"Worthington, a word with you in private, if I may," her uncle said.

Now what could it be? Grace tried to keep her countenance calm, but her panic must have shown. Uncle Herndon smiled reassuringly. "Just a formality, my dear. I need to discuss the settlements with Worthington."

"Of course, Uncle."

Matt kissed her cheek. "I'll be back soon."

The only thing she had of her own was her dowry, yet if her uncle wished to be responsible for making sure all was right, he was welcome to it.

* * *

Matt followed Lord Herndon to his study.

"Please have a seat. You may send your information to my solicitor. I wanted to tell you how Grace's portion and those of the children's were settled."

Matt didn't care if she was penniless, yet Grace wouldn't see it that way. "Very well."

"Grace has a dowry of around thirty thousand, invested in funds, from her mother's settlement. All the other girls have the same amount. The two younger boys have easy competences, enough for them to marry and command the elegancies of life. Still, their father wanted them to have a profession. The church, law, or the foreign office. Something of that sort." Lord Herndon rose and poured them both a brandy. "By the time Lord Timothy, Grace's maternal grandfather, died, two of his sons had predeceased him. He had a small estate in Cambridgeshire and a large fortune in investments. Before his death, he and I discussed the matter. He decided that his Cambridgeshire estate would go to Walter and the house on Half-Moon Street to Philip. Both properties are currently leased."

"I understand." Matt was relieved the children were taken care of.

"Grace, because she took the children, was to receive an additional amount upon Charlie attaining his majority. She'll still receive the bequest if she manages to keep the children together. I don't think she's ever thought about it. But old Lord Timothy wanted to ensure she had enough to live well on, if she never married."

"No, I'm quite sure she hasn't given the bequest a bit of thought."

Herndon fixed Matt with a stern look. "Grace is a wealthy woman."

He put down his brandy and stood. "Then she shall remain

so. Decide what you think right for any daughters she and I will have. I shall provide for our sons. Grace shall keep all her property. If anything should happen to me, I want her taken care of. Send me the figures and we'll speak again."

Lord Herndon grinned. "I understand you are also an heir to a marquisate."

"Indeed, but I don't expect anything to come of it." Matt shrugged. "My cousin is still young, and not at all reckless."

Herndon put a hand on Matt's shoulder. "I should dearly love to hear the story of how that came about."

"Someday I'll tell you." He grinned. Matt wanted to get back to Grace and take her home, hold her in his arms, and reassure her everything would be fine.

Chapter Sixteen

Grace's mind was in a whirl. The marriage she thought never to have would happen next week. But then what? Grace tried to breathe calmly but her heart fluttered.

Breathe, just breathe. Think of something else. Of how lovely it will be to have Matt with me every night.

"Grace, Grace?" Aunt Almeria hovered around her. "You are very pale, dear. Is anything wrong?"

Grace glanced up. "I can't believe it's happening so soon."

She'd spent years thinking about him. He claimed to have fallen in love in one night. Was she truly even that woman? Well, she admitted ruefully, part of her was. The part that was so wanton as to allow him, no, encourage him to take her anywhere. Had he mistook passion for love?

"Grace, is there anything I can help you with?" Aunt Almeria chaffed one of Grace's hands.

She passed her other hand over her brow. "No, I mean— I don't know what I mean. Worthington says he loves me— but—how could he know so soon?"

"Isn't it the same for you?"

"No—I remembered him from when I came out. He didn't remember me well at all."

"My dear, he was still in his twenties then. A boy in many ways. I am quite sure he is not the same gentleman he was then."

Did she not really love him then? Did she only love who she thought he was? "Yes, I see. I suppose it will all work out."

"Of course it will, my dear. Do not be upset if his ardor cools after you have been married for a while. It is normal for gentlemen, even the best of them, to have their *chères amies* and, of course, you must not expect him to be so attentive of the children. Once you are married and the guardianship has been established, he will not need to spend so much time with them."

Grace hadn't thought of that, and she should have. It happened to so many women. Her spirits sank lower. How could she have been so stupid to believe she could have what Phoebe and Anna had?

She was trapped. And the worst part of it was she'd trapped herself. Could she even enjoy the short time they'd have before he turned to another woman?

"You're right, Aunt Almeria. I can expect nothing more." She rose and went to the window. Grace stopped herself from crying, still tears pooled in her eyes. She took out her handkerchief. It wouldn't do to allow Worthington to see her like this. He'd hold her in disgust sooner if she became one of those women forever weeping and fainting. Maybe if she distanced herself from him. Then his eventual betrayal wouldn't be so hard to manage.

"Grace, my love." His deep voice washed over her.

Drawing on her breeding, she smiled brightly, before turning to greet him. "Are you ready?"

His eyes narrowed. "If you are. I thought you might like to rest for a while."

"No, no, indeed," she responded coolly. "I never sleep in the afternoon. Although, I would like some time to myself."

The confusion in his deep blue eyes cut her to the core. "Very well, if that's what you wish, I'll escort you home."

Maintaining a cool smile, she nodded. "Thank you, Worthington."

As they were bidding her aunt and uncle good-bye, her aunt said, "Remember what I told you, and you will not be disappointed."

The smile on Grace's face felt rigid as if it would crack if she wasn't careful. "Thank you, Aunt Almeria, I shall."

Matt—no, Worthington—Grace must remember to distance herself—glanced down at her. His brows drew together. Her heart skipped a beat, and she wanted to flee. Instead, she continued to smile.

He wanted to scowl. He greatly preferred his sometimes happy, sometimes panicked, but always passionate love to the coolly distant lady on his arm. What had her aunt said to her? How could he find out? He doubted Grace would tell him. But he knew three women he could ask.

On the way back to Berkeley Square, they made small talk about nothing. Once they arrived at Stanwood House, he ascertained that his stepmother had gone home after having been assured by Cousin Jane that she could take charge of the children. The house was strangely quiet. He missed the shrill voices and thumping feet. Matt kissed Grace's hand and left her in the hall.

His long strides took him across the grassy square and into his house. "Thorton, where is her ladyship?"

"Gone out, my lord. She doesn't expect to be back until late."

He started to walk away and turned. "You may wish me happy. Lady Grace has agreed to marry me on Tuesday next."

His butler bowed. "Then I do wish you happy, my lord. We shall look forward to your nuptials."

He grinned boyishly. "Don't smile now."

Thorton's face was a mask. "Smile, my lord?"

"You're an old fraud."

"As you say, my lord."

Matt left the hall. News of his marriage would run through the house like fire. He glanced at the clock. Not even time for tea. After a few hours, his sisters returned. He kissed them good night. Selecting a book, he began to read, but soon drifted off to sleep.

The following morning, his stepmother had not yet left her room when he rose.

Louisa pounded on his door. "Matt, do hurry, we shall be late."

"Late for what?"

"Breakfast. We are expected, and you are going to make us late."

She had to be the only female he knew who insisted on being on time. "I'll be down directly."

He should have realized from what Walter had said that they were now taking all their meals together. Just who had made the decision, he'd no idea.

When they arrived, Grace was already at the table orchestrating her brothers and sisters. Matt took a seat next to her.

She greeted him with a small smile. "Good morning, my lord."

Something was still wrong. If only he knew what it was. "Good morning." He waved a hand to encompass the table. "I take it this is to be an everyday affair?"

"Yes. Do you mind?"

He smiled. "Not in the least. The idea that I'll be able to see your charming countenance each morning delights me."

"Good." Grace sniffed.

What had he said? "May we discuss some matters after breakfast?"

Her head made sudden small shaking motions. "Not to-day. I need—there are some accounts I must review."

Simply wrong was quickly becoming very wrong. "Very well, then, later in the day or on the morrow?"

"Yes, of course. Perhaps then."

After he'd eaten, he left the children at Stanwood House and swiftly strode back across the square.

"In her parlor, my lord," Thorton said knowingly.

Drat the man! How the devil did he . . . ? "Thank you."

Matt entered without knocking.

"Worthington, what is this?" Patience glanced up, startled. "There is nothing wrong, I hope."

"There is, but I don't have any idea what." He sat heavily on a delicate French-backed chair that creaked slightly as he'd lowered his weight.

Patience frowned. "Did your conversation with Lord Herndon go well?"

"Yes, better than I'd expected. It appears that some of her father's relatives have been talking about her guardianship. Lord and Lady Herndon suggested we marry as soon as possible. We've chosen the Tuesday after Easter."

"Matt! That soon?"

"Yes, only family and close friends. I'll buy the license in the morning. Herndon and I discussed the settlements." He paused. "After that, Grace was different. I think it was something her aunt said." He fixed his eyes on Patience. "Do you know what it might have been?"

"Don't be silly." Patience raised her brows. "How should I know?"

"Did your mother say anything to you before you married?"

"Yes." She raised her chin haughtily. "She gave me some very good advice that I would have done well to take. But that is neither here nor there."

"Patience, I am sorry. I know you weren't happy . . ."

"Matt, that is not true, and don't you ever repeat it. I was a married lady, with more than enough pin money to see to all my desires. I had my children and you to keep me company. Now, if you will excuse me, I find I have some duties to attend to." She swept regally out of the room.

He shook his head. It wasn't true. She loved his father, and he didn't love her. When he'd been home, he was always attentive, but he had wanted more sons, and she'd given him daughters. Matt confronted his father once after he'd married Patience. Father admitted that he couldn't be at Worthington Hall without thinking of Matt's mother, and he never brought Patience to London because Worthington House had been Mama's pride and joy.

Widowhood had taken the sting out of Patience's marriage to his father. They did say widows were the most fortunate of ladies. He didn't want that to be true for Grace. He wanted her to be happy married to him. Matt stood. He needed answers sooner rather than later. Returning to the front hall, he donned his coat. Thorton handed him his hat and cane. He quickly made his way to Grosvenor Square and knocked on the Dunwood House door.

The butler bowed. "I am sorry, my lord. Lord and Lady Evesham had a matter of some urgency to attend to at Charteries. I expect them back by at the end of the week."

Damn, now what was he to do? "Be a good fellow and let me have a pen and some paper. I must leave a message."

The butler bowed again. "With pleasure, my lord. If you will follow me."

Matt wrote a note informing them of the marriage date. "Please have this conveyed to Lord Evesham as soon as possible."

"My lord, Lady Evesham asked me to give you this." The butler handed him a folded sheet of paper. He opened it—

ah, the list of entertainments. He tucked it into the inside pocket he'd insisted Weston put in his coat. "Thank you."

Quickly descending the steps, he turned toward Green Street, where the Rutherfords lived. If he had any luck at all, Anna would be there, and he'd ask her.

Matt was ushered into the study where he found both of them working at a huge partner's table.

Rutherford rose to greet him. "To what do we owe the pleasure?"

Worthington bowed to Anna. "I wanted to tell you Lady Grace and I shall marry next Tuesday. I—I also have a question for Anna." He glanced at her hopefully.

Giving him a curious look, she rose. "Come over here and make yourself comfortable. Rutherford, please ring for tea." She turned back to Matt. "Unless you'd like wine?"

"No, no, tea is perfect."

Anna sat on a love seat with Rutherford next to her. "Now, how may I help you?"

Matt felt the heat rise in his face. Damn, it had been years since he'd blushed. "I need not tell you that this must remain amongst us three?"

Shrugging lightly, Anna replied, "Of course."

Rutherford nodded.

"We, Grace and I, were at Lord and Lady Herndon's house yesterday. Lord Herndon and I went to his office to discuss the marriage settlements. When I returned to Grace, she was different. Colder. Just before we left her aunt told her to remember what she'd said. Whatever she told Grace, it affected her." He rubbed his eyes. "Do you have any idea what she could have said to make Grace distance herself from me?"

A small smile appeared on Anna's face. "I think I know. It is advice frequently given by ladies whose marriages are . . . not what they expected them to be."

He didn't like the sound of that. "Go on."

Anna grimaced. "Lady Herndon, with the best will in the world, probably told Grace to expect you not to be faithful."

"*What?*" He raked his hands through his hair. "Why? I don't understand what reason she would have to say such a thing."

"It's not uncommon. Lady Herndon probably wanted to spare Grace the disappointment she'd felt at one point."

Rutherford glowered. "Did your mother tell you that?"

Taking his hand, she patted it, and said serenely, "Of course, but by then I knew you didn't want anyone else."

"And I never shall," he answered gruffly.

"I'm very happy for the two of you." Worthington tried to keep his exasperation under control. "But how do I counter her advice? It's making Grace miserable."

Anna grinned. "You'll think of something. The best thing would be for you to get her to tell you what her aunt said, then you can speak openly about it."

Worthington strode back to his house scowling. Of all the ninnyhammered things to say to a woman who already had enough to worry about. Yet how to approach Grace?

"Thorton, I shall be in my study. I do not wish to be disturbed unless the house is burning down, or if Lady Grace should happen to visit, I shall see her. Only her, mind you."

"Yes, my lord." Thorton closed the door, and Matt leaned back in his chair, rubbing his temples with the tips of his fingers. Now he knew what advice Patience's mother had given her. Unfortunately in that case, her mother had been right. He'd need to give Grace all the affection and understanding his father hadn't given Patience.

Grace and Matt's love was more like his father's and his mother's. He'd cajole her out of her bad moods, and she would do the same for him. He'd protect her. But to do that, he needed to discover how to change what was going on in her beautiful, misbegotten head.

Jane needed a walk. Grace was upset and not ready to discuss whatever was troubling her. The children had their lessons, and Jane had some errands to run. At least that was the excuse she'd use if anyone asked. She'd always hoped Grace would wed, but now that the event would occur in about a week, Jane must seriously consider what she would like to do.

Though she had gone to Stanwood Hall to help Grace's mother and remained, she was not a poor relation. She chuckled to herself. Perhaps she should hire her own companion and travel. As much as Grace thought she would still want Jane to stay with the family, it was time for her to live her own life.

"Oy, lady. Watch where ye're goin'."

Before she knew what was happening, She was being hauled up and away from the street. A swift-moving sporting carriage passed where she'd been mere moments ago. Stupid, reckless driver. Did no one watch where they were going, and why was she still being held?

The scent of lemon verbena mixed with mint tickled her nose. No lady's perfume. Only one man she'd ever known used that particular scent, but he'd left years ago. She was slowly lowered to the pavement. The moment her feet touched the ground, she turned. A man, only a few inches taller than herself, gazed down at her with serious gray eyes.

The same color gray as a storm cloud, and just as changeable. "*Hector?*"

"Jane?" he said as if she were the only "Jane" in the world. "By all that is holy, it is you."

Long ago memories slammed into her, robbing her of breath. "How long have you been back?"

"Less than a week." He stared at her, yet she didn't know what to make of his look.

He had filled out in the last twenty years. His complexion, a reddish-brown, carried the remnants of India. Other than that, his dear face was the same, lightly rounded and cheerful. Older to be sure, but so was hers.

Surely he had married, but Jane found she could not ask the question. "How are you?"

"I'm much better now." He linked her arm in his. "Where are you going? I shall accompany you." When she hesitated, he asked, "Unless you're married, that is."

"No. I never married. You?"

His eyes sparkled with humor as they used to. "The same. I couldn't find a woman who could hold a candle to you, Janie."

The nickname only he called her took her back to days of her first Season, before her father had thrown him out of the house for daring to ask for her hand. If only she'd had the strength of character to elope with him, yet that would have been difficult as he hadn't asked. "I mostly left the house to think."

"Is it that noisy where you live?"

He said it as if she were living in a boardinghouse. Jane couldn't resist the temptation to tease him. "There are a number of children and more coming."

Hector stopped. His concerned gaze bore into her, still it was all she could do to keep from laughing. "Never tell me you're a matron at an orphan hospital!"

Jane patted his arm. "No, nothing so drastic. I have been acting as companion to one of my cousins who has guardianship of her brothers and sisters. There are a great many of them." He opened his mouth to speak, and she hurried on. "Now it appears that she will marry, and it is time for me to make my own life."

They began ambling down the street again.

"A paid companion." His tone was grim. "What the devil was your father thinking?"

"No, indeed. You mistake the matter." A giggle escaped Jane's lips. How good it felt to stroll with Hector again.

His tone was severe, but his lips twitched. He never remained solemn for long. "I have a feeling you're making a May game of me, Miss Carpenter."

"Well, perhaps a small one. I offered my assistance. My cousin needed help after her husband died, and I was free at the time. I stayed when she passed and her daughter, Grace, took over. Papa left me with a generous competence. As a matter of fact, before he died, he apologized for not allowing us to wed."

"I thought he had selected a husband for you?" The corners of Hector's lips turned down in a rare show of irritation. "If I'd had any idea you had been left alone all this time . . . well, let's just say I would have sent for you."

"I hardly call living in a house with seven children being alone."

"You know what I mean," he said, his voice gruff. "What happened to the husband?"

"I refused to marry the man." Jane felt herself straighten a bit. As she had when, for the first time in her life, she'd defied her father. "He refused to believe me until he dragged me into church that day, and I said no, I would not have that man as my husband."

Hector's deep laugh began in his stomach. The same laugh she had missed for so long. "I would have loved to see his face. Hoisted by his own petard."

"Exactly. The vicar asked why I'd changed my mind, and I told him I had not. I had never agreed to the marriage in the first place."

His face had regained its jovial mien. "I take it he didn't attempt to beat you?"

"No, you know, or rather knew Papa." She sighed. "He

would never resort to physical violence. There was a huge brouhaha, mostly my father shouting. He threatened to throw me out of the house, but my mother's aunt, I don't think you ever met her, a bluestocking who held weekly salons of artists and writers, said she'd take me in. Well, that ended that."

"Did he ever try to make a match for you again?" Hector's gaze slanted down at Jane.

"No. He made suggestions, of course, but I turned them down." She swallowed past the lump in her throat. "After all, how could I wed one man when I was already in love with another?" They had been walking on Maddox Street and had reached the corner of Davies Street. Hector had been quiet since she basically announced that she had waited for him. Jane's stomach was performing acrobatics. "I live in Berkeley Square."

"I shall do myself the honor of escorting you home."

She gave a tight nod. Perhaps she should not have been so open, yet seeing Hector again brought all the memories and feelings rushing back.

They had reached the square before he said. "Janie, I should like to court you. I know I'm not the specimen I used to be, and I'm an old bachelor with the attendant problems, but if you could see your way . . ."

His face had grown red. Tears pricked Jane's eyes. "I'm not the same as I was either, and I am a spinster and set in my habits as well, but there is nothing I would like more than for you to court me."

As they stared at each other, the years slipped away. Hector patted her hand twice. "I'm not sure how to go about this."

"You could ask me to walk in the Park, or take me to Gunter's for an ice cream."

"I ordered a curricle that will be delivered to-day. Would you ride with me in the Park to-morrow, Miss Carpenter?"

Where was her handkerchief when she required it? Jane sniffed and smiled. "I would be delighted, Mr. Addison."

Chapter Seventeen

Charlotte hailed Louisa from a bench in the middle of Berkeley Square. "It's no use. I knocked on Grace's door, and she sent me away."

"Matt's the same." Louisa bit her lip. "He's locked himself in his study and our butler won't even let us down the corridor. I did try to go through the garden, but was stopped." She plopped down on the bench next to Charlotte. "I wonder if they have quarreled."

Charlotte sat up. "I hope it is nothing to do with the guardianship."

"That would certainly upset them, but you'd think they would mope together."

"It's beyond me. If they do not work it out shortly, we will have to become involved. Do you go to Lady Huntingdon's party to-morrow?"

"Yes." Louisa smiled. "Our first real entertainment. I can barely wait for our first ball!"

A sporting carriage drove up to Worthington House and a gentleman with a many-capped greatcoat climbed down and threw the reins to a small boy dressed in livery. "Louisa, someone's just driven up to your house."

Louisa peered in the direction Charlotte pointed, then sat back. "Him? It is only Merton."

"I like his carriage, and his horses are very sweet goers. They look to be perfectly matched."

"No doubt they are." Louisa gave a bored sigh. "He insists *everything* be perfect."

Charlotte glanced at her friend. "That sounds a bit daunting. What is wrong with him?"

"It is not that anything is so very *wrong* with him. It's just that he is a marquis and *never* lets anyone forget it. *And* he is our cousin, so we are forever being reminded of it."

"Hmm, in that case, I suppose he's not worth knowing. I dislike anyone who is puffed up in their own consequence."

"That he certainly is. He is a couple of years younger than Matt and very high in the instep."

"I detest people who cannot be pleased." Charlotte glanced back over to Worthington House.

"I am in complete agreement. What are you wearing to-morrow evening?" Louisa asked.

"I think I shall wear my green muslin with the butterflies. Would you like to see it?"

"Since we will probably spend much of the evening together, let us coordinate our gowns."

Charlotte rose and signaled to her footman. "It will be more productive than anything else we could do at the moment."

"Agreed." Louisa stood, linking her arm with Charlotte's.

"If Grace and Matt do not start speaking to each other soon, I think Walter should scale the garden wall."

"While we keep Matt's butler busy at the front door."

"That should do the trick."

* * *

"I do not recall," Matt said, glowering at his butler, Thorton, "that a visit from the Marquis of Merton qualifies as the house burning down."

"No, my lord, but he was rather insistent."

"He always is." Matt resisted running his fingers through his hair. It was enough that Grace was still cool toward him, and now he had to deal with his cousin. "One would think a butler of your stature could be relied upon to keep upstarts from entering my study."

Thorton's teeth clenched together, as he bowed. "Yes, my lord."

"Your lips are twitching. I can see them." Damn, no reaction at all.

"My lord." He shut the door behind him.

The Marquis of Merton disposed himself gracefully in a chair.

Matt frowned. "Well, Dom, what do you want?"

"Is that any way to treat the head of the family?" Merton said in an aggrieved tone.

"You're not on about that again?" Matt, whose feet had been on his desk, moved them to the floor. He placed his elbows on his desk, leaned forward. "Since you seem to have forgot again, let me remind you. *You* are not the head of *my* family. The titles are separate. They always have been. I'll take leave to remind you that my title is older than yours. In addition, if you are going to take that tone with me, you may take your leave forthwith."

Merton flicked open his snuffbox with one hand and drawled, "What has you in such a foul mood?"

"If you must know"—Matt rose, made his way to the sideboard, poured two glasses of brandy, handed one to Merton, then resumed his seat—"it has to do with a lady."

His cousin raised a delicate brow. Worthington wouldn't be surprised if his valet plucked them. "My dear cousin, ladies are never worth the trouble."

He was going to wring Merton's neck. Actually, it would be the highlight of Matt's day. And probably do England a favor as well. "I'll thank you to keep your nasty tongue to yourself. I'm going to marry the lady in question."

Merton jerked up, almost sloshing his brandy. "*What?*"

Matt gave his cousin a wicked smile. If he couldn't see Grace, he might as well have some fun. "That got you off your high horse."

"With good reason." Merton tried and failed to resume a languid pose. "When did this come about?"

Rubbing his forehead, Matt glanced at his cousin. Why the devil did Merton have to show up now? "I should have married her years ago."

"Do I know her?" Merton took out his snuffbox, flicked it open again with one finger as if he was practicing, and took a pinch.

"Probably not. She is Lady Grace Carpenter."

His cousin frowned. "Stanwood?"

"Yes, the current earl's elder sister." *Who won't admit me into her presence right now.*

Merton saluted Matt. "To your health."

Matt grinned. "To my health. Are you going to tell me what brings you to Town? I thought you'd decided to travel abroad."

Merton sighed. "My mother. She's taken it into her head I must marry. Consequently, I'm here to look at the latest crop of young ladies."

"You're only twenty-eight, what is her hurry?"

"Lord, I wish I knew." He settled back into his chair. "You don't think she's got wind of your betrothal, do you?"

"Anything's possible. As long as you stay away from the two young ladies I'm responsible for, I wish you luck with the rest. It shouldn't be too hard. Just be sure to remind them you're a marquis."

Merton did rake his fingers through his perfectly coifed hair. "Am I never to live that down?"

Worthington grinned. "Not in this family."

"Fine way to treat the head of the family," Merton grumbled.

Matt's good humor fled, and anger he was an idiot for feeling, surged through him. "You," he bellowed, pointing at his cousin, "are not the head of *my* family."

Why was he even putting up with the man? He really didn't want Merton here now. Matt needed to figure out what to do about Grace. He'd be damned if she was going to treat him with that oppressive civility for God only knew how long.

"I told you they'd let his marquisship in." The sound of Theodora's disgusted tone carried from the other side of the door as only a child's can.

Matt chuckled as Merton rubbed his temples. Thank God for Theo.

Glancing up with a pained expression, he asked, "Which one is that?"

Good, let him have a headache. He'd caused enough of them. "Theodora and she probably has Mary with her."

"Mary?"

Merton was in for it this time. Theo didn't like him at all. "Yes, one of Grace's sisters."

"We wish to see my brother." Theo must be talking to Thorton. No one else would spend so much time arguing with her. "If you allowed his marquisship in, then we should be able to go in as well."

Merton groaned and tossed off his brandy. "She couldn't have been more than three or four. Doesn't anyone in your family forget anything?"

Matt laughed. "Apparently not." He smiled broadly. "Thorton, let them in."

Theodora, with Mary trailing close behind, rushed in the

room. His sister glanced intently at Merton, narrowed her eyes, then turned to Matt.

Although he appreciated the gesture, Patience would have his head if he let Theo get away with cutting his cousin. "Theo, stop and bid Lord Merton good day."

Her lips set tightly together.

Matt snapped his brows together. "If you do not do as I say, you will go to your room and remain there until the morning."

Casting him a resentful sidelong look, she curtseyed. "Good day your m—"

"Theodora. Properly."

"My lord."

Merton stood and bowed. Not an inkling of his consternation showed on his face. "Good day to you as well, Lady Theodora. I beg you to introduce me to your friend."

"Mary, allow me to introduce Lord Merton. My lord, this is my friend, Lady Mary Carpenter."

The two girls lost no time dashing behind the desk. Theo stood next to Matt, while he helped Mary climb onto his lap. He glanced from one girl to the other. "Now, what's so important?"

Mary gazed up at him with her big, blue eyes. "Grace isn't happy, and she won't let anyone in." She played with one of the buttons on his jacket. "And you wouldn't let anyone in. We can't go to the Park without permission, and we need to go run so we don't drive everyone to Bedlam."

"Ah-ha. Very well. I'll take you." He frowned. "Did you walk over here alone?"

His sister huffed. "No, we have a footman."

"Good girls. Go back over and tell everyone to be ready in ten minutes." He gave Mary a kiss on her head. Theo kissed his cheek. Once he'd set Mary down, he stood. "Merton, you may accompany us if you'd like."

"There is one small matter." Merton rose and addressed

Matt tentatively. "I wondered if I might stay with you for a bit."

Damn, damn, and double damn. "Why?"

Glancing down at his nails, Merton replied. "My mother is not coming to Town, and I don't wish to open Merton House up so that I can rattle around in it alone."

Matt's jaw clenched. *The devil!* "How long?"

Refusing to meet his eyes, Merton responded, "I'm not exactly sure."

"You may remain here for two nights. After that, we'll discuss it. You haven't picked the best time to visit, without even a letter letting me know."

"Of course, thank you. If it doesn't work out, I shall move to a hotel."

If Merton stayed for very long, it may not be the children driving Matt and Grace to Bedlam. "We need to go." He got Duke, strode out of the house and across the square. Merton trailed behind him. When he entered Stanwood House, the children were assembled in the entrance hall. Matt counted. "We're missing two."

Royston bowed. "No, my lord. Lady Charlotte and Lady Louisa have gone shopping."

Matt raised a brow of inquiry.

"My lord, they have taken their maids and two footmen. I expect them back any moment now."

He nodded. "Very well. Is Daisy ready?"

Daisy dashed into the hall and, in trying to come to a stop, slid on the polished marble tiles and landed inelegantly at his feet. Matt glanced down and was hard put not to laugh as she gazed up at him smiling. "Lead?"

"Here, my lord." Harold handed it to Matt. "Thank you. You take Duke. I'll see if I can teach this young lady some manners." He turned to the others. "The rest of you, two by two, holding hands. I want four footmen."

As the children filed out of the house, followed by the

liveried footmen, Merton had a pained expression on his face. "Eight children?"

"Eleven. As you no doubt heard, the two eldest girls are shopping. Stanwood is at Eton."

"Isn't this type of outing rather below your dignity?"

"Not at all." Matt grinned evilly. "And if you think it below yours, you may return to Worthington House, or do whatever else you'd like to do. Though you'll probably be ostracized as chickenhearted."

"I won't cry off." Merton ran a finger under his neckcloth. "A nice walk will be just the thing."

By the time they reached the Park, Matt thought everything was going so well, he was even in charity with his cousin.

"Good girl, Daisy." Matt patted the dog. Finally, she was heeling.

The children had paired off. Philip, Theo, and Mary were kicking a ball around. The boy who'd started the fight with Walter approached, said something, then held out his hand. He and Walter shook. *Good lads.*

Matt decided to spend some time training Daisy. After a few minutes, she pranced daintily beside him, showing off her new skill. Matt didn't understand why Grace had so many problems with the Dane. All she needed was a firm hand.

They'd almost made it to where the older girls were sitting when Matt's arm was practically jerked out of the socket, and he was in danger of falling. He hauled back on Daisy's leash, as she lunged again after a squirrel.

"Matt, are you all right?" The twins, Augusta, and Madeline rushed up to him.

He tightened his grip on the dog as she charged the squirrel, now on a lower branch of the tree chattering.

"Daisy!" He walked away from the tree, turning her so that she could not avoid looking at him, and used his most severe tone. "A well-behaved young lady does not attempt to dislocate her master's shoulder."

She gave him a sorrowful look, and he was tempted to delude himself into thinking she understood, but just at that moment, the damned rodent scampered down the tree, and she tried to take off again. This time he was ready for her.

Blinkers might be a good idea.

Grace hid in her study for the better part of the day. She was trying and failing to work on her accounts when the sound of Worthington and the children returning echoed through the house.

She'd been miserable before, during, and after breakfast. Worthington had been hurt by her coolness. Her aunt might be correct that he would lose interest. Perhaps she should try to forget her aunt's advice and enjoy his company while he remained attracted to her, storing up all the memories to keep her warm in the future.

The door opened and Worthington stood in the entrance gazing at her. With his hair slightly tousled, he was even more handsome than usual. Grace's heart thudded as she stared back. She'd missed him so badly and had been ill-tempered with everyone because she hadn't had his company. Not to mention his touch.

He strode in and took her in his strong arms. "I can't live with you being so distant."

Grace tilted her head up, and his lips met hers. Belatedly, she remembered she had on an old morning dress and very little else. His hands caressed her face as he kissed her more deeply. She wound her arms as far around his neck as she could and desperately returned his kiss. Their tongues tangled, and Grace ceded control to him. On tiptoe, she pressed against him. One of his hands roamed down to caress her tight breast. Only three thin layers of muslin separated his curious fingers from her nakedness, and she was rapidly losing her struggle not to make love as her desire overrode her brain.

"No stays?" he murmured against her lips.

"No." She ran her greedy hands under his jacket. "You have on too many clothes."

"I do." He chuckled deeply. "You, however, are perfectly dressed."

Her bodice loosened, and he peeled down each stratum of cloth covering her breasts.

"I've dreamt of these and how they tasted." He nudged her head back with his and lowered his mouth to her breasts.

Flames shot up and swirling desire captured her. All thoughts of denying herself of the pleasure of making love died when he sucked her nipple. "Ah, Matt."

"I won't do anything else. I promise."

The ache between her legs overwhelmed her. Oh God, how she'd missed him. Breathing became harder, and she panted. "Please, I want you."

Worthington raised his head and searched her eyes. "Are you sure?"

Not knowing how much longer she'd have him, Grace nodded. "Yes, yes, I'm sure."

"Come, we'll try something new. I'd really like to have you back in a bed again." His hand moved between them and his erection was free. Turning her so that she faced her desk, he said, "Rest your head on your arms."

He raised her skirts so slowly she thought he'd never finish. His hard hands heated her thighs sending sparks of anticipation shooting through her. By the time his fingers moved to her center and wetness pooled between her legs, Grace wanted to scream and tell him to take her as he continued his slow path. Worthington's fingers stroked, causing spikes of desire to drive her mad. A high moan escaped her lips. "Matt, please. I want you."

When he finally flipped up her skirt and nudged her legs apart, she was trembling with need.

"You're wet." Matt chuckled deeply. "Grace, do you have any idea how I've missed you?"

His teeth nibbled her ear, and she pushed back against him. "As much as I've missed you."

She wanted him so much. Relief coursed through her as Matt's shaft slowly filled and possessed her. His fingers found her most sensitive spot and rubbed. She struggled to breathe. A spark lit deep inside and his long, deep thrusts built her tension higher until her knees buckled and she convulsed around him.

Matt's groan and the way he held her when he came gave her hope that he wouldn't leave her soon.

He smoothed her skirts back down and carried her to the sofa. Holding her on his lap, he softly stroked her neck and feathered light kisses on her temple. She could stay like this with him forever.

"I wonder if you know how much I love you." Matt had never required a woman to complete him before. Yet he needed Grace. Not just to make love to. Though her responsiveness called to his inner beast and soothed it. He was driven to protect and cherish her. Matt had never wanted a woman who did everything well all by herself. Even though Anna and Phoebe were good friends, and he valued them, Grace was different, a strong woman who still required him. Giving him his purpose in life.

He shifted her around, pulled up her gown and petticoats, then retied her laces. Would she finally tell him what had been bothering her? Though he was sure Anna had been correct, Matt wanted Grace to trust him enough to say it. "Sweetheart, are you all right? There's been some constraint between us recently."

"It was something my aunt said." She nuzzled against him. "I'll try not to let it worry me."

"If you want to tell me?"

"No. It's not a concern that need bother you."

But he wanted her to tell him. How could he make her happy if he didn't know? "If you insist."

She laughed. "I do."

Matt tried to hold her closer, to let her know she could trust him. He tried again. "I would like to know."

She shook her head. "It's not important."

The hell it wasn't. It had made them both miserable. He'd find out what it was later. "My cousin Merton arrived today begging a room. I told him I didn't know how long he could stay, that I needed to discuss it with you first. I'm happy to kick him out on his ear, if you wish."

"How bad is he?"

"Completely insufferable. He never fails to get my ire up, and you'll hear my sisters refer to him as 'his marquisship.'"

Grace pursed her lips. "I have trouble picturing Patience allowing that."

"Normally she would not, however, he didn't endear himself to her, either. He came to visit us a few years ago, all puffed up in his own consequence. Thought everyone should be impressed that he was a marquis and acted as if he was making a duty visit to poor relations." Matt smiled. "He assured us that, as the head of the family, he would always be willing to help."

"Is he?" Grace's brow furrowed. "The head of your family, I mean. How could that even be?"

"No, my ancestor married a lady who held the title. After she died, their son became the earl. Merton's side of the family has never got over the fact that our side of the family became a new house."

"I do not understand. If he usually comes to Town for the Season, why must he reside with you?"

He wished Merton wasn't staying with them. "He was

supposed to go on his Grand Tour, but his mother sent him to Town to find a wife."

Grace frowned. "How old is he?"

Settling her back against him, he said, "Twenty-eight. You haven't met my aunt Merton."

She twisted around. "I beg your pardon, my lord, but I have. She's actually some sort of relation of mine, and not at all a dragon." Grace screwed her face up for a moment. "Is not his family name Bradford?"

"Yes. My ancestor took his wife's surname. The gentlemen in my line will do almost anything for the ladies they love." Matt resumed the original topic. "Could be they heard about us, and he doesn't want me to get the jump on him in setting up my nursery." He kissed her forehead and couldn't resist holding one of her breasts in his hand.

Grace blushed delightfully. "Maybe, though the news would have had to have traveled terribly quickly."

Enough about his cousin. "Do you know you're even more beautiful when you blush?"

The deep rose in her face deepened. "It is not necessary for you to pay me compliments."

"You're out there, my lady, it is essential." Matt captured her lips again.

Grace lay back in his arms, her eyes glazed with desire. "In that case, do you know how handsome you are with your hair tousled?"

He cruised her jaw with his tongue.

"You should invite him to join us for dinner."

"Grace, he's a bore."

"Nevertheless, he's part of your family and staying at your house. It's only proper. Besides, what is one more person at our table?"

"You do have a point." He took a paper from his pocket. "We must take a look at Phoebe's list of entertainments for the week."

"And compare them with where Charlotte and Louisa are going. What time is it?"

His stomach picked that moment to growl. "Time for tea."

Grace leaned her head back to look at the clock giving him perfect access to her neck. It was impossible not to nibble it. Her giggle rumbled under his lips. If he could only keep her this relaxed.

Chapter Eighteen

Dominic Sylvester Henry, Tenth Marquis of Merton, Eleventh Earl of Scarsdale, and Baron Bradford, frowned at the mirror.

"What is it, my lord?" his valet, Witten, asked.

"I thought I saw a spot, but I daresay it was a shadow."

His valet peered closely at the snowy-white neckcloth. "It must have been. I see nothing, my lord, and I inspect every piece of linen that comes back from the laundress."

Merton placed his gold-rimmed quizzing glass, pocket watch, and fobs about his person. Not too many, of course. One would not wish to draw Brummell's fire at Whites later. "I believe I am ready."

Witten opened the door and Dom stepped into the corridor, making his way to the grand staircase and thence to the drawing room where he'd been instructed to wait until the family was gathered. As it turned out, he was the last one to arrive.

"You are late."

He turned to find a tallish, fashionably dressed young lady glaring at him and bowed. "I beg your pardon, Lady Louisa, is it not?"

She curtseyed. "It is. Now we must be off." She took

Worthington's arm and led the other three sisters out into the main hall to the door.

Lady Worthington, the only one left, curtseyed, and Merton offered her his arm. "Good evening, my lady."

"Good evening, my lord." Her tone was slightly chilly.

Being in Worthington House must be similar to being in an enemy camp. Why had he even bothered to honor them with his presence?

He followed the others across the square, up the shallow stairs to Stanwood House, and into the drawing room.

A striking lady, not in her first blush, came forward to greet him. From the way Worthington gazed at her, she must be his intended.

She curtseyed. "Lord Merton, how very kind of you to join us. Your mama is a connection of mine. We shall consider you as family."

Thank the Lord. Someone who knew what was due his rank. He took the hand she offered and kissed it. "Lady Grace, how could I have stayed away?"

She smiled politely. "Obviously, you could not."

"Not if you wanted to eat, that is." Worthington smirked.

Leave it to his cousin to ruin the mood. "Thank you, Worthington, for your acute observation."

Lady Grace glared briefly at Matt. "I shall introduce you to the others. Some of whom I believe you've already met."

Merton was formally introduced to the children he'd met earlier to-day. He turned to meet the sister who'd gone shopping and was struck dumb. Standing before him was the loveliest young woman he'd ever seen. Her hair matched her elder sister's and her eyes were the same arresting deep sky blue, but there the resemblance ended.

Which was strange since they actually looked very much alike. Her skin seemed to glow with more luminescence.

Humor lurked in her gaze as she rose from making her curtsey. She was no taller than Lady Grace, but she was sylphlike in her carriage. Dom took her hand and kissed it, then forgot to give it back. "Lady Charlotte, I am enchanted."

Her perfect lips curved in a smile. "Thank you, my lord. We are pleased you could join us."

Her voice was musical, and he looked forward to a very pleasant evening in Lady Charlotte's company. Then his cousin Louisa joined them.

She took Lady Charlotte's arm. "Come along, Charlotte, he's very handsome, but not worth your time."

Lady Charlotte grimaced. "Excuse me, my lord. Louisa . . ." She was pulled away before she could finish.

He stood alone for a few moments feeling rather foolish, when the youngest girl, Mary, that was her name, came up to him. "Well, no matter what the others say, I think you're nice."

"Thank you." He smiled. "The others?"

Mary took him by the hand to a sofa. "The other side of the family, Matt's sisters."

"Ah. What do they say? Or should I ask?"

"Only that you are puffed in your own con—con—I don't remember the rest."

"That's all right. I think I have it. Lady Mary, may I escort you into dinner?"

Mary's chin rose higher. "Yes, you may, and you may also ask me about Charlotte if you'd like."

Merton choked. What did they say about coming from the mouth of babes? "Thank you for your very kind offer."

Grace gave Matt her arm. Charlotte's and Louisa's behavior had been an embarrassment. "I do not care what you think of him. While he is in my home, he shall be treated kindly. What Louisa did was not only rude, it was mean-spirited. Charlotte will hear from me concerning her behavior." Grace glanced over her shoulder. "I could not be more proud of Mary. She is the only one who has behaved just as she ought, and she's only five."

Matt frowned. "If I'd known he was going to cause a problem, I would have suggested he dine at his club."

"*He* was not the problem." Grace stopped until Lord Merton reached the dining room door. "My lord, we are dining *en famille*. However, you may sit next to me. Mary, you may sit next to Lord Merton."

Mary beamed. "Thank you. I'd like that."

Merton, with Mary on his arm, strolled to where she'd indicated.

Matt turned and whispered in Grace's ear, "At least his conquest is too young to be thinking of marriage."

"For your information"—she allowed her irritation to show in her tone—"no female is too young to think of marriage. Do try to behave. Where is Patience?"

Matt glanced around. "There." He indicated one corner of the dining room.

Patience was speaking in hushed tones to Louisa, and, for her part, Louisa hung her head. Grace nodded approvingly. "Good."

For the first time, it was clear to her that she could be of value to Matt's family as well.

When Charlotte had entered the drawing room, she hadn't expected to see Lord Merton. He was even better-looking up close. His golden-blond hair was expertly styled in a new windblown fashion, à la Vent. His coat cut to perfection across his broad shoulders. Merton wasn't as tall as Matt, but he was still much taller than she. He bowed elegantly, and when she gazed into his eyes they changed color, from gray to blue. She would have happily stayed, until Louisa pulled her away. Charlotte was glad her youngest sister had taken him in hand, and she tried not to watch him during dinner. She would apologize as soon as she could. She was sure Grace would expect her to.

Matt declined having port in the dining room, and he and Merton joined the ladies in the drawing room.

She made her way over to where Merton stood. "My lord?"

"Yes, my lady."

"I—I wanted to say that I should not have allowed Louisa to take me away."

His eyes widened, and Merton seemed to relax. "Thank you."

"You're welcome, and I'm happy that Mary made you feel welcome. She did, didn't she?"

"Yes, she did. She is very charming."

Charlotte laughed lightly. "Indeed, though sometimes embarrassingly direct."

He flushed a little. "I predict she will be one of those ladies who know just how to help everyone."

"You're probably correct. Tell me, do you spend much time in Town?" She led him to a chair and sat on the sofa next to it.

"I try to always be present for the parliamentary sessions."

"Indeed. I am very interested in politics. To which party do you belong?"

He stiffened a little. "Why the Tories, of course."

"Oh." That was a disappointment.

"I take it your family supports the Whigs?"

Charlotte smiled politely. "Yes, Lord Worthington does as well."

Merton raised a supercilious brow. "I would not wish to speak badly of my cousin, but he does have what I consider to be rather extreme views."

She struggled to maintain a pleasant expression. This is what Grace meant about using one's manners when one would prefer not to. "Indeed, and which of those views do you consider extreme?"

"I shall give you an example. All this talk of social reform. Why should the average man have a vote? They wouldn't know what to do with it. There is a reason our society is ordered as it is."

Charlotte spoke to him for quite a half an hour before tea was served. Though Merton was one of the more attractive gentlemen she'd seen, he didn't seem to have an original thought in his head. Did he truly believe the things he said? It was as if he was living in the last century. Such a shame. She allowed him to escort her to where Grace was pouring tea and took the cup he handed her.

Perhaps husband hunting was not going to be as easy as she thought it would.

Early the following morning, Charlotte knocked softly on her sister's bedchamber door. "Grace?"

"Charlotte, come in." Grace sat at her dressing table while Bolton put her hair up.

"Grace, what did you think of Merton?"

"I thought him very well mannered. Particularly after the provocation Worthington and Louisa offered."

"I agree that was not well done. But did you think him a little—well a little stodgy?"

Bolton finished, and Grace signaled to her to leave. "Yes, I think stodgy is the word I would use."

"It is not as if he is older."

"He is young and handsome, but stodgy, nonetheless." She grinned. "Some people are born that way, others learn it." Grace gave Charlotte a wry smile. "I would caution you not to expect him to change. Don't lose heart, he is only the first eligible gentleman you've met. There will be plenty more."

Charlotte couldn't keep her brows from drawing together. "What do you think I should do?"

"Look around. There is no reason for you to marry this year, unless you want to. Keep in mind that a handsome face and pleasant manners are not everything, and may, indeed, hide a number of sins. You must agree on how you wish to live your lives as well."

"Did you and Worthington do that?"

Grace paused for a moment. "We are fortunate in that we are both very liberal thinkers."

Charlotte nodded thoughtfully. Grace was almost always right, as she was now. Unless some being came along and magically changed Merton's views, he would not do for her. "Thank you."

"You're welcome, my dear." Grace grinned as she stood. "Come, let's go down to breakfast before the children pile in."

"Grace?"

"Yes, love?"

"Will we live at Worthington House?"

Her sister heaved a sigh. "I truly dislike the idea of uprooting everyone. I must take some time this week to go over the houses and discuss it with Matt. I'll also need to consider Lady Worthington."

"That's what is difficult about being a lady, isn't it?" Charlotte frowned. "Our homes are not truly ours. I never thought I would leave Stanwood. I see now that even if you were not marrying Matt, or I didn't wed, once Charlie marries, it would not be mine anymore."

Grace hugged her. "Very true. Or if you are a widow and your son marries. Although at that point, there is always the option of the dower house. Then again, there are women like the Dowager Lady Beaumont who can afford to set up their own homes. Before you wed, we shall discuss it in much more detail when we draft the settlement agreements. They are your protection in any marriage."

"Not that I would ever think of doing such a thing, but what if a couple elope?"

"In that case." The edges of Grace's lips tugged down. "The lady is completely dependent on the good will of her husband, as he will own everything she has, including her private possessions."

"I do not think I would care for that." Charlotte kissed her sister. "Thank you."

That was the best part of having Grace as her sister. She didn't push aside one's concerns. "I'm glad you and Matt will marry. You love him very much, don't you?"

Something passed over Grace's face, and when she smiled it was more beautiful than Charlotte had ever seen it. "Yes, I do."

Matt had already consumed his first cup of tea. He'd been about ready to send for Grace when she and Charlotte entered.

"You're here early, my love."

He stood, took her hands, and kissed her lightly on the lips. "Yes, I wanted to speak with you before the horde arrived."

Nothing even resembling a smile hovered on her lips. "Horde?"

Ah, that came under the category of "I may criticize my family, but woe to whoever else does the same." He kissed her again. "No, no, don't pull caps with me, my darling. Even you have to admit that it's impossible to carry on a serious conversation with everyone else here. I include my four sisters and stepmother."

Finally a rueful grin appeared on her lips. "You're right, I can't argue with that."

"Good." He helped her make her breakfast selections. If he could only wake up with her each morning, his life would be perfect. "My housekeeper would like to know when you are coming to inspect the house."

Grace took a breath. "I've been thinking about that. After breakfast I should think."

"Perfect. That will be one less item on our list." He signaled to one of the footmen. "Please have someone sent to Worthington House, and tell Mrs. Thorton her ladyship will be over in about an hour. She is to hold herself ready."

"Yes, my lord."

"An hour?" Grace shook her head. "I couldn't possibly be ready by then." She started ticking off the reasons on her fingers. "The children will barely be done eating. I must give Charlotte her assignments, get the children up to the school-room, dress, meet with the cook, and I'm sure there is something I've forgotten."

At times such as this, Matt felt as if he was pushing a boulder uphill. He pulled her chair out. "You are already dressed, and most fetchingly, I might add. You can give Charlotte her instructions while you eat. The cook can wait, and I shall take over here. I'm quite sure I am capable of getting them up to the school-room. After which, I shall join you at Worthington House." Grace poured his tea, and he took the cup. "I shall gladly give you a free hand with any redecorating you'd like to do."

"You will need to do something with the school-room and the children's bedchambers." Charlotte pulled a face. "It is really dark."

"Yes, you will." Louisa entered the breakfast room and grimaced. "The rooms are not nearly as nice as the ones here. Especially the school-room."

The rest of the children straggled in shortly afterward, with their eyes half open and yawning.

What was this? They usually had too much energy in the morning. "Why do you all look so tired?"

"We think it was the late night, my lord," Miss Tallerton said. "They were so overstrung none of them went directly to sleep. I don't think Town hours agree with them."

"Oh dear." Grace's brows furrowed in consternation. "I hadn't thought of that. I suppose we must continue to keep country hours when we dine alone."

Matt leaned back in his chair, taking a sip of tea. "They could eat in the school-room."

Several pairs of sleepy eyes glared at him.

"No, they cannot." Grace threw him an irritated look.

"Matt?" Louisa asked, using a warning tone. "Have you seen the school-room?"

He had a feeling he was about to get a lesson in humility. "No."

"There is not a place for a table large enough to fit all of them," Grace said. "When we have guests, they will dine early in here."

"I'm sorry. I suppose I should have taken a look first." That had not been well done on his part. "As you wish, my dear."

Breakfast was much quieter than usual. She dabbed her lips with the serviette and rose. "Charlotte, I would like you to practice your music. Perhaps Louisa can join you. I must go now if I'm to be ready for Mrs. Thorton."

Ah, he was to be trusted with the children. After Grace left, Matt glanced around the table with a sense of contentment. She was finally accepting their marriage and making decisions again. "After you've finished, you may all go back to bed for a nap. I'll not take grumpy children to the Park."

He waited until they'd gone, then ambled over to Worthington House.

* * *

The door opened before Grace knocked.

"My lady." Worthington's butler bowed. "Mrs. Thorton is waiting for you in the morning room."

"Thank you, Thorton."

Grace looked at the large entrance hall, tiled in black-and-white marble. An ornately carved grand staircase anchored the room, rising to a gallery on the first floor, then up again to another gallery. This was older and larger than Stanwood House. Flanking the entrance hall were two rooms. Two corridors, one on each side of the hall, led off to the back of the house. She followed Thorton down one of them to a pleasant, sunny parlor with French windows leading to a terrace and the garden beyond.

Mrs. Thorton was as short as her husband was tall. Pleasantly plump with a jovial countenance, she looked to be around fifty years of age. Grace hoped she'd be as easy to work with as she appeared.

The housekeeper bobbed a curtsey. "Welcome, my lady. I have my notebook and pencil. Where would you like to start?"

Grace smiled. "In the school-room. I imagine major renovations will be needed there."

Leading Grace out of the parlor and up the stairs, the housekeeper said, "I understand, my lady, that you have several brothers and sisters."

That was one way to put it. "Indeed, seven. Three boys, though the oldest is at Eton, and four girls. The eldest is making her come out this year. I shall need at least five bedchambers for the children and two sets of chambers for their tutor and governess."

Mrs. Thorton raised her brows. "Then you will have to remodel the entire floor."

Grace followed her up three flights of stairs to the school-room. It consisted of one room and two connecting bedchambers at the front of the house. A corridor with rooms on either side led to the back. Most of the rooms were very small and either empty or used for storage. "Where do the servants sleep?"

"The next floor up, my lady. Mr. Thorton and I have rooms in the other corridor on this side."

That was odd. If no one else did, the butler usually had his apartments downstairs. Grace pursed her lips. "Are you happy on this floor?"

"Well, my lady, to be honest, we were happier in the rooms downstairs."

"What are those chambers being used for now?"

"Mostly storage."

Then there would be no reason the problem could not be remedied fairly quickly. "Decide what you must have done to make them habitable again, and send me the list. In the meantime—" Grace opened the doors to the two front apartments, which were spacious. Each consisting of a bedroom, dressing room, and parlor. "They will do well for the governess and tutor. I'd like them painted and cleaned. Hmm, if we combine every second room, the bedchambers will not be so cramped." Grace put her fingers to her temples. "Art room with lots of windows and light, children's parlor. What else?"

"A nursery?"

Her cheeks warmed. "At the other end of the corridor, with rooms for a nurse and maids."

Mrs. Thorton made notes. "A new water closet?"

"An excellent idea. Two new water closets, and we can turn one of the small bedchambers into a bathing chamber."

By the time they were done, the list had grown remarkably. Strolling around the floor again, she hoped there was space for all of it. "When was the last time this house was renovated?"

"I've been here for over thirty years and this will be the first time anything more than the main rooms were redecorated."

"Well, I suppose there has not been much of a need."

"No, my lady. Not since his lordship's mother died."

It was almost one o'clock before they descended to the first floor. "Mrs. Thorton, I shall let you have your luncheon. We can meet again afterward."

"As you say, my lady." She dipped a curtsey, then bustled away.

Grace stood looking around and wondering how long it would be before she lived here. Were they doing the right thing by marrying when they each had responsibilities for their sisters and brothers? Charlie still had to learn to manage all the Stanwood properties and not be a stranger to them. She put a hand to her forehead. How was this all going to work?

Chapter Nineteen

Matt strode in the breakfast room as Grace and the children were rising from the luncheon table. He kissed her quickly to a chorus of *oohs, aahs,* and at least one *uck.* Wondering if the running commentary every time he kissed her would ever end, he fixed the children with a stern look. "You may all keep your opinions to yourselves."

Grace placed her serviette on the table. "And where were you all morning? I thought you were to join Mrs. Thorton and me?"

He tucked her arm in his. "I was going to, but decided procuring our special license, as I'd not had an opportunity to do it before, took priority. I understand you've not yet finished."

"I suppose so. Have you eaten?"

"Yes, and you need to complete your tour." He hurried her out the door.

Grace put her hand on her head and patted. "Matt, I can't go without my bonnet."

"You're just going across the street."

Thorton opened the door and bowed them in.

"Tell Mrs. Thorton we shall begin with the morning room," Worthington called over his shoulder.

When they reached the room, he whisked her in, closed the door, and pulled her into his arms. "I've wanted to do this all morning." His lips descended onto hers. When she opened her mouth to protest, he captured her lips with his own. "Don't talk. Just kiss me," he mumbled against her lips. "I'll hear Thorton coming."

When her arms went around his neck, he smiled. God, he loved how she responded to him. Moving his hands over her derrière, he held her flush against him, letting her feel his need. Her skin heated, and she was ready for him. If only they had the time. Yet his housekeeper was coming down the corridor. Matt reluctantly released her just as Mrs. Thorton knocked. Perhaps he'd tell Mrs. Thorton he would show Grace around himself. Maybe they could start with his bedchamber.

His arm was still around Grace's waist when Mrs. Thorton entered, took in the tableau, and narrowed her eyes at him. "If you will come with me, my lady, we'll finish up."

With lips still a little swollen, Grace smiled charmingly. "Of course, Mrs. Thorton."

Matt grinned. "I can take it from here, if you'd like."

His housekeeper's brows rose, just as they had when he'd been caught sneaking in one of the hunting dogs. "No, my lord, I would not like. What *I'd* like is to finish what we started this morning. Which won't happen if you take over."

Grace choked. "Indeed, Mrs. Thorton. Worthington, why don't you take a look at the drawing I made of the changes needed for the children's floor."

He placed his hand on the small of Grace's back and stroked downward. "I'll do it later. First, I want to be there when you see your chambers."

Her breath hitched. "If you wish. I'll call you when we get to them."

He scowled as Grace surveyed the morning room, then

left with Mrs. Thorton. He had plans for her to-day, and they did not include his housekeeper.

He followed them out. Grace could go over the renovation with him later. Staying out of their way, he noted the manner in which Grace dealt with Mrs. Thorton. She listened to his housekeeper's suggestions, melded them with her own, and came to a consensus. He vaguely wondered how much all this was going to cost him and dismissed it. Much more important to have a happy household.

When they reached the bedrooms, Grace turned to him. "Where are your sisters?"

"Taking lessons from your Miss Tallerton."

"Where's their governess?"

"For some reason, she didn't come. Yesterday, Patience told me she had received a letter that the woman had taken another position closer to her family." He and Grace had not discussed his sisters' lessons. Would she share her governess? The best idea was to give her the choice. "I suppose I'll have to hire a new one."

"Don't be ridiculous. We don't need two. Winters and Tallerton share the lessons. Her father was a cleric, and she was taught with her brothers as they prepared for Oxford. She also has all the usual accomplishments, drawing, harp, pianoforte, French and Italian. Winters has a degree in theology from Oxford. He is teaching them Latin, higher mathematics and alike."

"I see." To the best of his knowledge, his former governess didn't have half those accomplishments. "As long as Miss Tallerton and Mr. Winters don't object."

"Why would they?" Grace shrugged. "The girls are all close to the same ages."

Matt continued to follow until they reached the last room on their list. He opened the door to the countess's parlor. It was clean, but obviously had not been used in years. On one side of the room was a door leading to a large dressing area, with another door to a bedchamber, with views of the back garden.

Grace turned to him. "Does your stepmother not use these rooms?"

"No." He turned to Mrs. Thorton. "I think we can take it from here."

She nodded. "Yes, my lord. My lady, I'll put the lists in proper order."

He closed the door. "The last person to use this apartment was my mother."

Grace's eyes grew wide with confusion. "I don't understand."

Drawing her gently into his arms, he kissed her lightly. "My father and mother were just about inseparable. In fact, I don't remember them ever being apart, even overnight. After she died, he never slept in this bed or the one at Worthington Hall again. I have not slept in those rooms because I was waiting for a wife to share them with me." Matt kissed her again. "Father told me once he married Patience because he was lonely. Yet she couldn't fill the emptiness my mother's death caused. He never brought Patience here because he didn't love her."

"My parents were very much in love as well. If Mama had died first, I can't imagine Papa remarrying. I don't know if I feel worse for Patience or your father."

"I think I pity Patience more. My father had a chance to know deep, unending love. She was robbed of the opportunity." Matt shook his head. *Vivers men should only mate once.* "There is no separate bedchamber for the countess."

Grace's arm circled his waist. "I understand."

"Do you?"

She gazed up at him. "Indeed. My parents always shared a bedchamber. They couldn't bear to sleep apart."

Maybe now she'd tell him what Lady Herndon said, and he could make Grace understand she had nothing to worry about. "Do you love me like that, Grace? Because that's how I love you."

Tears welled in her eyes. "Yes, I love you exactly the same way."

With nimble fingers he untied her bodice and pushed her gown down over her hips. The muslin made a soft *whoosh* as it fell.

"Matt, what are you doing?"

"I need to see you. All of you." He pulled off her petticoats. He would have liked to truly take his time and unwrap her like one of those Russian boxes, one piece of clothing at a time. After untying her chemise, he stepped back. "You are the most beautiful woman I've ever seen."

The stays dropped to the floor, to join the rest of her clothes. Then he remembered to pick up her gown and put it over a chair.

Grace blushed but stood still, allowing him to look as he'd not been able to that first night. Her breasts were generous and firm. He traced one finger over her ribs to her waist then over the swell of her hips. The curls between her legs were the same color as her hair. She took his breath away.

He ached to possess her. To find his home inside her.

Matt gathered Grace into his arms and took the lips she offered him. She opened her mouth and her tongue drove him higher. His already swollen shaft ached and begged to be let free.

Her breath came in short gasps as she leaned back from him. "Do you have anywhere to go this afternoon?"

"No." Matt smiled and untied his cravat.

Grace pushed his jacket open, tugging it off. He allowed his hands to roam over her body. It was as smooth as the softest silk. Her nipples furled into tight buds, as she closed her eyes, allowing him to possess her. "You are perfect."

A sultry smile shaped her lips. "And you, my lord, have

too many clothes on. Hold still for a moment while I untie your cuffs."

After Matt had pulled the shirt over his head, Grace reached up and took his lips. It wasn't until they spoke of their parents that she realized the depth of her love for him.

The next thing she knew his erection was free and his pantaloons fell to the floor.

Matt backed them to the bed and sat, removing his boots and stockings.

When he rose, he was naked and beautiful. Grace reached out, pressing her fingers against his chest, studying it before she ran her hands through the thick, silky hair and down over his stomach. His body tightened beneath her touch. But he stayed motionless as she reached behind him and traced his back to his bottom. His body was all solid muscle.

Grace looked down at his shaft and touched it. Hard and so soft at the same time and, oh Lord, the pleasure he gave her. The throbbing between her legs increased, and she shuddered in anticipation. She didn't want to wait any longer to feel him inside her body. Trailing her hands up over his chest, she touched his nipples and licked them. They rewarded her by tightening. "Make love to me."

He picked her up, holding her like a child holds a favorite doll, and climbed in the bed. His chest hair abraded her already sensitive nipples. He settled between her legs, and she waited for him to enter her. When he didn't, she arched up, trying to encourage him. "What is it?"

He answered not in words, but by moving his lips, in soft featherlike kisses down her neck, over her breasts, sucking first one then the other. Tension wound inside her, and she gasped for air. She shook with a stronger, deeper desire than she'd ever known. The searing need for him that had started at the apex of her legs soared through her. "Matt, I need you inside me."

Chuckling wickedly, he moved his lips down over her stomach. Her mouth dried, and her breath became raspy. When he licked her core, Grace cried out and almost came off the bed.

"Do you like this, my love?"

That had to be one of the stupidest questions she'd ever heard. She tried to find the breath to answer but could only manage a high-pitched moan.

"I'll take that as a yes."

Grabbing at him, Grace tried to pull him up. As much as she liked what he was doing, she needed him now. Just the thought made her shudder again. "Please, Matt."

He licked his way up her body and just when she thought she'd die if she had to wait any longer, he plunged into her, withdrew, and thrust in again. She wrapped her legs around him, sobbing with need. Flames engulfed her, and her core ignited. Grace clung to him and spun apart as he pumped into her one last time and shuddered.

Matt held her close as her arms and legs relaxed. "I can't believe how lucky I am to have found you. This is your place."

He'd tucked her, limp and sated, in next to him. "My place?"

His lips pressed against her head tilted up. "Next to me. You fit perfectly."

When she gave it some thought, Grace discovered he was right. She was safe and secure being held by him like this. She rolled just enough to see his face. "What are you thinking of?"

He smiled down at her, his eyes more green now. "I was wondering if we'll scandalize the servants like my parents did."

Running her fingers lightly over his chest, she made her voice as sultry as she could. "What did they do to scandalize them?"

He kissed her and cupped a breast. "They made love whenever and wherever they wished."

She pulled his head down and ran her tongue over his lips. "I think we're already on our way. Until the children are here, that is."

"I'm not going to think about our brothers and sisters now." He kissed her slowly, tantalizingly. He was trying to keep from going too fast, but she wanted none of that. They were in a bed for the first time since that night and she intended to take full advantage of it. Pressing against him she moved one leg across his hip.

His eyes smoldered. "Again?"

"Again."

Grace dressed with care that evening. She wore a gown in *jonquille* silk. The neck was square and quite low, the high waist trimmed with a band of lace and seed pearls. Short epaulet sleeves left her shoulders mostly bare. The skirt flowed down and ended in a demi-train. Looping a long strand of pearls three times around her neck, she allowed one part to dangle lower. Pearls hung on gold wire adorned her ears.

Bolton dressed her hair high, pulling tendrils to fall past her shoulders, before securing the knot with combs. Grace collected her Norwich silk shawl, fan, and reticule.

"We haven't had you dressed so fine since you were last in London."

Grace stared at her reflection in the mirror. "I think you're right."

Bolton started to pick up then glanced over her shoulder. "You can tell his lordship for me that I'd appreciate it if he didn't crush your gown."

"*Bolton!*" Grace's face was immediately hot.

"Just like your parents, you are. Go on now. He'll be waiting for you."

Grace attempted to gather her dignity. "You are incorrigible."

"Yes, my lady."

Matt *was* waiting at the bottom of the stairs for her. When she reached him, the look in his face was all she could have wished for. His eyes, warm and loving. His well-molded lips tilted in a smile.

He took her still ungloved hand and kissed it. "You are amazingly beautiful. That color suits you. Though the bodice could be a bit higher."

His fingers hovered as if he'd try to pull it up. She rapped them with her fan. "I thought you'd like it."

"I do." He leaned closer and whispered, "And I'd like to take it off you."

Licking her suddenly dry lips, she remembered to breathe. "After we are married, you may."

"I'll hold you to that, my lady. You do realize that one week from tonight we will be man and wife."

She was about to answer when the knocker sounded and her aunt and uncle entered. "Aunt Almeria, Uncle Bertrand, I think the others are already in the drawing room."

Matt bowed to her aunt and shook hands with her uncle. "Yes, the girls and my stepmother." He turned to Grace. "The younger children would like to see you and their sisters before we go."

Of course they would. "I remember waiting to see my mama dressed for a party." She nodded to her butler. "Royston, please send them down."

"Yes, my lady."

A footman opened the door to the drawing room as Grace and Matt approached. She'd seen Charlotte earlier, but not Louisa. Charlotte's gown was of willow green, and Louisa wore light blue. They looked beautiful.

Matt grinned. "I know I told you before, but the two of you look lovely."

The girls blushed.

Grace scanned the room. "Where is Merton? I thought he was joining us."

"I caught him blowing a cloud in the house and sent him packing. I believe he's at Limners."

Grace squeezed his arm. "Just as well. I cannot abide cigar smoke. It's such a nasty habit. I hope it never catches on."

"I've also told him," Matt said in a wintry voice, "not to try to engage either Charlotte's or Louisa's attentions."

Grace raised her brows. "Thank you. Just don't tell them. It is always so that one immediately wants what is forbidden for one to have."

A wicked gleam entered his eyes. "Indeed."

A species of dread rose in her. Grace tried to keep her tone light. "And what happens when it is no longer forbidden?"

Matt's eyes undressed her before he pulled her closer. "This novelty will never end."

Her heart beat faster, and she prayed he was right. Still her aunt's words ran amok in her head.

It was at times like this when Matt knew Grace's confidence had suddenly and inexplicably fled. His compulsion to hold her and comfort her surged within him. He'd be perfectly happy to pick Grace up and carry her to his house, their chamber, and keep her there until they married. But he couldn't even take her in his arms with her aunt and uncle present.

Patience cleared her throat. "Do you accompany us or have you different plans?"

Grace turned to her. "We are attending Lady St. Eth's drum this evening. To-morrow we'll be at Lady Featherton's soirée."

Patience nodded. "That's a good plan. You will have a quiet evening with the political set, allowing the rest of us to drop hints about your romance. Then to-morrow you'll be present at the largest entertainment of the evening."

The rest of the children piled into the room. The girls exclaimed over their sisters' gowns, while the boys sidled up to Matt.

"They are very pretty, for sisters, I mean," Walter said.

Matt's gaze was drawn to Grace. "They are indeed."

Philip made a face. "If you like that sort of thing. I have more important things to do than look at gowns."

"I suppose you do." Matt had a difficult time maintaining a straight face. Philip's ideas would change dramatically in a few years.

Royston announced that all the carriages were ready. Grace and Matt waited until the others left before descending the stairs to her town coach.

He climbed in after her and gave the order to start. "Are you ready?"

"I'd better be. We've no choice."

Chapter Twenty

A half hour later, Matt and Grace were at the head of the receiving line at St. Eth House. Lord and Lady St. Eth greeted them, then they were directed to the ballroom.

Worthington scanned the other guests, recognizing most of those present. "I'll introduce you to whomever you don't know."

"Thank you. I am acquainted with several people, but it has been a while."

Through the expedient of twining Grace's arm with his, Matt kept her next to him. No point in allowing anyone to get the idea he would be a complaisant husband. If any of the gentlemen of the *ton* wanted to dally, they could find someone else's wife.

A moment later, two of his friends approached. "My love, allow me to introduce Lord Huntley and Lord Wively. Lady Grace Carpenter, my betrothed."

Huntley raised a surprised brow and smiled. "Lady Grace, Worthington, I wish you happy."

By this time, Wively, whose jaw had dropped, closed his mouth. "Yes, very happy, indeed."

Grace curtseyed and held out her hand. "I am pleased to

meet you. Any friend of Worthington's will be welcome in our home."

"Thank you, my lady." Huntley took her hand then slanted a look at Matt. "I'd kiss your hand, but Worthington might call me out."

He was surprised to find that he *had* been watching Huntley intently and gave a short laugh. "As long as you do nothing more than a salute, you'll be safe."

A wicked smile dawned on Wively's face when he bowed to Grace. "When is the wedding?"

Then the devil kissed Grace's hand, and Matt had trouble keeping a growl from escaping. At least she was wearing gloves. "One week from to-day."

"This is sudden," Wively said, unable to hide his surprise.

"No, not at all," Matt replied, smoothly tucking Grace's hand more securely in his arm. "We met a few years ago, but circumstances kept us apart." He was pleased to see Grace gazing lovingly up at him. "The minute I saw her again, I knew no other woman would do. We've no reason to wait and several very good reasons why we should not."

Huntley raised a brow in inquiry.

"Lady Grace's sister is making her come out, as is my sister. Having our wedding before the Season is under way makes it easier for us to chaperone them."

"Makes perfect sense to me," Huntley said, "four eyes are better than two."

Wively, though, grinned with unholy mirth. "You? Chaperone?"

Narrowing his eyes, Matt shot back. "I seem to remember you have a sister as well."

His friend lost his smile and closed his mouth. Good, Grace didn't need to know about Matt's peccadilloes. Particularily after what her aunt had most likely told her. And, after all, they were in the past.

Huntley gave a bark of laughter. "He's got you there, Will. When does she come out? Next year, isn't it?"

Wively emitted a sound that resembled a low snarl. "Yes. But it was not necessary for you to mention it."

Grinning, Matt turned back to Grace. "Shall we stroll, my love?"

Her eyes sparkled, and she inclined her head to his friends. "As you wish, my love."

As they started to leave, a lady in her late twenties strolled up to them. "Lady Grace, Lord Worthington, how good to see you here."

Grace stared for a moment, as if trying to place the woman, then smiled. "Lady Fairport. It's wonderful to see you again."

The Countess of Fairport was one of Phoebe's elder sisters.

"Is Fairport here?" Worthington asked.

"Yes, he'll be over in a moment. Phoebe asked us to look out for you, and we were happy to oblige." Her ladyship glanced at Grace. "I understand you are both interested in being more active in the party. We can always use a few more good political hostesses."

Grace nodded. "That is one of the things we wish to do. You know, of course, about the children. Still, we wish to be as active as we are able."

When Fairport joined them, Matt greeted him. Fairport's father had been one of his sponsors when he took his seat in the Lords.

Several moments later, Grace and Lady Fairport paused. Taking advantage in the break in their conversation Fairport bowed. "Lady Grace, I'm glad to see you back in Town."

"Thank you, my lord. May I say you haven't changed a bit? Neither of you have, my lady."

Fairport dipped his head slightly, and said in a low voice, "We're in for it now. Here comes Lady Bellamny."

Grace's arm tensed, and she glanced at Matt. "She will want all the details."

"We should have practiced our roles." He tried to make light of their pending doom. "Don't worry about a thing," he said with more bravado than he felt. "Agree with me, and we will carry it off."

"Gladly." Her eyes twinkled. "You are much more inventive than I."

"Charm, my love, I plan to charm her." Matt gave the old dragon his most elegant bow. "My lady, how nice to see you."

Lady Bellamny fixed her sharp, basilisk gaze on him. "Don't try to flummery me, Worthington. I've known you since you were in leading strings. You have no wish at all to see me. Am I to take it the rumors are true?"

"To which rumors are you referring, my lady?" he said with what he thought was sufficient sangfroid

Her cane struck the floor, missing his foot by a hair. "Are you or are you not betrothed?"

Lips twitching, he attempted to keep a broad smile from his face. "Yes. We are."

"Good." She turned to Grace. "I never did like the decision you made to remain single. Your mother wouldn't have wanted it. When is the wedding?"

Before Grace could say a word, he answered, "Tuesday."

Lady Bellamny's chins jiggled as she chuckled. "Giving her no chance to get away I see. Well done, my boy. What are you doing about Lady Grace's brothers and sisters?"

"I am applying for guardianship." Conversing with Lady Bellamny was like being interrogated by Bow Street Runners.

Her shrewd eyes studied him for a moment. "Excellent. The children need a man, and so do you, my dear."

Grace blushed deeply, and he wondered if she was thinking about this afternoon.

Smiling kindly, Lady Bellamny patted Grace's arm.

"You'll find out what I'm talking about soon enough. Now what story am I to put around?"

Grace cleared her throat, her voice a bit timorous. "I developed a tendre for him in my first Season . . . and now that we've found each other again, we see no reason to wait."

"That will work." Lady Bellamny nodded approvingly. "Anyone who counts knows Vivers men fall hard and fast. I shall do my part. I wish you happy. You have both made a very good match."

Grace curtseyed and Worthington bowed, as Lady Bellamny sailed off.

Lady Fairport covered her face with her fan and giggled. "She is the most embarrassing lady I know."

Unfurling her fan as well, Grace applied it to her face. "But she's well-meaning, and if anyone can scotch rumors we don't want, it will be her."

Fairport gave a low chuckle. "Indeed. No one has the nerve to gainsay her. I think your story is in good hands."

Matt covered Grace's hand with his. "Are you all right?"

She lowered her fan. Her eyes danced with merriment. "I don't know what to think about her comment that I needed a man."

Bending his head, he murmured in her ear, "I know what she meant."

He couldn't help smiling smugly when she blushed again.

They stayed through supper, then found Lady St. Eth and bid her a good evening.

"We had a wonderful time, my lady."

"We did, indeed," Grace said, as Lady St. Eth embraced her.

"If I can be of help"—she gave Grace a speaking look—"please send word, my dear. Your mother was a good friend of mine, as well as Worthington's. Don't hesitate to ask."

"We won't, thank you," Grace responded gratefully.

There scheme was going much better than he'd expected. Having Lady Bellamny on their side was a boon.

Several hours later, Matt helped Grace into the carriage. "Nary a hint of scandal. Does that make you feel better?"

"Yes." Grace gave him a half-smile. "I have to admit I was a bit nervous. Especially when your two friends questioned you about the timing."

He gave the signal to go, and the coach moved forward. Matt lost no time getting her back into his arms. "I promise. Nothing will hurt you."

For a few moments, Grace seemed preoccupied with smoothing her skirts, then she glanced up. "I know you would never do anything to purposely hurt me."

They were back to that. He wished she'd tell him what her aunt said so he could address her fears. All he could do was show her. He kissed her fully, trying to make Grace understand how precious she was to him.

Royston opened the door as they ascended the steps. "My lady, my lord, Lady Worthington, Ladies Charlotte and Louisa, and Lord and Lady Herndon are in the drawing room. Tea was just now served. Miss Carpenter asked me to tell you not to wait up for her."

"I wonder where Jane could have gone?" Grace handed her cloak to Royston.

"Probably visiting friends," Matt said.

A footman took his hat.

They entered the drawing room, eager to discover how the entertainment had gone for the girls.

Patience handed Grace a cup. "How was your evening?"

"It went well." Grace glanced around the room. "How was yours?"

Her aunt smiled broadly. "I haven't had so much fun in years. Charlotte and Louisa were, without a doubt, the loveliest young ladies present. I predict we will have gentlemen calling and leaving their cards by the dozens."

"I had several matrons ask me about your romance," Patience said in an excited tone. "Naturally, I told them I was vastly pleased that the two of you had found each other again, and that the wedding would be very small because of your duties to your sisters and the rest of the children."

Lord Herndon addressed Worthington. "One of the law lords was in the card room. He recommended you file before Good Friday. You'll need two witnesses to your betrothal. I shall be one."

Worthington nodded. "Thank you, sir."

"It was my pleasure. Take the children around this week. Not for the court but for the *ton*."

Furrowing his brow in thought, Worthington said, "Indeed. Perhaps a visit to the museum for Louisa and Charlotte and Gunter's for the younger ones."

"But Matt," Louisa objected, "Charlotte and I want to go to Gunter's as well."

Grace took his hand. "What about a trip to Richmond and a picnic? That would be the perfect outing for my landau."

He'd heard about her carriage, but couldn't understand why a younger lady would want one. "Why did you buy a landau?"

"I decided I needed one when Phoebe took us to the carriage maker's. There was one there I almost bought, but on further reflection, I had mine built so that it will hold all the children at one time." Grace raised her chin. "I realize they are thought to be for older ladies, but mine is very stylish, I assure you, and I am quite tired of everyone making fun of it."

"Well"—he grinned—"your stylish landau will have to have my crest put on it. Which reminds me, Lord Herndon, may we complete the settlements to-morrow or the next day?"

"Yes, yes, indeed. I received all your information and have a proposal ready. Grace?"

"Yes, Uncle?"

"Come around in the morning after breakfast, and I'll go over them with you." He smiled, taking a sip of wine.

"I cannot. I have a meeting with the architect for the re-modeling that must be done at Worthington House first thing. May I come after that?"

Matt had been paying only half an ear to the conversation as he sipped his brandy, but mention of remodeling caused him to sputter. "Architect?"

His betrothed opened her eyes wide. "Why yes, you told me to do as I wished. Don't you remember? It was when I tried to show you the plans."

It was when he'd been attempting to get her into his bed. Yet he had no intention of getting on her bad side now. "Of course, I remember. Do you mind if I join you?"

Her smile dazzled him, and he wanted to see it more often. "I would love for you to join us."

"Worthington," Patience asked. "Have you sent the an-nouncement to the *Post?*"

"No, I saw no reason to send a betrothal announcement this week and a wedding announcement next week."

"I agree, my love." Grace took his hand. "Everyone who is in Town already knows and the rest will learn of our marriage later."

He glanced at their sisters. Louisa and Charlotte were trying their best not to yawn. Both girls needed to retire. "Patience, why don't you take Louisa home, she's not yet used to Town hours."

Charlotte stood, kissed her aunt and uncle, then em-braced Patience and Louisa. "I think I'll go to bed as well. Aunt Almeria and Uncle Bertrand, thank you. I had a won-derful time."

Patience held her hand out to the Herndons. "Good night, my lord, my lady. Grace, do you mind if I take Char-lotte with us shopping to-morrow?"

"Of course not." Grace bussed Patience's cheek. "Shall I see you at breakfast?"

Patience grinned wryly. "If we are not too much trouble?"

"None at all. Good night."

"We shall go as well, my dear." Aunt Almeria rose. "It has been a very entertaining evening. I hope one day to come to one of your breakfasts."

Uncle Bertrand took her arm. "Then, my dear, you will have to arise far earlier than you usually do."

She rapped him with her fan. "Worthington, Grace, I wish you a pleasant evening."

After the Herndon coach left, Matt turned to her. "I should go as well. Will you show me the plans at breakfast?"

"Come a bit before. If I take them out with the children around, everyone will want a say."

He glanced around the hall and outside the still open door. Royston was busying himself with the coat wardrobe, and the street was empty.

Matt took her in his arms. "Very true. I'll come early." Her face was tilted up, and her lips were too tempting to be ignored. He kissed her. "Good night, my love."

"Good night, my darling."

"How did you like my friends?" Hector had finagled his good friends, the Robinsons, whom he'd met in India, into hosting a small dinner party for the sole purpose of having some reason to be with Jane. They were now ambling the few blocks from Hill Street to Berkeley Square. He sent up thanks to the deity that the weather had remained dry.

"I enjoyed it immensely." Jane's face glowed with pleasure as they passed under one of the gas lamps lighting the streets. "It has been so long since I've been able to discuss such a wide range of subjects. Grace, of course, is knowledgeable, but, what with the estate and the children, she is usually too exhausted by the end of the day to take pleasure in intense conversation. Are many of your friends in Town?"

"Not only in London, but in other areas of the country as well, Bristol, and Edinburgh mostly." Though the question was not where his friends were, but where Jane would like to live. He'd waited over twenty years to see her again. This time he wouldn't let go.

Her voice was quiet when she asked, "Have you given any thought as to what you would like to do now that you have returned home?"

That put him in a pickle. "I'm still considering my options. Much shall depend on a certain lady."

Her pace slowed. "Will it?"

"Why don't you tell me what you would like."

Her tone grew wistful. "If this war would ever end, I would love to travel."

"I wouldn't mind a few journeys to civilized places, but if you want to go to the Levant or anywhere like that, I'd be forced to object."

"Oh, no." Her laugh reminded him of the tinkling of silver bells. "I have no desire to travel the wilds."

That was a relief. After so many years in India, he didn't want to peregrinate too far from home. "Where would you wish to live?"

"I think," she said slowly, "that would depend upon my husband's and my combined fortunes."

If she thought he'd allow her to spend her funds on their living expenses, she was out. Perhaps now was the time to tell her he was a nabob. Though the Jane he'd known had valued honesty and caring over wealth. If she hadn't, she would have married long ago. Yet how to approach the topic? He couldn't very well blurt out that he could give Golden Ball a few thousand. "I don't think a house in Town and a snug property in the country would be out of the question."

"That sounds . . . like a lovely dream. Perhaps a better idea would be to rent a house during the Season."

He must tell her soon, but not on a public street. Mayhap it would be better to show her. "I'm currently residing at the Pulteney and am growing tired of not having my own place. I've made arrangements to view a couple of properties on the morrow. I'd be honored if you would give me your opinion."

By this time, they'd reached Berkeley Square, and Jane had come to a halt in front of a large town house. The door opened. A tall man dressed in black waited patiently. Hector slid around so that he stood in front of Jane, between her and the door.

"Will you come with me?"

She glanced up a bit shyly. "Yes, it sounds quite enjoyable."

Taking her hand, he raised it to his lips. "I shall fetch you at ten o'clock, if that is not too early."

"Ten o'clock is perfect."

Hector waited until she was in the house and the door had closed. He looked forward to to-morrow when he'd finally have some time alone with her. Now he just needed to find some entertainment for them to attend in the evening. Courting Jane now seemed to require much more thought and planning than it had when they were younger.

Chapter Twenty-One

Mr. Edgar Molton presented himself at the office of Chiswick and Chiswick, Solicitors, shortly after nine o'clock. A clerk took his coat, hat, and cane, then showed him to a room with a long table. He glanced around. The offices consisted of a small reception area and a corridor with at least three doors. All of them closed. He should have made Chiswick wait on him. The problem was that Edgar hadn't wanted the man to see where he was living. That would change shortly.

The clerk led him to a room lined with books and two small windows.

"If you'll wait here, sir, I'll see if Mr. Chiswick is available."

The young man left, leaving Edgar to wait without even an offer of tea. He drummed his fingers on the highly polished mahogany table. If this was the way they planned to treat him, he'd certainly change solicitors. He was a wealthy man now, and had no reason to tolerate such Turkish treatment.

It'd been almost a year since his father had died. Of course, the old man had one foot in the grave for years. It took almost three months for him to return after he'd sold everything he owned in the West Indies. What a relief to be back in England. Finally, he was a gentleman of substance.

The door opened without even a knock warning him. That settled the matter. Chiswick and Chiswick would receive no more of his business.

"Mr. Edgar Molton?" a well-dressed man asked with a confused expression.

He didn't offer his hand, but raised a haughty brow. "Mr. Chiswick, I presume. Shall we get this over with?"

Chiswick hurried forward and offered Edgar a seat. "Yes, of course, I have the documents for your signature right here. I am sorry to have kept you waiting. It's been several months, and I was unaware you would visit us to-day."

"Your letter took some time to reach me, and I had to wrap up my affairs in the West Indies before departing for England."

The lawyer positioned the documents, just so, on the table, and the clerk came in with an inkstand and pen. Once everything was in order, Chiswick glanced up, adjusting his spectacles. "Indeed. I am a little surprised you made the trip. We would have been happy to have organized the banking arrangements."

Edgar frowned. The man was an idiot. Why his father had kept the firm on, he didn't understand. "I do not know how you would expect me to manage the estate from the West Indies."

"Estate?" The lawyer's mouth dropped open for a moment. "Dear me. This is not good at all. It appears, sir, you did not receive my first letter to you. Allow me a few moments. I shall return immediately." Mr. Chiswick left the room. The clerk brought in a cup of tea and a plate of biscuits. A few minutes later, Chiswick returned. "This is a copy of your late father's will. You are aware that none of the estate was entailed?"

Edgar shoved back the sinking feeling in the pit of his

stomach. "Yes, of course, but I am the last male child. My father was a wealthy man."

"Yes, yes, he was." The lawyer adjusted his spectacles again. "However, he divided his property among his heirs. Your share is an allowance of one thousand pounds per annum."

"*One thousand pounds?*" There must be some mistake. "How the devil am I supposed to live on that? What happened to the rest of it?"

Chiswick motioned to the document on the table. "If you would like to read the will?"

Edgar seized the papers. His hand trembled as he perused the document. He'd received nothing under the will except for the income from certain investments, and he was not allowed to touch the principal. If he died without issue, the income would go back into the estate to be reallotted equally. The rest of the old man's estate was divided evenly among his other heirs. His sisters and their brats got everything. To be fair, that wasn't precisely true. His dead sister's oldest daughter was to receive an income of ten thousand pounds per year to be kept in a trust for her until she married or turned thirty as long as she kept the children together.

Edgar tried to keep a scowl from his face. Leave it to that damned old man to make his life as miserable as he could. He'd thought to have received most of the estate and had been living on the expectancy for months. His debts were mounting, and now, he had almost nothing. He had to find a way to get his hands on some of that money.

Chiswick's voice cut into his musings. "Mr. Molton, you have the quarterly income for the past nine months due you, and the next quarter day is coming up soon. If you would like, I shall arrange to have it transferred to your account as well as make the arrangements for the quarterly transfers."

At least he'd be able to meet his more pressing obligations.

"I'll need some flimsies now. You may open me an account at Hoare's. I take it the family still banks there?"

"Yes, sir, they do."

"Good. I'll send my direction." He turned to leave and waited for Mr. Chiswick to open the door. Edgar may not have any money, but he'd be damned if he let that black box treat him like he was nobody.

Mr. Chiswick opened the door then disappeared down the corridor. Edgar donned his hat. He was pleased to see the roll of soft in Chiswick's hands when he returned.

"Here you are, Mr. Molton. This money represents the amount due you for the past three quarters."

Edgar took the money and his coat and cane, then left. *One thousand pounds a year.* What the hell happened to the town house on Half-Moon Street? The thought of asking his sister to advance him some funds briefly crossed his mind, but that miser of a husband she married would queer him. Maybe he could gammon his niece, Grace. She wasn't married. Poor girl, she'd probably be happy to have her uncle help her with all the brats. Better check out the lay of the land first. He hadn't seen the girl since she was a child. She might be as much of a bitch as her mother had been.

He was on his way back to the small room he'd taken at a boardinghouse when he felt a tug at the pocket of his greatcoat.

Grabbing a small hand, he looked down to see a small boy dressed in a dirty shirt and breeches. "What do you think you're doing?"

The lad flushed and tried to pull out of his grip. "I didn't mean nothin', sir. An accident it t'were."

"An accident, eh?"

"Yes, sir." The lad nodded several times.

Molton would bet this boy would do a lot for the little bit he'd pay him. "How'd you like to earn a yellow George instead of stealing it?"

"Wha'd I'd haveta do?" the lad asked suspiciously.

"Just go watch a house. Come tell me who comes and goes."

His eyes narrowed. "Fer how long?"

Rubbing his chin, Molton responded. "Maybe just today. Maybe longer. Depends what you see."

The urchin held out his hand. "I wants the half bean now."

"Very well." Edgar held out a half guinea. "Here you go. Find Stanwood House in Berkeley Square, Mayfair. Come back here in the morning. What's your name?"

"Jem. I'll do jus that, gov." He took off running down the street.

Molton went in the house and climbed the two sets of stairs to his room. His luck was in. He knew it. He'd be living in better quarters soon.

Early the next morning, Matt left his home and crossed the square to Stanwood House. As he opened the door to Grace's study, she was bent over her desk giving him an excellent view of her enticing derrière. "Good morning."

She glanced over her shoulder, smiling beautifully. "Good morning to you. Come look at this." Grace adjusted her position, making room for him. "These are the plans . . ."

He couldn't manage to drag his gaze from her lush bottom. His breathing quickened as he imagined her skirts up and her bare to him. He ambled up behind her, keeping his voice low. "I'd rather look at something else."

Matt pressed against her firm buttocks. Holding her to him with one hand, he ran the other over her breasts and down between her legs. Her breath hitched and her skin flushed. *Halfway there.* Leaning over her, he traced the outer whirl of her delicate ear with the tip of his tongue.

She sighed, and her voice was sultry. "We must review the plans."

"Grace, please?" He pleaded, inching up her skirts. He caressed her inner thigh. Her legs trembled as his hand dipped into her curls.

A moan escaped her. "We—we don't have much time."

"We won't need much time." He slid two fingers into her hot, wet sheath. "You're ready." He smiled smugly to himself.

"Oh God, when am I not?" Grace's head dropped onto her arms.

Worthington chuckled and reached for the buttons on his fall. "That is one of the many things I love about you."

There was a gasp from outside. He turned toward the sound and saw what looked like a child run from the window. It damn well better not be one of theirs. Why in the name of God hadn't he thought of that before? "Stay here."

Bursting out the door to the garden, he rounded the corner of the house, just in time to see a small boy squeeze through the iron rail of the fence and into the street. "What the devil was that about?"

Grace ran out behind him. "Who was it?"

"I don't know. Some urchin. From the way he was dressed, he doesn't live in Mayfair."

"Matt, do you think someone is watching us?"

He drew his brows together. "I don't know what to think. Don't worry." Taking in her stricken countenance, he put his arm around her shoulders and led her back into the house. "Come show me the plans."

He couldn't think of anyone who'd be spying on them. Herndon said her relatives were relieved and happy about the marriage. Grace's other uncle was out of the country. Still, any further lovemaking would have to be confined to his bed. At least until they were married. Better to be safe than sorry.

A few minutes later, Matt was reviewing the architect's drawing for the renovations she'd done to Stanwood House.

Impressive indeed. Grace had thought of everything. "They're extensive."

"What I like is that they serve the purpose so well."

"May I see the rooms?"

"Naturally. Come with me."

They climbed the stairs to the school-room floor. The children bid him good morning. Despite the number of them—his younger sisters were there as well—everything was orderly. The common areas were large and well lit by sun streaming through floor-to-ceiling windows on the eastern side of the house. As he strolled around, he noticed that the window placements ensured the rooms would remain lighted until the sun set. It had an airy feeling he'd not experienced at either Worthington Hall or across the street. "This is nothing like what I expected."

Grace smiled proudly. "Do you like it? The children and their tutors find the area suits them."

"I think it's remarkable. Nothing like the dingy school-room I was used to and the bedchambers are larger. What's in here?"

"That is the art room. Next to it is a space for sewing, games, and reading." She took his hand. "At the end of the corridor on either side are the tutors' rooms. They each have a bedchamber, a small dressing area, and a parlor. There are two bathing chambers as well."

He peeped into the tiled rooms with copper tubs. "Remarkable. Is this what you have planned for Worthington House?"

"Something very like it. The school-room floor there is larger. What do you think?"

"It's perfect. How long will it take to accomplish the renovations?"

"We will have to discuss it with Mr. Rollins." She glanced at him and wrinkled her nose. "This took the last part of summer and all autumn. I don't believe the renovations can be completed this Season."

Clearly, she was in her milieu. He turned her toward the stairs. "What's your plan for where we would live?"

As they descended, Grace replied, "I thought we could reside here at Stanwood House for this Season. There is enough room for everyone. Of course, Patience would have to agree. Yet, if we began the work at Worthington House immediately, it could be completed in time for the Little Season." She glanced at him with concern. "You don't mind having the children with us when we are in London, do you?"

Matt came to a halt. Many people did leave their children in the country for the Little Season and sometimes during the primary Season. But the idea that they'd leave their bunch alone with only the servants and tutors filled him with foreboding. "No, I don't think I'd sleep a wink if we didn't have them with us."

Grace's laughter was musical. The only problem with her scheme was he didn't like the idea that she would not be in his home and in his bed. "Where would we sleep?"

She worried her bottom lip as she thought. "In my chambers?"

Wondering how long her bed was, he glanced at her skeptically. "Let's see it then."

Grace led him along a corridor and stopped at a room at the end. "Here it is." She opened a door to her parlor and kept on through a dressing room until they entered her bed-chamber.

There was little chance he'd fit the bed, but to be fair, he'd give it a try. "May I?"

She glanced at him and then at the bed, and gave him a dubious look. "Yes."

When he lay on it his feet hung over.

"Oh dear."

"My lady . . ." Bolton entered from the dressing room, stopped and stared at him. "That's not going to work, is it?"

Worthington smiled ruefully. "No."

Grace rubbed her forehead. "Perhaps we could have a larger bed made."

"It would be so long you wouldn't be able to walk around the bed." Bolton frowned. "My lady, why do you want to stay here?"

"We're renovating the school-room, and redecorating some of the other rooms at Worthington House. We can't live there while all that is going on. I thought it would be better if our brothers and sisters resided here until the other house can accommodate them."

Wrinkling her brow in thought, Bolton nodded. "I understand you not wanting to live across the street with all the racket, but you and his lordship could sleep there."

He bestowed his best smile on her. What a wonderful woman his affianced wife had for a maid. "Bolton, that's a wonderful idea."

Frowning, Grace glanced at her maid. "But what if one of the children falls ill or has nightmares?"

"My lady, you could be fetched immediately if you're needed."

Worthington sent up a silent prayer to stay on Bolton's good side.

Rubbing the bridge of her nose, Grace finally said, "Yes, I suppose it could work."

He'd been sitting on the edge of the bed and went to her. "If it does not, my love, we'll find a way to stay here."

Grace's eyes were soft as she gazed at him. "Very well. We shall try it."

Bolton disappeared back into the dressing room, and he took Grace in his arms. "We *will* make it work. Even if I have to have a bell-pull installed at the door so that Thorton can be awakened in the middle of the night."

Her eyes danced with merriment. "Poor Thorton."

Matt's stomach growled. "We must have our breakfast if we're not to be late for the meeting with Mr. Rollins."

They'd almost finished eating when Patience and Louisa entered the breakfast room.

His stepmother looked as if she was expecting bad news. "Well, how were they?"

"They were fine," Grace said reassuringly. "Everyone settled in, and we had no trouble at all. Not even any bad dreams. The children should be down soon. Louisa, why don't you go up and see what's keeping Charlotte?"

After Louisa left, Patience let out a sigh of relief. "I cannot express how pleased I am. The only thing concerning me about the wedding was the children. But it seems they have taken it upon themselves to behave."

Grace glanced at her with raised brows. "It has all been remarkably trouble-free. Almost too easy."

He covered her hand with his. "Let's not go looking for trouble."

"No, you're absolutely correct." She poured Patience a cup of tea. "I'll enjoy it while it lasts."

The sound of stampeding elephants echoed from the stairs. And he'd thought his sisters were loud. "I believe they'll be here shortly."

He wondered what Grace had done to keep the ceilings from seeming as if they were falling in.

"My lord," Royston said from the door. "A message has come that Mr. Rollins has arrived at Worthington House."

"Thank you, Royston. I'll go immediately."

Matt rose, kissed Grace on her cheek, and braced himself for the comments that usually accompanied his displays of his affection for her, but no one said a word, though Philip shuddered and Madeline sighed. "You finish eating, my love. I'll take him up. Do you want me to take the plans for this house with me?"

"No, it's not necessary. Tell him I want essentially the same design. I have made some other notes as well." She pulled several sheets of paper from her pocket. "Here, take these. I'll be over shortly."

Matt took her scribblings and left. It might behoove him to look at all the changes Grace was proposing to his house.

Chapter Twenty-Two

"Grace, what are you and Matt doing?" Augusta asked.

"We are remodeling Worthington House so that the school-room floor will be almost the same as the one here."

Alice and Eleanor glanced at each other. "But we all decided to live here."

Looking around the table, all eyes were on her. "We shall for this Season. The next time we come to Town, we'll live at Worthington House. By the time everything is ready, I promise you will like it."

Patience pulled a face. "I'm afraid it will take a great deal to accomplish."

It certainly would. Yet Grace wouldn't blame Patience, who'd never been encouraged to do anything with the house. "I agree." The children still appeared skeptical. "How would you like to have a hand in decorating your chambers?"

"Can my room be pink?" Mary asked.

"It can be any color you wish, sweetie."

Her announcement was the impetus for a great deal of talk among the girls.

Patience grinned and said, "Grace, if you want to join Worthington and the architect, I shall watch the children."

She looked at her empty plate and debated eating another helping. For some reason, she'd been so hungry lately. "I'll leave in a few minutes. I want Matt to meet with the architect alone first. It is his house after all, and he must be comfortable with Rollins."

"Grace?" Louisa asked. "How is this all going to work?"

Patience glanced up. "I'd be interested to know that as well."

"Some of the younger girls will have to share their bed-chambers. Louisa will take the chamber next to Charlotte's, and Matt and I will sleep across the street. Patience, you may live or sleep where you choose. Although I must warn you, there will be a great deal of noise and dust during the day at Worthington House."

Jane, who had joined them a few moments before, turned to Patience. "When we visited in early November, there was so such a din, one could not hear oneself think. Not to mention the dirt and workmen trailing in and out of the house."

Patience played with the fringe of her shawl. "Do you have a place for me?"

Although Grace always knew her soon-to-be stepmother-in-law would be affected by the marriage and changes to the family, she hadn't appreciated how displaced the other woman might feel. "We have a very nice apartment that I think would suit you. Jane, would you please show Lady Worthington the Yellow Chambers when you've finished?"

"I'd be happy to."

Grace took her last sip of tea and rose. "I shall see you later."

A few minutes later, Thorton opened the door and bowed to her. "They are in the school-room, my lady."

"Thank you, Thorton. Please tell Mrs. Thorton I'd like to have the list of fabrics we shall need, if it's ready."

"Yes, my lady."

As Grace entered the main room where she found Matt

and Mr. Rollins in close conversation. "Mr. Rollins, how nice to see you again."

Both men rose. Rollins bowed. "My lady. Thank you for thinking of me."

She sat at a low chair next to the table with the plans. "Will you be able to do something similar here to what you did at Stanwood House?"

"Yes, indeed. I've just been going over the plans with his lordship. May I also wish you very happy?"

Despite having been congratulated, told it was a good match, and happy wishes before a contented, joyful feeling filled her. As if she was able to believe it for the first time. "Thank you. I believe we shall be." She met Matt's eyes. There was so much love in them her heart beat faster. Perhaps her aunt had been wrong. Maybe this could work after all.

"My love?" Matt asked.

"I'm sorry." She took out her pocketbook as if she'd been attending to their conversation. "Were you saying something?"

His eyes danced with mirth. "I was saying that, after we've finished this floor, I'd like Mr. Rollins to make some other renovations. Such as a proper bathing chamber for us."

"What a lovely idea. I would like that immensely."

Rollins's lips twitched. "My lord, my lady, I'd like to stay here and take measurements. I'll have a complete diagram for you after the holiday."

Matt shook his hand. "Thank you, Rollins. I look forward to receiving them. My lady, shall we go?"

She took the hand he offered and rose. "Before I forget, I must visit the fabric warehouse to-day. Would you like to come with me?"

"I'd like nothing more," he said, as if they were going on a picnic and it would be a great lark.

Narrowing her eyes, Grace asked, "Have you ever visited a fabric warehouse?"

"No." He smiled broadly. "Though I anticipate an enlivening time."

He would be the first gentleman she'd heard about who thought so. "We shall see. Since you'll be with me, I'd also like to go to one of the furniture warehouses. Unless you like the Egyptian motif?"

His brows snapped together. "Are you telling me we have that horrible stuff here? Where is it?"

"In two of the major reception rooms." She closed her eyes for a moment. How could he . . . ? "Worthington, you followed Mrs. Thorton and me around them. How did you not notice?"

His eyes slowly pursued her from her head down over her breasts to her toes. "I was focused on something else."

Grace's cheeks grew warm, and her pulse beat faster. Drat him for always having this effect on her. "I see." Tamping down her desire, she quickly changed the subject. "Once the renovations are completed, and we are here for the Little Season, we shall need additional footmen and maids."

His gaze was still on her. "I'll let Thorton know."

"I thought we could keep on the ones I hired for the Season." She tried to ignore Matt as his eyes sparkled wickedly, and her body responded. Maybe if she kept talking . . . "Matt, did I tell you that Charlie will be home to-morrow? I plan to allow the children a holiday while he's here. I shall tell Miss Tallerton and Mr. Winters they may either stay and enjoy London or return home for the week." Despite her attempt to ignore him, her gaze dropped to his lips. Really, he was being impossible. They would never accomplish all their tasks if he had his way. "We must go if we are to meet my uncle after luncheon."

He opened a door and before she knew where they were,

he'd dragged her into his arms, and his lips urged hers to open. Fire rose as he caressed her, exploring her mouth. Throbbing started between her legs. "Matt, my love . . ."

"I've barely been able to think of anything but you since I awoke this morning. I need you so much, Grace."

How could any female not respond to that? "We cannot take long."

Glancing around the room, he waltzed her around until her back hit the wall.

He lifted her. "Wrap your legs around me, and hold on."

"Matt, don't crush my skirt. Bolton complained the last time."

"I won't." His ragged breath tickled her ear, adding to the sensations of his one hand. "I need to remain on Bolton's good side."

He rubbed that place that made her crave him and placed two fingers in her, stroking her. Sparks leapt deep within her and her breath was every bit as ragged as his.

"Please, now." She tried to stifle her cry of pleasure as he plunged into her. Sparks ignited into flames and the sun burst over her as her legs trembled, and she called his name.

He kept her from falling and thrust twice more. "Oh, Grace, my only love."

The warmth of his seed spread within her, and she missed him as he withdrew from her. If this loving could only continue, she'd be the happiest woman in England and Europe.

He slowly lowered her feet to the floor, while holding her so tightly, his chest pounded against hers.

He kissed her slowly and thoroughly as his hands stroked her back. "Are you sure you want to go shopping?"

The man was wicked. Gazing up at him, she lifted her hand to his cheek, returning his kisses more deeply, before murmuring, "I am *not* going to live with the Egyptian motif."

He groaned and lifted his head. "I suppose you're right."

Matt had called for his curricle to be readied, but when they walked out, a small town coach stood waiting. He glanced at his coachman and frowned. "What happened to the carriage?"

His coachman cast a gimlet eye at the sky and sniffed. "It's comin' on rain, my lord. You wouldn't want her ladyship to get wet."

A footman let down the stairs. Matt handed her into the coach and climbed in closing the door.

Grace tilted her head to gaze up at the sky through the window. "It doesn't look like rain."

He settled next to her. "If Tim Coachman says it's going to rain, it will. I've never known him to be wrong."

Matt was so large that he took up most of the seat. Giving up the battle to keep her distance, she settled against his shoulder. "It's no matter. I shall be able to bring back more packages in this."

Dislodging her, he frowned. "How much is this going to cost me?"

If she had known he was going to be such a problem, she would never have asked him to join her. Then again, they must learn to work together. She could not be expected to have his approval each time she purchased something for their home. "I have no idea." Grace patted his knee. "If you are short of funds, I shall make you a loan. Nevertheless, I will expect you to repay me on quarter day."

"Minx."

Jane stole surreptitious glances out the window of the pretty first-floor apartment she was showing Lady Worthington. Goodness, it was almost time for Hector to arrive. Nevertheless, when Patience had asked, Jane couldn't very well have refused to show Patience the rest of the house. A smart curricle pulled up in front of the house. "Patience, do you mind if I leave you? I have some other things I must attend to."

"Not at all, my dear. Please do not let me keep you from your duties."

Jane darted to her bedchamber, opening the door so quickly it bounced off the wall. "My straw bonnet with the green ribbons."

Her maid, Dorcus, rushed into and out of the dressing room, holding the hat. "What's got you in such a thither?"

"Mr. Addison is here. We are going for a carriage ride." That Jane was going to look at houses with Hector, she kept close to her chest. They had come so close to marrying the last time he courted her, she did not want to raise anyone's hopes. Especially hers. Although, that might be a lost cause.

Her maid placed the hat on Jane's head. "Don't let him get away this time."

She didn't *exactly* let him get away the last time. If only they had both had more gumption, when her father refused his suit and his father sent him to work for an uncle in India. Now, she had no one to please but herself. "We shall see."

Just as she reached the hall, the door opened. Before he could even ask for her, she sailed forward, took his arm, and led him down the steps.

"Is there a reason you do not want me in the house?" His tone was slightly aggrieved as he helped her into the carriage.

"It is nothing at all like that." Jane settled her skirts. "Until we . . ." How was she to explain this? "Do you have any idea what it is like living in a house with ten curious children?"

He gave the horses their office. "I can't say that I do, but trying to imagine it gives me a fright."

She slid a sidelong glance at him. The corner of his lips quivered as if he were ready to burst into laughter at any moment. "As it should. It is a wonder anyone can have a private thought."

"You care for them a great deal."

The tension of rushing out of the house before anyone saw her began to drain. "I do. I feel as if they are my own nieces and nephews."

He steered the curricle in a northerly direction, turning right around the square and onto Bruton Place. The carriage stopped before an elegant three-story white stone town house on the corner of Bruton and Barlow Place. Two bow windows flanked the front door.

"Here we are."

Poor Hector, he had been gone so long he probably didn't realize how dear the house would come. "It is lovely."

"That was my exact thought when I rode by it yesterday. You must be honest with me as to whether or not you like it."

How could she not? Still, it would hurt his pride if she adored the residence and he could not afford it. Mayhap the better idea would be to find fault. Jane held her tongue as they entered the hall, which was tiled pink marble; the columns and the wide, curved staircase were of the same material. Before she could stop herself, she'd exclaimed, "How beautiful!"

With his hands behind his back, Hector looked like the cat who'd eaten the canary. "I thought you might like it. When the fellow described it to me, I thought it would bring out your complexion."

"Bring out my . . ." Whatever was he thinking?

"Yes, it reminds me of the inside of a large shell I once saw." He twined his arm in hers. "Let's look at the rest of it."

Try as she might, from the well-appointed rooms, to the modernized kitchen, Jane could not find a thing wrong.

It even had a huge ballroom. He led her out the French windows to the walled garden. As they snoodled along a path, she fell in love with the property. Yet he was making a mistake, and she must say something. "What would you do with such a large house?"

"Live in it."

"But, Hector . . ."

He led her to a stone bench. Once she was seated, he sank to one knee. "I should probably wait longer, but I feel as if I—we have lost so much time already. Jane Carpenter, would you do me the great honor of being my wife."

Dorcus's words echoed in Jane's mind. Love and consternation showed in Hector's lovely blue eyes. "Yes. Yes, I will be your wife."

As he had once before, he touched his lips gently to hers. "You've made me the happiest of men."

His forehead was against hers when she said, "This house is wonderful, but maybe a bit . . ." Even now, she couldn't say it.

"Pricey?" He grinned.

A little gumption was what was needed. "Well, yes. To put it bluntly."

"My love." He pressed his lips to her forehead. "First, I will tell you that I will not allow you to cry off."

"Of course, I will not." She didn't understand. Why would she?

"I did well for myself in India. In addition to that, my uncle left me his fortune. We can not only afford to buy this house, but as many country properties as you wish."

She couldn't breathe. "Just how rich are you?"

"Let's just say, I am one of the wealthiest men in England."

That was horrible! Her heart dropped to her toes. "How can you wish to marry an old spinster like me? You must know that you could have almost any lady you wished. One who could give you children."

"Remember your promise. I told you the truth when I said I'd never found the equal of you. If need be, I have plenty of nieces and nephews to leave my property to." He punctuated his statement with a kiss. "I love you, Jane."

Tears started in her eyes as her heart swelled to at least twice its size. "I love you, Hector. I always have."

Chapter Twenty-Three

The pounding on the door finally penetrated Edgar's foggy head.

"Sir, sir, you want me ta'tell you what I seen?" Jem's high, penetrating voice speared through Edgar's temples. Once he had the money, he'd find a better quality brandy.

He rubbed his eyes and pulled on his dressing gown before opening the door. "You're early." He waved the boy in and sat in a chair. "Go on."

"Last night there was a bunch of rum morts and swells. They had three rattlers. I waited like you told me and later, they all come back. One rattler stayed on the street like. Then there's an old mort and a swell left, and two morts went across the street with a fart catcher."

Molton shook his head trying to clear it and keep up with the cant. "What you're telling me is that there were two men and several women who went off in coaches. The older couple kept their coach waiting and two ladies with their footman walked across the street?"

"That's what I jus telled ye," Jem said, disgustedly. "Then the last rum mort holds up her neb and it was all honey-moon with them."

"The last lady let the gentleman kiss her?"

"Don't know why ye keep repeatin' everthin'."

Edgar scrubbed a hand over his face and wished he'd had a cup of coffee before listening to this. At least his head didn't ache as badly as he'd thought it would. "Then what happened?"

"The swell left and went across the street."

Molton leaned back and frowned. "I don't know how interesting that is."

Jem jigged before him. "But it ain't all. I finds me a place next to the house to sleep and this mornin' the same swell that smacked the rum mort last night, had her ready to shag her."

Molton bolted up. "What's that you say? They were going to copulate?"

Jem frowned. "Don't know what that means, but his hand was under her skirt and . . ."

"Yes, yes, good job. Here"—he tossed the coin to the boy—"you've earned your other half bean. Keep watching the house and there's more for you." Getting money from his niece, assuming it was her, and possibly her lover, was going to be easier than Edgar had thought.

Matt entered the warehouse, took out his quizzing glass, and surveyed the rows upon rows of fabric set on racks against the walls and laid out on tables. There was everything from silks and satins to brocades and velvets. This was not what he'd expected. "How on earth do you expect to find anything in here?"

Glancing up at him, Grace took his arm. "The clerks will help."

A short, slender man with spectacles appeared out of nowhere and gushed, "My lady, so good to see you again."

"Mr. Quimby, thank you." Grace smiled politely. "Here

is my list. You will see the colors and types of materials listed with the amounts."

Worthington stared at the sheets of paper she handed to the clerk. How much fabric were they buying? And how much was all this going to cost him? Not that he couldn't afford it. Had Grace ever practiced economy? He prayed that she was not like Patience, always having to be reined in.

"Is there anything wrong with the materials you bought last year?" Mr. Quimby asked, concerned.

"Not at all. They are all perfect. Lord Worthington and I are marrying. This purchase is for his town house."

The clerk bowed. "If I may wish you very happy, my lady, my lord?"

"Thank you, Mr. Quimby."

Worthington murmured his thanks as well. This may be very dull work, but it was good he'd come. They'd be here all day if he wasn't there to move Grace along.

Quimby bowed again. "If you would like to have a seat, my lord, my lady, I shall fetch some rolls for you to inspect."

Turning to follow him, Grace said, "Thank you. I'm sure Lord Worthington would like some coffee while we wait."

The man bowed again. The only person Worthington had ever met who bowed as much as Quimby was a Chinaman he'd once encountered. "Of course, my pleasure. Tea for you, my lady?"

"Yes, thank you." Grace inclined her head. He wondered if he should be worried that the clerk knew her so well. How much shopping did she do here?

After assisting his affianced wife to sit and taking a chair himself, Matt leaned close to her. "Come here quite a bit, do you?"

Grace lowered her lashes. "Well, it wouldn't do to allow him to forget me." Her gaze lifted innocently to his. "Did you think you were marrying a nip-farthing?"

Eyeing her suspiciously, he retorted, "I think you're making a game of me."

"Well, of course, I am." She grinned. "If you will act as if I'm spending your whole fortune on fabric. I shall tell you, my lord, that I know how to hold house and have been doing so for several years now."

"Very well then." He let out the breath he'd been holding. "Carry on."

More quickly than he expected, several rolls of material appeared on a long table.

Quimby motioned Matt and Grace over. "My lady, if you would care to take a look?"

Worthington followed Grace, viewing the selections over her shoulder.

Glancing back at him. "Do you see anything you particularly like?"

He hadn't expected to be asked for his opinion. Maybe this wouldn't be so bad after all. "Am I allowed to choose as well?"

Grace looked up at the ceiling for a moment. "Don't be a noddy. Of course you may."

He took out his quizzing glass and inspected the fabrics with more interest. "Well then, I like these two."

Her lips formed a very kissable pout as she thought. "For which rooms?"

"My study and the library."

"I think they are perfect." Her eyes flashed approvingly.

He didn't know if it was his relief at knowing he could trust her, or one of those feelings that came with being in love, but he wanted to puff his chest out. This shopping was going extraordinarily well. "How often do we need to do this?"

"Every few years." She turned from the fabrics to him. "Curtains especially need to be replaced when they fade or begin to look shabby. I like to have two sets for each room and change them in autumn and spring. It gives the house a fresh look and the material lasts longer."

He tried to envision it. Then a thought occurred that didn't please him. "How often do you change furniture?"

Grace laughed. "I don't like to rearrange the furniture at all, once I have organized the rooms as I like, that is." She tucked her hand in his. "We'll do it together."

He enjoyed that she touched him the way she did. From the first night at the inn, he'd known they were meant to be together. "If we're able, I'd like to take you to Worthington Hall for a few days to meet the servants and decide what you wish to do."

Grace steered them to another table. "That would be wonderful. It will also give me an opportunity to stop at Stanwood Hall and make sure things are as they ought to be."

When they'd finished their selections from one table, they were taken to the next. In a surprising amount of time, they were finished. "Do we have time to go to the furniture warehouse?"

Grace glanced at her pin watch. "It is half past eleven. We can at least make a start."

They spent longer looking at furniture than they did with the fabrics. Matt was happy to find his love liked the cleaner lines of Sheraton and Hepplewhite. Once again she surprised him by having a list of items they needed.

He gave her full rein picking out the chairs, sofas, and tables. He discovered he liked the lion paw feet that were popular, but when she chose a narrow daybed he overruled her. "Do you have anything a bit wider?"

The clerk bowed. "Yes, my lord. If you'll just come with me."

Obviously not thinking along his lines, Grace asked, "Why do you want a larger one? I'm not sure it will look right."

He leaned closer and murmured, "It will look perfect with you draped on it."

Grace blushed fierily and choked. "I suppose the reason you want it larger is so there is room for you as well?"

He stroked her back from neck to bottom, enjoying her response as she tried to maintain her countenance. Matt smiled wickedly and whispered in her ear, "How perfectly you know me."

At two o'clock, Matt knocked on the door of Herndon House where he and Grace were shown into Lord Herndon's study.

Grace's uncle rose and greeted them with a somber mien. "My dear Grace, Worthington. I have bad news I must share before we discuss the settlements." He handed her a letter.

Taking it, she perused the contents with a deepening frown. "Oh dear. This cannot be good."

Matt read over her shoulder.

Dear Lord Herndon,

I regret to inform you that Mr. Edgar Molton has arrived in England. He did not receive my letter to him telling him of the disposition of Lord Timothy's estate, and he was not at all pleased. I have agreed to set up a bank account for him. Though, as you are aware, I shall not represent him in any legal matter.

Yr Very Obedient Servant,
Jos Chiswick

The ne'er-do-well. Matt wished he knew more about this uncle.

"My dear," Uncle Herndon said as she raised her eyes

from the note, "do not allow him in your house at all. Once there, it will be almost impossible to get him out." He grimaced. "As I have reason to know."

Biting her lip, Grace responded, "I shall inform the staff."

Herndon frowned. "Do not even allow him into a parlor to wait for you. It's a terrible thing to say about your aunt's brother, but he's not to be trusted in any way."

Grace's teeth firmly gripped her bottom lip. "I understand. My mother warned me about him when it was rumored he was in England shortly after my father died. When he was young, he had stolen a locket she cherished a great deal from her to pay gambling debts."

"That was the least of his faults," her uncle said in a wintry tone. "He was into moneylenders and had taken advantage of more than one innocent."

Damn the blackguard. Matt wanted to hold Grace close to him. Molton's timing couldn't be worse, showing up now when he could do the most harm. Matt had been racking his brain trying to figure out why that lad had been watching them. Could the boy have something to do with her uncle showing up? If so, what was Molton up to? Matt didn't like it one bit, and the only way to protect Grace was to have her safely married to him. The question was, would either she or her uncle agree to move up the ceremony again?

He searched her face. "My love, it's just occurred to me he may be behind the lad we saw."

She rubbed her brow. "Why would my uncle have sent him?"

"Worthington is correct, my dear," Uncle Herndon said. "He could be planning to break in."

Matt could have kissed Herndon. Much better that she did not think he could be after the children. "It's a possibility we can't dismiss. You daren't trust him at all." He took her hands and glanced at Herndon. "Grace, my lord, how would you feel about bringing the wedding forward?"

Her startled eyes flew to him. "What can you be thinking? With Easter coming, the only possible day would be to-morrow!"

"Yes. If we can finish the settlements, my lord, then Grace and I can stop in at St. George's and make the arrangements."

Her uncle lowered his brows as he thought. "No need to talk to the rector. I'll send a note around. My wife isn't the only one to have contacts at St. George's. One of the clerics is a nephew of mine. Do you have the license?"

Matt thanked God that he'd had the foresight to procure it. "Yes."

Grace's troubled eyes flew to his. "What about Charlie? He's not due to come home until to-morrow."

Heedless of her uncle, he drew her into his arms. "We'll send for him this afternoon. I'm sure he won't mind leaving school a day early."

"But, who will stand up with me? Phoebe sent me a note saying she'd be out of Town for a few days."

"Chartier is not far. I'll send a rider this afternoon, if need be." He smoothed her brow with his thumb. Somehow, Matt would make this rushed wedding up to her.

Herndon set out the documents for the settlement on a small writing table.

Matt guided Grace to the chair in front of the desk. She picked up the papers and, after a few moments, glanced up. Her gaze focused on him. "Are you sure this is what you want?"

He'd spoken with Marcus and Rutherford about the settlements they'd arranged with their wives. Neither of them had an heir closer than a second cousin and expressed concern over the treatment of their wives if anything were to happen and both had a normal marital settlement. Matt didn't trust his heir to care for his wife either. The conceited popinjay would like nothing more than to treat her as a poor dependent. That sort of rubbishing treatment wasn't going to happen to Grace. Matt had decided upon allowing Grace to place all her property in trust for her benefit made the most sense. "It is."

Herndon spoke up. "Since you gave me power of attorney to act for you, I've already placed your property in trust, my dear."

Taking a breath, Grace dipped the pen in the standish and signed the agreements.

After Matt added his signature, his mood lightened. He'd be married to-morrow. Nothing was going to stand in his way.

Grace glanced up at him with an innocent demeanor. "Oh dear, if my landau remains my property, should I still have your crest put on it?"

Her uncle gave a shout of laughter. "I am happy to see you joking again, my love, but I wouldn't push your young gentleman too far."

Matt shook his head and grinned. He was just coming to appreciate his Grace's wicked sense of humor. "No, sir, she's made enough of a May game of me to-day. Come, my love."

"Grace," her uncle said, "who is standing up with you?"

She gave him a wry smile. "Lady Evesham, but I fear we must send for her."

Herndon put the settlement agreements in his drawer. "That is one problem I can relieve you of. I saw traveling coaches arriving at Dunwood House not long before you arrived."

Grace heaved a sigh of relief. "Thank you for telling me."

Taking her arm, Worthington bowed to her uncle. "Let's go see if Phoebe and Marcus are receiving."

"Give me just a moment. I must send permission for

Charlie to be brought home." Grace scribbled a quick message and handed it to her uncle. "Thank you for taking care of this for me. You've been a great help through everything." She reached up and kissed his cheek. "I could not have done it without you."

Herndon hugged her, clearing his throat. "I'll have the permission sent now. Once I speak with my nephew, I shall give you the time of your wedding."

Grace rose and kissed her uncle again. "Thank you. You are the best of uncles."

"So you always tell me, my dear."

Matt had to agree. Absent her uncle's efficiency, he and Grace would have to wait, and he had a strange feeling that would be dangerous. Something was definitely afoot.

The Dunwood butler bowed to Grace and Matt, then showed them to the morning room at the back of the house.

Marcus helped Phoebe rise. "Grace, Worthington, how happy we are to see you."

"Phoebe, I'm so relieved you have returned." Grace and her friend embraced and bussed cheeks. "The wedding day has been moved up again. We are getting married to-morrow."

Eyes wide, Phoebe stared at her. "What happened? Why so soon?"

"My mother's brother, Molton, has returned, and he is a known troublemaker. He didn't receive what he expected to under my grandfather's will."

"I see." Phoebe's lips formed a thin line. "I take it you are acting on the advice of Lord Herndon?"

Grace smiled wryly. "Yes."

"In that case, there is no time to lose." Phoebe's chin firmed and a martial light entered her eyes. "We must go round to Madame's." She turned to Matt. "Fetch your stepmother, Charlotte, and Louisa. Grace and I will meet you at Madame Lisette's on Bruton Street."

Grace's mind had been rapidly making a list of what needed to be done for the next day. "I must inform our cook and both households."

"Worthington can do that. Let's be off." Phoebe looked outside. "Well drat, it's come to rain."

Matt grinned. "You may take my coach. I'll walk back."

Grace touched his arm. "No, we shall drop you off. It's on our way."

After leaving Matt at Stanwood House, they proceeded to Bruton Street.

She'd just finished the fitting when Patience and their sisters arrived. "Did Matt tell you?"

"Yes, there is nothing to be done for it." Patience embraced Grace. "I trust your uncle, and I agree with him. I am to tell you that Charlie has been sent for, and your staff instructed not to allow Molton in the house."

Part of the burden weighting Grace down began to lift. "Thank you."

"Do any of you have engagements this evening?" Phoebe asked.

"Yes, Lady Featherton's soirée."

"You must attend, there is no avoiding it." Phoebe paced. "I would not mention the wedding. There will not be any entertainments between Friday and Monday, and you were to have been married on Tuesday anyway."

Footmen held umbrellas as the ladies left the modiste's shop and scurried down the street to the milliner's for the hats to go with their new gowns.

"I hope the maids can finish the gowns for the girls." Her sisters and Matt's would be so upset if they did not have new gowns to wear. "The seamstress was to have had them ready for Easter, and now we need them three days sooner."

"It will all get done." Phoebe patted Grace's hand. "These things always do. I'll see you this evening."

"We'll help, Grace," Charlotte said.

Next to her, Louisa nodded. "Anything we can do to assist, and don't worry about our gowns. We have several new ones we can wear."

Grace's throat tightened. What had she done to deserve such wonderful sisters? "Thank you. Patience and Phoebe, you as well. I don't know what I'd do without all of you."

"My pleasure." Phoebe's eyes sparkled. "Haven't you been told that those of us in the married state like to help others along? Now we must select a bonnet worthy of your gown." Keeping her voice low, Phoebe spoke in Grace's ear. "Smile, you are marrying a man you love, who loves you."

"Yes, I am." Grace took another breath and smiled. She'd never been so happy and nervous at one time in her life. "A hat is just the thing."

Chapter Twenty-Four

The moment Grace entered Stanwood House, Matt pulled her aside.

"I have enlisted Miss Tallerton, and Jane, as well as a friend of Jane's, into addressing invitations for the wedding breakfast. They are in the morning room."

"Jane's friend? I suppose I know she has them, but who is the lady?"

"Come with me into the drawing room." His lips curved into a secretive smile. "I'll tell you after we discuss the wedding."

She chuckled lightly and allowed him to lead her. "What time is the ceremony to be held?"

"Ten o'clock. It appears there's another marriage at eleven." He grinned, but then shook his head. "I shouldn't be happy as it's quite shocking. A young couple brought back from fleeing to Gretna Green is getting leg-shackled after us."

Grace widened her eyes. It was her worst nightmare that one of her sisters would elope. "Do you know who they are?"

Pouring them both a glass of wine, he handed one to her. "No, your uncle didn't ask." His lips thinned. "I don't doubt we'll hear about it this evening, unless they've been successful keeping it quiet. I only hope Louisa and Charlotte don't decide it's romantic."

Rubbing her suddenly tense neck, Grace said, "I can only pray that I've done a good enough job of instilling in her the impropriety and danger of a runaway marriage." She took a sip of wine. "It would amaze me if it has been successfully hushed up. Those types of things tend to get out." She glanced at Matt. "As sad as it is, that should eclipse our rushed marriage."

He set his glass down and put an arm around her. "Grace, I've sent a message to both of our solicitors. The guardianship application will be filed immediately after the wedding."

She leaned into his strength and warmth. "Uncle Herndon will help."

Nuzzling her, he grinned. "I think he's already made plans to talk to one of the law lords."

"Now what is the secret about Jane's friend?"

"It is a he. A Mr. Hector Addison. They will also be marrying shortly."

"Never tell me he is the one she loved all those years ago?" Grace gasped, and had to stop herself from dancing a jig.

"The very same, from what I can gather."

"But I thought he'd died at sea."

"He sailed off to India and recently returned."

She threw her arms around Matt. "This is such good news. You don't know how worried I've been about her!"

"Believe me, I had a fair idea." Matt kissed her soundly. "I know you won't rest until you've met him."

"What is he like?"

"He is jovial, and, from the way he looks at Jane, very much in love."

"You'd better tell me everything you know, so that I won't discomfit them with too many questions."

"I don't know much." Matt held her hand as they ambled

down the corridor. "They have found a house not far from here, and, from their plans to purchase a country estate as well, I believe him to be quite warm. As to embarrassing him, wait until he meets the children."

Molton allowed Jem into his rooms and gave him a towel. "I stayed until the rain come. Weren't nothin' going on 'cept for this morning. That rum mort went across to the swell's house just after I got back."

"Did you see her leave?"

"She left wi' him in a rattler. Woulda followed but there were a fart catcher on the back."

"I see. It appears my niece has taken a lover." Molton rubbed his chin. "The court won't like that. Where did you say the gentleman's house was?"

"Direct across the square. Ye want me to go back?"

Edgar ambled to the fireplace. "No, I'll need someone who can act as a witness." He dug in his pocket. "Here's the rest of your money and a bonus."

The lad's face lit up. "Coo, guv'nor. Anytime ye needs somethin' ye call for me."

"Yes, thank you, I will." Edgar smiled to himself. It wouldn't be long before he'd not be in need of anything. Women really weren't very intelligent. He'd be interested to know who this lover was. Berkeley Square had never been one of his haunts.

After Jem left and the rain let up, Molton shrugged on his greatcoat, donned a beaver hat, and took up his cane. He made his way to the nearest lending library and found an old copy of *Debrett's*. Shortly thereafter, Molton had his answer. Very indiscreet of them. A plan started to form in his mind. He could blackmail both his niece and Lord Worthington for a tidy sum.

A few blocks away from the library, he saw a sign

announcing HARVEY COMBS, INVESTIGATOR. Exactly the type of person Edgar was looking for. Entering the building, he climbed the stairs to the second floor, knocked, and went in.

"Mr. Combs?"

"Who'd be wantin' to know?"

Molton took in the greasy-looking suit and dingy neck-cloth worn by Mr. Combs, who seemed only slightly less disreputable than his linen. "My name is Molton, Edgar Molton. I have recently returned from abroad and found that my niece, who has guardianship of my younger nieces and nephews, has become a woman of loose morals. I intend to file a suit in the chancery court, but I will need a man of integrity who can stand as witness to her depravity."

Combs straightened a little. "That would be me. Where do I find this woman?"

"Berkeley Square, Mayfair, at Stanwood House." He stopped to see if there was any change in the man's demeanor. A slightly feral look crossed Combs's face. Edgar wondered briefly what it meant, but didn't bother himself over much. What did it matter? "Her name is Lady Grace Carpenter. I have been reasonably informed that she is Lord Worthington's mistress."

"Ten pounds now and ten later."

The idiot had obviously taken Edgar for a flat. "Five now and ten later. If you argue with me, my offer will go down."

Giving him a pained expression, Combs whined, "I have me expenses."

Edgar looked Combs in the eye. "As do I. You may accept my offer, or I'll find someone else."

"Right then, you got a deal. When do'ye want me to start?"

"To-morrow morning. With what I think is going on, you'll have to watch all night and into the next day." Molton handed the investigator five pounds. "Don't think to run out on me."

"Wouldn't dream of it." The man pocketed the money. "I'm as honest as the day is long."

Edgar didn't believe that for a minute, but he'd make sure the man wouldn't cheat him.

It was still raining when Matt ushered his party out of Stanwood House and assisted them into the town coaches for the short drive to Curzon Street. Word of his and Grace's pending nuptials had apparently spread. Lady Featherton greeted them enthusiastically and wished Grace and him happy.

He escorted Patience and their sisters to a small sofa and chairs, then strolled the room with Grace. Approaching a group of gentlemen and their wives, they were shortly put in possession of the facts surrounding the couple who'd been attempting to elope.

"Would you believe it, my dear Lady Grace? They found the couple only a day from Gretna Green."

Grace's lips were pressed together. "Shocking and disgraceful. I sincerely hope it is not a romantic story. Who are they, Mrs. Stanley?"

"I fear you may be disappointed." Mrs. Stanley's dark brows drew together. "The girl is a Miss Snow, who was to make her come out this year. The gentleman is Alvanley's youngest, Lord William Hunt. Lord William's not got a feather to fly with, you know how it is with all the Hunts, and the young woman is an heiress."

"I remember being introduced to her." Grace placed a finger on her lips. "She was at Lady Bellamny's party."

Matt didn't like the sound of that. If Grace had met the young woman, Louisa and Charlotte would have been introduced to Miss Snow as well. He hoped the girls didn't find Miss Snow's behavior acceptable. "I had no idea Lord William was so avaricious."

Mrs. Stanley's eyes rounded in shock. "Oh, my, no indeed, and I would not have believed it if anyone had accused him of being a fortune hunter. It appears the two have known each other since they were children. With Miss Snow's looks and fortune, her father wanted a brilliant match for her. She is quite a taking little thing after all." Being at the center of attention, Mrs. Stanley glanced at the others gathered around before continuing. "I believe Mr. Snow knew of the attraction and forbade them to speak. Then it was rumored that he was trying to arrange a match for his daughter."

"As a result," Grace said, in a disgusted tone, "Lord William is now cast in the light of her hero."

"Well if Mr. Snow's daughter is an heiress," one of the gentlemen said, "I don't doubt he'd rather not be related to Alvanley."

"For my money," Matt added, "the matter was handled very poorly."

Mrs. Stanley continued, "Mr. Snow won't have a choice but to agree that his daughter and Lord William wed. Before he caught up with them, they were seen at an inn by Lady Cavendish."

Grace shook her head. "Well, if that's the case, there is no hope of keeping it quiet."

"Indeed, my lady." Mrs. Stanley paused and smiled. "Oh, but I've quite forgotten to wish you happy. It's a very good match for the both of you. And I hear you are going to marry quietly." She smiled knowingly. "I daresay you'll be busy with your sisters making their come outs. Worthington, you have your work cut out for you."

Glancing in the direction Mrs. Stanley was looking, he stifled a groan. The girls were standing with a group of several young men and women. Only the increased pressure of Grace's hand on his arm kept him from going over and making a cake of himself. And this was only the beginning of the Season. He'd be a wreck by the end of it.

Grace inclined her head. "Mrs. Stanley, no doubt we shall see you later in the evening. Thank you for the news."

"When I see you again, my lady, you will probably be Lady Worthington."

Smiling politely, Grace tugged on Matt and led them off toward another group. His attention though was not on where they were going, but on Charlotte and Louisa. "My love, you cannot go hieing off every time a young man addresses one of the girls."

"I don't like this elopement talk." Matt frowned. "It sounds much too romantic."

Grace nodded to some of their acquaintances. "Are you afraid one of our sisters will think it so?"

"Aren't you?"

She glanced at him in thought. "No, as soon as they understand the couple will have to retire to the country and not show their faces for the next couple of Seasons, they will not think it so enticing."

The expression on her face and her confidence reassured him. "Still, I would like to go home as soon as common courtesy will allow us to."

Grinning, Grace glanced at the girls. "First we must detach them from their admirers without them knowing what we're doing." She paused. "Charlie is the excuse we'll use. Charlotte will not want to miss the opportunity to welcome him and introduce him to Louisa."

When they returned to Patience, the girls were in a circle of their new friends, all talking animatedly. Grace's lips formed a moue. "The elopement?"

Patience's lips thinned. "Yes. The story is growing by the moment."

"Let's not make too much of it," Grace replied. "The less said, the easier forgotten."

"Of course you're right," Patience agreed. "When it comes up, we will pretend that we are not that interested."

Suppressing a growl, Matt took a deep breath and calmly took note of the young men with their sisters. He didn't know either of them by sight. Though the good thing about the *ton* was information would be forthcoming. "Grace, they should go down to supper with us."

"Yes, my dear."

When he would have ordered their sisters to accompany him, Grace glanced over and said, "Louisa, Charlotte, will you join us for supper?"

Charlotte turned. "Oh yes. We're glad you're back. Louisa and I have so much to tell you."

Grace smiled. "Then let us go down so I may hear it all."

A gentleman with black hair and a rather swarthy complexion, who had not been part of the group, bowed. At least Matt knew this one. "Lady Charlotte, may I have the pleasure of accompanying you to supper?"

Charlotte glanced at Grace, whose brow slowly rose in an imperious manner. "Excuse me. I do not believe we've been introduced."

The young man stuttered and bowed hastily. "Oh—oh, my lady. Excuse me. I was introduced to Lady Charlotte earlier in the evening."

"My love," Matt said, "may I present Lord Harrington? Harrington, Lady Grace Carpenter, my betrothed."

Grace inclined her head. "Lord Harrington. I'm delighted to meet you. The family was just going down to supper. Would you like to join us?"

Taking the hand she offered he bowed again. "It would be my pleasure, my lady, and may I wish you happy?"

"Thank you."

When he straightened, Harrington turned to her sister. "Lady Charlotte?"

She smiled brightly. "Lord Harrington. I'd be delighted to have your escort."

They turned to go when Worthington almost tripped over another young man. "Bentley?"

"My lord, I—I wanted to ask if Lady Louisa would accept my arm to the supper room."

Bentley was not much above medium height with light brown hair styled in curls. Worthington strove to keep from grinning. He'd never known Bentley to stammer. "Then you must ask her."

Bentley bowed. "Lady Louisa, will you . . ."

She stuck out her hand. "Yes, I'd be delighted."

Charlotte whispered to Louisa, "Let him finish."

Placing her hand on Bentley's arm, she murmured back. "He was taking too long."

Grace pressed her lips firmly together to keep from laughing and made the mistake of glancing at Matt, who was also struggling with his countenance. She took his arm and held him back, allowing Patience and the girls to precede them. "From the mouths of babes."

Shaking his head he replied, "I'm not sure I'm up for this."

Grace patted his arm. "We will become accustomed. After all, it's only the beginning of the Season." Grace glanced ahead and back to him. "What do you know about the young men?"

"Bentley is heir to the Duke of Covington. Harrington is heir to the Marquis of Markham. They are both in their late twenties. Old enough to think of settling down. Bentley is dependent on his father. Harrington has his own funds as well as the expectancy. I'll find out more if their interests are serious."

"They must have met the girls at an earlier party. I'll look to see if they've left cards. We were out and about so much to-day, I didn't have a chance."

A footman came up with a note on a silver salver. "Lady Grace Carpenter?"

Her hand began to tremble, and she braced herself in the event it was bad news. "Yes, what is it?"

The man bowed. "A message for you, my lady. Would you like me to wait?"

"Please." Grace's heart pounded rapidly against her chest as she opened the letter. Thank God. She took a breath and calmed herself. "Charlie is home safely. They ran into some problems with the state of the roads, but he is home now." She glanced up at the servant. "There is no reply."

"Thank you, my lady."

After the man left, Matt glanced down. "You looked frightened for a moment."

Terrified would have been a more accurate word. Taking a deep breath, she was glad for the comfort he brought. "I've never received a message at a party before. I—I thought for a moment some accident had occurred."

He placed her hand on his arm and they entered the supper room. "Would you like me to take you to the house?"

She did want to go home and see her brother, but Grace needed to think of the girls as well. "We'll have to ask Patience. I don't want to drag them home if they wish to remain."

"Let me get you something to eat and a glass of champagne. We will see how our sisters are doing."

Relieved to have him to share her thoughts and concerns, Grace glanced up. "Thank you. That's perfect."

Matt escorted her to the table where Patience and their sisters sat.

Patience looked at Grace. "What is it?"

"Nothing bad. Charlie is home safely. They were delayed due to the weather."

"Charlie's here?" Charlotte's face broke into smiles. "Oh Grace, may we go?"

Grace was relieved her sister would rather leave, but there were the proprieties to consider. "Charlotte, you know better. Now that you've accepted Lord Harrington's escort, you must remain with him through supper. We shall remain for a little while longer and then take our leave."

Charlotte sighed. "Yes, of course. I just so want to see Charlie."

"I know you do." Grace squeezed her sister's shoulder. "I do as well."

"I imagine all the children will be up now." Charlotte turned to Patience. "This is his first year at Eton. None of us is used to having him gone."

Patience smiled. "I understand. If Louisa wishes to stay, I shall, of course, remain here. If not, we may depart after supper."

Louisa leaned over the table. "I want to go as well."

Worthington, followed by Harrington and Bentley, came back with a footman in tow. "I think we've selected the choicest of the offerings for you."

Charlotte accepted the plate Lord Harrington offered. "Thank you, my lord. This looks delightful."

He took the seat next to her. "We got to the lobster patties before anyone else did, and snagged several of them. I hope you like them. Worthington didn't seem to know."

Looking at Louisa, Grace was pleased to see Lord Bentley hover solicitously over her, making suggestions.

"My love," Matt murmured, leaning over, "will you also try a lobster patty?" His lips grazed her ear. "You can finish it this time, as well as your champagne."

Rogue! How dare he have reminded her? Still, she smiled and was so happy tears started in her eyes. The last time she'd been in a supper room eating a lobster patty and drinking champagne was the evening he'd found her. "Yes, I would love to."

With the young couples settled, Patience turned to

Grace and Matt. "It has occurred to me that our living arrangements will seem very odd to our neighbors."

Matt leaned back in his chair and toyed with his champagne glass. "Yes, well, I suppose as long as we're not crossing the square in our nightclothes, they should be happy."

Grace choked. "That would certainly give rise to talk. Patience, are you settled in?"

She took a sip of champagne and nodded. "Most of my clothing and other items arrived by the time we returned this afternoon. I think all of Louisa's things are there. Grace, Louisa's chamber is lovely, and it was a wonderful idea to have Charlotte and her share a parlor between them. They seem to have so much in common and have become great friends."

Matt had arranged to have most of the work done while they'd been out to-day. Grace shot him a sidelong glance to find him grinning at her. "They actually chose the room. Still, I am pleased you agree. How are your apartments?"

"Perfect. I have even more room than I had at Worthington House."

She'd been worried that Patience might not feel at home at Stanwood House. "I'm so glad. Please tell me if you'd like to have your rooms at Worthington House redecorated or remodeled."

Patience smiled. "What a lovely offer. I shall take you up on it. Yet first, let's take care of the wedding and the children."

Grace glanced up to see Phoebe and Marcus coming to join them. She stood and hugged Phoebe.

After she'd seated herself, Phoebe grinned. "It has been so busy, I've not had an opportunity to look for you. You will be pleased to hear, I was barely asked a question about you. It seems as if the *ton* has a new interest."

Marcus caught Matt's eye. "I see you have prospects."

"Yes, I don't know who is more nervous, them or me."

"I am very pleased I have time before my nieces come out." Marcus chuckled.

Matt spoke to Marcus in a low voice, but not so low Grace couldn't hear. "Marcus, how do you like married life?"

"There is nothing better."

"I think it will be the same for me."

Phoebe nudged Grace. "You look far away."

"I was just thinking, to-morrow I'll be wed to the gentleman I always wanted to marry and everything is going so well."

Her friend nodded. "And you feel as if it cannot all be true?"

Maybe that was the fear she had tonight when the note came. "Precisely. As if something will come along to ruin it."

Phoebe covered Grace's hand with hers. "You and Worthington each have different strengths. Trust him when you don't trust yourself."

It seemed like a long time since she'd had someone to rely upon and Matt was already taking care of her and the children. Looking up she noticed some of the guests were leaving the supper room. "Louisa, Charlotte, we'll go and see Charlie now."

Charlotte turned to Lord Harrington. "Please excuse me. My brother is home from school and we haven't seen him in such a long time."

He helped her to her feet and bowed. "Then I shall not keep you, my lady. May I make plans to drive with you to-morrow afternoon?"

Charlotte's eyes flew to Grace. "I'm sorry. We—we have family plans."

"Then the next day?"

"Yes, I'd be happy to ride with you."

He kissed her hand and a light blush infused Charlotte's cheeks. "I shall come for you at five o'clock."

Though Grace was unable to hear, she was sure a similar conversation was going on between Louisa and Bentley.

Matt stood, took Grace's hand, and addressed Bentley. "We must be going. Although we all have a busy day tomorrow, I am sure the ladies will be at home the next day."

The young man bowed. "Thank you, my lord."

Grace smiled to herself as Matt herded them all to bid their hostess a good evening and called for the carriages.

The rain had finally let up, leaving a clear sky for their wedding in the morning.

Chapter Twenty-Five

No sooner had Matt, Grace, and Patience crossed the Stanwood House threshold than shouts from above for them to come see Charlie reached them. The children must have been watching out the window.

Charlotte and Louisa ran up the stairs, hoisting their skirts in a very unladylike manner, while he, Grace, and Patience followed at a more sedate pace. Matt reached the school-room to see both Charlotte and Louisa being hugged by a tall, lanky sixteen-year-old with the signature Carpenter hair and eyes.

The boy held Charlotte back. "Char, look at you. Have you been at a ball?"

"No silly, a soirée. This is an evening gown, not a ball gown."

Charlie hugged her again. "Well, you look as fine as five-pence." He glanced at Worthington's sister. "And you are Louisa. You're to be my new sister? Char wrote to me about you. How nice that you're both making your come outs together."

Alice pulled him away. "Here is Matt."

Mary jumped up and down. "We're all getting married to-morrow."

Charlie picked her up and twirled her around. "Are we?"

Suddenly, both Great Danes bounded through the door. Daisy tried to wrap herself around him. "Yes, yes, girl." He patted her head. "But what have we here? A friend for Daisy?" Charlie reached out to Duke and stroked his back. "How are you? You're a handsome boy." Duke's tail thwacked hard against the wall so hard, Matt was concerned either the wall or the tail would break.

Watching Charlie with the others made him understand, in a way he had not before, the reason Grace had fought so hard to keep her brothers and sisters together. He'd be here to help her now and to protect her and the children, his and hers.

Charlie broke away to hug Grace. "I've been told I am to wish you happy."

Nodding, she responded in a tight voice with emotion, "You are indeed. Charlie, this is Matt, Lord Worthington."

The boy stuck out his hand. "I'm pleased to meet you, sir. I feel as if I know you already. The twins and Walter said you'll keep us together."

Matt shook Charlie's hand. "I shall. That is a promise."

Charlie glanced at the children. "Thank you for agreeing to take us on and for my new sisters."

Laughing, Matt replied, "Don't thank me. I couldn't get your sister unless I took the whole bunch of you."

Charlie chuckled. "She does drive a hard bargain."

The Earl of Stanwood might be only sixteen, but he took his family seriously. Matt wondered what it was like for him to be the head of the family and have no control over the welfare of it. He and Grace would have to make a point of discussing the arrangements they'd made with Charlie.

"I think all of you need to go to sleep," Grace said, as she kissed each of the younger children. "Charlie will be here for three weeks, and we have a lot to do in the morning. You'll have circles under your eyes for the wedding if you don't go to bed."

They tucked the children in then took Charlie, Louisa, and Charlotte with them down the stairs.

Matt glanced at Charlie. "Did you learn of the marriage tonight?"

"No." He grinned. "I've been receiving letters."

"Indeed." That was odd. "Who's been writing to you?"

"Everyone." Charlie turned a solemn face to him. "I'm glad you are teaching Walter to box."

"He's a quick learner." Then a thought occurred to Matt. If the children had been telling Charlie everything about his and Grace's very short courtship, Matt didn't want those letters getting out. He raised a brow. "The letters?"

"I brought them home to burn." Charlie grimaced. "You do know they listen at the keyholes?"

Matt resisted putting his hand over his face and wondered, for the first time, what the children may have heard when he was in Grace's study. He sighed. "I seem to recall Alice saying something about it the first day I was here, then I forgot. I might just have every keyhole in Worthington House sealed."

As they descended the stairs from the children's floor, Grace saw Patience hovering at the bottom. "Patience, why didn't you come up?"

"I didn't want to intrude. Your Miss Tallerton and Mr. Winters are in the drawing room. Shall we join them?"

"Yes, we're going there now. They were probably driven out by the noise."

A footman opened the door. Grace walked in with Patience followed by Matt, Charlie, Louisa, and Charlotte. Jane and her Mr. Addison were in conversation with Winters and Miss Tallerton. "Are they making that much noise?"

Jane's eyes twinkled. "It has been mayhem since he walked through the door. Before then, we had thought they were sound asleep."

Matt put his hand on Grace's shoulder. "Wine?"

"Yes, please. The girls and Charlie may have a glass as well." She took a seat on the sofa. Charlie helped Matt serve the wine. It had taken her a while to accept that with him around, they were more of a family. Harder to admit was that she needed his help with the children.

Her brother gave Mr. Addison a quizzical look. "I don't believe we've been introduced, sir."

Jane blushed. "Charlie, this is my betrothed, Mr. Hector Addison. We have known each other for many years. Hector, Grace's brother, the Earl of Stanwood."

Charlie grasped Hector's hand, shaking it. "Please call me Charlie. Jane is very dear to us, and I'm happy to see her settled."

Matt handed Grace a glass and sat down next to her. "My love, we should tell everyone what we've decided."

Taking a sip, she addressed them. "Well, some of you know and some do not. Worthington and I will be remodeling his house. Accordingly, Lady Worthington and her daughters will live here with us. Worthington and I will sleep at his house, but otherwise live here." When she paused, he slid an arm around her. "My uncle on my mother's side has returned, and Lord Herndon believes he will attempt to make trouble. Because of that and the court case, Worthington and I are marrying in the morning." Everyone nodded, not surprised at her announcement. "Worthington's solicitor has instructions to file the change of guardianship after the wedding. My solicitor will immediately agree. Miss Tallerton, Mr. Winters, if you'd like, you may take a vacation for the next couple of weeks." She grimaced. "I doubt they'll get much studying done with all the changes and Charlie being home."

"Thank you, my lady," Miss Tallerton replied. "If you wouldn't mind, I'll visit my family for a few days at Easter, then return."

Mr. Winters nodded. "I have the same idea."

"Thank you. Do not feel as if you must hold lessons."

"Mr. Winters and I have discussed it. We would like to take the children to some of the more important sites in London." Grace and her family had been so lucky to find these two people. "If you are sure?"

Miss Tallerton grinned. "Very sure. It will give us an opportunity to see them as well."

Glancing at Jane, Grace said, "Jane, have you decided when you will marry?"

"It will take about a week or so to finalize the purchase of the house. We shall wed at that time." Her lips formed a moue. "Unfortunately the seller did not give his power of attorney to his solicitor and we must await his signature on the documents. In the meantime, I have some shopping of my own I must do."

"If you do not mind, I would like to hold your wedding breakfast here. We'll have had a great deal of experience."

Leaning across from her chair next to the sofa, Jane patted Grace's hand. "I would love nothing better. At least my being here for another week or so will give you and Worthington the option of taking more time together."

Matt glanced at Charlie. "Stanwood, do you have anything you'd like to add?"

"I think you've made a good decision to enjoy at least a little peace and quiet. After we move into your house, I suggest we lease Stanwood House for the Season until I'm old enough to live here."

Drawing her brows together, Grace asked, "Are you sure you won't mind?"

He shook his head. "No. It's not as if I'm leaving it forever." He came over to Grace and kissed her cheek. "If you'll excuse me, I'm off to bed."

Louisa and Charlotte bade them good night as well and followed him out.

Then Miss Tallerton and Mr. Winters rose.

"We'll bid you a good night as well," she said. "I hope the children are finally asleep."

"It appears we're all tired." Mr. Addison assisted Jane. "Good night. I look forward to seeing you in the morning."

Once the door shut behind Jane and Addison, Grace leaned her head against Matt's shoulder. He kissed her head. This was the last night he'd sleep without her next to him. "Marcus and Rutherford will come for me in the morning. We'll take the boys with us."

She placed her hand on his cheek. "I love you."

"I love you and adore you." He kissed her gently. "To-morrow, my love."

"To-morrow."

He left, knowing she watched him as he crossed the street. Worthington entered his empty house and was suddenly lonely. No thumping of footsteps marred the quiet, and he realized how much he was looking forward to having everyone here, under his roof. And Grace as his wife managing the chaos. This time next year, his house would be full with their brothers and sisters and, he hoped, a child of their own to add to the madness.

Grace rose early the following morning to hear Bolton rummaging around. Pulling back the bed hangings, she stared. "What are you doing?"

"Packing everything you don't need for the wedding. We got everyone else moved yesterday."

"I see. I'm going down to breakfast. When do you want me back?"

"If you're here by half past eight that will give me enough time. I'll order your bath for then."

"Very well." Grace swung her legs over the side of her bed. The last time she'd do so. She looked forward to sleeping next to Matt. Yet even though she hadn't spent much time here recently, it was her home. "It's a strange feeling, leaving."

"I understand, my lady. But you'll see, this was meant to be. Besides, you'll only be away at night."

Grace chuckled ruefully. "Perfectly true."

Bolton helped her into a morning gown and Grace went down to find the breakfast room empty. "Royston, where is everyone?"

"Come and gone, my lady. They were not allowed to wear their new clothes to breakfast, not even with smocks. You enjoy the quiet while you have it."

After pouring her tea, she helped herself to baked eggs and toast and wondered about the other changes the day would bring.

She'd finished her third cup of tea when her butler entered the room. "My lady, Bolton says you are to come now."

"Thank you, Royston."

She sank into the warm water as Bolton arranged items on the dresser. Grace caught a flash of light. "What was that?"

Bolton held up a delicate gold necklace set with amethysts and diamonds.

Peering at it closely, Grace shook her head. It wasn't hers or her mother's. "Where did this come from?"

"His lordship sent it over this morning with a pair of earrings, a tiara, and a bracelet."

"They are perfect. He really has done well." Water splashed as she stood and Bolton handed her a towel.

"There's a package from Rundell and Bridges in my dresser, please take it out and compare it to the necklace."

Her maid found the package, took out the pin, and grinned. "A perfect match, my lady."

"Crafty old man." Grace grinned. "I went in looking for something for Lord Worthington. I had almost selected a fob and the clerk said he had just the thing. I picked it up the next day." She'd never bought a gentleman a gift before and was concerned that Matt wouldn't like it.

"If you want my opinion, it was good thinking on his part."

"Indeed." Grace turned to the creation of Madame Lisette's hanging on the door. "How do you like my gown?"

"It's beautiful. The netting is just the right touch."

Bolton took the towel. Grace donned her chemise and stays. "We'll put this on you and cover it up while I dress your hair."

She raised her arms, and the soft, cream-colored silk floated over her. The bodice was cut in a low V in both the front and back, decorated with a band of embroidered gold ribbon. The gown had a small demi-train. Next came a short overdress in pale gold netting dotted with seed pearls and layered sleeves extending to her elbows. Bolton helped her into a dressing gown and then styled Grace's hair in a knot at the back of her head and secured with pearl combs. Her maid pulled out several tendrils allowing them to flow over Grace's shoulders.

Placing a small hat made of silk and lace on her head, Bolton said, "The hatpin belongs to Lady Evesham for something borrowed, old and blue."

A knock came on the door. "My lady, Lord and Lady Herndon and Lady Evesham are waiting."

"Thank you, Royston. I'll be right down." Grace put on the earrings Worthington had sent, and Bolton clasped the necklace around her neck.

"I do look well, don't I?"

"Yes, my lady, you do. Go now."

Grace rose and surprised Bolton by giving her a kiss on the cheek. "Thank you."

"Go on, out of here."

Grace hurried out of the door, down the stairs, and strode into the drawing room. "I am ready."

Uncle Bertrand grinned. "Then let us be off. The children left several minutes ago. They should have them sorted by the time we get there." He took out his quizzing glass. "May I say you look beautiful? Are those the jewels Worthington gave you? Perfect."

Her aunt's eyes swam in tears as she carefully hugged her. "My dear. The parure your mother left you is still being cleaned and reset. It should be delivered later this afternoon. You are lovely." A tear escaped her eye. "She would have been so happy to see you."

"None of that, Almeria," Uncle said gruffly. "We don't want to get everyone weeping."

Dabbing her eyes with the corner of her handkerchief, she smiled mistily. "Yes, my dear, of course, you're right."

"You have the hatpin?" Phoebe asked.

"Yes"—Grace's heart swelled with happiness—"Thank you for thinking of it."

"You're very welcome," Phoebe said. "Ladies, we should be going. We don't want the gentleman to think you've run off."

Matt stood chatting with Marcus, Rutherford, and Anna. At a noise from the other end of the transept, he turned. Grace entered with her aunt and uncle and Phoebe. After giving her cloak to a footman, Grace turned and smiled. His heart quickened and his throat contracted. He'd be lucky if he could say his vows. She was the most beautiful woman he knew, and she was *his*.

Grace floated toward him, and he held out his hand, unable to take his eyes off her. He thanked God and the Fates that he'd found her. There was no other woman he wanted to spend his life with. She was gazing in his eyes and smiling back at him.

"Shall we begin?" the vicar said.

From the corner of his eye, Worthington could see the very young cleric grin.

Lady Herndon took a place with Patience and the children. They all sat quietly and were smiling expectantly. Charlie, Louisa, and Charlotte were spaced out among the younger ones.

Glancing at Grace, Matt asked, "Are you ready, my love?"

She nodded. "I am."

"Yes, well then, let us begin. Dearly beloved, we are gathered together here in the sight of God . . ."

When Marcus handed Matt the ring, there was a rustling and a few titters from the children. The twins had managed to get one of Grace's rings for him so he'd know the size. The ring he had finally chosen was the one his father had given to his mother, and it fitted Grace perfectly.

She glanced down as he slipped the intricate gold-and-diamond band on her finger and looked back up at him. Tears started in her eyes, but she was smiling. After the vicar pronounced them man and wife he took her in his arms and held her until the rustling from the pews made him remember where they were.

Phoebe and Marcus went with them to sign the registry.

"I'll need a copy of the marriage lines," Matt said.

"You may take a copy now." The vicar smiled. "Uncle Bertrand said you would require them, so they are ready."

"Thank you."

"It was my pleasure, I assure you." The younger man flushed. "I should tell you, it's my first wedding ceremony."

Matt felt his smile broaden. "Ours as well. I wish you many more."

The cleric grinned. "And I wish you only the one."

Grace chuckled. "Come, my lord husband. You may take me home."

"With pleasure, my lady wife."

Aunt Almeria sobbed into her handkerchief. "You two are very silly. Now we must get the children home."

The level of noise rose and echoed through the church.

"Yes, yes, we all want to see Grace, but we shall have to wait until we are home again," Charlotte said, ruthlessly herding the younger ones.

Charlie's face was stern, but the corners of his lips ticked up as he took Mary and Theodora's hands. "Listen to Charlotte. Come, we must go. Jacques has treats for us when we get back. I for one am hungry."

"You're always hungry," Mary said. "I hope he has lemon tarts."

Marcus leaned over to Grace and Matt. "That's right, bribe them with food."

Louisa took her remaining sisters' hands. "Augusta, Madeline, come along."

Rutherford whispered to Anna, "How many children did you say you wanted?"

Anna shook her head and smiled, but forbore to answer.

Once the children were in the coaches, Grace heaved a sigh. "I think that went well."

"I agree." Phoebe took Marcus's arm. "Now if we can be as orderly as the children, we shall be back in no time."

Anna glanced at Rutherford. "I agree."

He took her arm. "I feel as if I'm being managed again."

Raising a brow, Anna said, "No, my love, I'll only manage you if you don't come, immediately. There is another wedding here at eleven."

"Ah," Rutherford replied. "The Gretna Green couple."

Chapter Twenty-Six

Grace and Matt arrived at Stanwood House and quickly formed a receiving line. They stood with her aunt, uncle, and Patience. Phoebe, Anna, and their husbands took charge of settling the children.

Lady Bellamny was the first guest to arrive. "Worthington, Lady Worthington, well done."

Lord and Lady St. Eth and Lord and Lady Dunwood were next in a steady stream of wedding breakfast guests. After a half an hour or so, Uncle Bertrand, Aunt Almeria, and Patience left to entertain the guests.

It wasn't until then Grace realized that no one had asked her about the entertainment. "Matt, please tell me someone was in charge of the planning for this. I thought we'd have only family and close friends."

"The Dowager Lady Worthington and your chef planned it. Or I should say, our chef."

"For how many?"

"Not over a hundred."

The blood rushed out of Grace's head, and she swayed. "I did tell you that I don't take surprises well?"

"Grace, are you going to faint? Here, lean on me and take some deep breaths." He caught Royston's eye. "Water."

After she'd had a few sips, Matt said, "I don't understand how it is you don't bat an eye at the antics of your brothers and sisters, but a change in plans can make you swoon."

"It's really rather simple. I expect the worst from them. As a result, I'm always relieved when it doesn't occur. Royston, how many more?"

He checked his list. "Two, Lords Huntley and Wively."

"They are always late," Matt said brutally. "Huntley and Wively can fend for themselves while we attend to the rest of our guests."

"Did I hear my name?" Huntley ambled through the door. "Sorry, Worthington, Wively will be right along. He and I were searching for the perfect wedding present. We finally found it, but it won't be ready until to-morrow."

Matt's eyes narrowed. "This had better be something appropriate."

Lord Huntley was the picture of innocence. "Of course considering the number of children you are now responsible for, we did think of a milch cow. But then thought it would present a rather odd sight in your back garden. Not to mention the necessity of hiring a milkmaid to manage the beast"

Grace started to giggle and had to cover her mouth to not laugh out loud.

Wively strolled up. "Yes, then we heard you're remodeling and that gave us a new idea. You'll see it in the not too distant future." He calmly took Grace's hand. "Lady Worthington, my pleasure. As a favor to me, I pray you will overlook Worthington's fits of temper. They don't usually last."

"Thank you for the advice," Grace replied, unable to keep her voice from trembling with mirth. "I shall bear it in mind."

Wively bowed, kissed her hand, and Huntley followed suit. Her husband's still-narrowed eyes followed them.

"I wouldn't worry, my love." Grace took his arm. "I am sure

it won't be unsuitable, and if it is, we can always put it away and bring it out when they visit."

The large reception rooms were opened up as well as the terrace doors. A string quartet played softly, and long tables were set in an adjoining parlor with canapés and other offerings. There'd been no time for a wedding cake; therefore, various tarts and small, square, iced cakes, Jacques called petits fours, as well as trifles, decorated one table. Glasses of champagne, lemonade, ratafia, and wine were carried by footmen.

Worthington snagged two glasses of champagne and handed one to Grace. "To us and our family."

She saluted him. "Yes, to us and our family."

Uncle Bertrand must have seen them as he called the guests to order and presented the first toast. He was followed by Marcus and Rutherford. Grace and Matt made the point of spending time with each of their guests, before she whispered, "I'm going to change. I'll meet you at the front door."

He kissed the tips of her fingers as she slipped out of the room. A few minutes later, he found Royston. "We're departing now."

"I shall inform Lord Herndon and, I think, Miss Carpenter, only."

"You're a good man."

Grace returned to him in a plain, muslin morning gown and took his hand. "Are you ready?"

Perusing her lush form, wrapping his fingers around her slender hand, desire swept through him. Causing his muscles to clench. They would have at least the rest of the afternoon and all night to themselves. Visions of her naked beneath him floated through his mind and his hand caressed her back. He drew her to him and whispered, "No stays?"

She gave him a sultry glance. "I didn't think I would need them."

He was more than ready. He'd dreamed about this for days.

Matt towed her out of the house, restraining himself from running across the square to his house.

Thorton opened the door and bowed. "My lady, welcome to your new home."

"Thank you, Thorton."

After that, Mrs. Thorton came to greet her. Did they have to take so long? Matt should have given his butler and housekeeper the day off so that he and Grace could be alone.

Scowling, he pulled at her hand and started up the stairs.

Thorton bowed again. "We shall be standing by in the event you require anything, my lady."

Matt was almost positive he'd seen his butler's lips twitch.

A few moments later, they were in his chamber—no—their chamber. He closed the door and faced her. His heart thudded. Finally she was his, and he couldn't think of a thing to say. The silence was only broken by the crackling of the fire.

Grace stood before Matt staring at him. "I know it's foolish, but I feel shy for some reason."

He touched her face lightly with the tips of his fingers, cupping her cheek. Heat spread through her, and she leaned into his hand. With a turn of her head, she kissed his palm.

Bending down, he kissed her lips lightly. "It's only because this is the first time we've planned it."

Grace shook her head slowly. He was wrong. "No. The first time, I planned for it to happen."

"Indeed?" Feathering soft kisses on her jaw, Worthington made his way back to her lips. "You may have, but I didn't."

She lifted her eyes to his warm lapis gaze. "No?"

He drew her closer, like he had the night at the inn. "No. When you kissed me, I knew you'd never been touched and had every intention of asking you to marry me before we made love."

"That was the reason you left me at my chamber. Was the kiss that bad?"

Worthington wrapped his arms around her. "It was innocent and perfect. I knew I was falling in love with you."

Grace relaxed, relishing the feeling of love and safety. This was what she wanted for the rest of her life.

"Grace, why did you come to me?" He kissed the top of her head. "Why take such a risk?"

Her throat closed in pain. "I—I'd never planned to marry."

Caressing her back, Matt asked, "Because of the children?"

She put her arms around his neck and nodded. "I thought if I could have just one night with you that would be enough. Then I could go back home, take care of the children, and not care if I never married."

He grinned ruefully. "But once would never have been enough for me. I had to find you." Kissing her lightly on the lips, he held her tighter. "Brown denied you were there. If I'd been alone, I might have thought you were a phantom. Thankfully, my groom was with me. I searched for you all along the road home."

The cold tears and despair seemed so long ago. "I cried until I arrived at Stanwood House."

He held her back a little and captured her eyes. "You should have stayed, Grace. I was so lonely without you."

Tears filled her eyes. She had to tell him, if she didn't do it now, she might never say it, and it would stand between them. Swallowing, she tried to straighten her shoulders, but she couldn't look at him. "I—I want you to know that I understand this—this passion may not last." She closed her eyes and forced herself to continue. "That—that when it is over, you will take mistresses." Her voice failed and tears started to roll down her cheeks.

There it was, at least she was finally telling him. "You think I'll take another woman? Whatever gave you an idea like that? Or should I ask whom?"

"My aunt said that even the best of gentlemen . . ."

All he wanted to do was comfort her, but he needed to hear it, and she needed to say it. "What else did she say?"

"That—that you would lose interest in the children."

Damn all well-meaning aunts.

"Grace, my darling. I cannot speak to her marriage, but, my love, my dear, dear, love. I shall never lose interest in you or the children."

When she tilted her head up, her beautiful woebegone face wrung his heart. He frowned. "That was the reason you were so cold to me when we left?"

"Yes, but then I decided I would take the love you could give me until you—you tired of me."

Holding her close to him again, he said, "My poor sweetheart. If only you'd told me."

"How could I have? I had so many doubts and everything was happening so quickly."

"I know she meant well." Matt kissed her. "Yet I can't help but wish she'd not spoken to you. My love, my parents did not have that sort of marriage, and it's not what I want with you." He kissed her temple and vowed he'd show her every day how much she meant to him. Grace and the children. "But my father did with Patience. I could never inflict that type of pain on you."

"Are you sure? Because if I let down my guard . . ."

"There is nothing more certain. I want you as my lover, my friend, and my wife."

Matt kissed her gently, deeply, and with all the love he could infuse into a kiss. "I vowed to-day to worship you with my body, and to keep myself only on to you. That is a promise I shall keep."

He brushed the tears from the corners of her eyes, then

took her lips, teasing them open. His tongue stroked hers and explored, slowly building a fire that he wanted to last for the rest of their lives. "I love you."

"And I love you."

"Grace, I'm going to make love to you."

"Yes."

He unlaced her gown and found only a chemise underneath. Slowly, he untied the ribbons and pulled her bodice down until the dress hung on her hips, exposing her perfect breasts. He held them reverently before moving his hands down over the indentation of her waist, then on to her hips. The chemise and gown fell in a *swoosh*. "Your turn."

Grace untied his cravat and let it drop. She unbuttoned his waistcoat and pushed to remove his jacket. "I need help. This jacket won't go down."

"Tug at the sleeves."

Going behind him, she pulled as Matt shrugged out of the jacket. He drew his shirt off over his head.

Grace unbuttoned the placket of his breeches. They dropped to the floor. He took off his shoes and stockings, standing naked before her.

Her eyes grew round and a small smile appeared to pull at her lips. Reaching out she ran her hands over him. "I love your chest."

"Do you think you could admire it just as well in a supine position?" Worthington picked her up and carried her to their bed.

Kicking her feet out, she toed off her slippers. "My stockings."

"In a minute." He feathered kisses over her throat and down her neck. Her skin warmed and flushed. He caressed her lips with his tongue, teasing until she put her arms around him and captured his mouth. The familiar heat rose between them. He sank deeper into their kiss and Worthington's senses threatened to scatter. His shaft had been hard since they reached the room, but this was not the time to take her quickly. He wanted to reacquaint himself with her body. His heart raced. Holding her head in his hands, he drove her further into their passion, until Grace was panting and writhing beneath him. Her legs embraced him, pleading for him to take her.

"Not yet," he managed to murmur.

Worthington's lips left hers and moved down to her breasts. He held one in his hand while his mouth ministered to the other. Grace shook with need. But his licking and tasting added a layer of pleasure to what she wanted. She cried out and this time he didn't caution her to be quiet. He left her breasts and traveled over her stomach to her curls. Oh, he hadn't done that since their first night, and she wanted it. When she moaned, her wicked husband chuckled deeply as she arched into him wanting more.

Grace shuddered and screamed when his tongue stroked and entered her. "Matt, Matt, please."

"Ah, so that's what I have to do in order for you to scream my name?"

Matt embraced his need for her. He'd not expected their union to be so strong this soon. Slumping down next to her, he ran his hand over her naked body. This was the lady he was meant to have, to live his life with. His woman, his love. For the second time, he settled her in the place next to him and pulled the covers over them.

Her skin was still flushed and dewed. Grace snuggled into him. "That was different, wasn't it?"

"Yes." He kissed her forehead. "It was different. How it's meant to be."

"I like being in a bed with you." Grace turned in his arms and captured him with her deep blue gaze. "I won't leave this time. I want to know what it's like to wake with you next to me."

Matt didn't think he'd ever known such joy. "Good. I don't want to have to go looking for you."

Mr. Combs woke early with a stuffy nose. His wife brought a hot cloth and laid in on his troublesome appendage. That always seemed to help. The job would have to wait until he could breathe again. He went back to sleep. By the time he woke it was late morning and sunny, and he could breathe. Combs dressed then found his wife in their small parlor, mending clothes.

"I'm on my way out." He leaned down and kissed her cheek.

"Just a minute. I made some pies for you." She bustled into the kitchen and was back a moment later. "Here you go. I'll send one of the boys to see how you're doing later."

"Don't want to say much now." Combs tapped the side of his nose. "But this job may make us more than the fee."

His wife grinned. "We can always use the money."

A few moments later, Combs took a hackney to Davies Street, just outside of Berkeley Square.

It was early afternoon before Combs could fulfill his agreement with his new client, Mr. Molton, and finally arrived in Berkeley Square. Carriages lined the streets and men in livery stood conversing. "Can ye tell me which one of these houses be Stanwood House?"

Once of the men pointed to a town house, two down from the corner.

Walking down the street a bit, he stopped to chat with two younger footmen. "What's goin' on here?"

A larger and older man wearing a different livery ambled up. "What's goin' on here is none of yourn business. If it was, ye'd know."

Shrugging, Combs said, "Didn't mean nothin' by it. Jus makin' conversation like."

"Go make it somewhere else, then. We're all on dooty here."

Combs walked into the parklike place in the middle of the square, leaned against a tree, and watched the door of Stanwood House. After a while, a young woman matching the description Molton gave him hurried across the square with a well-turned-out swell. "Bold as brass they are and in the middle of the day," he muttered.

After, the couple entered a house on the other side of the square. He made himself as comfortable as he could and waited, never taking his eyes off the house, until his son came to relieve him. "Mind, keep watch on that door." He pointed to Worthington House. "Yer lookin' for a young rum mort with yaller hair. Brazen-faced is she. Been in there most of the day. It's no wonder our swell don't want her to have charge of the children. Teach them all to be as loose as she be. She'd be better off at Miss Betsy's, if you know what I mean."

"They'd pay a pretty penny for her, and, the Lord knows, we could use it," his son agreed. "You better get home. Mam says she'll be waitin' for ye with dinner."

Combs stood and stretched. "I'll spell ye tonight."

Matt must have drifted off to sleep. When he glanced out the window, the sun was no longer visible.

He kissed Grace's hair, and she squirmed against him. "I'm famished."

"Mmm, I am too." He slid her under him.

"For food." Her stomach growled.

He heaved a sigh. "I suppose I don't want anyone to say I starved my wife."

"Should we call someone?"

"Wait here." Matt donned his dressing gown and gave Grace the colorfully embroidered silk banyan he'd bought for her. Stepping into the parlor, he saw a table set up with covered dishes, wine, water, and lemonade. "Someone has anticipated your needs."

Grace seemed to float into the room. She lifted one of the lids. "Roasted chicken, what else do we have?"

He uncovered the rest of the dishes. "Bread, cheese, fruit. Would you like wine?"

"Please. Will you carve the chicken?"

"With pleasure. By the looks of this, I don't think we are expected anywhere to-day."

"No, it appears not. I wonder if they'll bring breakfast or if we are eating with our family."

Grace plucked a grape from the bunch, slid it between her still swollen lips, and chewed.

Worthington's blood heated and desire rose again. He wished she'd remove her dressing gown. Though it was probably too much to expect her to dine in the nude, or allow him to eat grapes from between her breasts. Well, maybe eat the grapes. That shouldn't take too long to accomplish.

Taking another grape, she chewed and swallowed. "What are you thinking?"

"Come here." When she reached him, she had another piece of fruit between her lips. He bit it in half and licked the juice from her lips. "Of things we must do in the future."

"Oh, such as the guardianship."

"The guardianship of course, among other things." He lowered his lids and smiled slowly. "I've left a message that we are to be disturbed only if there was any problem with the filing. Because, to-day and tonight, I plan to concentrate on my wife, and I don't want her worrying."

Grace's eyes opened wide, her smile was sultry. "Oh, is your wife not allowed to worry, my lord?"

Running the smooth skin of the fruit over her lips and down her neck, before popping it in his mouth, he smiled.

"My wife will fret, it's her nature. My job is to make her less anxious."

"Then I predict your wife will be an extremely happy lady."

He carved the chicken. "Do you remember that first night, when I told you you'd be well pleasured?"

She swallowed and nodded. "Yes."

Placing a large piece of chicken on her plate, he grinned. "You need to eat."

Grace woke to find herself nestled into Matt in the same way she had been that first morning. When she started to slip out of bed, his arm clamped around her. "Where are you going?"

"Only to the water closet." She smiled. "I'll be right back."

He grunted.

Even though the room was a little chilly, she didn't don her dressing gown. Upon her return, she found he'd stoked the fire and added more wood.

Sliding back into the bed, she snuggled next to him to warm herself. Come to think of it, he was warm the last time. "Are you never cold?"

"Not really. You are though." He turned her so her back was to his chest and pulled the duvet closely around her.

In a few minutes, she was comfortable enough to think about other desires and pushed her bottom into his engorged shaft.

His lips nuzzled her hair and his teeth nipped at the outer whorl of her ear. She could feel his grin as Matt kissed her jaw. "Do you want something, my love?"

"Yes, if you don't mind." He slid his hand to her curls and stroked before his lips traveled over her breasts, over her stomach until he licked the tight nub nestled in her mons.

She shouted his name as the tension spiraled, winding her tighter.

Matt chuckled. "I love it when you scream."

She tried to laugh and couldn't. She'd scream all he liked if he'd just bring her the relief she needed. Bright sparks burst inside her. He moved back up her body. His hard shaft penetrated her, then he withdrew and entered again. Frissons of delight raced through her. Grace wrapped herself around him and the maelstrom built until she thought she would die. It flung her out and he shouted and pumped deeply into her. Hers, he was hers. He'd made his vows earlier, yet he'd also made them to her now. A bond she had never known could exist enveloped them, and she vowed never to let anyone else have him. Nothing would ever separate them.

The next time she woke, the sun poured through the window.

"I'm hungry." Grace started to rise.

He stopped her. "I'll go." Matt pulled the covers around her, then strode into the parlor. "Nothing. I assume that means we're expected across the way for breakfast."

She gave him her most sultry smile. "Hmm. Well, until Bolton and your valet arrive to dress us, you can come back to bed, my lord."

His eyes roamed over her body, and he grinned. "What an excellent idea, my lady."

Thus far, being married was a great deal of fun.

Chapter Twenty-Seven

Matt closed the door on his valet, then turned toward Grace. "Not only have I been advised we are expected across the street, I've been reminded that this is Good Friday, and we have a church service to attend." Matt gazed down grinning at what must be the most wanton-looking countess in London. Her hair, a riot of messy curls, was spread out over her and around the pillows as she sprawled naked on the sheets. "Bolton is here and has your bathwater ready."

Grace sat up, pushing back her hair. "I'm hungry."

He gave a bark of laughter. Other than making love, the only thing they'd done was eat. He took her hand and pulled her up. "You're always hungry. If you want food, you'll have to bathe. I cannot have my countess appearing at church appearing less than respectable."

Her eyes flew open. "Less than—what do you mean?"

He turned her toward a mirror. She was delectable, but he doubted she'd agree.

"Oh no. What a fright I look, and you didn't say a word."

"You look like what you are, a well-sated wife." He handed Grace her dressing gown. "My wife and I love you just as you are."

She pulled a face as she stared into the mirror. "You must be besotted if you like my appearance now."

Matt kissed her. "Considering I had something to do with it, I dare not complain."

"No. You're right about that." She turned into his arms.

"My lady, your water is getting cold." Bolton's voice boomed through the door.

"Coming, Bolton." Grace closed her eyes for a moment, then gazed up at him.

"My lord?" Timmons, his valet, called. "You must dress if you're going to be on time."

Matt grinned and imagined many mornings of these conversations. "Yes, I know. I'll be there directly."

Gathering her in his arms again, Worthington kissed her. "I'll see you soon."

Grace melted into his arms. "Yes."

Bolton grumbled as she combed out Grace's curls. "I don't suppose his lordship could have let you braid your hair?"

Grace laughed. "I don't recall the matter coming up." Though other subjects had. "I'll ask him, if you like."

"I'd be surprised if it'll do any good." Bolton shook her head. "I remember well your mother's maid complaining."

Grace donned the morning gown she'd worn yesterday, this time with stays, then returned to their chambers. How she loved the sound of that. She leaned against the door and watched as he tied his cravat. "Don't be long, will you?"

"No, it's just this cravat. I'll be along soon." He eyed her morning gown. "You're not wearing that?"

"Naturally, I am not, but I never dress until the children have eaten. It won't take me long." She blew him a kiss, left the house, and walked across the square. From Royston to the tweenie who cleaned the parlor, her household servants were lined up to wish her happy.

Her butler bowed. "My lady, the staff would like to congratulate you on your marriage."

Tears of joy started in her eyes as she greeted each one and thanked them. "Oh, my. I didn't expect this. Thank you so much."

A few minutes later, Matt entered and was congratulated as well. "Come, my dear. We must break our fast and go to church."

When they entered the breakfast room, Mr. Winters and Miss Tallerton stood and began clapping. The children joined in.

Charlotte rose. "We are so happy for you."

She nudged Charlie who jumped up. Louisa handed him a piece of paper. "Yes, we are and we, all of us have a toast for you." He raised his teacup. "'To Matt, our new brother, and Grace, our new sister, we wish you a happy marriage and'—just a moment—do you really want me to say this?"

"Yes," Louisa hissed, and resumed her smile.

Charlie's brows rose. "All right, 'we wish you many happy times together and a lot of children, because we want to be aunts and uncles.'"

Their brothers' and sisters' faces beamed. At the moment, Grace couldn't bring herself to think of additional children. She glanced at Matt who was fighting a valiant battle to maintain his countenance, and spoke for the both of them. "Thank you for all your good wishes. Now, everyone must finish breakfast. We are going to church again."

After filling her plate, Grace took her place at the foot of the table.

Her husband leaned down. "Do I have to sit at the head?"

"No, not during breakfast." She held her hand out to him.

"Good." Worthington took her fingers and kissed them

before visiting the sideboard. He came back with a plate piled even higher than hers.

Yesterday morning, she had felt so alone it had quite dampened her appetite; this morning she ate everything and went back for more. "I love breaking my fast with all of you. I only hope that by the time you have gone on to make your own lives, we shall have more children to join us."

Her brothers and sisters and his sisters all nodded in agreement. Worthington paled a little. "Indeed, my love, we shall hope for the best."

Grace took her last bite and her final sip of tea. "If you can stay and help get them all together, I'll see you in about fifteen minutes."

"Of course. I'll take care of them and have everyone ready."

She kissed him and left.

"Sir," Philip asked, "why must you always kiss Grace?"

Matt picked up his cup. What does one say to an eight-year-old boy about kissing? "She would be upset if I did not." The boy's brows drew together as if not quite understanding. Perhaps something more direct was called for. "It is obligatory to kiss one's wife."

Philip frowned. "Well, in that case, you won't mind if I don't marry, will you? I don't think I would like to always be kissing a lady."

Louisa and Charlotte hid their faces in their hands as their shoulders shook. Matt cast them a stern glance and noticed that Walter and Charlie were applying themselves diligently to their plates. Matt returned his attention to Philip. "Not at all. When you are of sufficient age to marry"—Matt slapped Louisa on the back as she made a choking sound—"and you still do not wish to kiss a lady, I'm sure Grace and I will have no objection to you remaining single."

Letting out a relieved breath, Philip smiled. "Thank you, sir."

"Er, Philip, you may call me Matt if you choose. I *am* your brother now."

"Umm, yes, sir. I mean, Matt. Thank you."

Walter fixed Matt with a look. "Very glad this all worked out. You marrying Grace, that is. Didn't much like her acting like a watering pot and hiding away."

Agreeing entirely with Walter, Matt nodded. "No, I can see how uncomfortable that would have been. I don't like to see her cry myself."

Charlie stood. "All right, you lot, time to go and finish getting ready."

Matt lounged in his chair. "She'll be at least a half an hour."

As he turned to look at him, Charlie's face took on an amused cast. "Still have some things to learn about Grace, I see. You'll look no how when she comes back and we're all still at the table."

Unable to believe what he was hearing, Matt said, "Go on."

Charlie grinned. "If she says fifteen minutes, that's what she means."

"Very well, off you go. I don't intend to spend my first full day as her husband in a bumble bath."

"Wise decision, sir," Walter added.

Grace appeared precisely fifteen minutes after she'd left. He would have dashed a hand across his eyes in relief, but he was straightening Philip's clothing.

"Is everyone ready?" Grace asked, sticking a pin into her hat.

"Yes," Matt said, turning toward the milling herd. "Everyone, hold hands with one other person and line up."

They sorted themselves out in short order and were ready. "My lady." He bowed. "After you."

Grace took his arm. "Where is Patience?"

"She went with your aunt and uncle."

"Very well, let us proceed."

"My love," Matt said, "are we going to walk to church every time we attend?"

"You have a choice," she said in an overly sweet tone. "We can walk, or you can see how much energy they have when we take the coaches. Do you remember yesterday?"

He frowned. "Yes, but that was only because of the wedding."

She cast him a sidelong glance. "If you truly believe that, we may take the coaches on Sunday."

He had a vision of eleven active children in St. George's—his active children—and capitulated. "You've done a very good job with Charlie. He appears to take his duties seriously, but in stride."

Grinning, his wife said, "He made it easy. When we went through the guardianship process, he realized, early on, that he would be responsible for the children and the estates upon his majority." Grace paused. "I wish he could have the opportunity to enjoy some freedom before taking up his duties, but it's not possible."

Matt covered her hand. "Many young men who've made that decision are very dull dogs. Charlie is not. I predict he'll enjoy himself in a fashion that won't harm his dependents."

"No, he's not a dead bore." Tilting her head, she smiled up at him. "And I think you are right. He will find a way to enjoy himself and not harm anyone else."

"Don't forget, he'll have both of us to help him now." Matt would do his best to ensure Charlie did not shoulder any responsibilities he wasn't ready for. All young men should have time to sow a few wild oats.

Combs relieved his son and at seven o'clock the next morning watched the lady walk back over to Stanwood House. The gentleman followed a few minutes later. "He'll have what he needs now, and we maybe could help him a bit more by getting rid of his niece." Combs sauntered out of the square and headed toward Mr. Molton's rooms.

Molton heard the banging at the door and tried hard to separate it from the banging in his head. He'd been at the Daffy Club last night, reacquainting himself with London's entertainments. He planned to be a very rich man.

"Mr. Molton, sir. I got the information ye need."

Combs. Of course, who else would be knocking so early? "Give me a minute."

He dragged himself out of bed and poured water in the basin. After splashing his face and brushing his teeth, he donned a dressing gown. In his considerable experience, people who woke up at the crack of dawn didn't like to smell gin or brandy on another person, and he required Combs's full cooperation.

Molton opened the door, welcomed Mr. Combs, and motioned him to a seat. After which, he rang for coffee. Once Molton had poured a cup for himself and the investigator, he took a chair. "Tell me what you found."

Combs took a large drink of the coffee and set the cup back down. "It were just like ye said. That niece of yourn's a regular doxy. Spend the whole night at that swell's house and come out as brazen as could be this morning. I'll testify to it. Can't have trash like her keeping innocents."

"Er, thank you. Well done." Molton rubbed a hand over his face. *Don't tell me the man's a bloody Methodist?*

"Thank ye. When I teld me rib what she done, she sez it's clear where me dooty be."

"Yes, yes, of course." Molton rubbed his jaw. "I shall, of course, attempt to reason with her. If she will not give up the children, I must file a suit in Chancery Court."

"Ye jus tell me, and I'll be there. Seen it with me own eyes. Me and my oldest." He nodded emphatically.

"Thank you again, and thank your son. I'll come by later to pay you."

"No need, no need a'tall. Won't be in the office to-day, as it's Good Friday. But me rib and me, we figure it's a mission of God to save those youn'uns."

Good Lord, the man was a Methodist. A starchier group of people he'd never met. "Truly, the work of the Lord." Molton said with what he hoped was proper piety. "You have a good day with your family."

The man wrung his hand. "Be seein' ye later I s'pect."

"Yes, yes, if she's not reasonable." Fate must be on his side. At least he saved some money. Though he wouldn't have to worry about being at low water ever again, not after he spoke to Worthington and let him know the game was up.

Once Matt and Grace arrived at the church with the rest of their family, Charlie, Louisa, and Charlotte helped settle the children. Patience and Lord and Lady Herndon joined them. A few moments later the Eveshams and Rutherfords stopped by.

Seeing the wives of his friends in a delicate condition, Matt wondered how long it would be before Grace was breeding. He must have lost his mind, but he hoped she was already pregnant.

St. George's was half empty, and he gave thanks for those who'd left London for Easter. The remaining congregants now paid little attention to them. They returned home to Jacques's roast beef and Yorkshire pudding. The chef was definitely remaining with them.

After dinner, Charlie took him aside. "I wanted to thank you, sir."

Worthington turned in surprise. "How so?"

Charlie grimaced. "The children, though I don't suppose

I should call Louisa and Charlotte children, told me that Grace refused you at first, but you kept at it until she said yes."

Clapping him on the back, Matt glanced at his brother-in-law and gave Charlie a serious look. "One must fight for what one wants."

"Yes, well you see, I knew she wanted to marry." He shuffled his feet a bit. "But she gave up all her dreams for us."

"Fate has a strange way of arranging things." Matt squeezed Charlie's shoulder.

"I suppose it does." He paused for a moment. "When I attain my majority, I'll take them off your hands."

This was not a discussion Matt intended to have now. "Let's see how everything goes." Glancing around and seeing Grace occupied with the older girls, Matt lowered his voice. "You wouldn't like to tell me, man to man, earl to earl, how to remain on Grace's good side?"

Charlie grinned. "Don't surprise her. She's held our hands through stitches and broken bones, and other things that would give another woman the vapors, but give her a surprise birthday party, and she faints dead away. Don't understand it myself. No reason I should. It's just the way she is."

"Like a game of billiards, Stanwood?"

"Wouldn't I just. I've had no one to play with since m'father died."

Matt clapped his hand on Charlie's shoulder. "Then come with me, young'un, and we'll see how much you know."

Walter and Philip joined them. Charlie knew the game and only needed practice and a few pointers. He helped Matt teach the younger two. As much as Matt loved his sisters, he enjoyed having younger brothers.

He gave silent thanks for Grace coming into his life.

* * *

Lord Bentley and Lord Harrington were ushered into the drawing room. Grace smiled as they made their bows and Louisa and Charlotte curtseyed.

"I know it's not usual to visit on a holy day," Bentley said, tugging on his cravat "though there are so few people in Town . . ."

Harrington nodded. "We—we thought we'd call."

Resisting the urge to laugh, Grace motioned for them to a sofa. "We are very glad you did. Please have a seat, and I shall ring for tea."

"No need to do so on our account," Harrington replied.

"Indeed," Bentley said. "We wouldn't want to put you to any trouble."

This must be the first time that either gentleman had done the pretty. "Thank you for your concern." She rang the bell-pull. "But we usually drink tea at this time of day."

Bentley swallowed. "Of course."

Even though Grace bid them to sit, they naturally remained standing until she sank onto the sofa.

By the time Matt joined them Charlotte was pouring the tea.

He took the place next to Grace, drawing her attention. "I suppose they will overcome their nervousness at some point."

Taking in the young men as they fiddled with their fobs, she hoped, for their sake, it was soon. "You are not to make a game of them and tell Charlie the same thing. They are being very courageous in trying to be the girls' first suitors."

He drew his brows together. "Do you suppose they stayed in Town because of Charlotte and Louisa?"

Grace looked at him over the rim of her cup. "A mere glance at the *Morning Post* would have revealed to you that their parents are at their country estates hosting large house parties."

"Which means they did."

"I think that is a safe assumption."

A loud *woof* and thumping came from overhead. Matt glanced up. "If you've got it under control here, I'll take the rest of the children and dogs to the Park."

More thumping and another deeper bark echoed down the stairs. "Good idea."

He left and a few moments later the sounds of the younger children, footmen, and dogs readying themselves could be heard. Matt strode back into the drawing room and brought her fingers to his lips lightly grazing her knuckles, before turning to leave.

"If you don't mind saying," Bentley asked, "what kind of dog is that?"

"Dogs. Two Great Danes. One is ours and the other is Grace's family's." Louisa smiled. "I suppose I should say our dogs as we are one family now."

"You don't say?" Harrington glanced up. "I'd like to see them," he said, adding nervously, "if you don't mind, that is."

Charlotte rose, a small smile tilting her lips. "No, we don't mind at all. Worthington will be down with them and the children in a few minutes."

"We usually all go to the Park together," Louisa added.

In very short order, Daisy barreled into the room, and Matt's deep voiced barked a command. "Daisy, halt."

Well, if she didn't actually stop, she did slow down. Grace smiled with relief. "Worthington, she is doing much better."

Her husband muttered something under his breath that Grace assumed was a curse and strode into the room with Duke. Bentley and Harrington went to meet the dogs.

Grace thought it was to their credit that neither of the young men was worried about the dogs leaning against them.

Then Bentley, who was petting Daisy, said, "My grandfather had Danes. Wonderful dogs. She's pretty young, isn't she?"

Charlotte came over. "Yes, she's just over a year. Duke is four."

Harrington grinned. "You've got a couple of more years of trouble with her then." Glancing at Bentley, he asked, "Would you mind if we accompanied you to the Park?"

Louisa and Charlotte exchanged excited glances, and Charlotte said, "We'll just need a moment. Matt, will you wait for us?"

"Yes, of course. Just hurry."

Before Grace followed the girls out of the room, she looked at Matt. "I think I'll come as well."

She was able to keep Louisa and Charlotte quiet until they reached Grace's old room, where one of her bonnets was. It was a good thing Bolton had decided to keep some of Grace's clothing here. "Now what is going on?"

"Grace," Charlotte said excitedly, "they asked us to reserve a waltz for them at Lady Sale's ball."

Louisa's eyes glowed. "I think that was very well done of them, coming here. They remained in Town just to ask us to dance."

Grace was so happy for them. They would both be great successes this Season. "They certainly got the jump on the rest of the young gentlemen."

As the children, Louisa, Charlotte, Charlie, and their guests, walked out of the square and down the street to the Park, Grace regarded the young men. Apparently both Harrington and Bentley intended to keep their lead on the competitors. They were attentive not only to the girls, but to their brothers and sisters as well as the dogs. Walter, though, had decided to have some fun by pulling faces and batting his eyes.

"Don't," Matt said. "One day, you'll be in the same position."

"And don't tease the girls either," Grace said.

Walter grinned good-naturedly. "You two are taking all the

fun out of this." He fell quiet for a few minutes, then said, as if a thought had occurred to him, "Charlotte could be married this year."

"Yes." Grace studied her brother. "If she meets the right gentleman, she could be wed before summer."

"Who's next then? Augusta?"

Matt nodded and suddenly his face had a panicked expression. "My God. Do you realize we have the twins and Madeline coming out the same year?"

Charlie gave a bark of laughter.

"You laugh now," Matt said darkly. "You won't think it's so humorous when you're drafted to help chaperone."

Her brother's face fell. "I don't suppose you have a tower at your estate, do you?"

Chapter Twenty-Eight

After they returned from the Park, Grace went to her study to sort through the mail she'd ignored during the past two days. She was in the process of answering a letter from her steward when Patience knocked on the door.

"May I come in?"

Putting down the pen, Grace sprinkled sand over the paper. "Of course. How are you settling in?"

Sinking gracefully into a chair next to the desk, Patience grinned. "Very nicely. I rather like not having many responsibilities. Do you have the account books for Worthington House?"

Searching through the ledgers on the bookcase next to her desk, Grace shook her head. "Not yet, is there something you wish to go over with me?"

"Not really." Patience grimaced. "I thought I should tell you they are not up to date. I never could make them balance, so I just gave up."

Was that the reason Matt had been so concerned about Grace's expenditures? "Oh dear. How long has it been since you've looked at them?"

Patience glanced at the ceiling and gave an airy wave of her hand. "I am not quite sure. Probably about six years."

Did Matt even suspect his household accounts had been ignored for so long? Grace dreaded the answer to her next question. "Do you still have all the receipts?"

"Every last one." Patience brightened, obviously proud of herself. "I thought I might need them at some point. For a while, I kept them all in a drawer, and when I ran out of room, I put them in boxes."

"That is a starting place." Despite her dread at having to trace back years of expenditures, Grace kept her tone even. "Tell me, does Louisa know how to hold house?"

"Ah, not precisely." The other woman's brows drew together. "I have never been able to teach her, and I did not want to bother Worthington."

Grace didn't want to think about what Matt was going to say. Yet now she could kill two birds with one stone. "If you show a couple of footmen where the receipts are and have them bring the boxes here, I'll use them to teach Louisa how to balance the accounts."

"Thank you, my dear." Patience rose. "I hoped you would say that. I shall attend to it immediately."

Not many moments later, Patience, accompanied by two footmen, strolled to Worthington House. She showed them where the boxes were stacked. As they were leaving the house, a gentleman, with the reddened face of one who had spent much of his life in dissipation, approached her.

"Lady Worthington?"

Whoever he was had a great deal of gall addressing her without being introduced. Raising an imperious brow, she used her coldest tone. "I beg your pardon."

He bowed. "I apologize. Please allow me to make myself known to you. Mr. Edgar Molton, at your service."

With a great effort, she maintained a look of unconcern. Matt would have to be told immediately. "Indeed."

Wondering what to do next, Patience stared at the man. Of course, Lady Herndon had warned them all that he might try to approach, but Patience really had not thought it possible. Whatever the man wanted, he wasn't going to receive any help from her. "How may I help you, Mr. Molton?"

A smile creased his face. "It's the other way around, my lady. There is a certain matter of which I have knowledge that may interest you."

Raising her other brow, she tried to think of what to say. No matter what, she must put him off. That would be the best course of action. "I doubt that very much. Good day, Mr. Molton."

When he stepped closer to her the footmen set down the boxes, flanking her protectively.

The man took two steps back. "Do you have any idea who I am, my lady?"

"Mr. Molton, I know precisely who you are, and I have been instructed not to have anything to do with you." She turned to one of the footmen. "Please, let us get the boxes and go."

"Is your husband in?"

She whirled back to him. For a moment, her mind was in a muddle, then it dawned on her that the man thought she was the current Lady Worthington. And if he had seen Grace and Worthington . . . Molton must be here to make trouble for Grace. "Lord Worthington is not home at present. I expect he will return later in the day. Now, you must excuse me."

Patience swept past him. Should she warn Grace? No, it

would only upset her. Worthington was well able to handle the scoundrel, probably without Grace knowing a thing about it. Yes, that would be best.

Patience took a breath to calm her rapidly pounding heart, and instructed the footmen to deliver the boxes to Lady Worthington. She then left a message for her stepson to attend her as soon as possible, went into the morning room and ordered tea. Fortunately, she did not have long to wait.

Worthington strode into the room with a frown. "Patience, you wanted to see me?"

She rose and held out her hands. When he took them, she said, "Oh, Worthington, the most dreadful thing—Grace's uncle, Molton, accosted me as I was leaving Worthington House."

Worthington's visage darkened. "What did he say?"

"Quite honestly, I did not give him a chance to say much at all, but he seems to think I am your wife."

"How in the world?" Leading her to the sofa, he continued to hold her hands, keeping her calm. "Here, sit down and tell me everything."

Patience told him what had happened. "He clearly does not have a copy of *Debrett's*, nor does he keep up."

"No, clearly not." Worthington shook his head. "When was this?"

"Not long ago. Less than an hour. I told him you would be home later. Where had you gone?"

"I received a message to meet with Lord Herndon." That was a bit of good luck. Matt had been shown the signed guardianship papers and was promised a copy as soon as one was made. As of late yesterday, he'd been awarded custody of Grace's brothers and sisters. No one would hurt either them or her.

"Worthington, are you listening to me? I said, I did not tell Grace."

He returned his focus to Patience. "Thank you. That was well done. If he can be taken care of without her knowledge, there is no reason to worry her."

Patience nodded happily. "Those were my thoughts."

He glanced at her. "Where is she?"

"In her study, attending to correspondence." Glancing up at him, she pulled a face. "I—I also had the household receipts delivered to her."

"That was a good idea." He smiled. "Patience, I have never blamed you for not being able to reconcile them. I only wish you would have told me sooner."

"You knew? Oh, Worthington, I was so embarrassed that I could not manage. But at least Louisa will not be as stupid as I am. Grace has promised to teach her."

"In that case, you no longer have to worry about them. It's all working out." He kissed her cheek. "If anyone asks, I'll be across the square."

About three hours later, Matt was in his office reviewing a letter from his steward when Thorton knocked. "My lord, Mr. Molton is here as you said he would be."

Matt grinned to himself. *Let's see what the here-and-therein wants.* "Show him in."

A few minutes later, Thorton returned with Grace's uncle.

Having the upper hand, Matt found it surprisingly easy to smile as he greeted the bounder. "Mr. Molton. Please take a seat." He waited until the older man lowered himself into a leather chair. "Now, to what do I owe the pleasure of your visit?"

"You may not be happy, my lord, when I've said what I intend to."

Matt raised an inquiring brow. "Indeed, sir, and why is that?"

Molton frowned. "I know what you've been up to and with my niece. I'm sure you wouldn't want your wife to know about it."

This was going to be more entertaining than Matt thought. He assumed a perplexed demeanor. "Your niece, sir? I understand you have several. To which one are you referring?"

"Grace, Lady Grace Carpenter." Growing agitated, the man spat out her name.

Matt placed his elbows on the desk and regarded Molton with spurious interest. "Oh, Grace, it is? I see, and what do you suspect me of doing with Grace?"

By this time, Molton's face was turning an interesting shade of reddish-purple. Matt idly wondered if there was a name for the color.

"You have ruined her," the older man proclaimed dramatically.

Matt regarded Molton over steepled fingers and widened his eyes. "Have I? I think you should make yourself plain, sir. I've no wish to go round and round with you. Exactly how have I ruined Grace?"

"Play the innocent all you want." Molton's eyes narrowed. "You will not get away with this perfidy."

"Until I know what perfidy you are speaking of, I don't know how I could get away with it, as you so elegantly phrased it." Matt wondered how much longer this was going to continue. Then again, it was rather like playing a fish on the line.

Spittle formed at the corners of the man's mouth. "I had a man watching this house, and he saw Grace enter yesterday afternoon and not come out until this morning."

Ah, now they were getting somewhere. Was it control of the children's funds or blackmail the man intended? Matt leaned back in his chair and grinned.

Molton's jaw dropped. "You don't deny it?"

Matt opened his eyes even wider. "But my good man, why should I? She did indeed spend the night with me. Although why it is any concern of yours, you have yet to explain." He lifted his hand and made a *come* motion. "You do intend to tell me, do you not? Or are you wasting my time?"

Half rising from the chair, he leaned forward. "I know she's attached to those brats of hers."

Suddenly, the fun of egging the man on was gone, and it was all Matt could do to stop himself from leaping over the desk and grabbing the cur by his neck. "I take it you mean her brothers and sisters?"

Settling back down in the chair, Molton replied, "I do. Seems to me, under the circumstances, you understand, that it wouldn't be hard to have them taken away from her."

Acting his part, Matt frowned slightly. "You don't strike me as the sort of man who is overly concerned with the children or your niece's morals."

"Couldn't care less about a bunch of kids. As for my niece, she can spread her legs for anyone she wants." The man's mouth twisted into a humorless grin. "It's not them I'm after."

"Your sense of familial affection astounds me," He drawled. Herndon was right. Grace's uncle was a bounder and a loose fish. "Why don't you open your budget and tell me what it is you do want."

"Money. I'll mind my own business for a payment on my bank account, say quarterly, until my niece is either married or until Stanwood comes of age. Then I want that ten thousand pounds she's getting."

Matt curled his lips as if amused. "Mr. Molton, the descriptions of you did not do you justice. It will, however, be a cold day in hell before I give you so much as a farthing."

Molton stood, scowling. "You'll pay, my lord, or she

will. I'll spread it all over Town that she's your mistress. One way or the other, I'll get what I want."

There was a shuffling in the hall and Grace's clear voice. "Don't worry, Thorton, I won't bother him for long."

Matt moved quickly toward the door and placed his hand protectively on her waist when she entered.

She stopped in surprise. "Forgive me. I was not aware you have a visitor. I shall come back later, if you'd like."

He put his arm around her and drew her closer. "It's no matter, my love. He was just leaving."

Grace's forehead puckered as she looked at Molton. "Do I know you?"

"You've grown up to be a fine-looking woman," her uncle said.

Grace glanced at Matt. "Who is he?"

Smiling wickedly, he replied, "Grace, allow me to introduce your uncle, Mr. Edgar Molton. Molton, my wife, the Countess of Worthington."

He paled and grabbed onto the chair he stood next to. "Wife?" he uttered faintly.

Matt hardened his gaze. "Wife."

"But—but there was no announcement."

Keeping his arm around Grace, he poured glasses of wine for himself and Grace. Molton could go thirsty. "It's been sent, but not yet printed. The holiday, you understand."

Grace took her glass and glanced up. "Worthington, I don't understand what is going on."

"Your uncle, my love, decided to blackmail us. He had a man watching the house yesterday. The person saw you enter and not leave until this morning."

"Blackmail? Not the children?" She gave a sigh of relief. "That is not at all what I thought he would do."

Grinning, he hugged her closer. He had been prepared for her to swoon. But blackmail was not her fear. It was having the children taken away. "No. It seems his needs are much simpler." He turned to her uncle. "Not that you deserve an explanation, but I shall give you one. We are renovating the house for the children. At present, my family, including my stepmother, the lady you approached earlier, and our brothers and sisters are living at Stanwood House. Grace and I sleep here."

Molton seemed to shrink into the chair. "All my plans, all my money, gone. I should have known it was too good to be true."

Matt tugged the bell-pull. "Mr. Molton, if you have no further business, I suggest you depart."

Molton seemed to have aged ten years. He stood. "Yes, yes."

"I understand one may live much more inexpensively overseas. I propose you think about it. If I ever see or hear of you near either of our houses or the children again, I shall have no difficulty in making your life decidedly difficult."

Thorton came and escorted Molton out.

Grace shook her head unbelievingly. "All he wanted was money?"

He took her glass and set it on his desk before drawing her closer. "Yes, he had no interest in the children at all, other as a means to get what he really desired."

"Then your petition will be granted without challenge."

Matt took Grace in his arms, twirling her around before kissing her deeply. "It's already been granted. Herndon sent for me earlier."

Melting into him, she returned each languid caress of his tongue with hers. He was moving her toward the daybed he'd had delivered, when Grace pulled back and her eyes widened. "Then—then we've nothing to worry about any-more?"

He gave a shout of laughter. "If you don't think having

two young ladies making their come out nothing to worry about, then I suppose you're right. I, however, am not quite so sanguine."

His wife opened her lips to speak, and he swooped to take possession of them. After kissing her thoroughly, he raised his head. "I shall rely on your good sense. In the meantime, we have more important issues to attend to."

She gazed at him. "Indeed, my lord, and what would they be?"

He pushed her gown and stays down, before taking her in his arms again. "Scandalizing the servants."

A discreet tap sounded on the door as Grace adjusted her bodice.

"My lord," Thorton said, "Harold is bringing Miss Daisy over for her lessons shortly. I thought you might wish to be ready."

Matt brushed his lips across Grace's. "He means presentable."

"I imagine he does. How is she doing?"

"Better now that I'm having Duke to show her the way."

"I'll see you back at Stanwood House."

He escorted her to the door. "I won't be long. She is unable to pay attention for more than twenty minutes."

The dogs were with Harold making their way through the square when Grace walked down the steps and onto the pavement.

"My lord?"

Matt closed the door. "Yes, Thorton?"

"Mr. Timmons wishes to know when you would—"

A woman's scream rent the air.

Grace!

Matt tore the door open and bolted down the steps, but

the old, black coach was already turning the corner, both Danes following.

The footman darted across the street. "*My lord, her ladyship's been taken!*"

Matt's blood turned to ice. "Harold, did they say anything?"

"I heard something about a Miss Betsy."

Damn. If Matt didn't get her back quickly, who knew what they'd do to her. Whoever was behind this would pay, and pay dearly. His long strides ate the distance back to his house. "Thorton, get my horse now. We don't have a moment to lose."

"Worthington." Jane gasped for air as she came running up. "We saw what happened. Hector's following in his curricle."

Matt nodded tightly. "Take care of the children until we get back."

"I shall. You just worry about rescuing Grace."

Matt strode through the garden, into the mews behind, just as his groom brought out his horse. Without saying a word he swung himself up on the large gelding. If Harold was right and the kidnappers were taking Grace to Miss Betsy's, he might be able to make it to Regent Street before they did. Even though the road was not completely finished, it would be their fastest route to the Covent Garden area where the brothel was located. The one thing in his favor was that the coach was not yet headed in the right direction. He rode at a fast trot out of the alley and onto Bruton Street.

With any luck at all, he'd be able to cut them off.

Chapter Twenty-Nine

Grace's bonnet was still askew as she jerked down her skirts and righted herself. Her heart raced causing her to feel vaguely ill. Either that or it was the odor from the two men. Other than a discrepancy in age, they looked very much alike.

The deep barks that had sounded from either side of the hackney had ceased. Were the dogs still with them or not?

Suddenly the driver shouted and the coach slowed. "Get off, you damned beasts."

"What's goin' on out there?" the older man next to her yelled.

"The blasted dogs are nipping at the horse."

"Call yer dogs off," the scoundrel growled.

The coach swung right, and Grace grabbed on to the strap to keep from falling off the seat. "Even if they listened to me, why would I wish them to stop?"

Suddenly Duke jumped up, lunging at the window, snarling.

The blackguard clutched her bare arm, sinking his fingers painfully into her skin. "Do what I'm tellin' you to, or I'll hurt ye."

The last thing she'd do was try to send the dogs away. If she could find a way out of this mess, they would likely be her only protection. "He only listens to Lord Worthington."

"Who?" the blackguard barked.

"The nob she's been shagging."

"My husband," she said with as much dignity as she could muster.

The older man began to turn red. "Yer what?"

"I told ye, Da—"

"Shut it. I asked her."

"My husband." Grace raised her chin and revised her opinion of boxing. She'd happily watch Matt pummel these men into the dirt.

"She's lying."

She narrowed her eyes at the younger man, and said in a voice laced with ice, "Someone is, but it is not I. If you know what's good for you, you will release me immediately."

Grace fought down a wave of fear and nausea, and prayed Matt would find her soon. The hackney jerked to a halt.

"What ye doin'?" the blackguard next to her bellowed. "Get moving."

"You ain't paying me enough for me horse to be ruined," the driver shouted back.

The younger man stuck his head out the window as a fist slammed into his nose. Blood spurted everywhere. Black spots danced in front of Grace. She would not swoon. Not now when she had to get away.

The cur next to her screamed as Duke lunged, snapping at the opposite window.

Abruptly, the carriage door was wrenched open with such force she thought it had been torn off its hinges.

Matt's strong arms were around her, dragging her out of the coach. Grace clung to him, trembling from head to foot.

He held her tightly, as he ambled toward a team of horses. "I've got you now. You're safe."

Finally the beating of her heart began to slow, then she started to tremble. "I never want to go through anything like that again. What did they want?"

His hand rubbed her arm, soothing her. "I'll find out." His voice was rough. "Addison here will take you home. Wait at Worthington House until I return."

"But I want—"

"Grace, what you don't want is a scandal. Trust me to take care of the matter."

She opened her mouth to argue, but he was correct. Anything that reflected on her would also reflect on their sisters. "Very well."

He lifted her up into the curricle. "Go to the mews and enter through the back."

Hector handed Matt a piece of paper. "In the event you'd like to see them depart our fair shores."

Matt waited until Addison's carriage had turned onto Bourdon Street, before turning his attention to the scoundrels who'd abducted his wife. The street was thin of company, but not deserted. Mac and three other grooms held the men, while Daisy and Duke stood growling and showing their impressive array of teeth. Matt unfolded the paper.

Captain Brumhill ship the Cabalva

He stepped over to the hackney and addressed the driver. "What did they tell you about this?"

The man rubbed his nose. "That she were a runaway."

His jaw ached, and he loosened it, trying to ease the pain as he speared the two kidnappers with a hard look. "Who hired you to abduct the lady?"

"Ain't no lady." The younger man, whose nose Matt had already broken, spit. "She's nothin' but a whore."

He rammed his fist into the man's belly. "She is my wife."

The older cur paled. His voice was whiney. "Wife? We didn't know—"

They must be the men Grace's uncle had hired to watch the houses. If he discovered Molton had planned this, Matt would hunt the man down and kill him. Opening his clenched fist, he bit out, "Who hired you?"

"No one. We thought . . . money."

The last word was said in a whisper. They would have sold Grace to a whorehouse because they wanted the money. A red haze descended around him. If he hit either of the blackguards again, he wouldn't stop until they were dead. Well, they were going to wish they were. Matt handed the paper to Mac. "Use this hackney, and take these pieces of filth to Brumhill before I kill them."

Matt mounted his horse. "Duke, Daisy, come."

The two dogs trotted next to him. A few minutes later, he handed the gelding's reins to a groom.

Thorton waited in the corridor as Matt entered the house through the garden door. "Her ladyship is in her parlor, my lord."

Matt took the back stairs three at a time. When he got to her parlor door, he stopped. What the devil was he going to tell Grace? Or did she already know what the blackguards had intended?

The door opened, and she flew into his arms. He held her face as he kissed her, breathing in her clean lemon scent.

"Why did they kidnap me?"

"They had been working for your uncle and got carried away." That was close enough to the truth. He wouldn't sully her with the rest of it. "They won't bother you again. I've seen to that."

She nodded, her forehead moving against his cravat. "Matt."

"Grace." They each said the other's name at the same time.

"Ladies first."

"I want you. Now." She stretched up, pressing her lips to his.

Thank the deity. That was exactly what he'd wanted to say. "Who am I to deny my wife?"

He carried her to their bed, laying her gently upon it. Her wrapper fell open, and he couldn't get out of his clothing fast enough.

Dear God, if anything had happened to her . . .

Sliding in next to Grace, he pulled her on top of him, devouring her lips, plundering her mouth, until her small sighs and moans were a symphony. He rolled her under him and entered her slick, wet heat.

Grace wrapped her legs around Matt, holding him tight. The swirling fog of fear she'd felt drifted away leaving only her love for him and the fire building inside her. He'd never taken her with such intensity. The curling tension drove her higher than ever before, and she shook with relief, at the same time he groaned, and collapsed next to her, cradling her in his arms.

She drew her fingers across his chest, playing with the soft curls. Despite what had happened, she had never felt safer. When she had needed Matt, he'd come, just like she knew he would. Years of dread and worry left her. There was only him and their family.

Family. Sisters. Oh no, what time is it?

She donned her wrapper, and tugged the bell-pull.

"What is it?" Matt lay on his side, his blue eyes sharp.

"We have a ball tonight."

Bolton entered the bedchamber. "Yes, my lady."

"The ball."

"Everything is under control. The Dowager Lady Worthington and Lady Herndon have taken Ladies Charlotte and Louisa to dine at Herndon House before the ball. Miss Carpenter arranged everything. Now, if you're hungry, I'll tell Cook."

Grace sank back onto the bed. "Yes, thank you."

Matt rubbed her back. "I would rather give the bare bones of the abduction attempt to the children, and then I believe I'll speak with Marcus and Phoebe about self-defense lessons for you and the others."

"I never actually agreed with it before"—Grace tilted her head as he worked on her shoulders—"yet I now think it's a good idea. Duke and Daisy were magnificent."

"I saw them running down the carriage horse as if it had been a wild boar. All their instincts took over." He stopped rubbing, and she wiggled her back for him to continue. "Are you all right, my love?"

She smiled. "I have never been better."

Two weeks later, Grace entered Jane's bedchamber. Her cousin was beautifully dressed in a pale yellow silk gown, with lace trim. "You called for me?"

"Yes." Jane's countenance had a pinched look, and lines bracketed her mouth. "This is silly, but I'm marrying in an hour, and I have no idea what occurs in a marriage bed. You are the only one I can think of to ask."

Grace took a breath. This was not the last time she would have to address that question, she'd better get used to it. "Have you kissed much at all?"

Her cousin's face softened, a soft smile appearing. "Oh yes, and"—a blush crept up Jane's neck—"a few other things."

"Has he been considerate?"

"Always, and so gentle."

"Then I believe I can leave it to your husband to show

you. Do not worry if there is some pain when you join. It only occurs the once." Grace hugged her cousin. "It will be lovely."

Jane nodded. It was a bit frightening, yet her cousin was correct. Hector would be gentle. "Yes. Thank you."

A light tap sounded on the door, and Charlotte poked her head in. "We've brought you some things."

"Please, come in."

The girls from both families entered.

Jane fought tears of happiness as Charlotte and Louisa clasped a strand of pearls around Jane's neck. "These are from all of us. Something new."

Augusta placed a pair of earrings in Jane's hand. "This is for something borrowed."

The twins and Madeline pinned a turquoise brooch on Jane's bodice. "Something old. You may keep it."

Jane couldn't keep the moisture from her eyes as Mary and Theo approached carrying violets. "These are blue for your hair," Mary said, handing Jane the slightly mangled blooms.

"And a ribbon," Theo added.

"I shall have my maid put them in my hair straightaway." Jane hugged them one by one, as the girls and Grace filed out of the chamber.

"Come now, miss." Dorcus led Jane to the dressing table. It was hard to believe that tonight she'd be in her new home with Hector.

"No crying now." Her maid handed her a handkerchief. "Your eyes will become red."

"I am being silly."

Dorcus arranged the violets, holding them in place with small pearl pins. "There now."

Jane made her way down the main staircase where her cousin and Matt waited. She had been relieved that he'd offered to take on the settlement negotiations and give her away.

Less than a half an hour later, she stood with Hector in the same place Grace and Matt had stood two short weeks ago.

Hector gazed into her eyes as he repeated his vows. His voice strong and steady. This day had been so long in coming. Happiness infused her tone as she made her promises to him.

Once they had been pronounced man and wife, the children gathered round. "Our house will seem quiet after this," Jane said.

Hector's large palm guided her out the door. "Perhaps if we're lucky we'll manage some of our own."

Later that afternoon, after the wedding breakfast guests had departed, Charlotte entered Grace's study holding a letter in front of her. When she dropped her hands, she was frowning.

"What is it?"

"Dotty can't come to Town. Her mother broke her leg. Now we won't be able to make our come out together as we'd planned."

Grace forbore mentioning her sister had Louisa. It was not the same. Charlotte and Dotty had been friends since they were in leading strings. "Let me see it."

After perusing the missive an idea planted itself in Grace's head. Of course, she'd have to ask Matt if he minded taking on another girl for the Season, but, under the circumstances, she did not think he would object. Perhaps she'd suggest it as practice for when the twins and Madeline came out. "I'm not making any promises, but let me see if I can come up with a solution."

Charlotte's countenance was wreathed in smiles. "If anyone can think of something, you can."

After Charlotte left, Grace rang the bell-pull. A few moments later, Royston entered. "My lady?"

"Please have his lordship attend me."

"I will hunt him down."

This was the problem with living in two households. She seldom had any idea where her husband was.

She was in the middle of a column when her door opened. A lecherous smile tilted Matt's lips. "You wanted me?"

She rose, meeting him halfway to the door. "I do. Unfortunately, not for that."

His face fell. "That is a pity. Perhaps I can interest you later. What is it then?"

"Charlotte received a letter from her friend Dotty." Grace explained her sister's friendship with the other girl, and how they'd looked forward to this Season for years.

He was quiet for several moments, then said, "Invite her to come."

That was exactly what Grace had hoped he'd say. "Thank you. I did want it to be your decision. You'll have to write her father. I'll write Lady Sterne and tell Charlotte."

A grin played around his mouth. "I'll do it immediately, after which I'll help you dress for dinner."

Grace slid her arms over his broad shoulders. "You may have to wait and undress me. We have a ball to attend this evening."

"Do we? Will Patience attend as well?"

"I believe so, why?"

"Perhaps I can find another empty parlor, my lady."

Epilogue

Two weeks later. Worthington House, Mayfair, London.

Matt and Grace strolled across the square from Stanwood House to Worthington House. The front door opened as they climbed the steps. The other house was in an excited uproar as Charlotte's and now, Louisa's friend, Dotty, was due to arrive that afternoon. Unfortunately, hiding from the shrill shrieks that would herald that event was not an option. The only quiet moment he'd have with Grace was the next hour. Even that had been stolen.

Thorton bowed and said in a dry tone, "My lord, two wedding gifts have arrived."

Matt was sure he'd never seen his butler looking that dour. Something was not quite right. He and Grace had been receiving presents since their marriage. What could . . . "From whom?"

Thorton's tone held a note of long suffering. "Lord Huntley and Lord Wivenly."

Matt groaned. "Tell me we don't have livestock in the garden."

Thorton gave a shuddering sigh. "No, my lord, but you may wish we did after you see what was delivered."

Grace stepped fully into the hall, stopped, and made a choking noise. "Oh, my!"

Trailing behind her, he followed her gaze. "What the devil is *that?*"

He took out his quizzing glass and scrutinized the large statue made entirely of jade, gold, and other precious stones. It appeared to be a woman, mostly naked, with several arms and eyes.

His butler handed him a card. "This accompanied the piece. There is also an interesting vase which I have placed in your bedchamber, not wanting any of the children to view it."

Matt opened the note.

My dear Worthington,

  Wively and I searched high and low for an appropriate wedding gift for you and your new countess. Luckily, we stumbled, in Wively's case literally, across this lovely lady. She is the Chinese goddess of fertility and newlyweds, as well as several other things. We thought she might be useful.

  The statue dates back to the Ch'ing Dynasty as does the vase we found, in the event you required a little extra incentive.

  All our best in your Endeavors to fill your Nursery.

Yr. Servants
Gervais, Earl of Huntley,
and William, Viscount Wively

"I'll murder them," he growled.

Grace twitched the missive from him and a moment later laughed. "Oh dear. I suppose now is not the time to tell you I think I am increasing."

*Thanks to their large extended family
and unconventional courtship,
the Worthingtons have seen
their share of scandal and excitement.
But nothing has prepared them for this . . .*

The Dowager Lady Worthington isn't quite sure what
to make of country-girl Dorothea Sterne.
As the granddaughter of the Duke of Bristol, Dotty is
schooled in the ways and means of the nobility. But her
sharp wit and outspoken nature has everyone in a tizzy.
Especially their cousin, Dominic, the Marquis of Merton.

Prematurely stuffy, Dom was raised by his cheerless uncle
to be wary of a host of things, including innovation,
waltzing, and most perilous of all: true love.
Still, there's something about Dotty,
beyond her beauty, that Dom cannot resist.
But the odds are against him if he intends to win her
as his bride. Will he choose loyalty to his family—
or risk everything for the one woman
he believes is his perfect match . . .

Please turn the page for an exciting sneak peek of
Ella Quinn's next Worthingtons historical romance,

WHEN A MARQUIS CHOOSES A BRIDE,

coming in September 2016 wherever
print and eBooks are sold!

Chapter One

Early afternoon sun poured through the windows of the large, airy school-room in Sterne Manor. The space was filled with bookcases, four desks, two sofas, and sundry toys.

Miss Dorothea Sterne sat on the larger of the much used sofas, threading a strand of rose silk through the embroidery needle. She had one more Damask rose to complete before the slippers she was making for her mother were finished.

But no matter how hard she tried, she could not escape the fact that the neighborhood was sadly flat now that her best friend, Lady Charlotte Carpenter, was gone. For years, they had planned to come out together, just as they had done everything else since they could walk.

In the meantime, there was a great deal to keep her busy. Since her mother's accident, Dotty had taken up Mama's duties. Dotty enjoyed visiting their tenants, talking to the children and their mothers and finding ways to help them.

"Dotty," her six-year-old sister Martha whined, "Scruffy won't stay still."

Scruffy, a three-legged dog Dotty had saved from a hunter's trap was resisting Martha's efforts to tie a ribbon on him. "Sweetie, boys don't like frills. Put it on your doll instead."

Fifteen-year-old Henrietta glanced up from the book she was reading. "She took it off the doll."

"Henny," Dotty asked, "aren't you supposed to be practicing your harp?"

Her sister stuck her tongue out. "No, I'm supposed to be reading Ovid in Greek."

Their father, Sir Henry, was a classical scholar and had been a rector before his older brother's death a few years ago. Much to Henny's dismay, he had decided to teach all the children Latin and Greek.

Dotty took in the book her sister held. The marble cover was a trademark of the Minerva Press novels. "*That* is not Ovid."

Puffing out a breath of air, Henny rolled her eyes. "Aren't ladies supposed to be fashionably stupid?"

"No, they are supposed to appear stupid," Dotty replied tartly. "Which is completely ridiculous. I refuse to marry a gentleman who thinks women should not have brains."

"If that's the case, you may become a spinster," Henny shot back.

"Lord Worthington likes that Grace is clever. I'm sure there must be other gentlemen who believe as he does." Dotty resisted a smug smile.

Charlotte's older sister, Grace, was now the Countess of Worthington. She had taken all five of the younger children with her to London for Charlotte's come out. Shortly after arriving in Town, Grace had met and fallen in love with Mattheus, Earl of Worthington. They had wed three weeks later.

Not long ago, Grace and her new husband had returned to Stanwood Hall for a few days so that Lord Worthington, who was now guardian to her brothers and sisters, as well as his own sisters, could inspect the property.

Before Henny could retort, the door opened. "Miss," Dotty's maid, Polly, glanced around the room, her gaze settling on Dotty, "her ladyship asked me to come fetch you."

Dotty pulled the thread through, secured the needle, and set the slipper down. "Is she all right?"

"Oh, yes, miss." Polly fairly jugged. "She got a letter from London and sent for you straightaway."

Dotty hurried to the door. "I hope nothing is wrong." There was nothing wonderful in receiving a letter from London. Practically everyone they knew was in Town for the Season. Mama and Dotty should have been there as well, yet the day before their planned departure her mother slipped and broke her leg.

"No, miss," the maid said as she hurried after her. "Her ladyship was smiling."

"Well, I suppose the sooner I get to her, the sooner I shall find out what she wants." A minute later, she knocked on the door to her mother's parlor and entered. "Mama, what is it?"

Waving a sheet of paper in her hand, her mother smiled broadly. "Unexpected and wonderful news. You shall have your Season after all!"

Dotty's jaw dropped. She closed it again and made her way over to a chair next to her mother. "I don't understand. I thought Grandmamma Bristol couldn't sponsor me because of Aunt Mary's confinement."

"*This*"—Mama waved the letter through the air again—"is from Grace."

Dotty's heart began to beat faster, and she clasped her hands together. "What—what does she say?"

"After dear Charlotte received your missive telling her you could not come to Town for your Season, she prevailed upon Grace to invite you. She says"—Mama adjusted her spectacles—"having you would be no bother at all. She is bringing out Charlotte and Lady Louisa Vivers, Worthington's sister, you know, and one more in a household of ten children will hardly be remarkable. She comments that your good sense will be very welcome." Mama glanced up. "Not that I disagree with her. You do have a great deal of sagacity, but I am sure Grace said that for Papa's benefit. You know how he does not like to be obliged to anyone." Mama went back to the letter. "And it would be a great shame for you not to come out with Charlotte as you girls have planned for years." Mama set the paper down with a great flourish and grinned. "What do you think of *that*?"

For what seemed like a long time, Dotty could think of nothing. Her mind had never gone blank before. It was almost too good to be true. She shook her head, and finally managed to find an answer. "I never thought . . . Well, I mean I knew Charlotte was going to ask Grace, but I never even imagined that Lord Worthington would agree. Although her last letter said she missed me dreadfully. Lady Louisa, Worthington's sister, even wrote saying she had heard so much about me that she felt as if she already knew me and wished I was going to be in Town."

Suddenly, the fact that Dotty was actually going to Town hit her. She jumped up, rushed to her mother, and hugged her. "I wish you could be there as well."

Mama patted Dotty's back. "Yes, my dear. I wish I could go too, but Grace will take good care of you."

"When shall we tell Papa of Grace's offer?" What if her father refused to allow her to go? That would be horrible. "I'm not sure he will be as happy as we are."

Her mother glanced briefly at the ceiling and let out a sigh of long suffering. "If he had his way, you would not come out until you were at least twenty. He has gone out somewhere. I left a message to have him attend me as soon as he returns." She pushed herself up against the pillows. "We have no time to lose. There is so much to discuss. Polly," Mama said to Dotty's maid hovering in the door. "Have the trunks brought down from the attic and start getting Miss Dotty's clothes together."

"Yes, your ladyship."

Once the door closed, Mama leaned forward a little and lowered her voice. "Papa will dislike the idea of you going to London without me at first, but don't worry, dear, I'll talk him round."

Dotty sat back down and folded her hands in her lap. They trembled a little with excitement. She was really going to be able to come out with her best friend in the whole world! "I should write to Charlotte and Grace to thank them."

"Yes, after it is all settled." Mama opened her pocket-book and wet the tip of the pencil with her tongue. "We must think of who will accompany you. Papa will not allow you to travel with only Polly. I believe Mrs. Parks said her sister was going to Town to visit a friend. I shall ask if she will look after you. After all, it will save her the trouble of booking and paying for another coach."

Dotty nodded. "Yes, Mama. I believe Miss Brownly is leaving in a few days. She planned to take the mail."

"Then she will be glad for a chance to ride in a private coach and break the journey at a good hostelry. Run along now and help Polly. I shall send for you after I have spoken with Papa."

Dotty kissed her mother before running in a very unlady-like fashion up the stairs to her room. Four trunks already stood open and her wardrobe cabinet was empty. She started folding the clothes she found on her bed. "Polly, I do hope Mama prevails."

The maid paused to think for a moment. "I don't think Sir Henry has a hope against her ladyship." She gave a decisive nod. "She'll get her way."

Dotty smiled. Her mother usually did. "Still . . . I'll feel much better when I know for sure that I'll be going."

* * *

Two hours later, Sir Henry Sterne frowned at the letter in his hand as he ambled into his wife's parlor. "This is from Lord Worthington. I suppose you have one from Grace."

Lady Sterne smiled. She loved her husband dearly, but there were times his self-sufficiency went too far. She had no intention of allowing him to spoil Dotty's Season. "I do indeed. I do not think I have ever been so pleased for Dorothea. She and Charlotte have dreamed of their come out for years, and all the new gowns we bought for her . . . Well, I would hate for them to go to waste."

Her husband appeared unconvinced. "Worthington promises to take care of Dotty as he would his sister Lady Louisa and Charlotte"—his scowl deepened—"but, Cordelia, we would be entrusting her to his care. *In London*. And we do not know him that well."

"Henry"—Cordelia used her most patient tone—"we know Grace, and Worthington was perfectly amiable when she invited us to Stanwood Hall to dine during the few days they were here. He has a good reputation. Nothing smoky about him at all, as Harry would say." Her husband's lips folded together, and Cordelia rushed on. "Besides, Grace would not have trusted him with *her* brothers and sisters if he were not a good man."

"But looking after three young ladies?"

She almost laughed at the look of horror on his face.

"You forget, Jane Carpenter, Grace's cousin is still with them and the Dowager Lady Worthington as well. The girls will be well chaperoned, and Grace commented on Dotty's good sense."

"Yes, well." He glanced at the missive and drew his brows together so that they touched. "As the Season is well under way, Lord Worthington asks for an immediate reply. I suppose I should write to him."

Cordelia smiled again. "Does that mean you'll allow Dorothea to go?"

A bit of humor entered her husband's eyes. "I know you, my love. If I say no, I will never hear the end of it. You are every bit as determined as your mother. How do you propose Dotty make the journey?"

"You cannot complain about that, my dear. If we were not strong-willed, you and I would never have been allowed to marry." Cordelia struggled to keep the triumph out of her voice. It was fortunate that the Sternes had been friends with the Carpenters for generations. "I shall make all the arrangements."

"Very well, then. I know you'll send Dotty off as soon as possible. I do want a word with her."

"Of course, my love." Cordelia tugged the bell-pull and called for her daughter.

Dotty's steps faltered as she entered Papa's study. Her stomach lurched as she took in his grim countenance. He was not going to allow her to go to Town. She may as well make the best of it. Getting into a state would not help. She took a breath and readied herself for the bad news. "Yes?"

"Your father wishes to speak to you." She whipped her head around, seeing her mother lying on a sofa.

Papa came around from behind his desk and took Dotty by her shoulders. "You may join Charlotte for your Season. However, you know my feelings about this. You are still young, and there is no reason you must marry anytime soon."

She kept her face as serious as her father's. "I know, Papa."

He cleared his throat. "If a young man is interested in you, have him apply to Lord Worthington first. He will know best if the gentleman is suitable."

Dotty nodded. Relief and excitement rushed through

her. Yet her father wasn't done yet. She waited for him to continue.

"With the number of inhabitants already in Worthington's household and the dogs, you must promise me not to bring stray animals or people to Stanwood House. They won't appreciate it."

"I promise, Papa."

"Now, I must make sure the coach is ready."

As soon as her father closed the door, she gave a little shriek and hugged her mother. "Oh, Mama! Thank you so much. I shall never be able to repay you."

She patted her Dotty's cheek. "Yes you will, by having fun. Though mind what your father said. With all those children and *two* Great Danes, the Worthingtons do not need three-legged dogs or half-blind cats, not to mention homeless children."

"Yes, Mama. I'll do my best." Dotty grinned. Everyone loved Scruffy. The cat was the best mouser they ever had, and Benjy was turning into a fine groom. People and animals only needed a chance in life. Nevertheless, her parents had a point. Bringing strays home to Sterne Manor was one thing, taking them to someone else's house quite another matter altogether. Dotty said a quick prayer that she would not meet anyone in need of help.

Chapter Two

Dominic, Marquis of Merton, settled into his apartment at the Pulteney Hotel. His pride still stung at having been ejected from his cousin, Matt Worthington's town house. Blowing a cloud was the latest thing. Not that Dom would attempt to smoke in White's, but he outranked Worthington and should have been treated as an honored guest, not summarily told to leave. Still, it was probably convenient that Dom did not actually enjoy smoking, as he was sure the Pulteney would not allow it either.

He should have gone on his Grand Tour instead of taking a bolt to Town. But his mother had received a letter informing her of his cousin's plans to wed, and he decided starting his own nursery would be the most responsible course. After all, the succession would not look after itself, and he had a duty to his family and dependents. Perhaps he would travel after he married.

Not that Dom truly wished to leave England. He liked an ordered life and travel was sure to disrupt the structure with which he was comfortable. He did not wish to visit France at all. Any land where the inhabitants would murder their betters held little interest for him. It all came back to the proper order of things. Life was much better when everyone followed the rules and knew their places.

He reconsidered opening up Merton House for the Season, but there was really no point when his mother was not here as well. Without her to act as his hostess, he would not be able to plan any entertainments other than for his friends. The hotel would be fine for the short time he planned to spend in Town. It should not take him that long to find a wife. He was a marquis. Even without his considerable fortune, he would have been a desirable *parti*.

"Kimbal," he called to his valet.

"Yes, my lord."

"I shall be dining at White's."

"Yes, my lord."

Dom scribbled a note to his friend Viscount Fotherby asking if he would like to join Dom for dinner. By the time he was dressed and had donned his hat, Fotherby's answer affirming the plans had arrived.

A short while later, just as a light sprinkle turned into a persistent rain, he handed his hat and cane to the footman at White's and found his friend lounging in the room which held the club's famous betting book. William Alvanley, another of Dom's friends, was seated next to the window with another man staring intently at the rain.

He turned to Fotherby. "What are they doing?"

"Five thousand quid on which raindrop will reach the bottom of the sill first."

Despite being close with many of the Prince Regent's circle, Dom could not abide the excessive wagers his friends made. Alvanley would end up ruining himself and his estates at the rate he was going. "Are you ready to dine, or are you waiting the outcome?"

"Famished." Fotherby tossed off his glass of wine. "Thought you weren't coming to Town this year."

"My plans changed." Dom and Fotherby entered the dining room. "I have decided to take a wife."

"Wife?" Fotherby choked. "Any idea who?"

"Not yet, but I have a list of qualifications. She must be well-bred, not given to fits of temper or strange starts, quiet, biddable, easy to look at, I must get an heir on her after all, know what is expected of a marchioness. And not prone to scandals. You know how my uncle hated them. I think that about covers it."

"A paragon, in other words."

Dom gave a curt nod. "Indeed. I could wed no one less."

Three days later, Dotty arrived at Stanwood House in Berkeley Square, Mayfair, just after three o'clock in the afternoon. From the letters she'd received from Charlotte, it appeared that the Carpenters and Vivers were getting along well. Louisa's mother, the Dowager Countess of Worthington, was also living with them. Lord Worthington, however, was the sole guardian of his four sisters.

Royston, the Stanwood butler, opened the door and was almost bowled over by a sea of children and the Carpenters' Great Dane, Daisy.

"We saw your coach arrive," one of the children shouted.

Daisy tried to wrap herself around Dotty as Charlotte and a young lady with dark chestnut hair, Dotty guessed to be Louisa, hurried forward. Dotty laughed. "I didn't know I would receive such an ecstatic welcome."

A deep bark came from the side of the hall.

"That is Duke," Charlotte said over the roar.

"Enough." Lord Worthington's commanding tone had everyone except Charlotte and Louisa, backing away from the door. "Let her in the house."

Once the younger children had moved out of the way, his lordship, a tall, broad-shouldered gentleman with the same dark hair as his sister, came forward holding Grace's hand. They made a beautiful couple. Grace, with her gold hair was a perfect foil for her husband.

"I did say we were looking forward to you joining us." Grace laughed as she hugged Dotty.

"Yes, you did." She grinned. It was wonderful to be with the Carpenters again. "That was quite a welcome."

Charlotte threw her arms around Dotty. "I'm so glad you're here. This is Louisa, Matt's sister and my new stepsister." Charlotte pulled a face. "Not technically, of course, but we had to call each other something."

Dotty held out her hand to Louisa but got kissed on the cheek instead.

"I am so happy to finally meet you." Louisa smiled. "The three of us are going to be the best of friends and have such a wonderful time."

Dotty remembered she had not yet greeted his lordship. He took the hand Dotty held out, yet when she would have curtseyed, he held her up. "There is no point in standing on ceremony here. Call me Matt, all the other children do."

"Thank you, sir. I can't tell you how happy I am to be here *and* that you wrote my father."

Before he could respond, Charlotte grabbed Dotty's hand. "We must show you to your room. It is next to mine. We'll let you clean up and change. Then we'll have tea before taking a stroll in the Park. Louisa and I have our own parlor, and now it will be yours as well."

Dotty followed her friend up the stairs. "After two days of sitting in a coach, I would love a walk."

"I completely understand." Louisa linked her arm with Dotty's. "I don't know how one can want to *rest*, when one has been cooped up in a carriage for more than a day."

Charlotte and Louisa showed Dotty where the small parlor was located and then escorted her to her chamber.

Once there, she was left alone to splash her face and wash her hands.

Polly came in from a door to what must be a dressing room. "Here you are, miss." She hung up a pink muslin walking gown and paisley spencer. "Let's get you changed."

A few minutes later Dotty entered the parlor and found Louisa and Charlotte looking over fashion plates.

"Come and tell me what you think of this." Charlotte patted the seat next to her.

She handed Dotty a picture of a lady in a cream ball gown decorated with lace. Charlotte had the same coloring as Grace, and Dotty thought it would look lovely on her friend. "Very pretty."

The tea arrived a few minutes later. Once they all had cups and a plate of biscuits, she was told about all the balls and other entertainments she could look forward to, including Louisa and Charlotte's come out ball.

"Grace and Mama agreed the ball will be in your honor as well." Louisa beamed, apparently not minding a bit that she would have to share her ball with yet another lady.

Dotty finished off a ratafia biscuit. "It will be so much fun. I can't wait to see everything. You two have such an advantage over me."

All her dreams had come true. Although, she'd received letters from Louisa proclaiming her friendship, Dotty really had not believed it until now. It would have been difficult if Louisa had taken it into her head not to like Dotty.

Before long, they were walking out the door to the Park with three footmen following a discreet distance behind.

Strolling in between her two friends, she commented, "Mama said she always had a maid with her when she walked in Town."

"Matt says footmen are more practical," Louisa responded. "If one of us is injured he can carry us home, whereas a maid cannot."

"And," Charlotte added, "If we go shopping they can carry packages more easily."

They arrived at the path around Hyde Park, which Dotty was told was referred to as "the Park."

Charlotte made a funny face. "One is supposed to pretend that one always knows everything and play at *ennui,* but I think that's nonsense. Why act as if you are not having fun, when you are?"

"It does not make much sense to me either." Dotty sighed. "Here I thought I was ready, but instead I have such a lot to learn."

"It was the same for Louisa and me," Charlotte assured her. "You will catch on quickly."

A few moments later, they were hailed by two stylishly dressed gentlemen who Charlotte and Louisa obviously knew. They stopped, allowing the men to approach.

"Miss Sterne," Charlotte said primly. "May I present Lords Harrington and Bentley. My lords, a friend of mine from home, Miss Sterne. She will be residing with us for the Season."

Both men bowed over the hand Dotty held out. Thank heavens for all the lessons in deportment she and Charlotte had shared. Dotty curtseyed. "I am pleased to meet you, my lords."

The gentlemen accompanied the ladies for a short while, begging them for dances at to-morrow night's ball. Once they had gone, Dotty gave herself a small shake. "I cannot believe I am already engaged for two sets."

"They are very nice, aren't they?" Charlotte blushed.

Louisa glanced slyly at Charlotte. "I think Lord Harrington will ask to court Charlotte."

"Well, from the looks of it, Lord Bentley is quite smitten with you," she retorted.

"I wish he would not be," Louisa cast her eyes to the sky. "He is a good man, but not one I wish to marry."

In the short time Dotty had known Louisa it was clear poor Lord Bentley was not up to her weight. She would need someone older and more sure of himself.

Dotty took Charlotte's hand and squeezed it. "How do you feel about Lord Harrington?"

Charlotte's face became even redder. "He is very charming, but Grace says to give it time."

They resumed ambling on the side of the path. Suddenly there was a commotion and a shout from behind. Dotty turned. A small dog had grabbed the tassel on a man's boot and was backing up growling with its tail wagging trying to shake its prize. Foolishly, the man kept kicking out at the dog, making the animal think he was playing.

She put a hand over her mouth to keep from giggling, yet when he lifted his cane to strike the poor little thing, she rushed forward. "Here now, sir! What do you think you're doing?" She bent to the dog who turned out to be nothing more than a puppy. Turning to the man, she narrowed her eyes and scowled. "Shame on you."

Dotty worked on releasing the tassel from the puppy's grip, but each time the man shook his leg, trying to get the animal off, the puppy held on harder, growling and shaking his head. "Stop moving. Are you so stupid you cannot see the dog thinks you are trying to play?"

"Get him off me," the man shouted in a voice growing higher in fright. "Someone will pay for this. Is he your beast?"

Determined to ignore him, she counted to ten, took a breath, and finally managed to release the gold bobble from the puppy's sharp teeth. "There now." Picking up the dog, she stroked its wiry fur. "Where is your master?"

Just then, two school-aged boys came running up. "Oh, miss. Thank you so much. We've been looking for Bennie all over. He got away from us."

By this time Bennie was snapping at the ribbons of her bonnet. Dotty laughed as she tried to free them. "Here now, sir. Those are not for you either." She saved the ribbons and handed the puppy to one of the boys.

"We'll pay you for the damage, miss."

"It's no bother." She smiled at both of them. "Use the money to buy a lead. That will keep Bennie from running away."

"He's only twelve weeks old," the other boy said proudly. "We didn't think he could run so fast."

"Or so far," added the other.

"Thank you," they both said in unison.

Ah, well. Puppies would be puppies and boys would be boys. "Run along now, and keep Bennie out of trouble."

"Wait just a minute," the man with the tassels growled. "You owe me compensation. Your vicious beast ruined my boots."

"Stuff and nonsense." Dotty closed her eyes for a moment before fixing the man with a stern look. "It was entirely your fault. If you had acted like a sensible person and just picked the poor puppy up, your boots would not have suffered any damage."

By this time Charlotte and Louisa were ranged beside Dotty. The footmen were close behind.

"Dotty, are you all right?" Charlotte asked.

"I am fine." She glanced at Louisa who seemed to be glaring at the man's companion, whom Dotty had not previously noticed.

The contrast between that man and his friend with the tassels was remarkable.

She knew now what her father had meant when he had spoken disparagingly about "Dandies." The man whose boots Bennie had attacked was obviously one of that set. His shirt points were so high he could barely turn his head. His waist was nipped in and his garishly striped waistcoat was covered by so many fobs and other ornaments one could hardly see the cloth. Whereas his companion was dressed with elegant propriety in a dark blue coat and buff pantaloons. No gold tassels adorned his boots, which were so highly polished the sun reflected off them. With stylish gold hair and deep blue eyes, he was very handsome indeed. Then his lips curved up in a mocking smile, ruining the favorable impression she'd had.

"Merton." Louisa infused her voice with a note of disgust. "A friend of *yours*, I suppose."

Merton cleared his throat. "I daresay, Fotherby, that the lady is correct. You should have been able to stop the animal before any damage occurred."

Fotherby turned to Merton, staring at his companion as if betrayed. Merton's masked eyes were unreadable to Dotty, but something in them must have made an impression on Fotherby for he turned to her and bowed slightly.

"Ladies, my deepest apologies for not acting promptly to avoid an unnecessary scene."

Never one to hold a grudge, Dotty inclined her head, "Your apology is accepted, sir."

Merton lifted one brow and looked pointedly at Louisa.

"Very well," she said, in no good humor. "Miss Sterne, may I present the Marquis of Merton, a cousin of mine. Merton, Miss Sterne, a longtime friend of Lady Charlotte's family."

Dom bowed and watched with appreciation as Miss Sterne gracefully curtseyed. He had not been paying much attention to her encounter with Fotherby, thinking her just another modern termagant, until she stood and faced him. Botticelli could not have painted such perfection. The glossy blue-black curls peeping out from her hat served as a perfect frame for her heart-shaped face. She gazed at Dom with bright moss-green eyes. Surreptitiously, he sucked in a breath. He'd seen many beautiful women this Season, including Lady Charlotte, but none came close to equaling Miss Sterne.

But, *Dotty*, what a horrible name. It must be short for something. He prayed it was short for something. If not, the name would have to change.

Cousin Louisa had not given him an indication of Miss Sterne's station, other than that she was a lady. However, a Miss Sterne could possibly be the daughter of a viscount. That wouldn't be bad. Anything lower in rank would not do. Unless her bloodlines were superior. If that was the case, he could make an exception. He had the consequence of the marquisate to consider.

Bowing over her hand, he grasped her fingers. "It is my greatest pleasure to meet you, Miss Sterne. I pray you will allow me to call."

"Well," his cousin said in a voice intended to dampen his spirits, "only if you care to come to Stanwood House. Miss Sterne is residing with us for the Season."

He repressed a shudder at the thought of having to face that brood again, especially Theodora, Worthington's youngest sister. He kept a smile pasted on his face. "Perhaps, I shall."

The animosity between the two families was such that Worthington had told Dom in no uncertain terms that he was not welcome to court any ladies under his guardianship. Of course, at the time, only Ladies Charlotte and Louisa were at issue. He wondered if that prohibition applied to Miss Sterne.

Books by Bestselling Author
Fern Michaels

___The Jury	0-8217-7878-1	$6.99US/$9.99CAN
___Sweet Revenge	0-8217-7879-X	$6.99US/$9.99CAN
___Lethal Justice	0-8217-7880-3	$6.99US/$9.99CAN
___Free Fall	0-8217-7881-1	$6.99US/$9.99CAN
___Fool Me Once	0-8217-8071-9	$7.99US/$10.99CAN
___Vegas Rich	0-8217-8112-X	$7.99US/$10.99CAN
___Hide and Seek	1-4201-0184-6	$6.99US/$9.99CAN
___Hokus Pokus	1-4201-0185-4	$6.99US/$9.99CAN
___Fast Track	1-4201-0186-2	$6.99US/$9.99CAN
___Collateral Damage	1-4201-0187-0	$6.99US/$9.99CAN
___Final Justice	1-4201-0188-9	$6.99US/$9.99CAN
___Up Close and Personal	0-8217-7956-7	$7.99US/$9.99CAN
___Under the Radar	1-4201-0683-X	$6.99US/$9.99CAN
___Razor Sharp	1-4201-0684-8	$7.99US/$10.99CAN
___Yesterday	1-4201-1494-8	$5.99US/$6.99CAN
___Vanishing Act	1-4201-0685-6	$7.99US/$10.99CAN
___Sara's Song	1-4201-1493-X	$5.99US/$6.99CAN
___Deadly Deals	1-4201-0686-4	$7.99US/$10.99CAN
___Game Over	1-4201-0687-2	$7.99US/$10.99CAN
___Sins of Omission	1-4201-1153-1	$7.99US/$10.99CAN
___Sins of the Flesh	1-4201-1154-X	$7.99US/$10.99CAN
___Cross Roads	1-4201-1192-2	$7.99US/$10.99CAN

Available Wherever Books Are Sold!
Check out our website at www.kensingtonbooks.com